Praise for Debby Holt

'Thoroughly enjoyable . . . Had me smiling from start to finish' Erica James

'A wickedly comical read' *Heat*

'A fabulous novel which addresses real-life issues with wit and humour' *Closer*

'From the author of the superb *Ex-Wife's Survival Guide* comes another wicked treat' *Daily Mirror*

'This fast-paced romantic comedy is perfect bad-weather escapism' *She*

'Clever and surprising' *Daily Mail*

'A deliciously funny, gently ironic novel, Jane Austen-like in its elegance and playfulness' *Women's Weekly*

'I absolutely love this book. It is as funny as it is wise and I couldn't put it down' Katie Fforde

'One to curl up with on a winter's evening' *Oxford Times*

'Laced with wise and witty humour, this is great fun' *Woman*

BY THE SAME AUTHOR

*The Ex-Wife's Survival Guide*
*Annie May's Black Book*
*The Trouble with Marriage*
*Love Affairs for Grown-Ups*

ABOUT THE AUTHOR

Debby Holt was a shambolic supply teacher until she (and her pupils) were saved by her writing. She lives in Bath with her nice husband and her horrid mortgage.

Visit www.debbyholt.co.uk

# RECIPE FOR SCANDAL

*Debby Holt*

POCKET BOOKS

London · New York · Sydney · Toronto

A CBS COMPANY

First published in Great Britain by Simon & Schuster, 2010
This edition first published by Pocket Books, 2010
An imprint of Simon & Schuster UK
A CBS COMPANY



1 3 5 7 9 10 8 6 4 2

Simon & Schuster UK Ltd
1st Floor
222 Gray's Inn Road
London WC1X 8HB

www.simonandschuster.co.uk

Simon & Schuster Australia
Sydney

A CIP catalogue record for this book
is available from the British Library

ISBN 978-1-84739-654-9



Typeset in Plantin by Ellipsis Books Limited, Glasgow
Printed and bound in Great Britain by
Cox & Wyman Ltd, Reading, Berkshire

*For Sara*

# ACKNOWLEDGEMENTS

Sir Richard Mottram corrected my confusion about political honours. The glamorous Sophie Douglas Bate of Edible Food Designs in London and the stunning Angie Brooker of the bath deli in Bath were incredibly helpful about the catering world and I would recommend their services to anyone! The extremely cool Phil Hill of Cargo Records and the fairly cool William Feeny gave me valuable information about the music industry. Daniel Feeny gave me a great idea and it's possible that Jack Feeny did too. My brilliant agent, Teresa Chris, proved yet again why she is brilliant. As always, thanks to all at Simon & Schuster, especially Kate Lyall Grant and also Libby Vernon, whose contribution was massive.

*Love and scandal are the best sweeteners of tea*

HENRY FIELDING

# CHAPTER ONE

## *Bad Evening with Black Rocks*

Later – much later – it occurred to Alberta that if she hadn't been presiding over the most excruciatingly awkward evening of her entire life, she would definitely have asked Tony about his phone call; they would probably have talked about it and the subsequent course of her life could possibly have been very different.

Alberta did not ask Tony about his phone call because, like a bee floundering in a honeypot, she was struggling to escape the consequences of her own inadvertent folly. Like the bee, the more she struggled, the worse her situation became.

Alberta did not normally give dinner parties. As joint partner of *Bounty of Bath, for fabulous food for large or small functions*, her job involved cooking delicious food for people who had no time to cook for themselves. Consequently, the idea of using her precious free time to prepare a three-course meal for a variety of guests who didn't know each other, had about as much appeal as a doctor would find in spending a jolly evening listening to friends recounting their physical ailments.

The impulse for the party – gratitude – made the subsequent debacle all the more sad. Alberta and Tony had met Erica Wright at the Sixth Formers' Parents' Evening, held in the first week of the summer term. Ms Wright had recently joined the school as Head of Sixth Year and was the first teacher not to think that Jacob was infuriating or self-opinionated or possessed of an over-inflated view of his abilities. In fact, Ms Wright declared he was charming and quirky and perceptive and said he possessed an original mind. Alberta and Tony looked at their son with new respect and left the school hall in rather dazed good spirits, followed by a smugly smiling Jacob.

A week later, on the first of May, Alberta met Jacob's teacher again, this time at a Pilates class. Normally, Alberta would never have approached a woman like Erica. Erica was at least six inches taller than Alberta, whose own stature could generously be described as diminutive. Erica's hair fell like shimmering silk onto her shoulders. Alberta's hay-coloured locks were tied up on top of her head while her grown-out fringe refused to stay neatly behind her ears. Erica, tall and slim and svelte, looked amazing in her pale grey tracksuit and pink T-shirt. Alberta, short and slimmish and cursed, as she saw it, with big breasts, looked entirely unremarkable in her leggings, her oversized white polo shirt and her long blue cardigan.

Nevertheless, the balm-like memory of Erica's judgement on Jacob propelled Alberta towards unusually assertive action. At the end of the lesson, she went up to Erica and said, 'Ms Wright? My name's Alberta Granger. We met at the parents' evening . . .'

Ms Wright smiled. 'Please call me Erica. You're mother of the lovely Jacob.'

There was no sarcasm in Erica's voice. Erica obviously *did* think Jacob was lovely. Alberta felt a rush of appreciation for such amazing perspicacity. She said quickly, 'We so appreciated your comments about him. Do you have to dash off or can I buy you a drink?'

Erica hesitated. 'I have a mountain of marking but . . . Oh why not! It can wait another half-hour.'

Ensconced in a nearby wine bar with fat glasses of Chenin Blanc, the two women sat side by side while Alberta strove to explain the conundrum that was Jacob. 'We are so used to feeling utterly crushed at those evenings. I don't know what it is but Jacob seems to have this habit of thoroughly annoying all his teachers. I mean, I know he's quite unusual in some ways . . .'

'He's a clever boy,' Erica said, 'and he has a delightfully off-centre way of looking at life.'

'Yes,' Alberta said vaguely, omitting to mention that more often than not she found her son's views on life quite impenetrable, and when she *could* penetrate them they invariably made her feel uncomfortable. Sometimes, she felt she and Jacob inhabited different universes.

'What I like about Jacob,' Erica said, 'is that he shows no signs of the usual adolescent tendency to introspection or testosterone-fuelled fantasies. He seems to have an extraordinarily objective attitude to his peers and his school and his family.'

'He certainly does,' Alberta agreed. Although not entirely convinced, she was heartened that Erica thought Jacob's objectivity was a good thing. She still had, in one of her folders, an essay he had written for his homework when he was ten. The title was 'My Mother' and Jacob had divided his piece into two sections, *Advantages* and *Disadvantages.* There had been five advantages and seven disadvantages, one of them being, '*My mother does not posess much general knowlidge*'. It was encouraging that Erica thought Jacob's detached viewpoint was praiseworthy and Alberta knew she was lucky not to have the sort of teenage son who yelled that he hated her, as her nephew used to do to her sister-in-law. On the other hand, her nephew had grown into a charming young man. Indeed, Alberta had witnessed him giving his mother an affectionate hug at Christmas. Alberta couldn't remember the last time she'd been hugged by Jacob.

She decided they had talked enough about her son and asked Erica whether she was enjoying her new job. Erica said she was enjoying it very much although she missed the friends she had left behind in her old school in Northampton. Alberta had the impression that there was no Mr Wright but that there had at some stage very probably been a Mr Wrong.

'In fact, I'm glad I moved to Bath,' Erica said. 'I needed diversion.' She moved her glass and rested her arms on the table. 'You have a daughter, don't you? I seem to remember Jacob mentioning a sister.'

'Yes,' Alberta nodded. 'She's his half-sister actually. I was married before I met Tony. Hannah, my daughter, lives in London now.'

'Well, you'll understand how I feel. There's nothing like a mother and daughter relationship. Sadie tells me everything.'

Alberta nodded wisely as if she knew exactly what Erica was talking about, although the truth was that Hannah had never told her everything and most of the time told her very little at all.

Erica took a sip of her wine. 'It's been just the two of us for years. I've been dreading the time when she would go off to university. That was one of the reasons why I decided to apply for a new job. Sadie went off to Nottingham at the same time that I came here. I've been working too hard to worry about her too much. I *do* worry, of course. I had a phone call from her before I came out tonight and she was so upset. She'd met some boy and he'd stood her up. She said she'd waited for ages outside the cinema. I felt like going up to Nottingham and strangling him.'

Alberta nodded again, but this time with genuine understanding. 'I know what you mean. One feels so powerless to help! Hannah is very clever but she's always gone for boys who treat her badly. She had a boyfriend at school called Martin. He had lovely blond hair – all her boyfriends have blond hair – but I couldn't see what else she saw in him. He always seemed to grunt rather than talk. I could never understand anything he said and he never seemed to *wash*, if you know what I mean. She adored him. I knew he'd break her heart and he did. And then at Oxford she met a boy called Ludovic who had this habit of smirking every time I said anything. He smirked every time Hannah said anything too. He was most unpleasant.'

'Is she still with him?'

'No, thank God. For the first time ever, she's involved

with someone who's quite charming. He's the brother of her best friend and I used to know him when he was a boy. So I'm sure things will work out for your Sadie too, but it doesn't stop you worrying *now* of course.'

'It wouldn't matter so much,' Erica said, 'but this boy is the first one that she's really liked since she arrived at university. She thought she'd found her soulmate.'

'It all sounds horribly familiar,' Alberta said, pausing to take a sip of her wine. 'The same thing happened to me. After more than a quarter of a century, I can still remember it quite clearly. I was in Mallorca with my parents. I was waiting for them in a bar and this gorgeous English boy with flaming red hair started talking to me. We were only together for about twenty minutes but it was the most wonderful twenty minutes I had ever had. And – I'm sure you'll think this is daft –' Alberta could see from Erica's amused expression that she probably *would* think it was daft and she wished she'd never begun the story, but it was too late to stop now – 'I found myself falling in love with him! I had to go out to dinner with my parents – it was Pa's birthday – and the man was supposed to be going off to some party. But he asked me to meet him at the same bar the next evening and so I did. I waited for over an hour and he never showed up. I felt quite desolate. I was so certain he liked me.'

'When I was at school,' Erica said, 'there were two boys who made a habit of standing girls up. They would go and watch their victims waiting for them and they would bet on how long the girls would wait.'

'How *sadistic*!' Alberta exclaimed. 'How can people behave like that? I wonder if those boys are *still* like that. I wonder if they regret their past behaviour.'

Erica sniffed. 'I expect they're big, fat merchant bankers with too much money and sad little wives who see them once a fortnight when they're not screwing their secretaries. I bet there are quite a few men like that round here.'

'Well,' Alberta was slightly thrown by the unmistakable note of venom in Erica's voice, 'I expect there *are*, but there are lots of nice people too. I'm sure,' she added hesitantly, 'you'll like Bath when you get to know it.'

'I'm sure I will,' Erica said without much conviction. 'It does seem to be a very *rich* place. It has a great many big houses! I'll feel more at home once I've made a few friends.'

'Of course you will,' Alberta said warmly, 'and you should start by coming to supper with us. Can you come next Saturday? We have a big house too but it belongs to Tony's parents.'

'You live with your in-laws? Is that easy?'

Erica seemed to be genuinely interested and Alberta, who was always happy to praise her in-laws, responded with enthusiasm. 'We moved in with them when Jacob was a baby. We were going mad in Tony's tiny flat in London and suddenly, thanks to them, we had half a house and the run of the garden. Tony stays in London three or four days a week and his parents have always been happy to babysit when necessary.'

'You're lucky to have such support,' Erica said. 'Jacob's often mentioned his grandparents. He's also told me about his father's independent record company. It sounds fascinating.'

'Then you *must* come to supper and talk to Tony about

it!' Alberta said, trying not to wonder if Jacob had told Erica about her own thriving catering business.

Later, when Alberta was trying to recall Tony's reactions to his phone call, she remembered she had been apprehensive about inviting Erica. She was grateful to Erica, she admired Erica, but she wasn't at all sure she liked her. There was a bitterness and a hardness that Alberta found decidedly intimidating. Consequently, she prepared for the evening with a great deal of care. And it did start so *well*. The house looked great. Alberta had cut sprigs of cherry blossom for the sitting room; their dense clusters of pale pink flowers seemed to positively proclaim the full promise of spring. Jacob had removed his bicycle from the hall and returned the wellington boots to their home in the cupboard under the stairs. Lionel had polished the cutlery and the candlesticks. Evie had prepared bite-sized smoked salmon sandwiches. Tony had bought a generous selection of wine and Alberta had created a spicy fish curry and grilled vegetables that smelt as good as they looked.

Erica arrived, looking fabulous in black velvet trousers and a pale green cashmere jumper. She was greeted with enthusiasm by the family.

Tony shook her hand fervently and told Erica how happy she'd made them all. 'Let me introduce you to my parents,' he said. 'This is my mother . . .'

'. . . Evie Hart,' Evie clasped Erica's hand. 'As a besotted grandmother, I can only salute your wisdom. It is a delight to meet you!'

'And I am Lionel Hart, Jacob's grandfather.' Lionel rose from his armchair, removing his generous girth with some difficulty. 'I understand you teach English?'

'I do,' Erica said, accepting the older man's outstretched hand.

'Whatever you do,' Tony warned, 'don't get my father started on English Literature. And on no account talk to him about Rupert Brooke . . .'

'I have no intention of talking about Rupert Brooke,' said Erica. 'I'm afraid I am not a fan of his poetry.'

'You are clearly an excellent English teacher,' Lionel said. 'I think the man wrote appalling poetry. He was only famous because he had the face of an angel.'

Jacob came in and said hello to Erica. As usual his light brown hair looked as if he'd just got out of bed and he wore a sweatshirt he'd long since outgrown.

Erica beamed and said, 'Hi, Jacob, how nice to see you.'

Alberta sighed happily and went out to the kitchen to get the glasses and wine.

It was good to come back and find the room was a buzz of conversation and laughter and even better to see Jacob, who invariably avoided his parents' social occasions, still present and sitting on an arm of the sofa.

Lionel hailed her cheerfully. 'Alberta, thank goodness you've brought the wine. Evie has climbed on one of her hobby horses and refuses to get off!'

'It's a very important hobby horse,' Evie retorted. 'We live in a society that has lost the art of bringing up its children. We've closed down the playing fields, we've glorified computers! Our children pulsate with energy and have nowhere to expel it!'

'I do agree,' Erica said. 'Someone said in a staff meeting only last week that if all the kids had an hour of games at the beginning of every school day, discipline problems would disappear instantly.'

'That's all very well for kids who are *good* at games,' Tony said. 'I hated games at school and I wasn't the only one.'

Evie waved a dismissive hand. 'I know, dear, but it kept you out of mischief. You can't argue with statistics. Do you know that NHS spending on hyperactivity drugs has tripled in five years? There are four hundred thousand children in this country, aged between five and nineteen, who take them on a regular basis. That has to be wrong.'

'Evie is a psychotherapist,' Alberta told Erica. 'Quite a few of her clients are teenagers.'

Erica looked at Evie with new respect. 'Do you ever intend to retire?'

'Not as long as my brain holds out,' Evie said cheerfully. 'It's fascinating work. I'm only seventy-eight. My mother gave her last piano lesson at ninety-five.'

'Why did she stop then?' Jacob asked.

'She had no choice,' Evie said. 'She died.'

Erica smiled. 'I am beginning to understand why Jacob is so exceptional. He has an amazing family.'

The amazing family gave a collective smirk. And that was when the doorbell rang.

In months to come, when Alberta looked back on this event, she could see that this was the moment when everything started to go wrong. From this point in the evening, she would be incapable of dwelling on anything – even Tony's unusually protracted phone call – other than the car crash that was her dinner party.

It was a mistake to invite Colin. In hindsight, it was

foolish to invite Philip as well. And in retrospect, it was utter madness to invite poor Graham. As with so many people who precipitate disasters, Alberta had meant well. She had sensed that Erica was lonely. She *knew* that Philip and Colin and Graham were too. All three of them were clients who used her meals-for-one service. It was possible, she had thought hopefully, that among so many singletons, a little sexual chemistry might emerge.

If there was *any* chemistry in the air, the mix turned out to be sulphurous. Poor Colin was the first victim. While Alberta served up the curry, Colin tried to engage Erica in conversation. 'So,' he said, 'you're a newcomer to Bath.'

'I believe I mentioned earlier,' Erica said, 'that I arrived here in September.'

'So you did!' Colin smiled. 'Are you living on your own?'

'My daughter's at university. She comes home in the holidays. I cannot imagine ever wanting to live with anyone *other* than my daughter.'

Colin's smile lingered heroically. 'Really? How interesting.'

Erica's eyebrows rose. 'Do *you* live on your own?'

'I have for the last three years,' Colin said, 'since my divorce. I have a twelve-year-old son. He comes to see me once a month, or rather,' he gave a melancholy smile, 'he is *supposed* to come and see me once a month. I live in hope that one day I will meet some lovely lady and start anew.'

'I wouldn't bank on it,' Erica said. 'If I were you, I would learn to start appreciating life on your own.'

Alberta gulped. 'I'm sure that's unnecessary,' she said

with a nervous laugh. 'I'm sure someone will soon snap Colin up!'

She could hear the phone ringing in the sitting room and hoped Jacob would answer it. With any luck it would be Erica's headmaster telling her that the school was burning down and he needed her over there as soon as possible.

Tony grinned. 'That's what the Seeds of Persephone say.'

Colin blinked. 'I beg your pardon? Did you say the seeds of Persephone?'

'They're one of my newest finds,' Tony said. 'Their first single was called "Snap Me Up". They're very big in Sweden.'

'I'm afraid I don't know much about contemporary music,' Philip said. 'Give me Liza Minnelli any day!'

Erica gave a snort and tossed her head.

Philip managed an uncertain laugh. 'I take it you're not a fan of Liza Minnelli?'

Erica said, 'How very perceptive of you.'

'May I ask why you don't like her?' Philip asked.

Erica raised an eyebrow. 'I can quite see that Liza Minnelli is a perfect female icon for men who are frightened of women. She's so vulnerable and pathetic, her lower lip is perpetually wobbling and she makes up her face to resemble a china doll. In reality, I'm afraid, she's an archaic aberration of femininity.'

Erica did not look afraid. Erica looked terrifying. A dumbstruck silence followed her pronouncement, broken by Jacob who came in brandishing the phone. 'Mum, it's Uncle Christopher. He wants a quick word.'

Alberta's brother, a thoughtful academic who specialized

in medieval English Literature, had never delivered a *quick* word in his life. Alberta sighed, murmured her apologies to her guests and took the phone out with her to the sitting room. 'Hi, Christopher,' she said, 'I can't talk long, I'm in the middle of a dinner party.'

'Jacob told me,' Christopher said. 'I won't keep you a moment. Helen and I are planning our annual gathering of friends and colleagues. We thought we'd better check that you can provide your usual sterling service and do the food for us. Will you be able to come and stay?'

'If it's the last weekend in September, like last year, I can,' Alberta said. 'I've already pencilled it in.'

'That's wonderful,' Christopher said. 'Helen and I shall proceed with our planning. Will you make those delicious little cottage pies you made last time?'

'I'd be happy to make anything you want,' Alberta said. She could hear Erica's mirthless laugh issuing from the dining room like a blast of cold air and added, 'Look, I must go . . .'

'Do tell me,' Christopher asked, 'what are you giving your guests tonight?'

'We're eating spicy fish curry at the moment and then Black Forest gateau.'

'Are you?' Christopher said wistfully. 'I haven't had a Black Forest gateau in years.'

'I suppose it's a bit naff,' Alberta said, 'but it's very popular at the moment and I'm trying different recipes.'

'Your guests are very lucky. What have you got in the curry?'

'Christopher, I *have* to go, I'll speak to you soon.' Really, it was extraordinary that Christopher and Helen were both so clever and both loved food so much and yet had as much idea about cooking as would a five-year-old.

Back in the dining room, she put the phone on the sideboard and took her place at the table, noting with relief that Lionel was now holding forth.

'I know Tony will *howl* with disapproval,' he said, 'but my favourite performer has always been Suzi Quatro.'

Erica's face softened. 'I think that does you credit,' she said. 'I took Sadie to see her a few years ago. She's an icon for all serious feminists.'

'Actually,' Lionel confessed, 'I think I just liked all that leather.'

'The trouble with *you*,' Tony said, 'is you haven't listened to music *since* Suzi Quatro.'

'If you mean, I don't appreciate the groups you promote,' retorted Lionel, 'with their incomprehensible music and their incomprehensible names, you are absolutely right.'

'You won't even give them a chance,' Tony protested. 'The Seeds of Persephone are superb.'

The double act that was Tony and Lionel had swung into action. Thank God for Tony and Lionel! Alberta's heart, which had been pulsating wildly, began to slow down. It was funny, she thought, looking at the two men, how very different they were. Tony looked much younger than his forty-eight years. His blue eyes, framed by preposterously long eyelashes, were set wide apart. He was shorter than his father and slight of build with tousled blond hair through which he threaded his fingers whenever he was animated. Lionel was large and rotund with a shiny egg-shaped head and a booming voice that dealt only in certainties. He was a cheerful, optimistic soul who believed in the essential goodness of Man while relishing the absurdities he saw around him. Tony was soft-voiced and a better listener than his father. He was also deeply cynical. With any luck, he and Lionel would get on to politics and keep talking for the rest of the meal.

For a time her wish seemed to be coming true. And then, during the Black Forest gateau, Graham made a fatal mistake. He tried to join in the conversation.

'What people always forget,' Lionel was saying, 'is that for centuries European countries have been fighting each other. They don't any more, thanks to the European Union. Germany is as likely to invade France as we are to invade Italy. I do sometimes think that there is unnecessary pessimism about the state of the world in the twenty-first century!'

The phone on the sideboard burst into life and Tony leant back to pick it up. 'Hello?' he said cheerfully, pushing back his chair, 'We're in the middle of a . . .' and then, standing up, 'Can you hang on a moment?' He gave an awkward nod to his guests. 'I'm so sorry. I have to take this phone call. I won't be long.' He threw a half-apologetic, half-defensive smile to Alberta and left the room quickly.

Graham cleared his throat. 'Well, personally,' he said, 'I think we should start electing women leaders. That will stop all this macho posturing!'

Inwardly, Alberta groaned. It was obvious that Graham, attracted by Erica's fiery personality or perhaps her close-fitting velvet trousers, was trying to gain her good opinion. Alberta glanced uneasily at Erica, who looked like a lion that had just seen a particularly tasty wildebeest.

'Do you really think that?' Erica asked. 'Are you sure that Margaret Thatcher and Golda Meir, to give just two examples, were gentle, peace-loving folk?'

A rabbit who thrust his head out of his rabbit hole and discovered a tractor was bearing down on him would have looked less afraid than Graham did at that moment. 'No,' he said, 'my goodness, no, they were strong, they were very, very strong.' He rubbed one side of his head nervously. 'They were as strong as any man.'

Alberta, sensing catastrophe, looked meaningfully at Evie for help but Evie was studying Erica with the same expression that Alberta sometimes caught Jacob directing at *her*: the expression of a scientist regarding a particularly unusual blob of bacteria.

Erica gave a long sigh. 'I think it was Virginia Woolf who wondered why it was that women were so much more interesting to men than men were to women. I have to say that . . .'

Alberta did not take in what it was Erica had to say. All she knew was that it took Erica a great deal of time to say it. She wished Tony would come back. He'd been on the phone for ages. What the hell was he doing? She glanced around the table and knew that her three single male guests had, like her, given up the struggle. Only Lionel and Evie seemed to be enjoying Erica's extremely long dissertation on the deficiencies of the male gender since they occasionally chipped in with various questions and comments.

Alberta was pretty certain she was not the only one to breathe a sigh of relief when Tony came back to the dining room. 'I do apologize for being so long,' he said. 'Have I missed anything exciting?'

'Erica's been most interesting,' Lionel said, standing up and then directing a concerned glance at his son. 'I say, my boy, are you all right? No bad news, I hope?'

For a moment, it seemed to Alberta that Tony looked like someone who was trying to remember how to smile. 'No, no. Now, can I get anyone more wine?'

Lionel gave a slightly theatrical yawn. 'Not for me, thank you. I'm afraid I'm going to have to go to my bed, I'm too old for late nights.' He turned to his wife. 'Are you coming, my darling, or do you want to stay?'

Evie rose from her seat and smiled at Alberta. 'It's been a fascinating evening, dear, quite fascinating.'

'Fascinating,' Lionel agreed. 'So nice to meet you all. Erica, I look forward to not discussing Rupert Brooke with you on a future occasion!'

'Actually,' said Graham, 'I must be off too. I have a busy day tomorrow, a really very busy day. Alberta, the food was delicious. Please don't get up, I can see myself out.' He almost shot out of the door.

Within ten minutes, Erica and Colin and Philip also remembered they had a busy day ahead of them. None of them wanted coffee, all of them wanted to go home.

After waving goodbye to their last guest, Alberta closed the door and followed Tony back into the dining room, rubbing the small of her back as she did so. 'That was, without qualification, the most excruciating dinner party I have ever given. I shall never have another dinner party in my life.'

'Can I have that in writing?' Tony asked. 'I reckon everyone had a terrible time, except perhaps my parents and that's only because they like weird social experiences. As Nick

Cave and the Bad Seeds almost said, it's been a long, strange evening.'

Alberta shuddered. 'I thought it would never end. And you were out of the room for *ever.* Was it really necessary to have a marathon phone conversation in the middle of a dinner party?'

'I'm sorry,' Tony said. 'It was—' He stopped and rubbed his forehead with his hand. 'Shall we have a last drink before we start clearing up? I could do with a bit more wine.'

'I could do with a *lot* more wine,' said Alberta forcefully, passing her glass to Tony. 'I'm completely shattered. While you were out of the room, Erica let rip about the evils of men. I thought Graham was going to cry.'

Tony reached for the bottle and filled their glasses. 'Bertie,' he asked mildly, 'what possessed you to invite *three* unattached men to dinner with Erica?'

'I don't *know*!' Alberta said wretchedly. 'I thought she seemed lonely and I thought she might like to meet some people!'

'So why didn't you invite any of your female clients?'

'I don't know! I thought— Oh I don't know what I thought! I was only going to invite Philip but then, when I delivered a couple of pies for Colin, he was so sad because his son couldn't visit this weekend, and then Graham's cat died and it all got out of hand. How was I to know Erica was a man-hating ball-breaker?'

'I get the feeling she wasn't too excited about being set up with three random men.' Tony took a sip of his wine and leant back in his chair. 'And they were all non-starters anyway. The man with the tie looked like he was already depressed at the beginning of the evening and that was before Erica said anything. The man with the corduroy jacket was terrified of her and the one with the ears is gay.'

'Philip is gay? How do you know he is gay?'

Tony shrugged. 'He likes Liza Minnelli.'

'Oh,' said Alberta. She took a generous swig from her glass. 'I feel awful. They're all such nice men. And Erica was horrible to them! Tony, I am never going to match-make ever again!'

'Can I have that in writing as well?' Tony asked.

'I'll tell you what this evening was like,' Alberta said. 'It was as if Erica kept hurling big, black rocks onto the table. No one could relax. Even Lionel couldn't wait to get away.'

Tony grinned. 'It was quite funny, though. It was like that fairy tale where the icy princess dismisses each suitor in turn.'

'It was *not* funny,' Alberta exclaimed. 'It was *gruesome*! This has been the worst Saturday evening of my life! And it wasn't helped by your excessively long absence from the dinner table.'

'Well, let's make sure we have a good evening next Saturday. We'll have a nice, simple supper with Dylan and Jacob and Mum and Dad.'

'Oh,' Alberta said in the carefully neutral voice she always used when talking about her stepson, 'I'd forgotten Dylan was coming down.'

Tony gave a sudden laugh. 'Can you imagine if Dylan had been here tonight? I don't think he and Erica would have hit it off.'

'I don't even want to imagine it,' Alberta retorted and

promptly did so. And the possibilities of such an encounter were so horrific that she quite forgot to ask Tony who it was that had kept him on the phone for such a very long time.

# CHAPTER TWO

## *True Grit*

When Hannah was nine, an ostrich-faced boy called Robert Lee accused her of being a sheep-shagger. Hannah had no idea what had made him say this. She didn't have a clue what a sheep-shagger *was*, but from the look on his face she could see that it wasn't very nice.

The sheep-shagger memory resurfaced during an unpleasant meeting with Mr Kennedy at work. Mr Kennedy looked at her with an expression that was uncannily similar to that of Robert Lee and warned her that being too clever was just as counterproductive as being too stupid. As with the odious Robert, Hannah had *no* idea as to why he said this.

Such mysteries were not uncommon in Hannah's life. At primary school, she failed to acquire any friends but frequently gathered enemies for reasons she could not understand. Secondary school was different because, on her first day, she met a soulmate in Kitty and Kitty, whose ferocity when provoked was terrifying to behold, was more than a match for those tormentors of Hannah who joined her from primary school.

Hannah might have been bullied less often, but party invitations continued to be conspicuous by their absence. She often pondered the reasons for her unpopularity. She was clever of course and, even worse, was never any good at concealing her cleverness. She was as hopeless at keeping her hand down in class as she was at pretending to think Gary Jessop in the year above was hot.

But, actually, Hannah was pretty sure that these failings only partly explained why, without Kitty at school, she would have been a virtual social leper. Her peers could sense she was odd. It had taken Hannah a long time to understand this but the truth was that her emotional barometer was wayward to say the least. Who else could feel like bursting with happiness simply because she finally got the point of a Shakespearean sonnet? Who else would be so stupid as to be unable to eat for nearly three days simply because Lucy Gale told her her hair was the colour of dog poo, particularly since it quite clearly *wasn't*?

The last year of her school life was blighted by Martin Runner, a boy whose intemperate moodiness she mistook for romantic depth of feeling. There was one occasion when he leant forward and murmured, 'Do you love me?' and she whispered, 'Yes, I do,' and he sat back thoughtfully and said, 'I don't think I love *you*.' Hannah could almost feel her heart break.

She had never said any of this to her mother because her mother would not have understood. Hannah's mother was blessed with a sunny temperament that would always, like a cork in water, find its way to the sunlight. Hannah was convinced she inherited *her* temperament from her father's side of the family. Her father's parents had never recovered from the sudden loss of their only son and both of them died just a few years later and within eighteen months of each other, one from a brain haemorrhage and the other from a heart attack.

Hannah was only three when her father died in a car crash. She could remember walking into her parents' bedroom and finding her mother face down on the bed, her whole body shaking with grief. And yet six months later, she had met Tony.

Tony had been good in all sorts of ways. For a start, her mother started smiling again and they moved out of the gloomy mausoleum that was her paternal grandparents' house. Tony's flat was small and untidy but it was always full of music and Tony never minded if she left her toys on the floor. Tony taught her to play Snap and the Memory Game and when she beat him, he'd slap his head with his hand and make her laugh.

When Jacob came along, Hannah expected to be jealous. Instead, she felt a pure, unconditional love as soon as her mother put him in her arms and he looked up into her eyes.

Jacob did not disappoint her as he grew older. When Martin Runner finally dumped her, Jacob came into her room and stood in front of her while she wept. 'I want to say two things,' he said, taking off his glasses and rubbing them on his sleeve. 'One: if I weren't your brother I would want to go out with you, but if I were a girl I would not want to go out with Martin. Two: if you look at Martin's head very carefully, you will see his hair is thin on top. Mark my words: he will be bald before he's thirty.'

Hannah had found herself smiling, not just because Jacob had to be the only twelve-year-old in Bath who used phrases like 'mark my words', but also because it was funny to imagine Jacob scrutinizing Martin's hair.

Hannah had intended to go to Durham University along with Martin. Now, she changed her plans and decided to try to get into Oxford, partly because no one from school was going there and partly because her form teacher suggested it. She had no desire to spend her gap year in Bath and found a job with a health education pressure group in London.

It proved to be a good decision. She got involved in fund-raising, organizing media events, designing posters and even talking to pupils at schools. She wasn't very good at designing posters but she was very good at marshalling arguments and statistics.

She lived in Tony's London flat and that was fun too. Often, she'd go with him to various gigs in dark little pubs or the odd music awards evening. When Tony was away in Bath, she would plough through the enormous reading list she'd been sent from Oxford.

She was sorry to leave the job and Tony's comfortable little flat. She assumed Oxford would be as depressing as school had been. Indeed, she assumed Oxford would be worse than school since Kitty would not be there.

But Oxford turned out to be a great place for Hannah. She might not have Kitty, but she did have Harrison Mills.

Harrison was the first student she met at Oxford. They both arrived at Lady Margaret Hall at the same time and met while standing by the porter's lodge with suitcases and mothers in tow, checking the photographs on the display board. Her first impressions were of a wonderful smile and a very odd jersey. Having quickly ascertained they were doing the same course, they speedily dispatched their mothers and set about getting to know each other.

Harrison was not particularly good-looking. He was of average height, with regular features apart from a chin which was a little too big for the rest of his face. He had an infectious smile that instantly activated a set of dimples on either side of his mouth, and he and Hannah got on immediately. Until she met Russell, three hours later, she thought he was extremely attractive.

As it happened, the one good result of her relationship with Russell was that she did *not* become romantically involved with Harrison. If she had done they would undoubtedly have broken up within a few weeks – none of Harrison's relationships lasted more than a few weeks. Instead, Harrison became and remained a superb friend. She had no idea why Harrison liked her: they were totally different. Harrison was relaxed and easy-going and a great social animal. He insisted on dragging her along to meet people he liked and invariably she found that she actually enjoyed herself. Because she went with Harrison who thought she was marvellous, his friends seemed to like her too, and for the first time in her life, Hannah discovered what it was like to walk into a party and *not* feel the usual pangs of fear and apprehension.

In fact, life at Oxford would have been almost completely perfect, had it not been for Russell and Ludovic, both of whom were blond and beautiful and surprisingly brutal.

Russell was a tall, second-year student, a star debater in the Oxford Union, whose charm and confidence were initially focused on Hannah with such force that she was dazzled. When he stood for President of the Union two terms later, she could quite understand why he was markedly less attentive – he had so much to do, after all – and she went out campaigning for him whenever she could. One evening, he told her that his running mate was a perfect partner as she was so charismatic and clever. The next night was the election, and at five in the morning Hannah was with Russell and his friends when he was told he had won. Hannah was about to go up and fling her arms round him when she noticed that his running mate was not only doing just that but was also following it up with a kiss of such epic proportions that it could probably have made the *Guinness Book of Records*. She waited for Russell to break away and it was only when he didn't that she understood that when he had told her his running mate was a perfect partner he had expected her to understand that his running mate was the perfect partner.

Hannah's humiliation and misery were overwhelming and when she met Ludovic, she was glad to find he had no time at all for Union politics. Ludovic had no time at all for quite a lot of things. He had no time for shampoo or small talk or clean sheets or television or films that didn't illuminate the human condition. His favourite group was Radiohead, his favourite writer was Jean-Paul Sartre and he believed only stupid people were happy. He was actually rather depressing. When, after graduation, she got her position at Associated Metals, he told her she had proved to be as conventional and predictable in her actions as she was in her conversation.

It was Harrison who pointed the way. Just before he set off for Vietnam, he asked her if she was sure she wanted to be with someone who made her miserable all the time. It was such an obvious question and there was only one sensible answer. One month after she moved up to London, she finished with Ludovic. Now, eighteen months later, she couldn't believe she had put up with him for as long as she had.

Harrison had left Oxford straight after his finals to take up a job with Oxfam in Vietnam. He sent Hannah fascinating emails. Apparently, Vietnam was in greater danger from global warming than almost any other country. The World Bank believed that a tenth of its towns and cities would be swamped by rising seas by the end of the century. Harrison's job was to help upgrade national flood early-warning systems.

For a time, Hannah feared he'd settle abroad permanently but now he'd come home. He'd been in London for three weeks but she'd only seen him once, in a pub in Camden, and then she'd had to share him with a crowd of their old university friends.

Tonight, Hannah had him to herself and she couldn't wait to see him. This evening, she left the plush offices of Associated Metals much earlier than usual and raced towards the tube station.

They had agreed to meet at a pub called the Copper Arm. It was a big, spacious place with black leather sofas, high-backed settles and old gilt-framed mirrors. Hannah glanced around and smiled as she recognized Harrison's jersey. He was standing with his back to her at the bar and was wearing an old favourite, a salmon-coloured creation he had picked up at a Help the Aged charity shop.

She tapped his shoulder and he turned round and grinned before giving her a hug. 'Hannah Granger!' he said. 'It is very, *very* good to see you! I've just ordered our drinks . . .'

'I'll pay,' Hannah said. 'You can do it next time. Oh, Harrison, I have missed you!' She was aware that she was starving, probably because she'd had no time for lunch. When she paid for the drinks, she bought peanuts and crisps as well and led Harrison to a seat by the window. 'You haven't lost your tan,' she said. 'It suits you.'

'I can't get used to your hair,' he responded. 'I like it.'

'At first I thought it was a bit extreme but I'm used to it now. I had it cut after I broke up with Ludovic.'

'I am *so* glad you said goodbye to Lanky Ludovic. He was *so* boring.'

'He was not!'

'He was. He talked so quietly, I could never hear what he said. And he gave this funny laugh every time he stopped speaking and because I couldn't hear him I couldn't tell if it was a ha-ha-ha sort of laugh in which case I ought to join in or a huh-huh-huh sort of laugh in which case I ought to feel crushed. Anyway, I definitely like the hair. It makes you look like a small Audrey Hepburn.'

'Didn't she have long hair?'

'She had both but even when she had long hair she looked like a woman with short hair. Never mind about her. Tell me about the new man. I presume he is tall and blond and revoltingly good-looking?'

'Yes, but . . .'

Harrison shook his head. 'You are so predictable. Tell me everything.'

'Well –' Hannah paused to open the crisp packet with her teeth – 'do you remember me telling you I planned to buy a flat with the money my father's parents left me? Well, I did. It's in Stoke Newington and I can't wait to have you over. It's got lovely big sash windows and every room is light and bright and the floorboards are stripped and polished – I love it. Kitty came to live with me and a few months ago her oldest brother came back from Hamburg and asked if he could sleep on our sofa while he found a flat. I never really knew him in Bath – he's six years older than Kitty – but when he walked into the flat, it was weird, it all happened so quickly . . .'

'That's not weird,' Harrison said. 'Things always happen like that with you. You'd only met Lanky Ludo for about five minutes when you decided he was the love of your life. What does this one do?'

'He's an actor. You've seen him! Do you remember we watched that film called *The Sons of Cain* because it had Kitty's brother in it? That was Alfie. He was the first son, who got killed off quite early.'

'I remember,' Harrison nodded. 'He was the one who narrowed his eyes in a macho way every time he was about to rape someone.'

'He's a very good actor,' Hannah said severely.

'I'm sure he is. He was certainly good at narrowing his eyes. Hannah?' He leant forward and whispered, 'Why are you covering your face with your hand?'

'I've just seen Dylan,' Hannah hissed. 'I know I've told you about him. He's my stepbrother. Tony was married to a glamorous lawyer before he met Mum and somehow they produced Dylan who is probably the most annoying person in the world. I can't believe it. If Dylan's discovered this place, I'm going to have to give it up. Perhaps he won't see me.'

'Does Dylan have dyed blond hair?'

'Yes,' Hannah whispered.

'Then he's seen you.'

Hannah turned round reluctantly and watched as Dylan and his posse came towards them. His three friends all had earrings in their left ears as did Dylan, and they all had smirks on their faces as did Dylan.

'How you doing, Hannah?' Dylan said. 'I never thought I'd see you in a pub.'

'Really?' Hannah said. 'And why is that, Dylan?'

'I never imagined you having a social life. I'm glad to see you enjoying yourself.' Dylan grunted something unintelligible at his friends as they moved towards the bar, and raised an eyebrow at Hannah. 'Are you going to introduce me to your companion?'

Hannah sighed. 'Dylan, this is Harrison. Harrison, this is my stepbrother.'

'It's very touching to hear you call me that,' Dylan said, 'but since your mother and my father have never married, you aren't actually my stepsister.'

'It saves explanations,' Hannah said. 'I would hate people to think I actually *chose* to know you.'

'Isn't she a sweetie?' Dylan said to Harrison. 'It's been a pleasure to meet you. I didn't think Hannah had any friends.' Dylan's eyes veered briefly towards the mirror opposite him and he smoothed his hair. 'I'll see you around.'

Hannah watched as he moved away. 'The trouble with family,' she said, 'is that you have to put up with people you would never normally talk to in a million years.'

'I'm sure Dylan would agree with you,' Harrison said. He opened one of Hannah's bags of nuts. 'I think you're rather lucky with your relatives. I liked the ones I met in Bath and I *love* your mother.'

'That's because she invited you to have lunch with us every time she came up to Oxford.'

'I just like her,' Harrison insisted. 'She's fun and she's kind. I'll never forget how good she was about the red wine I spilt on her carpet at your twenty-first birthday party. I don't know how she got rid of those stains.'

Hannah nodded. 'She's brilliant at stains.'

'She's like you,' Harrison said.

'I don't know anything about stains.'

'No, but—'

'She's nothing like me apart from the fact that we're both really short. She's got blonde hair, I've got dark hair.'

'I don't mean looks. I mean she's like you. Does your brother still treat her as a human guinea pig?'

On Jacob's last visit to Oxford, he had talked about a book he'd been reading which applied exotic animal-training techniques to humans. He had more or less admitted that he'd found these worked very well at home.

'I have my suspicions,' Hannah said darkly. 'A few months ago, Mum was worrying about the fact that Jacob spent so much time at his girlfriend's house. Then, suddenly, she started worrying instead about the fact that Jacob was supposedly being bullied at school.'

'Don't you think he *was* being bullied?'

'I doubt it. Jacob's so immersed in his peculiar Jacob world that he probably wouldn't notice even if he was.'

Harrison shook his head. 'Jacob's like those scary alien children in *The Village of the Damned*. He'll be one of those creepy television hypnotists who make women fall in love with them.' He smiled at Hannah. 'I wish I could do that.'

'You'll be fine,' Hannah assured him. 'After Ludovic, I despaired of ever finding anyone and now . . . I've met Alfie. He's perfect for me.'

'That's wonderful,' Harrison said. 'I remember you saying that about Russell.'

'I didn't!'

'I remember you saying that about Ludovic too.'

'This time,' Hannah said firmly, 'it's different.'

Kitty was only a few inches taller than Hannah. Short-sighted and thin, she looked as fragile as a feather in the wind. In her case, appearances were definitely deceptive. Her clear blue eyes, behind her circular glasses, were fierce and focused and in a previous incarnation she could have been a Boudicca or a Joan of Arc. She was always ready to fight cruelty or unfairness. For someone like Kitty, it was a form of torture to keep silent in the face of injustice. At the moment she was in no position to do anything else. In the last fourteen months, she had walked out of two jobs and been sacked from a third. The marketing job with Envers Production Company was her last chance to prevent her increasingly battle-scarred CV going into free fall. It was therefore particularly unfortunate that on her first morning there she discovered she had the boss from hell.

When Hannah arrived home, she could tell that today

had been particularly bad. Kitty was lying on the sofa, watching *Four Weddings and a Funeral* with her red woollen hat jammed over her corkscrew curls. The only time Kitty wore her red woollen hat was when she was particularly upset.

On the television screen, Andie McDowell was trying on different wedding dresses and twirling in front of Hugh Grant, who was trying very hard to act as if he couldn't keep his eyes off her.

'I can't believe you're watching this,' Hannah said.

'Remind me again,' said Kitty, without blinking an eyelid, 'which of us it was who burst into tears when Hugh Grant sang to Drew Barrymore in *Music and Lyrics*?'

'That was different,' Hannah said, 'I was very tired at the time.'

'Well, so am I,' said Kitty. 'And when I'm tired, the best thing in the world is to sit and watch Andie McDowell simpering at Hugh Grant.'

Hannah cast her friend a sympathetic glance. 'What happened at work?'

'I can't even talk about it. If you want any supper, I've left half a jar of tomato sauce on the table and there's loads of pasta.'

'Thanks.' Hannah picked up a pristine new book from the table and considered the cover. The title, *Confessions of a Retired Schoolmistress*, was written in lurid red colours over a photograph of a grey-haired teacher with her back to the camera. The teacher was talking to a class of good-looking, sulky teenage boys. One hand, grasping a piece of chalk, was held aloft and the other, clutching a whip, was hidden behind her back. The teacher wore a sensible tweed jacket but her desk hid from the children the fact that she was also dressed in a tight black skirt, fishnet tights and red stiletto heels. 'Kitty!' Hannah said. 'This looks utter rubbish!'

'I know,' Kitty said. 'I can't wait to start reading it. And, anyway, the cover's misleading. It's the true memoirs of a schoolteacher. It's very educational.'

'Yeah, right,' grinned Hannah. 'So how *was* it today?'

Kitty grimaced. 'It was hideous. It was unrelentingly hideous. I am counting the days till I go away. Melanie told me off in front of everyone and Conrad looked like the cat that got the cream. She actually asked me if it was "that time of the month" and when I asked her what time of the month she might be referring to, she gave everyone a knowing smile and said that it obviously was! I know what she's doing. She is *trying* to make me lose my temper. She *wants* me to flare up and walk out. I didn't say anything. You'd have been proud of me. I am doing my best to keep my temper until I go on holiday. I nearly lost it today but I could see that it would please Conrad too much. I hate Conrad. I hate Melanie and I hate Andie McDowell. I'm sorry I'm in such a foul mood. I'll be better soon.'

Hannah put a sympathetic hand on Kitty's shoulder and went through to the kitchen. She felt extremely sad about her friend's predicament but there was no doubt that Kitty was an expert at hating people. One of the pleasures of living with Kitty was hearing about the many individuals who daily drove her to apoplectic levels of suppressed rage. And of them all, Melanie and Conrad were at the top of the hate chart. Conrad had joined the company the same day as Kitty and her feelings for him were only marginally less vitriolic than her hatred for Melanie. Most days she came home with a tale of some new and appalling act of pettiness or backbiting or insult. She was off to Croatia in three days with two of her girlfriends from university and Hannah knew she would miss her.

Hannah had a quick supper, allowed herself a fifteen-minute break with Kitty and Hugh Grant and then retreated with her laptop to her bedroom. After Ludovic, she had been grateful for the fact that she had a demanding job with finance exams to work for. When Alfie came into her life, it was impossible for her to continue to be so single-minded. She had been relieved when he got a small part in the play at the Bush Theatre since it meant that he was out every evening and she could catch up on her work. She was guiltily aware that she wished the play wouldn't close until her exams were out of the way.

Tonight, it was proving difficult to concentrate. Perhaps she was too excited about seeing Harrison again. He'd been odd this evening, though. She'd suggested fixing another date for a drink and he'd gone into a long ramble about various commitments and they'd ended up not fixing anything. He was waiting to hear about a job interview he'd had a few days earlier and he'd got another interview on Monday. She'd give him a ring in a few days' time.

At eleven, Hannah sighed and decided to give up the increasingly difficult battle to keep her brain fixed on the computer screen. On her way to the bathroom she glanced at the television. Kitty was watching *Notting Hill* now.

Hannah felt compelled to point out that it had exactly the same plot as the previous film. Kitty said she didn't care and that at least Julia Roberts was a better actress than Andie McDowell.

Twenty minutes later, Hannah was in bed with a thick file and soon after that she heard Alfie say, 'Hannah! Hannah, are you asleep?'

Hannah opened her eyes and said of course she wasn't, she'd been waiting up for him. Most nights, Alfie came home on a tide of energy, bounding into their bedroom as if he'd been shot from a cannon. Tonight, there was an added excitement about him that was almost tangible.

'Poor Hannah!' he cried, coming over to kiss her. 'You work so hard! You have such determination! Do I ever tell you how much I admire you?'

He did, often. It was one reason why she loved him. Alfie thought she was strong and tough and remarkably like the Sigourney Weaver character in *Alien*. She reached up to stroke his face. 'How was the play? Did you have a good audience?'

'Very good.' Alfie sat down beside her. 'And they liked me. I could tell they liked me. I wish I had a bigger part. Am I *very* vain?'

Hannah nodded. 'You are *grotesquely* vain. You'll be quite impossible when you're famous.'

Alfie pulled off his shoes and swung his legs onto the bed. 'I want to talk to you about that.'

'You want to talk about being impossible?'

'I saw my agent this morning. She's got me a very exciting audition. Have you ever heard of a queen of England called Isabella?'

'Yes. She was married to Edward the Second, whose death involved a red-hot poker.'

'Very good. Only now, some people think he escaped abroad and ended his days as a monk. There's going to be a six-part serialization of Isabella's life and it's going to be *huge* and I am going to audition for the part of Gautier d'Aulnay.'

'Who was he?'

'A sexy Frenchman who comes to a very nasty end. Isabella's father is King of France and she goes over to visit him and notices that her two sisters-in-law are having affairs with two handsome brothers, one of whom is Gautier. Isabella tells her father. Her father throws the girls into prison and the brothers are publicly castrated, partially flayed alive, broken on the wheel and finally decapitated.'

'That'd show them.'

'Quite. My agent's very excited. She says it's a part that could really make me. This time next year, I could be earning a fortune!' He swung his feet back onto the floor and stood up. 'I'm going to let you sleep. I'm too wide awake to go to bed. I shall watch something very bad on the television in the company of my sister, who's looking even more bad-tempered than usual.'

'I love you,' Hannah said. She watched him blow her a kiss before leaving the room and then she put her file down on the floor, switched out her light and snuggled under the duvet. She felt very happy. Alfie had been fretting for weeks about the fact he had nothing to do once the play was finished. If he got this job and his career took off, who knew what would happen? And it was wonderful to have

Harrison back in her life. London seemed an infinitely more attractive place now he was here. Life, Hannah thought sleepily, was really pretty good.

# CHAPTER THREE

## *Duel in Jacob's Bedroom*

Dylan was an unlikely Cupid but it was undoubtedly true that he was responsible for bringing Tony and Alberta together.

Alberta was sitting in St James's Park, watching Hannah chasing leaves and trying to catch them with her fishing net. (Who had given Hannah the net and why had they brought it to the park? If she had known in later years that her memory would become so faulty, she would have kept a diary.) Hannah, in navy dungarees and a pink and white top, with dark hair flying, screeched with delight while Alberta looked on.

The happy scene was torpedoed by a small boy with tufty brown hair and a green boiler suit who ran towards Hannah, snatched the fishing net and ran away. Alberta leapt from her bench and Hannah screamed with indignation and continued to scream until the boy came back, holding the net in one hand and the hand of a slim young man in the other. The slim young man assured Hannah that Dylan was very sorry for behaving so badly.

Dylan did not look sorry at all. The man told Dylan to

return the net and the little boy responded by clasping the net to his chest. Hannah resumed her screams and the man looked to Alberta for help. Alberta sensed the boy was the sort of child for whom the taking was more exciting than the having; she suggested he could play with the net for a few minutes while she and Hannah and the man worked together to make . . . Alberta's eyes roamed frantically for inspiration . . . a massive leaf mountain!

The man looked at Alberta with respect. Hannah agreed she would like to build a massive leaf mountain and happily began instructing the man and her mother on the best way of going about it. Dylan began to run around with the net. A few minutes later, having discovered that no one was paying him any attention, he came over, dropped the net and said *he* wanted to make a leaf mountain too. Hannah graciously allowed him to help her and the adults were able to step aside and introduce themselves.

The man was called Tony and Dylan was his son. Dylan was, Tony conceded, a rather demanding three-year-old, but he was going through a difficult time. He couldn't understand why Tony no longer lived with him and his mother. How could one explain divorce to a three-year-old?

Alberta nodded in sympathy and said she quite understood: her daughter was also three and was also a little demanding, probably because it was impossible to explain death to a three-year-old. Her husband, she told Tony, had recently lost his life in a car accident and she and Hannah were lost without him. They were now living, she added rather forlornly, with her late husband's parents.

A few months later, Alberta and Hannah moved in with

Tony. Tony said they had saved him from becoming a sad, embittered loner. Alberta knew this was not true: Tony was far too good-natured to be embittered and he had a huge circle of friends. Alberta told Tony she hated the dark, miserable home of her in-laws and he had saved her from going mad. Tony laughed. Alberta laughed too but had the uncomfortable thought that her comment was not entirely without credibility.

In their first year together, Dylan stayed with them most weekends. It seemed so fortunate that he and Hannah were the same age and could keep each other company. The truth was, however, that they had little in common. Hannah was an unusually articulate, opinionated little girl who liked reading and loved jigsaws. Dylan was a boy who couldn't sit still, was easily bored and loved smashing things up, especially jigsaws. Alberta explained to Hannah that Dylan did not mean to be unkind but he was probably jealous of her because she lived with his father and he did not and she must therefore try to be extra kind to him. Hannah said it wasn't *her* fault that Dylan didn't live with his father and she was very sure that Dylan *did* mean to be unkind. Alberta looked anxious and said with as much conviction as she could muster that she was sure Hannah was wrong.

As time went on, Dylan's visits became less frequent. Tony was dismayed but accepted his ex-wife's explanation. Lydia said that Dylan was at an age when he wanted to be with his peers. He liked swimming and football and sleepovers with his friend, Sam. Surely Tony couldn't expect him to give them up in favour of cramped weekends in a tiny flat with a stepsister who made him feel inadequate. Tony told Lydia he had never been aware that Dylan felt inadequate beside Hannah and that Dylan had never said anything to him to warrant such a view. Lydia assured him that Dylan had never said anything to her either but that she could just *tell*. Tony suggested he could take him out on his own at weekends and Lydia said that would be very nice but actually it didn't change the fact that Dylan still wanted to go swimming and play football and have sleep-overs with his friend, Sam.

With the birth of Jacob and the subsequent move to Bath, Dylan's visits dwindled still further. Tony tried to make a habit of seeing him regularly when he was in London, either by going over to Lydia's house or by taking Dylan out. Dylan continued to visit during the school holidays but these visits were never very satisfactory. Dylan and Hannah had a working relationship by this time which basically involved them having as little to do with each other as they could possibly manage. Tony hoped that Dylan would develop as good a relationship with his little half-brother as the latter enjoyed with Hannah. These hopes were not realized. Dylan enjoyed kicking a ball in the garden while Jacob preferred sitting on the lawn, building towers with his bricks. Too often, Dylan's ball would somehow end up knocking down Jacob's towers. Alberta assured Tony that by the time Dylan was a teenager, Jacob would worship him.

When Dylan *was* a teenager, Alberta was profoundly relieved to find that Jacob showed absolutely no signs of worshipping his older half-brother. When Dylan came to stay, he told loud, interminable stories about the parties he went to, the girls he was seeing, the teachers whose classes he disrupted and the drugs he implied he was taking. Hannah would roll her eyes and disappear up to her room. Jacob, who adored Hannah, would immediately roll his eyes and disappear too. Alberta would find him later, sprawled on Hannah's bed with his exercise book and his pencil box, absorbed in the creation of ever more intricate rockets. Alberta did her best to encourage her children to be more friendly but was handicapped by the knowledge that in their position she would want to avoid Dylan's company too.

Dylan's mother was half-French and Alberta heaved a secret sigh of relief when he decided to move to France after he left school. Dylan spoke excellent French and liked the idea of working on his uncle's vineyard in Epernay. After a couple of years, he decided he didn't like working on his uncle's vineyard after all. He was now in his second year at university, studying photography, and it was photography that was the reason for his forthcoming visit.

Dylan was arriving on Friday and staying until the following Wednesday. He had often expressed his disappointment that his grandparents had chosen to live in a rambling nineteen thirties house when they could have acquired an elegant Georgian terrace. Now, he wanted to put together a portfolio of what he called 'proper' houses; in particular, he planned a series of photos of the various Georgian crescents in the city.

Tony told Alberta that it was good to see Dylan taking his work so seriously and that perhaps he was really growing up at last. Alberta agreed this was quite likely and forebore to mention that Tony had expressed the same sentiments in the same hopeful tone at least four times in the last two years.

Tony rang Alberta when he was back in London and told her he and Dylan would travel down together on Friday. He added that he had rearranged his diary so that he could work from home while Dylan was in Bath. Alberta, meanwhile, had decided a weekend in Dylan's company was as much as she could stand.

Alberta's mother, known to all her family as Marma, had never invited either of her grown-up children to stay with her, her argument being that since they knew she would always love to see them, it was up to them to invite themselves. Fortunately, Tony wasn't aware of this.

Alberta, improvising wildly and feeling horribly guilty, said, 'Tony, I've had a call from Marma. She's invited me to go and stay on Monday for a few days. I haven't seen her and Pa for ages. Dylan won't mind if I go, will he?'

'No,' Tony said. 'We'll be fine.'

Tony's compliance made her feel ashamed but not so ashamed that she didn't then go off and make two phone calls. The first was to her mother to tell her of her imminent arrival. The second was less easy.

Alberta had met Diana Bounty fifteen years ago, when their younger children were at the same play school. They discovered they had both been professional cooks and were both anxious to return to the job market. When they set up *Bounty of Bath*, they envisaged a small-scale business in which they delivered good, home-cooked meals to people who couldn't or wouldn't cook for themselves. Gradually, as their confidence increased, they began to accept bookings for parties and even wedding buffets. When their client-base expanded, Diana pointed out that they no longer needed the paltry income brought in by what she called TCCs (time-consuming clients). Now that they were so much in demand for corporate functions, it was absurd to go on cooking individual meals for old ladies and helpless widowers. Alberta, however, had grown fond of her TCCs and knew how much they valued her meals. For a time it looked as if the two women might go their separate ways. Alberta felt they were like an old married couple who discover they no longer have the same interests. Alberta had gone into partnership with Diana in the belief they would provide a service as well as making a living. Diana was only interested in having the most successful catering business in Bath.

A compromise solution was reached. Alberta agreed that Diana's friend, Pam, could join the business with a view to becoming a third partner in a couple of years. Diana agreed to the retention of small clients on condition that Alberta took responsibility for them.

In order to achieve a temporary break from Jacob, Alberta had to ask Diana to cook for and deliver to three of her TCCs on Tuesday. She had anticipated an unenthusiastic response and she was right. She had to endure an eight-minute rant in which the phrases 'unbusinesslike behaviour' and 'thin end of the wedge' were repeated at least three times. And then, when Diana finally agreed to Alberta's fairly modest request, she had the nerve to tell her she had just accepted a booking for a twenty-first birthday party – food for one hundred and ten people – in June and Alberta might like to write down the date as she, Diana, would be away on holiday in Turkey at that time.

As if the phone call with Diana was not enough, Alberta had to face a barrage of complaints from Jacob. 'Dylan's staying for almost *a week*?' he complained. 'Do you realize it's my last ever school half-term? He's spending my entire half-term here? I'll go and stay with Maud.'

Maud was Jacob's girlfriend. Jacob's family had been surprised when he acquired a girlfriend. They were less surprised after they met her since she and Jacob seemed to be so exactly right for each other. Maud was an angular, beetle-browed girl who wanted to be either a forensic pathologist or a detective since she had a keen interest in the lives of serial killers. Maud was a child of progressive parents who took Jacob to their hearts and were quite happy for him to stay over whenever he wanted.

Alberta had never liked to ask Jacob what the sleeping arrangements were and although she could not imagine her son was enjoying full carnal pleasures, she did talk to Tony about the need for A Talk. Tony duly took Jacob to one side and began with a careless, 'Jakey, about Maud . . .' only to be stopped by his son who said simply, 'It's all right, Dad, you don't need to give me the condom talk.'

As Tony said later to Alberta, it would take a stronger person than *him* to pursue the subject after that. Alberta couldn't help agreeing that it would take a stronger person than *her* to say anything at all after that.

She was adamant, however, that there was no way Jacob could waltz off and stay with his girlfriend while his half-brother was staying in Bath. 'Tony would be most upset. Dylan doesn't come down very often. You can't just go AWOL for the duration of his visit. And anyway it's not a proper half-term. You're supposed to be revising for your A levels. You have to stay at home.'

'*You* aren't,' Jacob pointed out. 'You're going to stay with Marma and Grandfather.'

'That's different,' Alberta said. 'Marma . . . Marma asked me to go.'

Jacob raised his eyebrows, took off his glasses and wiped them with his T-shirt. 'If I stay here,' he said, 'Dad will make me have dinner with them every evening. I'll come with you.'

'You can't do that,' Alberta protested. 'We can't both go.'

'Why not? It's the holidays. I always go and see Marma and Grandfather in the holidays. And I can really work there. And anyway, I told Marma I'd come.'

'You *told* . . . ! *When* did you tell her?'

'I can't remember now,' Jacob said airily. 'I was chatting to her on the phone and she told me she'd invited you and she invited me too.'

Alberta opened her mouth and then, very slowly, shut it again.

'By the way,' Jacob said, putting on his glasses again, 'I won't be in for supper tomorrow. Maud's going to be on her own and I offered to go round. Her mother says she'll leave some chops for us. I feel rather bad really. I'm always eating their food.'

'I'm making a couple of quiches in the morning,' Alberta said. 'I'll make one for you and Maud if you like.'

'Mum,' Jacob said earnestly, 'that is *so* considerate. How *very* kind of you.'

'That's all right,' said Alberta.

As she left her son's room she wondered why it was that conversations with him always left her feeling so disconcerted.

For the next few days, Alberta was imprisoned by gloom, trapped between the recent memory of the dinner party for Erica and the dismal anticipation of the forthcoming weekend with Dylan. It was at times like this that she was glad Tony decamped to London in the week. Where Dylan was concerned, Tony was plagued by an unquenchable guilt, which was quite unwarranted as Alberta had told him too many times; it was, after all, Lydia not Tony who had ended their marriage. Tony made endless excuses for his older son's behaviour and Alberta had long ago decided she had no right to interfere or to judge. This did not of course prevent her from judging but at least she had never revealed to anyone what that judgement *was*.

Meanwhile, she continued to brood over the ghastliness of the Erica fiasco. She tried to talk to Evie and Lionel about it but their responses proved less than satisfactory. Lionel was rarely discomposed by the behaviour of other people, however extreme or unsettling that behaviour might be. He regarded his fellow humans as a cabaret show, set on Earth to entertain him. He thought Erica was a tremendous character, full of *spunk*, an independent spirit who proved that not all women needed a man in their lives to be happy.

This was fine except that, in Alberta's febrile state, his implication seemed to be that *she* was a woman who needed a man in her life and had tried to impose her own conservative views on the free-thinking Erica. Evie, at least, conceded that Erica had behaved very badly but she too made excuses for her, observing that poor Erica might have been able to accept the presence of *one* single male but to accept the presence of *three* was asking too much of such a proud woman.

On Thursday evening, Alberta went to Pilates with a beating heart and didn't know whether to be glad or sorry that Erica wasn't there. On Friday morning, she received a polite missive from Graham, thanking her for a 'stimulating' evening; this only made her feel more wretched.

In the evening, she changed out of her jeans and sweatshirt before going to the station to collect Tony and Dylan. These days, Alberta always wore a skirt in the company of her stepson. Two or three years ago, he had been staring at her corduroy trousers when he abruptly observed that only women with fat legs wore trousers. Alberta might be too short and have hair that would never stay put, but she *did* have good legs. Tonight, she put on her denim skirt and a blue and white striped top.

When they came out of the station, both Dylan and Tony were wearing jeans, T-shirts and trainers. The only difference was that Dylan's trainers were probably a hundred pounds more expensive than those of his father. Alberta got out of the car and said brightly if untruthfully, 'Dylan, how nice to see you.'

'Hiya, Bertie,' Dylan said, handing her his camera bag. 'You're wearing the same skirt as that woman over there.'

They all looked at the woman over there. The woman was indeed wearing a denim skirt. She also wore grey, wrinkled tights and a dirty T-shirt, and her long, greasy hair clung to her scalp like oil. Alberta said, a little less brightly, 'What a coincidence! Shall we go?' Not for the first time, she wondered how Tony, who was so agreeable, could produce a son who was *not.* After a particularly unpleasant evening a few months ago, Tony said that Dylan had never got over his resentment of his father's second family. Alberta responded that she quite understood. She *did* understand but she also felt that it was high time Dylan came to terms with the situation.

As Alberta drove home, Tony talked about the weekend in the tone of slightly exaggerated enthusiasm he usually adopted in the presence of his older son. 'I've told Dylan I'll drive him round Bath on Sunday morning and give him an idea of places he'd like to photograph. And, tomorrow, I thought we could all go to the Bath Spa. Jacob will enjoy that and the views from the top should be great.'

'What a lovely idea,' Alberta enthused. 'I've wanted to go there for ages. Diana took her sister-in-law before Christmas and says she's never stopped talking about it. How very exciting!'

'Very, very exciting,' said Dylan in a tone that made Alberta wince. The evening, she thought glumly, was going to be very long.

In fact, it was not too bad. Only Alberta noticed that Jacob was less than excited by the prospect of the Bath Spa expedition the following afternoon and that as the evening wore on, he became increasingly mute. It was, to be fair to Jacob, difficult to be anything else. Dylan had never understood the art of conversation and either talked endlessly *at* people or said nothing at all. Tonight, he hardly drew breath. His father and grandfather smiled indulgently and enjoyed their wine while Evie occasionally interjected a 'Very good, Dylan!' or 'That's wonderful, Dylan!'

Dylan described his recent project on London's bridges, the praise he had been given by his tutor, the praise he received from his fellow students, the famous pop star with whom he was now good mates at his local pub and the three clubs which were currently his favourite meeting places.

For Alberta, listening to Dylan had the same effect as lying on a beach while trying to ignore the ghetto-blaster behind her. Dylan's words always sounded as if he'd chewed them first and they issued from his mouth in the form of a one-note bark with no inflections or hesitations. Still, she was grateful that he was at least in a good humour.

It was only during pudding that the atmosphere became a little constricted. Having finished his lemon tart in record time, Jacob stood up and announced with an impressive appearance of regret that he had to go upstairs and do some revision.

Dylan looked up and grinned. 'All work and no play,' he said, 'makes Jacob a very dull boy!'

'Tell me, Dylan,' Jacob asked, 'what A level grades *did* you get?'

Dylan leant back in his chair. 'I did enough to get by,' he said. 'There is more to life than examination results. You want to have a bit of fun, go to a few parties, meet a few girls.'

Fortunately, the telephone chose that moment to leap into action and diverted Jacob from responding to his brother's suggestions. Instead, he said, 'I'll get it,' and charged into the kitchen. He returned a few moments later, presented the phone to his father, waved vaguely at his family and sped towards the stairs.

Tony said, 'Hello? Kenny? . . . Right . . . Right . . . No, I hadn't forgotten . . . Right.' He turned off the phone, put it down on the table and said, 'Hell! I forgot!'

'I like your friend Kenny,' Lionel said. 'He's an interesting chap. He always has something new to say. Last time I saw him, he told me that the two richest men in the United States have as much money between them as have thirty per cent of the entire American people. Isn't that appalling?'

'Kenny loves facts like that,' Tony said. 'He also has a garden shed that needs putting up tomorrow. I won't be able to go to the Bath Spa.'

'Can't you do it another time?' Alberta asked.

'I promised I'd help him. I've already put it off twice and Kenny gave up a whole weekend when our fence blew down.'

'Never mind,' Dylan said. 'Jacob and I will take Bertie to the Bath Spa. We'll all have a *jolly exciting* time, won't we, Bertie?'

'We certainly will,' Alberta said. 'And now, I think it's time for coffee. I'll just go and see if Jacob wants some.'

Jacob, surprise, surprise, was not doing his history revision. He was lying on his bed, reading *How to Win Friends and Influence People.*

'Jacob,' Alberta said, 'Tony can't come with us to the Bath Spa tomorrow.'

'Fine,' Jacob said, 'I won't come either.'

'I knew you'd say that.' Alberta advanced purposefully towards him. 'You *have* to come.'

'No, I do not.'

Alberta sat on the edge of the bed and very deliberately

pulled up her sleeves. 'If you don't come,' she said, 'I'll tell your father I think you should stay here on Monday rather than come with me to Hampshire.'

Jacob narrowed his eyes and pulled back his own sleeves. 'If you do that,' he said, 'I'll tell Dad you weren't actually invited to Hampshire at all.'

'You wouldn't do that.'

'I would.'

Alberta folded her arms and raised her chin. 'If you don't come with me to the Bath Spa, I'll tell your father we don't have to go to Hampshire after all and then we'll both have to stay here instead.' She stared unflinchingly at her son and he stared right back at her.

'You've got me,' he said at last. 'I'll come.'

# CHAPTER FOUR

## *Bad Company*

Alberta had wanted to go to the Bath Spa for a long time, not least because of the huge publicity that accompanied its development. Designed to be the jewel in the crown of Bath's tourist treasures, it soon acquired an unwelcome notoriety. The Three Tenors came to Bath to celebrate its opening with an open-air concert but it continued to remain stubbornly closed due to ever-increasing construction problems. Conservative and Liberal Democrat councillors blamed each other, the builders, the decorators, the architect and anyone else they could possibly think of. The general consensus among the long-suffering tax-payers of the city was that it would always be an albatross around Bath's neck. Even Lionel, normally the most placid of men, had seen fit to fire off a couple of angry letters to the *Bath Chronicle*.

When it did at last open, it received a positive reaction. Its glass structure fitted surprisingly well amid the honey-coloured Georgian buildings. Tourists came and saw and were, for the most part, conquered. On the first floor there was a vast, natural thermal pool, on the middle floor there were four glass steam rooms infused with natural oils. On the roof there was an open-air pool with staggering views of the city and surrounding countryside. It was the perfect place in which to chat and gossip with friends or canoodle with lovers.

It was less perfect as a venue for two half-brothers who had never got on. In the queue at the entrance, Jacob stood impassively while Dylan loudly told him what was wrong with his trousers and his jacket. Alberta stood and inwardly railed at Tony for suggesting the outing and then absenting himself from it.

Dylan's good humour took a nosedive when he came up against the hi-tech lockers in which one deposited one's clothes. Alberta also found them difficult to negotiate and as Jacob came to their rescue with an air of long-suffering patience, Alberta felt a novel sense of comradeship with her stepson. This lasted for as long as it took for Dylan to unwind his towel from around his loins and reveal his red bathing shorts with the legend 'F*** OFF!' written across his buttocks.

She felt better when they walked into the first chamber and she slipped into the warm, thermal water of the baths. Jacob made straight for the Jacuzzi while Dylan made for the cascade of water shooting from a steel funnel by the side of the pool. For a few minutes, Alberta enjoyed the sensation of drifting in the current while low, relaxed conversations gently buzzed around her. Then she heard a loud, familiar voice rend the air with a shout of, 'Hey, Jacob, come over HERE!'

Jacob, bobbing among the bubbles, froze and initially tried to ignore the yells of his half-brother. Finally, goaded beyond endurance, he made his way over and reluctantly joined Dylan under the chute of water. A few minutes later, irritated by Jacob's lacklustre efforts to frolic in the water, Dylan came over to Alberta and said he was ready to go up to the next level.

Alberta had the feeling she was not going to enjoy the second level. Her apprehension proved to be well-founded, which was a pity since the four steam capsules looked enticingly mysterious. She followed Dylan into the first, labelled 'Pine', and was not surprised to see Jacob career off into a different one. Once inside, she sat down next to Dylan. There were six other people in there. Two of them were women who had their eyes shut and looked as if they might be meditating; the other four were a group of friends who were talking to each other in hushed voices as if they were in church.

Dylan wiped his forehead with his hand and said loudly, 'I bet this place is dead unhygienic.'

'Oh, I don't think so,' Alberta whispered, wishing he would keep his voice down.

'I bet it is,' Dylan said. 'It's really hot and humid. I bet all sorts of germs flourish and fester in here. I mean, I had flu all last week. I bet my germs are flying all over the place.'

The two women who might have been meditating opened their eyes and directed them at Dylan.

'I'm pretty sure,' said Alberta firmly, 'that you don't have any germs to spread when you're in the *final* stages of flu.'

'Not true,' Dylan said with an authoritative shake of the head. 'I can almost feel my germs expanding in the atmosphere.'

The two women who might have been meditating exchanged glances and with one accord stood up and left the glass room.

'Anyway,' Alberta said, 'this place is designed to be health-giving. They wouldn't construct a room that allowed germs to fester, even,' she added pointedly, 'if they *are* your germs.'

'I've been told these sorts of places are very bad for you,' Dylan said. 'I think we should go up to the next level.'

'All right.' Alberta stood up and left, aware of a collective sigh of relief from the other occupants. When she'd bought the tickets, she'd been told they could stay for a maximum of two hours. At this rate, they'd be in and out within twenty minutes. She extracted Jacob from the Frankincense room and they all made their way up to the roof.

Which was *fantastic*. Even Jacob thought it was fantastic. Even *Dylan* thought it was fantastic. A shimmering blue pool surrounded by sun and sky and the roof of the Abbey and the hills of Bath, it was, quite simply, stunning. The three of them stepped into the water and grinned at each other as they did so. A soft breeze stroked Alberta's skin and soothed her frayed nerves. There must have been at least thirty people in the pool, but there was plenty of room to glide around. Alberta's resentment towards Tony faded. May was, after all, the perfect month in which to visit the place.

Jacob made straight for the bubbles in the corner while Alberta pointed out to Dylan what she thought might be the roof of their house in the distance.

Dylan didn't seem that concerned about the location of the house. He interrupted Alberta with, 'I'll be back in a minute,' and made his way towards a couple of girls who were giggling together a few feet away.

Alberta bobbed about happily in the middle of the pool, idly watching newcomers as they waded into the water. There was a rather sweet Japanese couple who held hands and then smiled at each other as they stepped into the pool. Another couple came in after them. The woman, dressed in a floral costume with a red towelling band to hold back her hair, had a Botox complexion with a robot-like sheen. The man was what could only be described as a mature hunk. He had a mane of black hair, flecked with silver. He was tall, broad-shouldered, lean and tanned and his charcoal-coloured bathing shorts left little to the imagination, or rather, Alberta thought appreciatively, they left a great deal for the imagination to be going on with.

Her eyes travelled up his torso and then on to his face and she was appalled to realize that *he* was looking at her looking at *him.* She turned quickly to hide the fact that her face had gone the colour of his wife's hairband. She wished Dylan would come over and tell her he wanted to move on, but he had made contact with the girls and was, for the first time that afternoon, looking as if he was not eager to be somewhere else. She glanced across at Jacob who was now busy in conversation with the Japanese couple, his eyes blinking rapidly, a sure sign that his interest was engaged.

Alberta made her way to the side of the pool and, resting her arms on the rim, sat back and shut her eyes for a long time. When she opened them – very slightly – she glanced airily around her with a smile that she hoped transmitted the fact that she was completely at peace with the world. The Botox woman was talking to an attendant who was crouching down to listen to her and the man was – oh God! – the man was looking at her looking at him *again*! And now, horror of horrors, Mature Hunk was making his way towards her and now, horror of horror of horrors, he was standing in front of her.

'Excuse me,' he said, 'I couldn't help noticing you looking at me. Do I know you?'

Alberta swallowed. 'I don't *think* so,' she said, 'but actually –' and even as she said it she felt it must be true – 'your face *does* look familiar.' It was true. His face did look familiar, she was sure it did.

'Does it?' His grey eyes were twinkling at her, they were definitely twinkling. 'I didn't think it was my face you were looking at.'

Alberta's bosom swelled and she caught Dylan's eye. She waved blithely at him, knowing that her complexion was now the colour of blood. She swallowed again and said furiously, 'I really don't want to talk to you any more.' She turned and collided with the enormous chest of a bald-headed man. 'I am *so* sorry,' she murmured miserably. She spotted Jacob and, with as much dignity as she could muster, waded through the water towards him.

Jacob was quite happy to go. Dylan said he was going to hang out with the girls but would probably be home in time for supper.

Alberta was relieved that Jacob spent the first half of their walk back home talking to Maud on his mobile. It gave her time to inwardly absorb and digest the encounter with Mature Hunk and transform her acute embarrassment into righteous rage at his appalling behaviour. She had received various overtures over the years, mainly from hopeful married men. She had always declined them politely, without taking offence. She had never, till now, been made to feel that *she* was a lascivious predator, and the injustice of such a judgement made her seethe with rage.

The second half of the walk was spent in an argument with Jacob who wanted to go over to Maud's house for the evening. Disagreements with Jacob almost always began the same way these days. He would begin by saying, 'You are absolutely right,' before going on to prove that she was absolutely wrong. Having pointed out that Dylan wasn't even certain he *was* coming back for supper, he added that it was quite unfair to expect *him* to stay and give up a stimulating evening with his girlfriend, particularly since they had planned to help each other with revision. Alberta had to admit that he did indeed have a point and said finally that as long as he cleared it with his father, he could go.

She was preparing the salmon in the splendidly distracting company of Johnny Cash's *The Man in Black* when Tony came home. His sweatshirt looked like it had been through a mud bath. He had just started telling Alberta about the huge difficulties involved in erecting a garden shed when Jacob walked in and immediately pleaded his case for abstention from supper. Tony agreed, rather too readily for Alberta's liking, that Jacob could go out and on being told that Dylan had struck up a friendship with two girls, responded with a proud 'That's my boy!'

Alberta said rather waspishly that she would not have purchased such a big piece of salmon if she had known that Jacob would not be eating and that she wouldn't have bought salmon at all if she had known that Dylan would probably be absent too since she had only bought the salmon because it was Dylan's favourite food. And furthermore, she added, staring at Tony as he cut himself a second doorstep of bread, if he carried on stuffing his mouth like that, it would only be her and his parents who would end up eating the salmon anyway.

Tony stopped spreading the butter onto his bread long enough to glance at Alberta and ask shrewdly, 'Do I detect you didn't have an afternoon of undiluted happiness at the Bath Spa?'

Alberta gave a reluctant smile. 'No, it was lovely. You'd really enjoy it.' She paused to glance through the doorway to make sure her son had truly gone and was not hanging around the dining room. 'You know what Dylan and Jacob are like together. Going anywhere with them is never entirely stress-free.'

'It's good for them to spend time together,' Tony said. 'By the way, I have some good news. I saw Erica Wright when I was walking back from Kenny's. She wanted to apologize. She said she has a terrible temper and she felt very bad but she thought you were setting her up.'

Alberta grimaced. '*That's* supposed to be good news?'

'You'd have been proud of me. I said you never meant to invite any of the three suitors. I said you only invited one of them because his dog had just died—'

'It was his *cat* who had died.'

'Whatever. I said you only invited the other two because they were both depressed about ex-wives and stuff and I said you were very upset about the whole evening. It was great. I made her feel *really* guilty. Next time she sees you, she'll be grovelling at your feet. Haven't I done well?'

'Yes,' said Alberta uncertainly, 'except it's not really true.

You're making her feel guilty for thinking I was setting her up when in fact, if I'm totally honest, I suppose I *was* setting her up. It's not very fair . . .'

'It's perfectly fair. She behaved badly and she knows it.' Tony returned the butter to the fridge and yawned. 'I'm going to have a bath. It took ages to put up Kenny's shed.' He eyed the salmon greedily. 'If Dylan doesn't come back for supper, I'll eat his portion.'

Dylan *did* come back for supper and arrived when Tony and Alberta were having a drink in the sitting room with Evie and Lionel. Dylan was in a very good mood, having agreed to meet his new friends in town later that evening. 'They come from Croydon,' he said. 'They're sisters. They're staying with their grandparents for a few days. They don't know anyone down here. I said I'd take them clubbing. Apparently,' he smirked and glanced round at his audience, 'they woke up this morning and heard their grandparents having sex. They said they've been in a state of shock all day.'

Evie sipped her sherry. 'They must be very easy to shock,' she said.

Dylan gave a knowing laugh. 'I don't think they're easy to shock at all. I think they're scared their grandparents might get overexcited and have heart attacks.'

'In that case,' Evie said crisply, 'they are remarkably ignorant about sex. The only danger of a heart attack would be if they did it straight after a good meal. That would be dangerous because a heavy lunch diverts blood away from the heart towards the stomach. In fact, statistics show that only one per cent of heart attacks are triggered by sexual activity and these cases usually involve the excessive excitement caused by sex with a *new* partner. Sex is *extremely* good for you. It helps stop you getting prostate cancer, it lowers blood pressure and it keeps depression at bay.'

'That's all very well,' Dylan said, 'but their grandfather is really old. If I were him, I'd stick with a bit of hand-massage, if you know what I mean.'

'Never mind, old boy,' Lionel said sympathetically. 'I'm sure you'll find a girlfriend soon.'

'For God's sake,' Dylan spluttered, 'I wasn't talking about *me*!'

'I think,' said Alberta quickly, 'it's time for supper.'

Of course, Dylan had no one to blame but himself since he had initiated the subject in the first place but Alberta couldn't help feeling sorry for him. It was in the spirit of purest sympathy that she embarked on a different topic of conversation as they all tucked into the salmon. 'We had a lovely time at the Bath Spa today,' she said brightly. 'It was an incredible experience, wasn't it, Dylan?'

'It was cool,' Dylan agreed, piling a great mound of rice salad onto his plate. He gave Alberta a sly smile. 'Who was that man you were chatting up in the roof pool?'

Alberta looked at him coldly, inwardly deciding that that was the last time she would ever feel sorry for him. 'Which man was that?'

'You mean there was more than one?' Tony asked.

'I mean I was *not* chatting him up. He was very rude. I didn't like him at all.'

'How very interesting,' Evie said. 'What did he say? Why was he rude?'

'I was sitting in the pool, minding my own business, just watching the other people in the pool – I *love* people-watching – and this couple came in and I was mainly interested in the woman not the man because the woman had obviously had some Botox done and I was wondering why women have that done when it only makes their necks look even more scraggy and then I just happened – in a casual sort of way – to glance at her partner . . .'

'And he was the man who was rude to you?' Evie asked.

'Yes, and I was just idly looking at him . . .'

'For a middle-aged man,' Dylan said, 'he was pretty fit.'

'I wasn't looking at him because he was *fit*!' Alberta protested.

'Ah,' said Tony, 'so you admit he was fit?'

'Yes . . . No . . . I don't know! I wasn't thinking about that! I just looked at him and then I looked at him again because I thought I'd seen him before and I was trying to work out where and then he suddenly came over to me and asked me why I was staring at him! I mean, it was so unnecessary! And so I told him I thought he looked familiar.'

'And he thought you were *being* familiar?' Tony asked helpfully.

'Yes, I think he did. He obviously thought I fancied him and—'

'And you didn't,' Tony said, 'because you weren't thinking of anything like that.'

'Tony,' Alberta said, 'you are being very irritating!'

'You went bright red when he talked to you,' Dylan said.

'I went bright red because I am not used to horrible men. I think he was the rudest man I've ever met.'

Tony helped himself to a dollop of Hollandaise sauce. 'You always said that Hannah's boyfriend at Oxford was the rudest man you ever met. What was his name?'

'You mean Ludovic,' Alberta said. 'Now he's the second rudest man I've ever met.'

'I saw Hannah the other night,' Dylan said. 'She was in a pub with some man.'

'Really?' Alberta said. 'Was it her boyfriend?'

'I don't know. I only said hello. I was with my friends.'

'Oh,' said Alberta. 'I expect it was Alfie. What did he look like?'

'He wore a disgusting jersey. It was the colour of vomit. We all reckoned he was gay.'

'Of course he's not,' said Alberta, adding hastily, 'not that it would matter if he were.'

'It would,' said Dylan, 'if you were Hannah.'

'Alfie's an actor,' Evie told Dylan. 'Hannah says he's getting lots of work.'

'He was on television last month,' Lionel said. 'He was in a rather unpleasant police drama about prostitutes. He only had a small part but he was very good. He was supposed to be a computer expert. He really *managed* to look as if he were clever.'

'I'd never have thought Hannah would go out with an actor,' Dylan mused. 'I always thought she'd go for people like *doctors* or *accountants* or *lawyers.*'

'I can't think why,' Alberta said. 'Hannah has an artistic streak. She won a poetry prize when she was fourteen. And the boyfriend she had before Alfie claimed he was an anarchist. I must say, Alfie's a huge improvement. And he seems to get quite a lot of work. It wouldn't surprise me if he became really famous.'

'Let's hope so,' Tony said, 'and then he can make loads of money and look after us in our old age.'

'Hannah will be the one to do that,' Evie said. 'She already gets paid more than I ever did.'

'She's a very clever girl,' Lionel said, 'and she works very hard.'

Alberta's heart glowed like a log fire. She was always careful to refrain from singing her daughter's praises in front of Dylan in case it might draw attention to the fact that Hannah was so very satisfactory while Dylan was so obviously not. There were many times she wished she was closer to her daughter but she could at least comfort herself with the knowledge that she had taught her the importance of having a proper career. Hannah had always taken an interest in her mother's business and had even designed the logo: a tart with a cherry on top.

'I work very hard,' Dylan said, 'but no one pays me anything.'

'You're a student,' Tony said. 'Students are supposed to be poor.'

Evie tapped her grandson's arm. 'That jacket you wore last night did not look as if it came from a charity shop.'

'Mum bought it for me,' Dylan explained. 'She always buys me something when she wins a case.'

'Your mother,' Lionel pronounced, 'is a clever woman too. What is she working on at the moment?'

'She's been doing some fraud case for months now. She's going to get married when it finishes.'

Alberta threw a startled glance at Tony but his face was devoid of any expression, his eyes apparently fixed on his glass. She looked away quickly and tried to conceal her dismay. He knew! He knew and he hadn't told her!

Lionel repeated, 'She's going to get married! Why didn't

you tell us that before? Who is she going to marry?'

Dylan shrugged. 'Another barrister. He's called Haydn and he wears weird cufflinks.' He passed his plate to Alberta. 'Could I have some more salmon?' He was aware that his grandmother was staring at him. 'What?' he asked.

'Is that all you can tell us?' Evie asked. 'His name is Haydn and he wears weird cufflinks? Is he older or younger than Lydia? Is he a QC like she is? Do you like him? Do you dislike him? Has he been married before? Have they been together long?'

'I dunno,' Dylan said. 'Now I've got my own flat in the basement, I don't see Mum very much. He's old like she is. He's all right.'

Evie threw up her hands in despair. 'Dylan,' she said, 'you are such a *man*! Put two women together for an evening and they will go home knowing about the other's love life, domestic life, job and state of mind. Put two men together for the same amount of time and all they will know at the end of the evening is what the other thinks about cricket!'

'That's not true,' Dylan said. 'I never talk about cricket.'

In bed that night, Alberta lay looking out at the stars. There were only two that she could see but one of them outshone the other. They reminded her of that old battery commercial where one soft toy with the good battery goes on dancing long after the poor soft toy with the bad battery has given up. When she had first moved in with Tony, she had found it difficult to get used to the fact that he liked to sleep with the curtains drawn back. Now she couldn't imagine ever wanting to close them.

Beside her, Tony lay quite still. His breathing was slow and measured and didn't fool her for a minute. Ever since Dylan had dropped his bombshell about Lydia, Tony had hardly said a word.

She turned towards him and put a hand on his arm. 'Tony,' she said softly, 'you knew about Lydia, didn't you? When did she tell you?'

At first, she thought he might continue to pretend he was asleep. At last he said, 'She rang the night Erica came to dinner. I forgot to tell you.'

She had forgotten that phone call. Why had it taken so long for Lydia to give Tony the news? What had Tony said to her? And why hadn't he mentioned it later? He had known for a whole week and he actually believed she would accept the idea that he had *forgotten* to tell her.

Alberta wanted to say: I might think that Lydia is a stuck-up, pretentious, self-satisfied, condescending cow, but I do know that she's the love of your life. You do *not* need to pretend that you're not upset. I know you are and I really, really wish you weren't.

Instead, Alberta said nothing at all, which was perhaps a mistake.

# CHAPTER FIVE

## *The Rare Breed*

Lord and Lady Trussler lived in Framley Barton, a small village in Hampshire surrounded by fields full of ponies and horse-jumps. It took about an hour and a half to get there from Bath and Alberta was preparing to come off the motorway when Jacob suggested stopping at the Fleet Services so he could buy some flowers for his grandmother. Touched by Jacob's thoughtfulness, Alberta readily agreed.

She left Jacob to choose from the selection of bouquets and wandered over to the paperback section. By the time Jacob joined her, she was immersed in *Confessions of a Retired Schoolmistress* – a 'shocking exposé of what really goes on in boarding schools' according to the blurb.

Jacob was carrying a bunch of preternaturally stiff red roses, a Paul McKenna paperback and two books of Sudoku exercises. 'I forgot to bring my book,' he said. 'The trouble is I only have enough money for the flowers . . .'

'You don't need to buy anything to read,' Alberta said, putting back the schoolteacher book. 'There are tons of books at The Gables.'

'I know,' said Jacob, 'but I've gone through most of them and I'm not interested in Marma's gardening books and I'm definitely not interested in her books about God.'

'She's given them all to Oxfam,' Alberta said. 'She gave up on God months ago.'

Alberta's mother was a woman of strong, if somewhat transient, enthusiasms. She had at various times been fascinated by Existentialism (Alberta owed her name to the fact that she had been born on an anniversary of Albert Camus's death), Socialism (inspired by conversations with her son, this was a cause she had had to support with some discretion since her husband was at the time a Conservative Member of Parliament), writing novels (effectively torpedoed by the long, hot summer of 1976), Feminism (another pursuit she had had to support in total secrecy since her husband was at the time a Conservative Minister of State), Gardening (the only interest that had continued to inspire her), and lately Religion.

'In that case,' Jacob said, 'you should definitely buy the Sudoku books. Marma will be looking for a new interest and Sudoku will be perfect. It's very good for old people. It exercises the brain and arrests the onset of dementia. You should start doing it.'

'Thank you, Jacob,' Alberta said, delving into her shoulder bag for her wallet and joining the queue for the till. 'I'm so glad you're looking out for me.'

When they turned into the long drive of The Gables thirty minutes later, Alberta felt the usual sense of anticipation. When Hannah was a toddler, Michael Trussler had decided for no apparent reason to sell the comfortable family home in his Surrey constituency and replace it with a dingy terrace in Carshalton. Since his third-floor apartment near Westminster was hardly child-friendly, this had been a disaster for Alberta whose consequent visits to her parents with Hannah and then Jacob had proved to be less than relaxing. On his retirement as a Member of Parliament, he had acted with similar decisiveness when an old friend told him he was putting his house in Hampshire on the market. Michael made an immediate offer and this time his purchase had been an instant success.

The Gables was a place of exquisite peace. The wisteria-draped walls under a clay-tiled roof exuded comfort and stability. The view across the village to the church and the surrounding countryside of hedge-trimmed fields was reassuring in its constancy. Now, as Alberta parked the car in front of the house and stepped onto the gravel drive, she stretched her arms above her head and then waved them in the air as her mother called, 'Alberta!' and came out to greet her.

Alberta felt the usual mixed reaction to her mother's patent enthusiasm. There was guilt that she couldn't respond with the same simple pleasure, but the guilt was allied to a conviction that Marma's behaviour in the past had justifiably forfeited any uncritical devotion on her part.

Age had been kind to Philippa Trussler. Tall and generously proportioned, she had retained a splendid figure. She had a round face that displayed few wrinkles; her cornflower eyes were as bright as ever and her cream-coloured, shoulder-length hair showed no signs of thinning. Today, in her customary uniform of jeans and over-sized shirt, she looked almost a decade younger than her seventy-three years. 'Alberta! Jacob!' she cried. 'Such a treat to have you here! Jacob, come and give me a hug!'

Jacob, never the most demonstrative of mortals, submitted to her embrace with calm resignation. Alberta took their bags from the back seat of the car and smiled at her mother. 'I love being here in May,' she said. 'I must plant some wisteria in our garden. The house looks like it's been decorated with lilac streamers.'

'Wisteria floribunda,' Philippa said. 'Isn't it beautiful? And have you seen the clematis on the far wall?'

But Alberta's attention had been diverted. Lord Trussler, celebrated peer of the realm, one time Government Minister, director of sundry companies, author of *Why England Needs Europe*, and occasional television pundit, emerged from the house looking dapper in brown trousers, white shirt and pale green cardigan.

Alberta put down her bags, ran over to him and hugged him tightly, breathing in the habitual scent of sandalwood. Michael was neither conventionally handsome nor obviously imposing. Slimmer than his wife and only slightly taller, he had a narrow face and a small, thin mouth. Yet women had always adored him, and at parties he had an indefinable presence, an un-showy air of authority that affected everyone who talked to him. Certainly, he was the only person Alberta knew who could dent Jacob's aura of self-possession.

'Hello, Jacob,' Michael said. 'Are you still giving your teachers hell?'

'I'm trying much harder not to,' Jacob said.

'Glad to hear it. I look forward to receiving an uncensored version of your scholarly progress at supper.' He put a hand on Alberta's shoulder. 'Forgive me if I disappear for a little while. I have another three paragraphs to write and then I am free.'

'Supper's at half past seven,' Philippa said. 'Jacob, be a love and take those bags from your mother. Let's go in. You're both in your usual rooms.'

Staying with her parents was like booking into a five-star country hotel. (Not that Alberta had ever actually stayed in one, but she was sure she knew what it would be like.) Her bedroom was a haven of lemon and cream, coordinating perfectly with the chains of wisteria that framed the stone-mullioned window. There were glossy magazines on the bedside table, along with bottled water and a glass. A small jug containing yellow roses stood on the dressing table. Alberta finished her unpacking, breathed in the scent of the roses and went downstairs.

Philippa was busy by the Aga and beamed at the sight of her daughter. 'Can you be an angel and shell the broad beans? The Cartwrights are coming to supper. Joan says she hasn't seen you for ages.'

'She's right. It must be almost a year.' Alberta sat down at the table and pulled the colander towards her. 'Has Jacob come down yet?'

'I asked him to pick some mint for me. He went off to the kitchen garden, clutching his mobile. Does he still have his girlfriend? I can't quite picture Jacob with a girlfriend. But then I remember being very surprised when I read that Bertrand Russell had great success with the ladies. I suppose you can never really understand these things. Hitler had hordes of female admirers.' Philippa dipped a spoon in her soup, had a quick taste and added as an afterthought, 'Of course I'm not for one moment comparing Jacob to Hitler. I'm just saying . . .'

'I know what you're saying,' Alberta said, splitting a pod and releasing the broad beans from their spongy casing, 'and I agree with you. But if you saw Maud, you'd think they were very well-suited. She's not your usual teenager. Her favourite place of all time is the British Museum. She told me she intends to die there one day.'

'What a lovely idea,' Philippa said. 'It would be rather nice to expire in the company of all those Greek statues. A friend of mine died two weeks ago.'

'Oh, Marma, I'm sorry.'

'It was a lovely death actually. She was playing Mah Jong with a couple of chums. She'd won two games in a row and was feeling very pleased with herself, when she keeled over and died. That's so much better than festering away in some filthy old hospital. I visited Harriet Appleby last week – you remember my headmistress friend from Surrey? It was most upsetting to see her lying in a ward that was so grimy and grey. And talking of teachers,' Philippa poured a bowl of new potatoes into the kitchen sink, 'we had your brother and his wife here last weekend.'

'You're very honoured,' Alberta responded. 'They've not been down to Bath since last summer. They're always so busy. I can't imagine how Helen fits in her Amnesty stuff with everything else she does.'

'They're both so thin.' Philippa sighed. 'As far as I can make out they eat nothing but cheese and biscuits. You'd think one of them would have learnt to cook by now. They ate everything I put in front of them and Helen was over the moon when I gave her a quiche to take back with them.

How they produced a strapping young man like Richard is beyond me.'

Alberta smiled. 'Christopher's booked me in for September as usual so I can cook for their annual party. I anticipate weekly emails suggesting ever more elaborate dishes.'

'Dear Christopher so adores good food.'

'Helen does too.' Alberta looked up. 'Do you want me to do all these beans?'

'Yes please, your father loves them. Have you heard from Hannah lately?'

'She rang a couple of weeks ago. I don't like to call *her* because she's always so busy. She works terribly hard.'

'She's so clever. You should be very proud.'

'I don't think I can take any credit. It's in her genes. She's so like her father. She has his drive and his single-mindedness.'

'So do you.'

'No, I don't. I'm not single-minded at all.'

'That's because you have children. You can't be single-minded once you have children. But you do have drive. You have just as much drive as Ed did.'

Alberta opened her mouth and shut it again. Marma rarely referred to Ed and when she did so there was always a slight edge to her voice. Alberta felt a quiver of irritation. 'It's ten past seven,' she said. 'I'll go and drag Pa away from his work.'

The study had a different character to the rest of the house. It had a blue carpet and dark, wine-coloured walls with two long, heavy oak bookcases, crammed with books and files. Michael sat with his back to the window, behind a vast leather-covered desk on which sat his computer and a silver-framed photograph.

Alberta knew the photograph well: it had been taken shortly after Ed had asked her father for her hand in marriage. There, frozen for ever in a moment of time, stood the two of them smiling broadly, on either side of Alberta. She could remember the occasion as if it were yesterday. Every time she saw the picture, she felt the same combination of pride and pain.

She smiled at her father and sat on the brown leather armchair. 'I've come to tell you we want a drink,' she said. 'Do you have to go on working?'

Michael took one last look at his screen and then with a flourish pressed the Save button. 'I'm getting old,' he said. 'It never used to take so long to write a fifteen-hundred-word article.'

Alberta laughed. 'If it's any consolation, I couldn't *begin* to write even a five-hundred-word article.'

'Ed could,' Michael said, moving the frame slightly. 'He once wrote me a speech in twenty minutes. It was a very good speech. He was the best assistant I ever had. I wish I had him here now. I still miss him.'

'I know you do,' Alberta said.

Michael smiled. 'At least I have *you*! You're looking well. How is Tony? Does he continue to pollute our airwaves with hideous music?'

'He does. He loves his job.'

'Well, I suppose that's all right then. And how are you?' He took her hands in his. 'You look tired.'

'I'm fine, especially today. It's wonderful to enjoy a few days of peace and tranquillity here.'

'I don't know about that,' Michael said. 'Your mother has invited the Cartwrights and I think I can hear them now.'

Maurice and Joan Cartwright lived in a seventeenth-century cottage in the centre of Framley Barton. Alberta knew that her parents regarded them as their closest friends in Hampshire, although she could never quite work out why. They were, after all, so different from her parents. Maurice was a sweet man who could talk happily to Philippa for hours about the correct way to take cuttings. He was not a man of strong views and whenever he did express an opinion, was instantly ready to retract if challenged. He was totally under the thumb of his wife and tended to keep quiet in her presence. Unlike her husband, Joan had strong views about absolutely everything and she loved nothing better than to engage Michael in political discussions. She was a tactile woman with everyone except her husband and was particularly flirtatious with Michael after a second gin and tonic. With no children of their own, the Cartwrights had always taken a great interest in the lives of the Trussler children and grandchildren and Maurice especially was a great favourite with Hannah and Jacob.

She was, after all, being unfair, Alberta thought, as she went through to the hall to greet the Cartwrights. Who was she to think that the Cartwrights were unlikely friends? There were people, Tony included, who couldn't understand why *she* was so friendly with Diana, still less why she'd gone into business with her; it was true that Diana was bossy, loud-mouthed and impatient. She was also efficient, entertaining and decisive. It all depended on how one looked at people.

It was in this spirit of understanding that she kissed Maurice, of whom she was fond, and Joan, of whom she was not, and said it was lovely to see them.

'So, Alberta,' said Joan, settling herself on the large lime-coloured sofa which seemed to pale into insignificance beside her purple satin suit, 'how is your *boyfriend*? When is he going to make an honest woman of you?'

Alberta gave a polite laugh, just as if she had not heard Joan ask this every time she saw her. 'I'm afraid we have no plans at present.'

'Well, don't leave it too long, dear, you never know what will happen.' Joan reached forward for the peanuts on the coffee table. 'We have some rather sad news. My brother-in-law died at the weekend.'

'Oh, Joan, I'm so sorry,' Philippa said. 'He was such a sweet man.'

Joan sniffed. 'He had some very odd habits, but then, one shouldn't speak ill of the dead. Poor Sheila is very upset. I've told her to sell up and come and live with us. We have plenty of room for her and she's a splendid cook.'

Michael sat down next to Joan on the sofa. 'Would Sheila want to move away from her friends?'

'She lives in *Birmingham*, dear,' said Joan. 'She's going to put her house on the market as soon as the funeral's out of the way. I shall enjoy having her down here. I'll have someone to talk to at mealtimes.'

'Don't you talk to Maurice?' Jacob asked in a tone of genuine enquiry.

'Hush, Jacob,' Philippa murmured, 'Joan is only joking.'

'No, I'm not,' said Joan, taking a slug of her gin. 'Maurice ran out of conversation years ago, didn't you, darling?'

Maurice nodded. 'I can't remember the exact date.'

Philippa smiled. 'Now you *are* joking!'

'He's not,' Joan said, 'and answer me this, Philippa, how often does Michael ask your opinion about topical events?'

'Well,' Philippa began, and then with Joan's beady eye on her, confessed, 'not very often.'

'Exactly,' Joan said, 'and that's because either he already knows what you think or he has no interest in finding out. That's marriage for you.'

'In that case,' said Jacob, 'why do you think my parents should marry?'

For a moment, Joan's eyebrows shot up like question marks and then she gave one of her bark-like laughs. 'You have a point, Jacob. You are a perceptive boy – two words that do not usually sit credibly together.' She put her hand on Michael's knee. 'What do you think of marriage, darling? Do you think it's a good institution?'

'It's been very good for me,' Michael said. 'I live in a comfortable house with a beautiful garden, for both of which my wife is entirely responsible.'

'That's all very well,' said Joan, 'but a housekeeper and a gardener could do the same.'

'No,' said Michael. 'No one could look after me better than Philippa.'

'Hear, hear!' said Maurice.

Joan swivelled round to face her husband. 'Are *you* saying you can't imagine anyone having a better wife than Philippa?'

'I'm saying,' said Maurice, 'that I can't imagine *Michael* having a better wife than Philippa.'

'I will say no more,' said Joan with more conviction than truth, 'except that I *could* make some very interesting comparisons about husbands and—'

'My goodness, look at the time!' Philippa said. 'We must go and eat. My soup will be bubbling away to nothing. Come along, all of you!'

There was an immediate exodus to the dining room and soon all were seated round the well-polished oak table. Jacob helped Philippa to pass round the soup. Conversation never flagged and covered subjects as diverse as Joan's friend's nephew's sex-change operation, the state of Conservatism in Britain today, the appalling halitosis of the local vicar and the future of space travel.

Really, Alberta thought, old people – well, at least these old people – could be very strange. If she and Tony had sat around discussing their relationship in the way these four had done over drinks, she would have felt pretty bruised. Yet here they were, happily wolfing down Philippa's smoked salmon tart. Joan and Michael were at one end of the table, berating Jacob for his lack of interest in party politics and down at the other end, Maurice and Philippa were almost tripping over their words in their enthusiasm to tell Alberta how very important it was to have ponds in gardens. Perhaps it was something to do with growing up during the Second World War. There was no doubt about it: these pensioners were a lot tougher than her generation.

This perception was reaffirmed the next morning when Alberta came downstairs at half past eight and learnt that her father had already spent an hour at his desk while her mother had just finished preparing a casserole for supper.

After Jacob finally staggered downstairs two hours later,

they went off to Marlborough for lunch, followed by a pleasant walk along the River Kennet. While Jacob talked to his grandmother about his tentative gap year plans, Michael told Alberta he had started writing a memoir, provisionally called *A Politician's Life*. He wanted her to know he was devoting an entire chapter to his late son-in-law. This made Alberta feel quite emotional and she squeezed his hand and glanced at his face and saw that perhaps he wasn't quite as tough as she had thought.

Despite the fact that they had been out for most of the day, Philippa still produced another splendid meal at supper. Jacob and Michael began a lively but good-humoured argument about Europe during the watercress soup and carried on with it into the next course. Michael thought that the trouble with today's politicians was that none of them had been alive during the Second World War; if they had been, he said, they'd have more respect for the importance of a united Europe and a United States of America. Jacob retorted that it had been a united Europe and a United States of America that had been responsible for a peace treaty in 1919 that had led to the rise of Hitler. Marma said that she did agree with Jacob that small was better because their parish council was extremely effective, although it had to be said that the chairman of the parish council ran it like a dictatorship.

There was a slightly bemused silence after this intervention, ended by Michael telling Marma she didn't know what she was talking about. Jacob said that on the contrary he thought Marma had made a rather sophisticated and indeed a complex point. Michael said that although he often found Marma's points incomprehensible, he had never found any of them either sophisticated or complex. Jacob said that he thought Marma was a very complicated woman with remarkably complicated ideas. Marma told Jacob she was extremely grateful for the compliment, if indeed it was a compliment, and that now she would go and get the apple crumble.

The following day, after a lazy afternoon in the garden, Alberta hugged her parents and set off with Jacob for home. Jacob was in a forthcoming mood. They discussed the grace with which all his grandparents had adapted to the ageing process. They talked about Sudoku, which Jacob had unfortunately forgotten to introduce to his grandmother; but in fact, he pointed out, she had told him while they walked along the river that she had recently discovered the delights of Yoga, so Sudoku could clearly wait. Conversation on Jacob's somewhat fantastical plans for the summer holiday was interrupted by a text from Maud which necessitated a long text from Jacob and a further one from Maud, by which time they had reached Bath.

There was a message from Evie in the kitchen.

*Hello! Hope you had a lovely time! Tony rang to ask me to get something for supper as he has a friend coming over. I've put fresh pasta and tomatoes in fridge. Lionel and I are at cinema with friends. Tell Jacob there's a programme on BBC1 this evening about neuro-linguistic programming.*

*Love Evie*

'Great,' Jacob said, and then, 'I'm off to see Maud. I'll have supper with her.' He disappeared before Alberta could tell him to take his bag upstairs.

Alberta took his bag, along with her own, upstairs. She changed out of her shirt and top, put on her jeans and a T-shirt, and went downstairs into the kitchen, wondering whether to give herself a cup of tea or a glass of wine. She was still wondering when she heard the front door slam and Tony call, 'Bertie?'

She went through to the hall, said 'Hiya . . .' and then stopped, her smile freezing on her face. Behind Tony, staring at her with an air of quizzical amusement, was Mature Hunk from the Bath Spa.

# CHAPTER SIX

## *There was a Crooked Man*

'Bertie,' Tony said, 'this is Daniel Driver. Daniel, this is Bertie.'

'I rather think,' Daniel said, 'I've had the pleasure of meeting Bertie—'

'Alberta,' Alberta said through gritted teeth. 'My name is Alberta.'

'I beg your pardon,' Daniel said. 'I think – indeed, I *know* – I've had the pleasure of meeting Alberta before. We met in the Bath Spa.'

Tony stared at Alberta and then at Daniel and began to laugh. 'I don't believe it! Of course, this all makes sense now. Only you could be so rude to a woman you've never met before. *You're* the man who thought Bertie fancied you, aren't you?'

Alberta folded her arms tightly and stared up with great interest at the hall ceiling. The fact that Tony found Daniel's behaviour so amusing was almost as annoying as the fact that Daniel clearly found it funny too.

'That is an extremely unfair question to ask me,' Daniel

said. 'If I say no, you'll assume I'm lying. If I say yes, you'll think I'm an arrogant bastard.'

Alberta's eyes returned instantly to Daniel. 'I'm sure we'd never think that,' she said, hoping that her steely gaze would lance his conscience.

'That's kind of you to say so,' Daniel said with an air of contrite humility that did not fool her for a moment. 'You give me courage to confess the truth. I have to admit I was under the clearly absurd impression that you couldn't keep your eyes off me.'

'Please don't think I'm rude,' Alberta began, 'but—'

'Please don't hesitate to be rude,' Daniel assured her. 'I'm sure I deserve it.'

'Thank you. I was only going to say that if I had seen *you* looking at *me* in the pool, I would simply have supposed there was something wrong with my appearance. I just think it's rather interesting that *you* automatically assumed that I . . . that I . . .'

'. . . That you fancied me? Put it down to wishful thinking!' Daniel said carelessly. 'As a matter of interest,' he added, 'why *were* you looking at me? *Was* there something wrong with my appearance?'

'Not that I can remember,' Alberta said. 'But I thought . . . I had the impression . . . I thought that I had met you somewhere before.'

'If we had done,' Daniel said, 'I am sure I would have remembered.'

'Now that I've talked to you,' Alberta said, 'I am sure I would too.'

'Let's have a drink,' Tony said, leading the way through to the kitchen. 'Where's Jacob? He'll be fascinated by this.

Our son,' he told Daniel, 'is a great one for theories. He believes there's no such thing as coincidence. I can't quite remember his argument but he'll no doubt explain it to you.'

'He won't,' Alberta said. 'He's gone to see Maud.' She took an apron from behind the kitchen door and put it on, tying it tightly round her waist.

'That's a pity,' Tony said, taking a bottle of Sancerre from the fridge. 'Daniel, you'll find some glasses in the cupboard behind you. Bertie, did you get my message? It's all right if Daniel has supper with us, isn't it?'

'I know you've been visiting your parents,' Daniel said, 'so I'm sure the last thing you want to do is cook for some stranger . . .'

'Don't worry about Bertie,' Tony said, 'she's used to cooking for any number of people. She's a professional cook!' He threw her a good-natured grin which she chose to ignore.

'It'll only be pasta and tomato sauce,' she said. 'If I'd known we were having a visitor here, I'd have been better prepared.'

'Well, in that case,' Daniel said, 'I'm glad you didn't know. I would hate you to have dressed up for my benefit. You look quite charming as you are.'

Alberta's eyes narrowed, she opened her mouth to speak, thought better of it, took the glass of wine that Tony had put in front of her and had a therapeutic gulp. Then, resolutely ignoring both men, she set about collecting her ingredients together.

One of Tony's less endearing characteristics was his failure to recognize when he was in the doghouse. He pointed

Daniel to a chair and sat down himself. 'I met Daniel in town,' he told Alberta cheerfully. 'I thought he wasn't coming till next week. He's staying here for a month.'

'He's staying *here*?' Alberta said sharply. 'He's staying with *us*?'

'Unfortunately not,' Daniel said. 'I already have somewhere. You may recall the woman I was with at the Spa?'

'I can't say I remember,' Alberta said.

'She's my landlady,' Daniel explained.

'Really? She didn't look like your landlady.' Alberta, realizing too late that she had just contradicted herself, set about peeling a carrot with exaggerated concentration.

'She and her husband are old friends. They're putting me up while I'm here.'

'Daniel's down here to produce an album for me,' Tony said. He shook his head. 'I can't believe you're the man from the Spa! I *do* wish Jacob was here!'

Alberta, recalling Jacob's theory on coincidence, was profoundly glad he wasn't.

'I'm sorry to have missed him,' Daniel said. 'He went with you to your parents, didn't he? Tony says you're very close to your father.'

Alberta began to chop her carrot. 'You make it sound as if that's really peculiar. Aren't most people fond of their parents?'

Daniel shrugged. 'I'm not.'

Alberta looked up and frowned. 'Why not?'

'They're dull.'

Alberta gave a short laugh. 'That's rather harsh. I wonder what they think about *you*.'

'I think they have a pretty poor opinion of me,' Daniel

said equably. 'At least, they did the last time I saw them. Mind you, that was over twelve years ago.'

'Twelve years ago?' Alberta repeated, putting down her knife and staring at him in amazement. 'You haven't seen them in twelve years? That's appalling!'

'Why? I don't like them.'

'They're your *parents*.'

'And they don't like *me*.'

'I'm sure that's not true.'

'I assure you it is.'

'Well!' said Alberta, reaching for an onion. 'Well!'

Tony opened the fridge door and took out the Sancerre again. 'You may not realize this, Daniel,' he said, refilling the glasses, 'but you are responsible for a very unusual occurrence. You have rendered Bertie speechless.'

Sometimes, Tony could be very irritating. Alberta was glad to hear the phone ring. 'I'll get it,' she said. She didn't care who it was – even if it was a double-glazing salesman – she would have a long and in-depth conversation with the caller. She picked up the phone and marched into the dining room. 'Hello,' she said, sitting down on one of the chairs.

'Alberta?' said a low, husky voice that could only belong to Tony's ex-wife. 'It's Lydia. How are you?'

'I'm extremely well,' Alberta said. 'I understand you're getting married. Congratulations.'

'Thank you. I must say I'm ridiculously happy.'

'How lovely. And how's work? Are you as busy as ever?'

'You would not believe how busy I am! I'm involved in this case . . . There's no point in explaining it to you, you'd never understand, but it's taking over my *life*! I'm up at five every morning at the moment. I sometimes wish I had a nice little cleaning business like you do! How *is* the cleaning business, by the way?'

'It's fine,' said Alberta, with super-human restraint, 'although it's catering, not cleaning.' Talking to a double-glazing salesman would be far more fun than talking to Lydia. She stood up. 'I'll get Tony for you.'

'Thank you. And thank you for entertaining Dylan. He got in about half an hour ago. He's very pleased with the photos he's taken. He says Jacob is odder than ever.'

'Does he?' Alberta said tonelessly, returning to the kitchen. 'I can't think why. Here's Tony.' She passed the phone to Tony. 'It's Lydia,' she said.

'Oh,' Tony stood up. 'I'll take it outside.' He walked out of the kitchen, shutting the door behind him.

Alberta began to dissect the onion and then, annoyed by the silence in the room, looked up at Daniel. 'Is there anything wrong?' she asked.

'Not at all,' he said politely.

'You are looking at me in a funny way,' she said accusingly.

'I do apologize,' Daniel said. 'I was simply wondering why you hate the woman on the phone.'

'I don't hate her!' Alberta put down her kitchen knife. 'Are you always like this with people you've just met?'

'Like what?' Daniel asked.

'I said barely five words to you at the Bath Spa before you accused me of staring at your private parts and now you've told me I hate my partner's ex-wife. I suppose what I'm asking is: are you usually this rude to people you don't know?'

Daniel leant back against the sideboard and folded his arms. 'No,' he said thoughtfully, 'I'm really not. I don't know why I am with you.'

'Nor do I,' Alberta said tartly, dropping carrots and onion into the pan along with a dash of butter. 'And for your information, I don't hate Lydia. It's true I don't like her that much. She has a way of saying things that make one feel rather small. I expect you'd get on with her famously. Anyway, I'm very pleased for her. She's getting married soon.'

'Will you and Tony go to the wedding?'

'I have no idea.'

'The best wedding I ever went to,' Daniel said, 'was that of my second ex-wife. Her bridegroom hired a castle for the reception. It was magic.'

Alberta stared at him. 'How many wives have you had?'

Daniel stared up at the ceiling as if trying to remember. 'I'm on my third now.'

'Your third? How long have you been married to your third?'

Daniel thought again. 'About twelve years.' He sighed. 'Mind you, I haven't seen her for a long time.'

'Well!' Alberta said. It occurred to her that despite Daniel's cavalier attitude, he might be genuinely upset about his marital difficulties. She said more softly, 'Well, I am very sorry.'

She reached for the bag of tomatoes and began to cut them into small pieces. Aware that he was looking at her, she returned his gaze. '*Now* what are you wondering?'

'I was thinking,' he said, 'that you are an exceptionally nice woman.'

She knew she was blushing and was relieved that Tony came back, thus relieving her of the necessity to reply. For some reason, Tony had switched into work mode and began questioning Daniel about his timetable for the next few weeks in the recording studios. Alberta was happy to opt out of the conversation and concentrate on cooking the meal.

Over supper, the two men swapped stories about various bands. Tony seemed to be as relaxed and good-humoured as ever. Only once did Alberta catch him staring at nothing in particular and she was pretty sure his mind was on his latest phone call from Lydia and her forthcoming nuptials. She was distracted from further contemplation by Daniel who asked her if she could remember the first record she had ever bought.

'It was either "Sugar, Sugar" by the Archies or it was "Two Little Boys" by Rolf Harris.' She sighed thoughtfully. 'I think it was "Two Little Boys". It still makes me cry.' She could see the two men exchange glances and raised a defiant chin. 'Thousands of people bought that record.'

'Thousands of people,' Daniel said, 'think Celine Dion can sing.'

'Well, I was very young when I bought it,' Alberta said. 'What was the first record you ever bought?'

Daniel pushed his plate away and gazed dreamily at her. '"Let's Spend the Night Together",' he said.

Alberta blinked. 'I beg your pardon?'

Tony nodded approvingly. 'That is a *great* record.'

'It's all right,' Alberta said, recovering quickly. 'The lyrics are pretty repetitive, though.'

Tony looked for sympathy to Daniel. 'This is a woman whose favourite pop group was Wham!.'

'In fact,' Alberta said, happy to prove him wrong, 'my most favourite pop group was Showaddywaddy, especially when they sang "Under the Moon of Love".'

Daniel put a hand to his forehead. 'You liked "Under the Moon of Love"?'

Tony grinned. 'There's no point talking to Alberta about music. She hated the Sex Pistols, she's never heard of the Ramones or the Damned and she thinks Boney M were musical geniuses. Oh yes, she also preferred Gary Glitter to David Bowie.'

Daniel shook his head and murmured a soft, 'Wow!'

He left, straight after coffee, having extracted a promise from his hosts that they would allow him to take them out to dinner the following Friday.

'So,' said Tony as they cleared the table, 'have you forgiven him for his behaviour in the pool? What did you think of him?'

'It doesn't matter what *I* think of him,' Alberta said. 'He clearly thinks he's fantastic.'

'I thought you got on rather well with him. He certainly liked you.'

'Of course he likes me. He thinks I'm in thrall to his beautiful body. I bet he thinks *all* women are in thrall to his beautiful body. I can't believe he hasn't visited his parents in twelve years! And he hasn't seen his *third* wife in ages! What sort of marriage is that?'

'Do you remember me telling you about Jason Ringwood who wanted to buy me out a few years ago? He's a great mate of Daniel. He says the third wife was a coke-head. Daniel was too for a while. Then he cleaned up his act, which is very good for me because he's a great producer.'

'What happened to his wife?'

'I seem to recall she went off with the drummer from the Jam Biscuits.'

Alberta gave him the tray of coffee cups and followed him through to the kitchen. 'What a terrible name for a band,' she said.

'They were a terrible band full-stop,' Tony said.

Alberta laughed and gave Tony a sidelong glance. 'What did Lydia want?'

'She wants me to keep an eye on Dylan when she goes on her honeymoon.' Tony began to load the dishwasher. 'How are your parents?'

'They're very well. They sent you their love.'

'Did they?' Tony gave one of his lopsided smiles. 'I'm sure your father was heartbroken I wasn't there.'

'He is fond of you,' Alberta said awkwardly. 'It's just that . . .'

'. . . I'm not the right son-in-law, am I?' Tony shut the dishwasher and straightened his back. 'I think I'll go and do my emails.'

Alberta was not surprised to find that sleep eluded her. Her mind seemed to be overflowing with disjointed thoughts. She turned to one side, then to the other and finally lay on her back, having plumped up her pillows for the fourth time in half an hour.

On the other side of the bed, Tony stirred. 'Can't you sleep?'

'No.' Alberta opened her eyes. 'Did I wake you?'

'No.'

'Tony,' Alberta said, 'is everything all right?'

'Everything's fine. I enjoyed this evening. I like Daniel. He fancies *you*.'

'That is *ridiculous*.'

Tony yawned. 'No, it isn't.'

'Men like Daniel,' Alberta said confidently, 'don't fancy women like me.'

'Why not?'

'Daniel is the sort of man who only looks at women who are twenty years too young for him. I'm far too old.'

Tony said something but since his face was now buried in his pillow, it was impossible to understand him.

'Tony?' She nudged his back. 'What did you say?'

Tony briefly raised his face from his pillow. 'I said I think you underestimate him. And now I want to go to sleep. Goodnight, Bertie.'

'Goodnight.' Alberta frowned in the darkness. She wished Tony hadn't told her Daniel fancied her. She would *never* get to sleep now.

Later, of course, she could see how clever Tony had been. He had realized that she, in her sleepless state of mind, would want to quiz him about *his* state of mind concerning Lydia or her father or both of them. He had conducted a quite brilliant pre-emptive strike, producing a sentence that was bound to kick her off-course. '*He fancies you.*' Result: he had been able to go to sleep, without having to talk about what was really on his mind.

For the next few days Tony managed to give a fairly good impression of a man who was untroubled by anything. There were a couple of cracks in the veneer. He snapped at Alberta for failing to remind him that they were going to dinner on Saturday evening with Diana and her husband, a criticism which was particularly unfair since he had failed to tell *her* that he'd invited Daniel to supper on Wednesday. He also became extremely tetchy after a visit to Homebase, but that wasn't so very surprising. She was always tetchy after a visit to Homebase.

Perhaps he was just tired. There was probably nothing to worry about. The weekend had gone far too quickly. She had long been used to waving him off on Monday mornings but this time she wished he would stay a little longer so they could get a chance to have a proper talk. The problem with relationships – any relationships – was that month by month, unwritten rules slowly, almost imperceptibly, developed and as year followed year, it became increasingly difficult to deviate from them.

It had always been the case that certain areas were pretty much off-limits. In the early days, when they'd first moved in together, Tony had desisted from talking about Ed because he hadn't wanted to upset her and *she* had desisted from talking about Ed because she didn't want Tony to think she was comparing him constantly with her dead husband. She had also desisted from talking about Lydia because she hadn't wanted him to think she was prying or curious. The difference was that Ed was dead while Lydia was very much alive and was often on the phone to Alberta about weekends and holiday arrangements for Dylan. Tony had never said anything, but she could tell that he hated it when she complained about Lydia's tendency to overturn carefully laid plans; she had learnt to refrain from making any personal comments at all.

And so Lydia, after all this time, was remarrying and Alberta knew Tony was upset. On the one hand, she wanted to help him and she couldn't. On the other, she was upset that *he* was upset. It was funny, the way one could live with someone for years and still have such limited access to his feelings. She wished Tony would *talk* to her instead of pretending he was fine when he patently wasn't. Hannah was just the same. Alberta had always been able to tell when her daughter was unhappy and yet Hannah rarely confided in her. Did they think she was stupid? They probably did think she was stupid. And as for Jacob, Alberta had no idea at all what Jacob thought about. Then there was her mother. But Alberta did not want to think about her mother. Thinking about her mother when she was in this sort of mood was never a good idea.

She wished she didn't feel so *fractious*. She wished Tony hadn't made that silly remark about Daniel. It was ridiculous but it continued to pop up in her mind. Which it shouldn't, because Daniel was exactly the sort of preening, alpha male she despised. She hated the fact that he obviously thought she fancied him, she hated the fact that she did indeed fancy him. Not that that mattered or meant anything at all. But it was mildly upsetting to find she could be attracted to a fine pair of shoulders even when they were attached to such an unprepossessing character. It was even more upsetting to realize that the unprepossessing character was currently keeping her awake.

Friday evening did not begin well. Tony rang at six to say he was on his way to Paddington and that he would meet her at the restaurant. 'Daniel's booked a table for eight,' he said. 'Try to be punctual.' He rang off before she could point out that he was the one who was in danger of being late.

She went upstairs to have a shower and then took more care than usual over drying her hair. As a result, she was able to let her hair down. For once, it undulated becomingly over her shoulders and she shook it back from her face so she could apply her kohl pencil to her eyes. Later, when dressing, she took out her green dress but it had an infinitesimal stain on it and so she decided to wear what Tony called her Sex on Legs dress.

It *did* make her look good. It was short in length and a little low in neckline and it fitted her figure with extreme snugness. Alberta looked at herself in the mirror and was satisfied. The fact that she had taken such care over her appearance was of course nothing to do with the fact that she would be seeing Daniel. It was simply that she needed to boost her morale a little. There was definitely something a little confidence-sapping about having a partner who was depressed about the remarriage of his ex-wife.

She arrived at the restaurant punctually at eight and could see no one resembling Daniel. A charming young man came up to her and she said, 'I'm meeting . . .' and realized she had no recollection of Daniel's surname. 'I'm meeting,' she began again, 'I'm meeting . . . a man –' she saw him nod encouragingly – 'and I'm sorry, it's stupid but I can't remember his surname. He's tall with a lot of hair and he's about my age and he's quite good-looking . . .'

'Mr Driver's upstairs,' the man said. 'Follow me.'

Alberta did so, trying not to think what the nice man would be thinking about her. He probably thought she was on a blind date. Oh God, of course he thought she was on a blind date. Daniel was sitting at a table, studying the menu. He wore a white linen shirt with his sleeves rolled back, exposing a silver chain round his right wrist. He looked, Alberta thought nastily, just like a man who was producing a record by a band with a silly name.

The nice man led Alberta to Daniel's table. 'The lady told me she was looking for a good-looking man,' he said with an arch smile at Alberta. He obviously saw himself as Cupid. Alberta did not smile back. She could cheerfully have hit him.

Daniel rose from his seat. 'I'm flattered,' he said with an odious smirk that made Alberta want to hit him as well.

'The wine's on its way,' the man said. 'I'll bring another menu.'

Daniel waited for Alberta to sit down and then returned to his own seat. 'You look amazing,' he said, 'like a pocket Venus.'

'Thank you,' Alberta said stiffly. 'I'm afraid Tony might be a little late. He's coming straight from London.'

'Then I have you to myself for a bit,' Daniel said. 'How very satisfactory.'

Alberta didn't think it was satisfactory at all. 'I didn't tell the man you were good-looking,' she said. 'I told him you were *quite* good-looking.'

'In that case,' Daniel said, 'I am *quite* flattered.'

Alberta's phone came to life in her handbag. She reached down for it quickly.

'Hi, Bertie.' Tony's voice sounded a little out of breath. 'I'm at the station.'

'Well, Daniel and I are both here. Don't bother to walk. Get a taxi.'

'I can't. I'm at *Paddington* Station.'

'Paddington?' Alberta repeated, swivelling away from Daniel and lowering her voice. 'What on earth are you doing at Paddington?'

'I was going to catch the earlier train,' Tony said, 'but Lydia rang and wanted to meet for a quick drink. So . . .'

'Tony, how could you? Why didn't you tell me before?'

There was a pause. 'Because I knew you'd be angry.'

Alberta gripped the phone hard. 'I'm angry *now*.'

'I know,' Tony said, 'but you're sitting in a restaurant and you're sitting with Daniel so you can't show it too much.'

'Don't count on it,' Alberta growled.

'Bertie, I'm truly sorry. I'm getting the next train in a few minutes. Have supper without me and I'll join you both for coffee.'

'I expect,' Alberta said icily, 'we'll have gone home by then. Do you want to speak to Daniel?'

'I'd better go. Tell him I'll be there as soon as I can.'

Alberta put the phone back in her bag. 'That was Tony,' she said.

'I rather thought it might be.'

'The thing is . . . I'm very cross . . . he's still at Paddington. He was held up. I'm so sorry.'

'I'm not,' said Daniel. 'I'll be seeing loads of him in the next few weeks. I don't need to see him now.'

'Yes, but . . .' Alberta hesitated, 'you invited us to supper because Tony is your friend . . .'

'No, I didn't. I invited you both to supper because

I know and like Tony and I would like to get to know *you.*'

'That's very kind but I feel I'm here on false pretences. I am so, so sorry—'

'Alberta,' Daniel said, 'I find apologies tedious at the best of times. I have told you there is nothing to be sorry about. Can we change the subject?'

Alberta was relieved that the waiter appeared at that moment. She sat bolt upright while he gave her a menu and poured the wine. As soon as he had gone, she applied herself to the menu with an air of rapt concentration. A slight cough from her companion made her raise her eyes before returning her attention to the card in her hand.

There was another slight cough and this time Daniel spoke. 'Alberta,' he said, 'I beg your pardon. I have offended you. I seem to be making a habit of it. Please feel free to go on telling me how sorry you are.'

Alberta's mouth gave an involuntary twitch but she responded sternly. 'I would be far too frightened of *boring* you.'

'You would be incapable of boring me. Are you ready to order?'

The waiter had come back again. Alberta handed him the menu and said, 'I don't need a starter. I'd like the linguini, please. And may I have some tap water?'

Daniel, sounding suspiciously subdued, ordered steak and chips and a bottle of Pinot Noir.

Alberta gave a little sigh after the man had departed and asked Daniel how he was enjoying Bath.

Daniel's eyes twinkled but he replied with equal gravity. 'I'm enjoying it very much. I could wish for fewer hills.

Wherever I go, I have to climb a hill. I could never be old in Bath.'

'On the contrary,' Alberta said, 'there are plenty of healthy old people here. My daughter maintains that a twenty-minute walk in any direction here is better than any work-out.'

'I didn't realize you had a daughter. I assumed Tony only had the one child.'

'I suppose it's a little confusing. Tony and I have one son and Tony has another son by his ex-wife. Hannah isn't Tony's daughter. I was married before I met Tony.'

'How interesting to find that you too have exes in your life.'

'Hannah's father was never an ex,' Alberta said. 'He died.'

'What did he die of?'

Alberta took a sip of her wine. 'He had a car accident.'

'That must have been hard.'

'Yes.' Alberta took another sip. 'Do you have any children?'

'I have a son,' Daniel said. 'He's rather nice.'

'How old is he?'

'I'm not sure. I think he must be about eighteen or nineteen. He's doing a bit of travelling at the moment. He's either in North America or in South America.'

'There's quite a difference,' Alberta said severely. 'If I may say so, you are extremely cavalier about your familial relationships. You don't know which part of the continent your son is in, your poor parents are probably aching to hear from you . . .'

'I assure you they're not. I can't actually remember a

time when my mother was pleased to see me. I couldn't wait to get away. My mother had an extraordinary knack of turning every house we lived in into a mausoleum of spectacular gloom.'

'Did you move often as a child?'

'Every few years. My father worked for Barclays Bank and got transferred quite regularly. We lived in Surrey when I was very young, then—'

'I lived in Surrey!' Alberta said. 'Where did you live?'

'A place called Redhill. I don't remember much about it. I went to a funny little nursery school run by a large lady with very red lipstick. She usually wore skirts with spots on them.'

'Mrs Grander!' exclaimed Alberta with excitement. 'You must have been at Mrs Grander's!'

'Was I?' Daniel asked. 'I don't remember her name. The school was in her house and her poodles kept coming into the classroom.'

'One grey and one black! You were at Mrs Grander's!' Alberta said. The full significance of this revelation made her clutch his arm. 'You see? I was right! I *did* know you! I know just who you are. You are Disgusting Daniel!'

'Am I?' Daniel asked. 'Was I?'

'You must be him. How old are you?'

'I'm forty-five.'

'So am I!'

'Are you?' Daniel looked surprised. 'You don't look it.'

'Thank you. This is amazing. You must be him! There was no other Daniel there then. Disgusting Daniel had this funny blue cap and he refused to take it off.'

'That was me,' Daniel nodded. 'Why was I disgusting?'

'The first time you arrived, you stuck your tongue out at me. You were always sticking your tongue out at me.'

'I'm so sorry.'

'You were a horrid little boy,' Alberta said cheerfully. 'Once you deliberately poured water over my painting of a crocodile and after that I called you Disgusting Daniel.'

'That doesn't sound like me. I must have been having a bad day.'

'You were *always* having a bad day. I remember all sorts of things about you.' Alberta was enjoying herself now. She gleefully prepared to recall the numerous offences of the young Daniel and was only stopped by the arrival of their food.

Daniel fell upon his plate as if he hadn't eaten for a week. After a few mouthfuls, he looked enquiringly at Alberta. 'How's the linguini?'

'Superb. It's such a treat to have a meal cooked by someone else and—' She stopped abruptly. 'I've remembered something else!'

'Oh dear,' said Daniel. 'I thought you might. How come you have such a terrifying memory?'

'I don't know,' said Alberta. 'I don't remember lots of things. But I do remember you.'

'I feel honoured,' said Daniel, 'and grateful. At least I think I do. Without your memory I'd have no idea of my past crimes.'

'Well, I must say I think it's interesting,' said Alberta, taking a sip of her red wine and then nodding appreciatively. 'And it's all coming back to me. After you ruined my painting, my mother had a word with your mother and your mother wouldn't have a word spoken against you. She insisted you were probably trying to help improve the crocodile! She was quite fierce! So there you are!'

'Where am I?' asked Daniel.

'I have proved beyond doubt that you are being unfair to your mother. She defended you, she took your part, she cared about you. Really,' Alberta muttered as much to herself as to Daniel, 'parents get a very bad press from their children.'

'I take it you get on brilliantly with your parents,' Daniel said.

'I certainly haven't ignored them for the last decade, if that's what you mean.'

'Tony says your father was a politician.'

'He's Lord Trussler,' Alberta said proudly. 'He used to be a Minister in the government.'

'That's very impressive.'

Alberta looked at him with suspicion. 'I may be being paranoid,' she said, 'but you have a way of talking that sounds as if you're making fun of me.'

'You *are* being paranoid.'

He was still shovelling food into his mouth as if there were no tomorrow. She curled the linguini round her fork and said, 'You have some gravy on your chin.'

'Thanks.' Daniel rubbed his chin with his napkin and smiled. 'You can tell a lot about people by the way they eat.'

Alberta said severely, 'You certainly can.'

'You, for example, eat very neatly,' Daniel said.

Alberta rolled her eyes. 'This is the traditional defence of men who can't eat properly. I am obviously repressed while you are a man of gargantuan sexual appetites.'

'Alberta,' Daniel said, 'you're flattering me again.'

Alberta tried and failed to suppress a laugh. 'Do you always have an answer to everything?' she asked.

'No, I do not. Tell me about you and Tony. How did you meet?'

'We met in a park. He was with his little boy and I was with my little girl. He was in the process of getting divorced from Lydia. My husband had died and Hannah and I were living with my parents-in-law.'

'What was that like?'

'It was not great. Actually, it was terrible. I'd have gone mad if I'd stayed there much longer.'

'So you moved in with Tony? That was convenient.'

'Yes,' Alberta said, 'I suppose it was.'

'How long have you been married?'

'We're not. We've both been there, done that.'

Daniel reached over to fill Alberta's glass and raised a hand for the waiter. 'Personally,' he said, 'I'm a great believer in marriage. To me, it's the ultimate sign of commitment.'

Alberta's mouth twitched. 'So much so that you've done it three times.'

'Exactly.'

The waiter arrived at the table. 'Is everything to your satisfaction?' he asked.

'Everything is perfect, thank you. We'd like another bottle like this one.'

'Certainly. I'm glad you're both enjoying yourselves.'

Alberta glanced up at him sharply and then proceeded to attack the last strands of linguini on her plate. She was aware that Daniel was watching her and looked up at him. 'What is it?' she asked.

He grinned. 'I wish you could have seen your face. It really upsets you that he thinks we're a couple.'

'Given your behaviour at the Spa,' Alberta retorted, 'you can hardly blame me.'

'I'm sorry I was so rude,' he said. 'In my defence I didn't know that you were Tony's wife – I beg your pardon, his *partner*.'

'What has that got to do with it?'

'I wasn't trying to be rude, you see, I was trying to chat you up.'

'*That* was chatting me up? I'm amazed you found one wife, let alone three.'

'I'm sure,' Daniel said sadly, 'that my wives would agree with you.'

'I'm sorry,' Alberta began and then, catching his twinkling eye, said, 'Do you *always* tell lies?'

'Let's play a game,' Daniel said. 'I shall make three statements about myself and you have to guess which is true.'

'All right,' said Alberta, a shade warily.

'One: I wish you were single. Two: I find you very attractive. Three: I'd like to go to bed with you.'

Alberta blinked at him for a moment. 'I don't think any of them are true.'

'Now who's telling lies?' Daniel said softly. He straightened up as the waiter approached and said, 'Shall we have pudding?'

'I shouldn't,' Alberta said.

'Go on,' Daniel said. 'Be a little wicked.'

He was flirting with her. She shouldn't encourage him but it did wonders for her confidence. Dammit, she would have a pudding!

She felt completely relaxed with him now. The wine might, of course, have had something to do with that but it was impossible to be nervous in the presence of a man who turned out to be Disgusting Daniel. He made no more outrageous suggestions, confining his questions to studiously neutral subjects, like her career and her children. He never took his eyes away from her. It was rather gorgeous to be made to feel so attractive and she actually felt a twinge of regret when Tony at last arrived.

'I'm sorry I missed dinner,' he said, taking off his jacket and sitting down next to Alberta. 'My punishment was probably the worst egg sandwich I've ever eaten on a train.'

Daniel poured him a glass of wine. 'Here,' he said, 'it will take away the taste.'

Alberta's phone bleated once more and she reached into her handbag and pulled it out.

It was her brother, only it didn't sound much like him. Instead of his usual measured tones, his voice sounded anxious, a little out of breath and definitely upset. 'Alberta, where have you been? I've left at least three messages on your answerphone.'

'Hi, Christopher,' Alberta said, 'I'm in a restaurant. I've had my mobile on.'

'I know. It's silly. It didn't occur to me to try that until a moment ago.' He paused. 'Are you sitting down?'

'Well, of course I'm sitting down, I'm in a restaurant. What is it? Is there something wrong?'

'Yes,' said Christopher, 'yes, I'm afraid there is. I wish I didn't have to tell you this over the phone, I don't like using the phone at the best of times but—'

'Christopher, you're beginning to frighten me. Will you please tell me what has happened?'

'It's Pa. I'm afraid I have some rather bad news. Actually, it's *very* bad news. I wish I knew how to tell you this. I suppose there isn't a good way of telling you this. Alberta, you have to be very brave. Pa died in the early hours of this morning.'

Alberta gave a little cry and clutched the table with her free hand. She felt as if her entire body was being squeezed by giant pincers. She managed to whisper to Tony, 'Pa's dead!'

Tony took her hand. 'Daniel,' he said urgently, 'will you get a large brandy for Bertie . . . as quick as you can?'

'Alberta, speak to me,' Christopher demanded. 'Alberta, are you all right?'

'Yes,' she gasped, 'but I don't understand. He died this morning? Why didn't Marma tell us? How did he die? Was he in bed? Was Marma with him?'

'No,' Christopher said, 'it wasn't Marma who was with him, it was someone else.'

'What do you mean? Where was he?'

'He was in Streatham,' Christopher said. 'He was in a brothel in Streatham.'

# CHAPTER SEVEN

## *River of No Return*

When Tony rang Hannah, she was sitting on her bed, trying to recall every minute of the evening she had spent with Harrison two and a half weeks earlier.

A great deal had happened in those two and a half weeks. First, of course, there was Alfie's brilliant news. He was the first to concede he'd been lucky. He had been offered the part of the adulterous French prince because the producers were desperate.They were already filming when the up and coming young actor who'd been slated to play him had been rushed to hospital with peritonitis. At the audition, Alfie had been asked if he'd be available to start work almost immediately and he was able to assure them that the play in which he was currently acting was closing that very night. Even better, Alfie discovered there were at least three high-profile names in the cast which meant the production would hopefully receive loads of publicity.

It was all pretty amazing. Hannah had rung Harrison to tell him the news and had suggested he come over to help them celebrate but Harrison had been doing something else. She had suggested they meet for a drink later in the week but Harrison said he couldn't.

Meanwhile, Kitty had gone on holiday to Croatia and returned a week later. The vacation was not a success. Her two girlfriends had both met fabulous, caring, sexy, funny men within the last month and spent the entire week talking about them. Kitty had at least been chatted up on her second to last evening but her admirer was only eighteen and eventually admitted that he was only trying to impress one of the girls in his party. (Rather sweetly, he sought her out the next day to say the girl had indeed been impressed and he was very grateful.)

When Hannah came home from work to find her flatmate reading a book called *How to Be Happy on Your Own*, she decided it was time for action. It occurred to her that Harrison would be perfect for Kitty. They had met only once, at Hannah's twenty-first, and they had both been seeing other people at the time. Hannah was sure they'd get on. She rang Harrison and invited him to supper on Friday. Harrison didn't seem that keen but Hannah refused to take no for an answer.

The evening started so well. Within twenty minutes, Kitty was telling a sympathetic Harrison about her holiday and by the time they sat down to lasagne and salad, she was on to the subject of Melanie.

After dinner, they went back to the sitting room and opened a second bottle of wine. Things were going *so* well that Hannah suggested she make coffee. Both Kitty and Harrison said they were quite happy with the wine. Fortuitously, Alfie chose that moment to ring Hannah, so she was able to make a tactful retreat to the kitchen after all.

Alfie was filming in a part of Norfolk which was, according to the director, just like medieval France. He was now deeply in the character of the adulterous French prince. He'd met Princess Blanche, who was much younger than he'd thought she'd be. He'd also met his French brother and had liked him very much. The two of them had spent all afternoon being tortured, which had been quite interesting but very hard on their facial muscles. They were hoping to finish the torture scene the following morning after which he was going to learn how to ride a horse.

It was after Hannah had finished talking to Alfie and was making coffee for herself that she thought she heard the front door slam.

She *had* heard the front door slam. Kitty was sitting on her own in the sitting room, helping herself to more wine. When she saw Hannah, she said quickly, 'He's gone and it wasn't my fault,' and held out the bottle.

Hannah glanced at the door as if she expected Harrison to come back at any second. 'Why did he go?' she asked. 'And why didn't he say goodbye to me?' She took the bottle from Kitty and poured wine into her glass.

Kitty looked as if she didn't have a clue. 'He told me he was sorry he had to rush off and he'd loved the lasagne.'

'But *why* did he rush off?' Hannah persisted. 'Did you have a disagreement?'

Kitty shook her head violently. 'No, we were having a great time. At least, *I* was having a great time. I was very nice to him. Perhaps that was the trouble. Perhaps I was too nice to him.'

'What do you mean?' Hannah had a vision of Kitty

jumping on a startled Harrison. Perhaps Kitty had overdone the alcohol.

'We were talking,' Kitty said, 'or perhaps I was talking, I can't remember. And then Harrison said you were being a long time in the kitchen and I sat closer to him and said you were probably being tactful and then I looked up at him and he looked down at me and then he stood up and said there was something he'd never told you and then he stopped and then he said he was really sorry but he had to leave. And then he left.'

'I don't understand,' Hannah said. 'What was it he never told me?'

'He didn't say,' Kitty said. 'He looked like he couldn't wait to get out of the place. Perhaps I made him nervous. I don't suppose . . .' Kitty put down her glass and drew her knees up under her chin. 'Do you think it's possible he's gay?'

'*What?*' Hannah laughed. 'That is rubbish! Harrison's had lots of girlfriends! None of them has lasted very long but I think that's because they tend to choose *him* rather than the other way round. I *know* Harrison. And even if he were gay, which he isn't, why wouldn't he have told me?'

Kitty shrugged. 'I don't know. But he wears pretty odd clothes for a card-carrying heterosexual male. I'm pretty sure that that pink jersey he wore tonight is a woman's top.'

'It's quite likely it is,' Hannah said. 'He buys all his clothes in charity shops. That doesn't make him a transvestite. Perhaps he suddenly felt ill.'

'In that case,' Kitty said, 'it's funny that he only wanted to leave after I put my hand on his thigh.'

'You put your hand on his thigh?'

'I put my hand on his thigh! I put my hand on his *inner* thigh! And don't look at me like that, Hannah Granger. Can you look me in the face and tell me you weren't trying to set us up?'

Hannah sighed. 'I'm sorry. I thought . . .'

'It was a nice idea,' Kitty said, 'and I appreciate the effort you made even if it did end in disaster.' She rose unsteadily from the sofa. 'It only goes to show that we never know people as well as we think we do.'

It was this half-serious remark that continued to reverberate in Hannah's mind long after Kitty had gone to bed. The trouble was that Harrison was one of the few people who Hannah felt she *did* know. To think that Harrison might be as incomprehensible as everyone else made her feel surprisingly bereft and vulnerable. If she couldn't be sure of Harrison, who *could* she be sure of?

When she went to bed, she knew she wouldn't be able to sleep. Instead, she sat cross-legged on top of her duvet, frowning with concentration, trying to remember if there'd been any clues as to Harrison's strange behaviour at their last meeting. She kept glancing at her mobile, willing it to ring. She had sent him a text with the simple question 'What happened?' but either he had his phone switched off or he didn't want to talk to her.

Until this evening, she would never even have considered such a possibility and she sighed with relief when her phone did at last ring. But it wasn't Harrison, it was Tony. 'Hi, Hands-Off,' he said.

Hannah smiled. Tony had called her that ever since her sixth birthday when she'd got overexcited during a game of Twister and had kept shouting 'Hands Off!' at her stepfather. 'Hi, Tony, what's up?'

'I'm sorry to ring you so late. You weren't asleep, were you?'

'No. I invited Harrison to supper. He and Kitty are both single so I thought . . .'

'You're as bad as your mother. These things never work out.'

'I won't try it again, I can tell you. What have *you* been doing tonight?'

'I've just put your mother to bed. She made me promise to ring you. She didn't want you to wake up and hear it on the radio or read it in the paper . . .'

'Read *what* in the paper?'

'It's your grandfather,' Tony said. 'I hate telling you this over the phone, Hands-Off. He's dead.'

For a moment, Hannah sat looking stupidly at the phone before exclaiming. 'Grandfather's *dead*? But he's always been so healthy! No one would believe he's over eighty! Why is he *dead*? When did he die?'

'I think it was about four or five in the morning. He had a heart attack.'

'I'm so sorry!' Hannah could feel her eyes filling with tears and swallowed hard. 'Poor Marma! How terrifying for her! Did she wake up in the morning and find him dead?'

'That's the trouble,' Tony said, 'that's why it might be in all the papers tomorrow. He wasn't at home when it happened. He was in bed with someone else. He was in a house in Streatham. Apparently, he's been a regular . . . client there for a long time.'

It took Hannah a few moments to understand the implication of the word 'client'. She took a sharp intake of breath. '*Grandfather?* Are you saying Grandfather's been visiting prostitutes? It doesn't make any sense! He's eighty-two, for heaven's sake! And besides, he's . . . well, he's *Grandfather*.'

'There's more . . . Are you all right, Hands-Off?'

Hannah gulped and gripped her phone. 'What is it?'

There was a pause. 'The house in Streatham specializes in sado-masochistic practices. I suspect the delightful British press will have a field day.'

'I can't believe it! Poor Marma! Is she all right? And what about Mum?'

'She's not too good. I've managed to get her to go to bed. She's convinced it was all some horrible misunderstanding. As for Marma, Christopher says she's very calm. She wants to sort out the funeral arrangements on her own. She doesn't want anyone to be with her at the moment. It's difficult to know what to do . . .'

'Is there any chance that Mum's right? Could this all be some ridiculous mix-up?'

'Christopher seems pretty sure of his facts. He's spoken to the police. He's spoken to the woman who . . . who was in bed with him at the time. The thing is,' Tony stopped to clear his throat, 'I can't pretend I'm an expert on this sort of thing. And I know we're in a state of shock at the moment. It'll be some time before we know all the facts. Try not to get too upset by anything you read in the papers. They'll make most of it up. Look, I'd better go and see if your mother's all right. I'm sure she'll ring you tomorrow. If she doesn't, perhaps you could ring *her*. She's going to find this very difficult.'

'Of course I will. Give her my love. Goodnight, Tony.'

'Goodnight, Hands-Off. You take care.'

Hannah put down the phone and turned out the light. She tried to imagine her grandfather lying underneath some whip-wielding madam. Would they have talked first, exchanged opinions about the weather or the Prime Minister's latest pronouncements? None of it made any sense. Hannah shut her eyes and waited without much hope for sleep to come.

It seemed no time at all before the phone rang again. In fact, when she looked at her bedside clock, she saw that it was nearly eight. She propped herself up on her elbow and reached for her mobile.

'Hannah,' her uncle said, 'I presume you've heard the news?'

'Yes.' Hannah pushed back her hair. 'Uncle Christopher, I'm so sorry, I . . .'

'It's a terrible business. Helen and I have been talking about it most of the night.' He did indeed sound exhausted. 'We were hoping you could do us a very great favour. I know how busy you are but I wondered if you would consider going down to see Marma today? I know you have your finance exams in a few weeks.'

'I'd be happy to go. It's Saturday, after all. I'll give her a ring.'

'No,' Christopher said quickly. 'Don't ring her. Just turn up. The trouble is, I had a long talk with her last night and she made me promise that Alberta and I would leave her alone for a few days. She was most insistent that she wanted to be on her own. And I suspect your mother's too upset to go anywhere at the moment anyway. The point is, I'd rather you didn't ring Marma because if you do, she'll tell you not to come and Helen and I really feel someone ought to be with her this weekend. The place will be awash with tabloid reporters. Marma says she can cope but . . .'

'Don't worry, I'll go. How was she when you talked to her?'

'She sounded . . .' Christopher hesitated, as if he wasn't sure of the answer. 'I thought she sounded *business-like*.'

'That doesn't sound like Marma.'

'I know. I found her a little unnerving, to tell the truth. She'd spoken to the police and to a doctor. She was about to ring the vicar concerning the funeral. She said she didn't want any help with the arrangements. She said it was such a pity he had died when he did because the Siberian irises had just come out and he had always enjoyed the display they made.'

Hannah smiled. 'Now, that *does* sound like Marma.'

'Yes.' Christopher sounded a little less worried. 'It does, doesn't it? You will ring me after your visit?'

'Of course I will. I suppose there's no doubt about the circumstances of Grandfather's death?'

'None at all, I'm afraid. It's such a *tawdry* way to go. I find it very difficult to forgive him. I'd better go. Goodbye now.'

He rang off abruptly, leaving Hannah looking at the phone in consternation. He'd sounded so *angry*. She had always regarded her uncle as a quintessential academic: mild-mannered, measured, cautious.

She should ring her mother. She decided she needed a

strong coffee first and then a shower and then another strong coffee.

When she rang, forty minutes later, she got Tony and told him she was going down to Hampshire.

'Christopher told me. You're a star. Are you sure you can spare the time?'

'I'll take my laptop with me. I'm glad to be useful. Can I speak to Mum? How is she?'

'Well,' Tony said carefully, 'she's not too bad. She's watching *High Noon*.'

Hannah glanced at the kitchen clock. 'She's watching television?'

'It's a DVD,' Tony said. 'You know how Bertie loves Westerns. Can you ring her in an hour or so?'

'I'll ring her from the train. Does she know I'm going to see Marma?'

'I'll tell her,' Tony said. 'I'll tell her after *High Noon*.'

Tony seemed to find it quite natural that a woman should respond to a much-loved father's sudden and scandalous death by watching a cowboy film. But then, Hannah thought, how *should* one respond to such an event? At least *High Noon* was better than tranquillizers.

She meant to ring as soon as she got on the train but the carriage was full and instead she looked out of the window and watched the suburbs give way to countryside. She didn't even try to do any work. She took out her phone and sent a text to Alfie. At Reading the carriage emptied and she rang home. This time she got Jacob.

'Hi, Jacob,' she said. 'Can you believe any of this?'

'Yes,' Jacob said. Jacob could always be expected to say the unexpected. 'I couldn't at first but I've been thinking.

Grandfather looked so immaculate and he was always so polite to everyone. Have you ever heard him *not* thank Marma for a lovely meal? He was good on television: he looked so wise and so calm. No human being can be that perfect, or at least no human being can be that perfect without having some place in which they can be completely un-perfect.'

'You're probably right,' Hannah conceded, 'but I still don't see why he had to go to prostitutes to unwind. Why couldn't he drink too much or shout at a football team or play golf or something? I feel so sorry for Marma. How's Mum?'

'She's been watching *High Noon*. After lunch, we're going to watch *Shane* or possibly *The Magnificent Seven*.'

Hannah lowered her voice. 'Jacob, I know Mum loves Westerns but isn't this behaviour a bit odd?'

'Actually,' Jacob said modestly, 'it was my idea.'

'I might have known it. Go on then. Explain why you're force-feeding our mother with Westerns.'

'Mum is upset,' Jacob said. 'I mean, Mum is *really* upset. I've never seen her like this. I came back last night and she was crying. She wouldn't *stop* crying. Dad kept making her tea and hot chocolate and still she cried. It was horrible.'

'Oh, Jacob!' Hannah breathed, 'I'm so sorry. Poor Mum.'

'I went to bed,' Jacob said, 'and I tried to think what I could do to help. I've been reading this book about economics. It's rather good. It makes one see that one should never underestimate the power of irrational behaviour. Basically, its thesis is that we can't be relied on to do what's best for us and that government doesn't do us any favours by thinking we *will*. Government should *nudge* people into doing the right thing. In other words, if you *tell* people—'

'If you tell people what to do, they won't do it,' Hannah said impatiently. 'I can see that. How does all this help Mum?'

'I'm coming to that,' Jacob said. 'But don't you think it's an interesting idea? There's an example in the book about managers at Amsterdam's airport who wanted to reduce cleaning costs in the men's loos. So what did they do? They did *not* put posters up asking men to be more careful. Instead, they had a fly drawn on the porcelain of each of the urinals. As a consequence, they improved the accuracy of penile aim by eighty per cent. What do you think?'

'I think it's amazing you can remember a statistic like that. How does this apply to Mum?'

'Mum's upset. Mum's upset because Grandfather has died and she's even more upset because he has died in circumstances which suggest he wasn't as fantastic as she thought he was. Mum loves Westerns. Most Westerns have heroic cowboys who are brave but, crucially, are flawed in some way. Ergo, watching Westerns will help Mum come to terms with the fact that her father also had failings.'

'Jacob,' Hannah said, 'I hope you'll always be around to help me when I need you.'

'I hope so too,' Jacob said. 'I can hear my mobile going so I'd better go. Do you want to speak to Mum? She's in bed now. I'm taking you up to her. See you soon.'

There was a pause of a few seconds and then a pale voice said, 'Hello, Hannah.'

Hannah gripped her phone. 'Mum, I'm so sorry! Jacob tells me you're in bed. That's good. You've had a terrible shock. You need to rest.'

'Everyone is being very kind. Evie's making one of her soups. I can't believe it's happened. Your grandfather was such a *vital* man. I could never imagine a time when he wouldn't be here.' There was a long silence which Hannah didn't like to break. 'Tony told me you're going to see Marma. That's kind of you.'

'Have you spoken to her yet?'

'I tried but I got her answerphone.' There was another long pause. 'I shall try again when my headache goes.'

'Have you taken something for it?'

'He was a wonderful man, you know, Hannah, and he was such a good father. I couldn't have had a better father.'

'And that's what you must remember. All that other stuff . . . that's not important.'

'There is no other stuff. It's all a mistake. You'll see. It's a mistake.'

'Yes, but all I'm saying is that if it isn't a mistake—'

'It *is* a mistake. I watched *High Noon* this morning. Did you ever see it? You must have seen it.'

Hannah smiled. 'Of course I've seen it, you made me watch it about one thousand times.'

'Well, that's what your grandfather was like. Had he been in that situation, he would have been just like Gary Cooper.'

'I'm sure you're right and all I'm trying to say is that if Gary Cooper in *High Noon* had had, for example, an eating disorder or a . . . a tendency to like young girls, it wouldn't have detracted from the fact that he was very brave and—'

'He didn't have an eating disorder and if you remember he was in love with Grace Kelly.'

'Yes.' Hannah gave up. It was much better to leave the psychology stuff to her brother. 'Mum, I'll give your love to Marma and I'll ring you tomorrow. Try to get some sleep now.'

'I will.'

Hannah put the phone in her bag and looked out of the window at the green fields and the oak trees and the picture-perfect villages. But of course they weren't picture-perfect. The ancient churches were no longer used, the quaint little cottages contained all manner of misery and discontentment. Nothing was what it seemed.

She had been useless on the phone just now. She wished she could talk to Harrison. He was so sensible and so kind and he would know what to say to *her* and, more important, he would know what she should say to her mother. But even Harrison, apparently, was not what he seemed. He had certainly acted in a very un-Harrison-like manner last night.

She could hear her phone. Hannah pulled it out quickly, looked at it and then relaxed as she saw the name and number of the caller.

'I've just heard,' Alfie said. 'I'm so sorry. You poor old thing. I wish I was with you. How *are* you?'

And Hannah, who had thought she was fine, burst into tears.

# CHAPTER EIGHT

## *Pale Rider*

Hannah wasn't sure what she had expected: a swarm of paparazzi perhaps or a black-robed Marma weeping over the Siberian irises. There was no sign of Marma and the garden was as tranquil as ever. As she walked up the drive, Hannah could hear the bees buzzing busily as they hoovered up the pollen from the delphiniums. In the distance, a wood pigeon cooed unhurriedly. Hannah stopped to admire a green dragonfly that zigzagged over the roses before making for the pond and skimming the sun-dappled water. It seemed absurd that the owner of this pastoral idyll – the grandfather who had played croquet with her on the lawn – could have died in a seedy brothel in Streatham only yesterday.

Hannah rang the doorbell and almost immediately heard her grandmother's voice: 'I'm coming! Just a minute!' And then, a few moments later, the door was opened and there was Marma, looking bright and summery in a short-sleeved cream-coloured shirt and brown linen trousers. 'Hannah!' she exclaimed. 'What a delightful surprise! Have you come to stay?'

'Just for the night, Marma, if that's all right. Tony rang me about Grandfather and I wanted to see you.'

'How *very* sweet! Have you had lunch?'

'I'm not hungry.'

'So you haven't,' Marma said. 'Come on in.'

Hannah followed her grandmother through to the kitchen and stopped as she saw two men and a woman sitting round the table. She took in the cameras and the notebooks and felt a steely anger rise in the pit of her stomach, made worse by the fact that one of the men leered at her in a way that he quite clearly thought was irresistible.

'Are these friends of yours, Marma?' she asked.

'I don't know them from Adam, dear,' Marma said.

'My name is Moira, Moira Crewe,' the woman at the table said. She fixed Hannah with a dazzling smile that exposed every tooth in her mouth.

'Christopher said I shouldn't talk to the press,' Marma said, 'but these three have been standing in the garden for hours and I thought I should make them some coffee.'

Moira smiled again. 'We don't want to intrude in this time of grief . . .'

'I'm glad to hear it,' Hannah said.

'We simply wanted a brief word with Lady Trussler.'

Hannah frowned. 'Why?'

The man with the creepy smile said, 'Look, love, it's a big story. People want to know—'

'People have a right to know,' said the other man. 'Lord Trussler was a public figure. The public wants to know what his wife has to say.'

'My grandfather had retired from public life. The public has no right to know anything about his private life. And you have no right to trick your way in here and harass a poor grieving widow –' she glanced at her grandmother who was busy pulling cheeses and pâté and pickle from the fridge – 'who has only just lost her husband and is clearly in a state of shock.'

'Do you like hummus, dear?' Marma asked.

'Yes please, Marma. So,' Hannah said, pulling out her phone from her bag, 'unless you leave in one minute, I shall take photos of the three of you and make sure that as many papers as possible receive my own personal account of the persecution of Lady Trussler.'

'Now, look,' Moira said, 'there is no need to be unfriendly. All we want is—'

'I am starting to count now,' Hannah said. 'One . . . two . . . three . . .'

'Lady Trussler was quite happy to see—'

'. . . ten . . . eleven . . . twelve . . .'

'We're going,' Moira said, 'we're going right now. You can stop—'

'. . . eighteen . . . nineteen . . . twenty . . .'

The men picked up their bags and followed Moira out of the kitchen, through the hall and out onto the drive. Hannah strode after them, holding out her mobile like a talisman and shouting, 'Don't you *dare* come back!' For a few moments she stood, catching her breath, and then she turned and went back into the house.

Her grandmother had finished laying the table and was cutting some slices from a small brown loaf. Really, Hannah thought, her grandmother was incredible. It was somehow so like Marma that she would not behave in the predictable way. If she didn't know better, she would find it hard to believe that Marma had discovered less than twenty-four hours ago that her husband had died in the bed of a prostitute.

'Come and sit down, dear,' Marma said. 'There's some apple juice on the table; it's very good – they make it at the farm shop. Thank you for getting rid of those people. I was finding them dreadfully tedious. You reminded me of Jesus when he sent the moneylenders from the temple – very impressive!'

'I don't feel like Jesus,' Hannah said. 'I could have happily strangled them. How dare they pester you like that! You should never have let them into the house.'

'I know, I was very stupid, but the Moira woman said she needed the loo and the man with the unpleasant nose said their editor wouldn't let them leave until they'd had a few words with me. Do have some cheese, Hannah; that Cheddar is particularly fine.'

'You shouldn't be here on your own. I bet there'll be more reporters coming. Why don't you go and stay with Mum or Uncle Christopher for a few days? They'd love to have you.'

'Nonsense, I have a funeral to organize. And anyway, Michael's sister is threatening to come and stay. She'd scare anyone off.'

This was true. Great-Aunt Hilda might be seventy-nine but she was built like a pit bull terrier and had a temper to match. 'Well, if she doesn't come,' Hannah said, 'I'm sure Mum would love to come and stay. She could help you do the food.'

'I've been thinking about the funeral,' Marma said. 'I've spoken to the vicar. He's a very sweet man and has offered to do a little eulogy on Michael but I'd very much rather he didn't. Michael can't . . . couldn't . . . stand him and would loathe the idea of a eulogy from the pulpit. I thought perhaps I could call on you and Jacob to say a few words. Unfortunately, your cousin won't be here. He was quite prepared to come back from the States but I told Christopher to tell him to stay there. I'm sure you and Jacob can manage on your own.'

'We'd be delighted.'

'Good. And as for hymns, we'll have "Jerusalem", of course, and "Praise, My Soul, the King of Heaven". And Michael loved "Dear Lord and Father of Mankind".' Marma cleared her throat and suddenly burst into song:

*'Dear Lord and Father of mankind,*
*Forgive our foolish ways!*
*Reclothe us in our rightful mind,*
*In purer lives thy service find,*
*In deeper reverence praise,*
*In deeper reverence praise.'*

She stopped and said, 'I think that's rather appropriate, don't you?'

'I do,' said Hannah, wondering if now might be a good time to bring up the particularly foolish ways of her grandfather.

'And then there are the readings,' Marma said. 'I couldn't sleep last night, so I wrote down some suggestions. Would you like to hear them?'

'Yes,' Hannah said. 'May I have some more apple juice?'

'Of course, dear, help yourself. I'll go and get my notebook.'

Hannah watched Marma bustle out of the kitchen and frowned thoughtfully. She had always assumed her oddness came from her father's side of the family. Now, she wondered if she'd blamed the wrong side. There was her mother watching Westerns and her grandmother acting like she was organizing a birthday party. But then, of course, all of that paled into insignificance beside her grandfather and what he'd been up to. Her grandfather was the oddest of all. Hannah replenished her glass and cut herself another piece of cheese.

Marma returned with notebook in hand and reading glasses on the end of her nose. 'All right, dear, first off is the Dylan Thomas poem about death. Do you know the one I mean? I love those lines where he tells us to rage against the dying of the light. Isn't it a wonderful poem?'

'It is wonderful,' Hannah said, 'it's also seriously depressing and I know that everyone will be pretty depressed anyway so perhaps one wants a little more . . . I don't know, something a little less negative.'

'You see, I thought it was rather grand, the idea of Michael raving and raging . . .' Marma paused. 'Perhaps you're right. Well, there's always *Hamlet*, you know, "To be or not to be . . . " Such an interesting cogitation on the merits of suicide.'

'Yes, but Marma,' Hannah shifted in her seat, 'Grandfather didn't commit suicide and we don't want the congregation to think we necessarily endorse the idea.'

Marma flicked another page. 'What about *Macbeth*? "Nothing in his life became him like the leaving it . . ." That's nice.'

'Marma!' Hannah cried, then paused while she tried to think of a tactful way to phrase what she wanted to say. 'Do you *want* people to dwell on the way in which he left his life?'

Marma put her head to one side and then gave it a little shake. 'You see,' she said, 'I keep forgetting exactly *how* he died. So silly.'

'Actually, I think it's very sensible,' Hannah said, 'but I still don't think you can use that quote.'

'I shall do some more research,' Marma said. 'I think— Is that the phone?' She stood up. 'I shall take it in the study. Help yourself to more bread, dear, you need to eat more, you're far too thin.'

Hannah sat back in her chair. *Nothing in his life became him like the leaving it.* The press would have had a field day with that. Her mouth twitched. She noticed the *Daily Telegraph* on the dresser and stretched out an arm. She unfolded it and scanned the front page. On the bottom right-hand corner there was a photograph of her grandfather and a caption underneath.

*Lord Trussler, 82 years old, statesman, writer and pundit, was found dead in a house in Streatham in the early hours of Friday morning. See page 3 for full story.*

The article could have been worse. It referred to his position in Edward Heath's government and his pivotal role in taking Britain into the EEC in 1972, his ministerial positions under Margaret Thatcher and John Major, his appearances on *Question Time* and *Newsnight*. It praised his fluency and his courtesy as a debater, and even mentioned that he and his wife had always been regarded as one of the more stylish couples at Tory party conferences. Only in the last sentence was the manner of his death referred to. 'Eighty-two-year-old Lord Trussler apparently died of a heart attack while staying in a house of dubious repute in Streatham.'

Poor Marma. She was being amazing but Hannah suspected the grim truth of the situation hadn't sunk in yet. Perhaps all these funeral plans were as much a displacement activity as watching Westerns.

Hannah closed the paper and looked again at the photograph on the front page. There was her grandfather, his hair slicked back, his eyes looking confidently at the camera. He looked so handsome, so distinguished. Why would such a man want to go to some seedy establishment in Streatham and pay for kinky sex with a stranger?

She heard the study door close and quickly returned the paper to the dresser. As soon as Marma entered the kitchen, Hannah knew there was something badly wrong. Marma's face was flushed, she was blinking rapidly as if she had something in her eye. 'I'm sorry I was so long,' she said. 'I've had a rather disagreeable conversation with Joan Cartwright. She says she and Maurice have decided not to come to the funeral.'

'Why not?'

'Oh,' Marma waved an impatient hand, 'silly reasons. It never occurred to me that Joan of all people would be so sanctimonious. I'm sure Maurice will come.' She straightened her shirt and clapped her hands. 'It's a beautiful day. I'll make some coffee and then I think we should go for a walk.'

On the train back to London the following day, with the Sunday papers spread out about her, Hannah thought back to that walk and knew she would never forget it. Marma had made straight for the village, with Hannah walking beside her like a handmaiden. Every time they passed an acquaintance or even spied an acquaintance, Marma would call out, 'Hello there! Have you heard that Michael is dead? His funeral's on Friday! See you there!'

Reactions ranged from the nervously effusive – 'Oh, Philippa, I was going to ring . . . I read about it . . . I heard about it this morning, so sad, and this must be your granddaughter, aren't grandchildren a blessing in times like this?' – to the terse or the just plain panic-stricken. As they approached the church, one woman who was tending a grave saw them coming and promptly disappeared from view. Marma was ruthless, peering over the stone wall and catching her victim squatting on the ground.

'Ah, Marjorie,' she said, 'have you heard about Michael? He's dead.'

Marjorie looked up, with a face as red as the roses on the grave. 'I heard,' she said. 'I saw it in the . . . I'm so sorry.'

'The funeral's on Friday,' Marma said. 'See you there!'

Remembering Marjorie's hounded expression, Hannah gave a soft chuckle. Marma had been magnificent. Hannah hated leaving her.

Now she sat on the train, leafing through the Sunday

papers. The *Sunday People* had a lurid article titled LORD TRUSSLER TRUSSED UP! which provided a graphic description of the many services provided by 'the House of Sin in Streatham'. The *News of the World* had an exclusive interview with a young woman called Sukie Starlight. Sukie had been in bed with Lord Trussler at the time of his heart attack and declared she would never recover from the shock. Michael, she said, was a darling, he was a regular customer, ever so polite, he always thanked her every time she spanked him. Some people might call him a pervert but Sukie didn't care. He was just a man who needed love and he couldn't perform without a good spanking. And he liked the handcuffs too but she hadn't used them that night. Sukie said he was a sweet old man and she enjoyed making him happy.

Worse by far was the piece by Moira Crewe in another paper. Underneath the headline 'MEN WILL BE MEN' SAYS KINKY MINISTER'S WIFE! was a photograph of Marma looking confused. Moira, while purporting to be deeply sympathetic, suggested that Lord Trussler had been driven into the arms of a prostitute by the coldness of his wife who, Moira felt after an in-depth interview, cared only for her garden and her home. Moira concluded that Lady Trussler's headline-grabbing explanation for her husband's behaviour betrayed a lack of sexual understanding that was symptomatic of women of a certain age and class. In Moira's view . . .

But Hannah had had enough of Moira's views. She closed the paper and sat back, recalling once again the walk through the village. The only time Marma's resolve had faltered was on the way home when they encountered Maurice with his dog. He had looked at Marma with a pathetic and pusillanimous expression, half-pleading, half-smiling. Marma had waited for a moment before raising her chin and going on her way.

Throughout the next few days, the quality press picked up on the men-will-be-men comment. The opinion pages had a plethora of earnest articles about the exact meaning of those words. Had Lady Trussler known about her husband's private peculiarities? How many men had these particular needs? Did prostitutes provide a necessary role in the preservation of many marriages? How many octogenarians had these particular urges? How many octogenarians had any urges? *Should* octogenarians have urges?

On Friday, Hannah set off for the funeral. Kitty had said she'd be happy to go with her, and Alfie, who was still filming, had said he could probably come down in the evening. Hannah was grateful but had rejected both offers. She knew Kitty had planned to go to Cheshire for the weekend and as she said to Alfie, 'Marma would love to meet you but the evening of Grandfather's funeral is not the right time. I'll stay the night with Marma and come back the next day. I'll be fine.'

In fact, she did not feel fine. The funeral and the party afterwards were terrible. There was a gang of photographers by the church gates who were only temporarily quietened when Great-Aunt Hilda waved her stick at them. Inside, there were rows of empty pews. As the small congregation sang 'Praise, My Soul, the King of Heaven' the voices could hardly be heard above the sound of the church organ. Hannah felt better once she'd given her small speech about Grandfather. Her uncle read the first reading, an extract from an essay by Montaigne. His hands were shaking when he put on his reading glasses but he spoke the words in a fierce, ringing tone as if he were declaring war.

The second reading, a lovely piece by Edna St Vincent Millay, was voiced, far more gently, by her mother and all went well until she spoke the last two lines:

*'"Quietly they go, the intelligent, the witty, the brave.*
*I know. But I do not approve. And I am not resigned."'*

At this point she burst into tears and had to be borne away by Tony while from the right side of the church, Great-Aunt Hilda could be heard snorting indignantly, although whether at the words or at the tears, no one could be certain. The ceremony ended with a poem and then a final hymn, 'For Those in Peril on the Sea', a strange choice of hymn for a man who had such a well-known aversion to boats of any kind. The poem, 'The Soldier' by Rupert Brooke, was read by Great-Aunt Hilda. It had been chosen because Rupert Brooke was Grandfather's favourite poet but was not perhaps the wisest of choices. It had the celebrated words 'If I should die, think only this of me: that there's some corner of a foreign field that is forever England' – quite inappropriate since Grandfather was being buried in a Hampshire graveyard, and Great-Aunt Hilda's booming emphasis on the word 'foreign' made the choice of material even less comprehensible.

Back at the house, the vast array of cakes and sandwiches only underlined the paucity of guests. There couldn't have been more than twenty people there and most of them were family. Tony, Lionel and Evie were terrific, passing round food, engaging all and sundry in conversation. Jacob, on a one-man mission to eat his way through the feast, said very little. Hannah saw her mother leave the room at least three times, returning minutes later with suspiciously red-rimmed eyes. Hannah was almost relieved when Tony decided it was time to take his party back to Bath.

By now the only people left with Marma were Great-Aunt Hilda, Uncle Christopher, Aunt Helen and Hannah. Marma suggested a sherry in the garden and Hannah immediately volunteered to collect together the necessary glasses and bottle. It was good to be alone in the kitchen for a few minutes. She stood looking at all the sandwiches and the little quiches and the cakes and felt a rising fury against the so-called friends of her grandparents who had stayed away. She took a few deep breaths. Anger would not help Marma, she thought. Pull yourself together, Hannah.

She was looking for the sherry in the larder when she heard her grandmother call her. She returned to the kitchen and saw the sherry in Marma's hands.

'Sorry, darling,' Marma said. 'I'd put it in the sitting room in case anyone wanted anything stronger than tea. If you take the tray of glasses, I'll bring the bottle. And Hannah?'

'Yes, Marma?'

'Christopher and Helen are driving back to London in about half an hour and I think you should go with them.'

'I thought I'd stay the night here. I could help with the clearing up.'

'I'll have Hilda for company. I know you all think she's difficult but I'm actually very fond of her. And as for the clearing up, it's simply a case of putting food away. You go off home and spend some time with your nice boyfriend. Didn't you tell me he was coming back tonight? I'll be fine here with Hilda.'

Hannah looked out through the kitchen window. She could see Great-Aunt Hilda sitting on her chair on the terrace. In her green silk dress, she resembled a giant toad. 'Well,' Hannah said, 'if you're sure.'

Hannah sat in the back of the car, behind her uncle and aunt, and turned to wave at Marma. As Christopher turned into the lane, he spoke for them all when he said, 'Thank God that's over.'

For a time, Aunt Helen tried to lighten the atmosphere by asking Hannah in her soft Canadian accent about her job and her flat and Alfie.

Uncle Christopher suddenly erupted. 'That bloody village. The number of times they've eaten and drunk in that house and today only seven of them turned up! Those bloody people!' He reached for a CD and said, 'Please forgive my language! Do you mind if I put some music on?'

And so it was that they drove back to London accompanied by the heartbreaking sounds of Faure's *Requiem*, and for the first time since she had heard about her grandfather's death, Hannah allowed herself to think about him and mourn his passing.

When her uncle finally pulled up outside Hannah's home, he tried to apologize for his lack of conversation.

Hannah interrupted him quickly. 'Uncle Christopher,' she said, 'that music was just what I needed.' She got out of the car, went round to his window and kissed his cheek.

That was why music was important, she thought as she opened the door and went up the stairs to her flat. Great music allowed one to forget all the rubbish and appreciate the greatness of a life, of any life. She wiped her eyes and unlocked the door.

The sitting room light was on and she frowned until she saw Alfie's battered old case on the floor by the sofa. She took off her jacket and put it on the sofa along with her bag. She frowned again. She could hear sounds coming from her bedroom. The light was on in there too. She began to move forward and then heard another sound and then another. She took off her shoes and walked through to the bedroom.

For a moment she had the feeling she had wandered onto the stage of a French farce. There, facing her, on her bed, was a stranger, a naked girl on all fours, groaning with pleasure, her blonde hair falling like windswept curtains across her face. As Hannah's gaze rose to meet Alfie's, it seemed to her that her lover bestrode the girl like Ben Hur on his chariot.

Alfie stopped in mid-thrust and gasped, 'Hannah . . . hello there!' He stopped to catch his breath. 'We're in the middle of rehearsing a scene. This is Princess Blanche.'

Below him, Princess Blanche managed an awkward smile. 'Hiya,' she said.

# CHAPTER NINE

## *Run for Cover*

The night after the funeral, sleep remained stubbornly out of reach for Alberta. She had not slept much in the nights before the funeral and at the moment she felt she would never sleep easily again.

The event itself was both better and worse than she had anticipated. The hymns had been old stalwarts, good barn-storming tunes that she remembered from her childhood: 'Praise My Soul, the King of Heaven', 'For Those in Peril on the Sea', 'Dear Lord and Father of Mankind' . . . Alberta did not need to look behind her to know that members of the congregation were eyeing each other meaningfully as they sang the line, 'Forgive our foolish ways'.

Jacob and Hannah both paid their own tributes to their grandfather. Hannah made a confident speech, attributing her ambition and determination to her grandfather's example and to his belief in her. She ended on a touchingly defiant note, affirming in a ringing voice that she would always be proud of him.

Jacob's speech was rather different. Unlike Hannah, who had spoken without notes, he had a few pieces of paper which he shuffled from time to time. He told the congregation that he had done some research on famous prime ministers and politicians and had unearthed some interesting facts. Gladstone had entertained prostitutes with tea and cakes. Churchill's father died of syphilis before he could become Prime Minister and Churchill himself was afflicted by depression and perhaps as a consequence drank too much. In the first two years of the First World War, Prime Minister Asquith was infatuated with a young friend of his daughter and wrote epic-length letters to her on a daily basis. In the fifties, Harold Macmillan endured the misery of knowing that his wife was having an affair with Lord Boothby throughout his premiership.

At this point, Jacob cleared his throat and adjusted his glasses. He suggested that most people had secrets and that some secrets were more reprehensible than others. 'I agree,' he concluded, 'with Bertrand Russell who said that no one ever gossips about other people's secret virtues. My grandfather, for example, was very good at teaching me how to play card games. As a result I am an extremely able poker player.'

Jacob sat down so abruptly that the vicar was taken by surprise and dropped his prayer book as he stood up. He sent a vague smile in Jacob's direction, seemed to contemplate saying something, opened his mouth, shut it again and then opened it to announce that Christopher would now read from an essay by Montaigne.

Alberta had listened to Montaigne's words with intense concentration. One of his sentences still remained in her mind: 'We do not know where death awaits us: so let us wait for it everywhere.' That was the problem. She had never been prepared for death. She had never thought her father *would* die. He had seemed to be immortal and now that he was dead, the entire world seemed different without him.

She wished she hadn't made such a mess of her own reading. She had been the only one to make such an exhibition. Pa would not have been pleased.

This was hopeless. She had never *been* so wide awake. Alberta slid out of bed, careful not to wake Tony. Taking her dressing gown, she went downstairs to the kitchen and put some milk in a saucepan.

What was so upsetting about the funeral was its *modesty*. The congregation should have filled every nook and cranny of the church. There should have been Cabinet Ministers past and present, bishops and BBC dignitaries. Instead, there was Aunt Hilda shouting at reporters and a church that was two-thirds empty. Not even the Cartwrights had come. That had upset Marma more than anything; she had thought, right up to the last minute, that Maurice at least would come.

Had Pa killed anyone? No. Had he defrauded anyone? No. His crime was to be an old man who paid for sex. That fact, Alberta now accepted after a long and difficult conversation with Christopher, was true. She took the pan off the Aga and poured the contents into a mug. Was *she* upset about the revelations? Of course she was. She had always taken the view that men who paid for sex were men with an indefensible and repellent attitude to women. She had also always assumed that men who paid for sex were unattractive individuals who couldn't get close to a woman in any other way, and yet women had always loved Pa.

She had tried to talk to Marma about it. She had asked her why she had made that ridiculous comment to the press about men being men. Marma said it was the first thing that came into her head. When Alberta persisted, suggesting that Marma's response seemed to imply a familiarity with or a tolerance of Pa's secret life, Marma had been uncharacteristically dogmatic. 'I knew nothing,' she said, 'I knew nothing at all. I don't *wish* to know anything and that's the last time I shall mention the subject.'

Alberta took her mug to the table and sat down. Perhaps Marma wanted to avoid the subject because she knew only too well why Pa had felt the need to go elsewhere for his sexual satisfaction.

For years now, Alberta had tried to put behind her the memories of those horrible months after Ed's death but, like bad smells, her dismay and resentment at Marma's behaviour had persisted. Perhaps, in order to understand Pa's behaviour, it was necessary to revisit that time and face what Marma had done, or rather what she hadn't done.

Alberta's husband died in a car accident and left Alberta widowed with a three-year-old daughter. At the time, Marma was staying with Christopher and Helen in Canada. Did she make a call to her grieving daughter? Did she make plans to rush back to England? She did neither of these things. For a year, she neither wrote to nor rang Alberta. For a year, she stayed in Canada, helping her daughter-in-law with her baby and not helping her daughter at all. It seemed more than likely to Alberta that a mother who could ignore her daughter's grief could well be a wife who ignored her husband's physical needs.

None of this justified Pa's actions. But at least, according to that loathsome interview in the *News of the World*, he hadn't been the one who did the spanking. So that was sort of all right. It might be true that he liked wearing funny clothes and enjoyed being spanked on the bottom. Well, thought Alberta, sipping her milk, at least he hadn't wanted to hurt anyone.

If, and it was a very big if, Marma hadn't wanted Pa to go near her for years and years, perhaps he had just reacted – admittedly in a rather extreme manner – by going off to the spanking lady in Streatham. Alberta sighed. The truth was she would probably never know. It was all supposition. There was no point in raising her theories with Christopher. She and Christopher had not been able to talk properly about Marma for years. He was Marma's champion; but then *he* had never been let down by her.

At home, everyone had tried to be kind. Lionel had, as always, tried to find something positive to say, suggesting that at least Pa had died from an excess of pleasure and that that had to be better than dying slowly from some horrible illness. Evie had told her she should take as long as she needed to mourn her father, which was sweet but then Evie had been unable to conceal her concern at Alberta's wish to watch Westerns all day. Hannah had done her best to be sympathetic and supportive but Alberta knew her exams were imminent and felt it was wrong to distract her from her studies.

Funnily enough, of all her family, it had been Jacob who had helped her the most. He had joined her on the sofa while she watched *High Noon* and had even squeezed her hand when Gary Cooper discovered he had to face the gunfighters on his own. He had brought her a cup of tea while she watched *Bad Day at Black Rock* and agreed that Robert Ryan was a brilliant baddie. He had watched some of *Shane* with her and had even refrained from making his usual comments about Alan Ladd's lack of stature.

In fact, Jacob had been a star. She had been touched by his speech at the funeral. The vicar might have been shocked by Jacob's references to syphilis and adultery but Alberta had been cheered by her son's spirited defence of his grandfather.

As for Tony, he had tried to be sympathetic but she knew he had been glad to get back to London and work on Monday. She could see it was difficult for him to join her in her grief. Pa had never disguised the fact that he viewed Tony as a very poor second to Ed and Tony, not unnaturally, had always felt correspondingly uncomfortable in Pa's company.

Alberta finished her milk and took the mug over to the dishwasher. There was only one person who would have understood what she was going through now and she missed him more than ever. She began to cry, whether for Pa or for Ed or for both of them she wasn't sure.

Alberta was woken the next morning by the sounds of the Growlers streaming up from the kitchen and the appearance of Tony by her bedside. 'I've brought you a cup of tea,' he said. In fact, it was a mug, one of the many that had lost their handles over the years, but she appreciated the gesture.

She opened her eyes and struggled to sit up. 'What's the time?' she asked.

'Half past ten.' Tony sat down on the edge of the bed. 'Do you want any breakfast?'

'No, this is great.' Alberta sat up and pushed back her hair. 'I can't believe it's so late. I couldn't sleep last night.'

'Evie suggested we all go out for lunch. I think it's a great idea. I've booked a table at the Moon and Sixpence. And Diana rang. She wants to know if you're ready to go back to work this week. I said you'd ring her.'

Alberta groaned. 'Can you do me a favour? Will you ring and tell her I need another week off? I can't face it at the moment. Will you ring her now?'

'Do you know how much that woman terrifies me?' Tony protested but he stood up and went to the door. 'I may be some time,' he said mournfully before disappearing from view.

Alberta took a sip of her tea and lay down. She pulled the duvet up over her face. What she would really like to do was stay in bed all day with the duvet over her face and speak to no one at all. If she lived on her own, she would hibernate for a week or a month or a year and only get up when she stopped feeling like the sun had disappeared. She shut her eyes and concentrated on breathing deeply. With any luck, she would fall asleep again.

No such luck. Tony came back and sat on the end of the bed. 'I don't know how you can work with that woman,' he said. 'Just speaking to her gives me indigestion and I ate breakfast an hour and a half ago. The good news is she says if you need another week off, then you shall have another week off. The bad news is that she *is* rather concerned that you might have forgotten she's going to Turkey in ten days.'

'She's been talking about nothing else for weeks.' Alberta pushed herself up and had a sip from her now tepid tea. 'Tony, do you mind if I opt out of the lunch? I'm not really in the mood for company and I can't face any food at the moment.'

'Don't you think . . .' Tony hesitated, 'it would do you good to get out and about rather than just wallow in—'

'I'm not wallowing and even if I am, aren't I *allowed* to wallow for a little while? Pa died just over a week ago! Is that it? Am I now expected to get on with my life as if nothing had happened?'

'Of course not. I know how much you loved your father. I just think you might find things a little easier if you don't spend so much time dwelling on—'

'I *want* to dwell on him. He was my father! It's just a week! I know it's very boring and terribly tedious but I need to mourn my father and I can't do that by going along and having a jolly time in a restaurant. I think it's a great idea that you all go out for lunch. I shall have a nice, brisk walk on my own and when you come back I shall hopefully be all nice and jolly again. All right?'

Tony stared at her without expression. 'All right,' he said.

When Alberta came downstairs, Cat Power was on the CD player and Tony was sitting at the table, reading the paper. When he saw Alberta, he closed it a little too quickly.

'Is there something else about Pa?' she asked. 'You might as well show me.'

Tony opened the paper and passed it over. Alberta sat down. There was a big piece by one of the regular columnists. The title was 'MEN WILL BE MEN,' SAYS LADY TRUSSLER. IS SHE RIGHT?

'Oh, for God's sake!' Alberta fumed. 'What on earth possessed Marma to ever say such a stupid thing?'

'It's not easy to think of something clever to say when you're being hounded by reporters.'

'She didn't have to think of anything clever to say. She shouldn't have said anything at all!' Alberta looked indignantly at Tony. It annoyed her that he never failed to find excuses for Marma's wayward behaviour; yet he had not made any real attempt to understand the circumstances that might have led Pa to that house in Streatham.

Tony raised his eyebrows and said nothing, which annoyed her even more.

'I'm going out,' she said. 'I need some fresh air. I'll see you all later. Have a good lunch.' She stormed out of the kitchen without waiting for a response, grabbing her jacket from the coat stand in the hall.

She walked briskly along the pavement, crossed the road and walked on to the National Trust fields. For once, the view of the city with its church spires, its Georgian terraces and the Abbey dominating the centre, failed to please her. She sat down on the bench and took a couple of deep breaths. She could imagine the tone of the article: What makes a man like Lord Trussler seek out prostitutes and indulge in unnatural practices? She knew there would be nothing about his role in taking Britain into Europe, his brilliance at debate or his attempts to wean the Conservative Party from its intermittent habit of self-immolation. The press should be mourning the loss of a true statesman. Instead, it was only interested in going over and over and over a small, secret part of his life, and it was so mean and it was so unfair.

She stood up and walked down to the small church at

the bottom of the field. She thought about all the stories that lay behind the gravestones and she swallowed as she remembered the newly dug grave in the Hampshire graveyard. Tony would say she was wallowing. Stuff Tony!

She walked up to the fields above Prior Park. She wished she was clever enough to write an appropriate response to all the miserable words written about Pa in the last week. If Ed were alive, he'd know what to write. If Ed were alive, he'd be furious. He had adored Pa as much as she had. If Ed were alive, he'd be speaking out against all those who traduced his reputation. If Ed were alive . . .

Alberta stopped and decided to go home. It was time now to stop thinking. She would go home and watch a film. She would go home and watch *The Good, the Bad and the Ugly.*

Tony rang Alberta from London on Tuesday evening and said, 'How's it been today?'

'I'm sorry you had to walk to the station this morning. You should have woken me.'

'That's all right. So, what have you been doing today? Did you watch another film?'

'Yes. I watched *The Man from Laramie*.'

'I can't remember that one.'

'It's where James Stewart tries to find the gunrunner who sold weapons to the Indians who killed his brother's cavalry detachment.'

'I don't think I've ever seen that one.' There was a pause. 'What else did you do?'

'I made Jacob a cooked breakfast. He had an English exam this afternoon.'

'How did it go?'

'He said it was easy.'

'That's good. Do you have any plans for tomorrow?'

'I thought,' Alberta said, 'that I might watch *My Darling Clementine.*'

'Right. Well, I'd better go. I'll ring you tomorrow.'

Alberta put the phone down. It was obvious from Tony's voice that he had stopped himself from saying more. She could imagine what that more would have been: pull yourself together, stop watching stupid films, get a life. He didn't have a clue, she thought, he didn't have a clue.

In fact, Alberta didn't watch *My Darling Clementine* the next day. She did not watch any film at all.

At half past eleven she had a visitor. It was Daniel Driver. He wore white leather shoes, blue denim jeans, a green jersey over a white T-shirt and a charcoal jacket. For a moment, Alberta was aware of her shapeless grey tracksuit trousers, her shrunken black T-shirt and her scuffed trainers. She said, 'I'm afraid Tony's in London.'

'I spoke to him this morning,' Daniel said. 'I came to see *you.*'

'Oh,' Alberta was nonplussed. 'That's very kind of you but I'm not the most brilliant company at the moment.'

Any normal person would have taken the hint. Daniel nodded at the shrub in the big terracotta pot by the front door. 'I like that thing in that pot. What is it?'

'It's an acer,' Alberta said. 'It's a Japanese maple.'

'I'd like one of those,' Daniel said.

'Look,' Alberta began and then sighed. 'Do you want to come in?'

'All right,' Daniel said, as if he was responding to her earnest entreaty.

She took him through to the kitchen and motioned him to a chair. 'Do you want some coffee? I've just made a fresh pot.'

'All right,' Daniel said again. He went across to the window. 'I really like your garden,' he said. 'I've never had one. I have a courtyard at home. Your maple thing would look good in my courtyard.'

'I'm sure it would.'

'Most of the time I'm quite happy with my courtyard. It's only when I see gardens like this, I feel I'm missing out. You're very lucky.'

'Oh yes,' said Alberta, putting two mugs on the table, 'I'm *very* lucky.'

Daniel turned his back on the window and scrutinized Alberta's face. 'I'm sorry,' he said. 'That was a stupid thing to say.'

'Not at all.' Alberta shook her head. 'I'm afraid I'm over-sensitive at the moment. I expect Tony's told you I'm being a complete pain. I suppose I'm finding all the publicity a little relentless.'

Daniel pulled out a chair, sat down and raised his hands behind his head. 'It's no big deal,' he said.

'What's no big deal? The fact that I'm being a pain or the fact that my father is currently scandal of the month?'

'The fact that your father went to a prostitute. It's no big deal.'

'Well, that's reassuring. Thank you for that. I'm sure you're right. Perhaps you sleep with prostitutes on a regular basis. I'm sure I shouldn't mind that my father's private life is being dissected and discussed by thousands of people who've never met him but there you are. I do. I'm funny like that. Do you want milk in your coffee?'

'No, thank you. Did you know that Swedes drink more coffee than any other nationality?'

'No, I didn't know that. Do you have sugar?'

'No, thank you,' Daniel said. 'You do realize that every family has its scandals? You wouldn't believe what my mother's father got up to.'

'No,' Alberta said, sitting down opposite him, 'I probably wouldn't.'

'I never met him but my mother always said I looked very like him. He killed my grandmother.' Daniel took a sip from his mug. 'This is excellent coffee.'

Alberta put down her mug. 'Are you making this up? Because if you are . . .'

'Why would I do that? My grandfather got drunk and smashed his car and my grandmother died. Mind you, so did my grandfather.'

'That's terrible.'

'I know. The car was a write-off. It was custom-made as well.'

Alberta stared at him incredulously. 'Do you ever take anything seriously?'

'Not much.'

Daniel sat there with his legs stretched out in front of him and his mug between his hands. He looked mildly amused by Alberta's indignant response and she felt all the barely suppressed rage of the last couple of weeks rise to the surface of her mind like a dam about to break. 'Do you know something? You haven't changed at all. You are just the same as when you were Disgusting Daniel all those years ago. Surely even you can see what that must have done to your mother?'

'Yes, it made her miserable. And she's gone on being miserable ever since.'

'Well, can you blame her? To lose both her parents like that . . . It must have been horrific for her.'

Daniel shrugged. 'Stuff happens.'

Alberta's eyes narrowed. 'Well, that's a very profound opinion. Stuff happens. What a pity you weren't alive at the time so you could have told her that. I bet that would have made all the difference in the world to her. She might even have been able to have a good laugh about it.'

'I doubt it,' Daniel said. 'She's never had a great sense of humour.'

'Well, how extraordinary! What a surprise! I wonder why *that* is! What a pity we can't all be like you. I suppose I should find the idea of my father dying in a brothel quite funny too.'

'Well,' Daniel said, 'I suppose—'

'Daniel,' Alberta said, rising from the table, 'please don't say anything more. Thank you very much for visiting me. It's been so interesting to compare your sordid family secrets with my sordid family secrets. But now, if you don't mind, I have things to do. I did warn you I wasn't feeling very sociable at the moment. I'll see you out.' She marched past him and made straight for the front door which she opened wide, keeping her eyes fixed on the road until he had crossed the threshold.

'Thanks for the coffee,' Daniel said. 'I'm afraid I didn't finish it.'

'I don't mind at all.'

'And for the record: I've never been with a prostitute.'

'Really?'

'Really. You may find this hard to believe but, unlike your father, I've never had to pay anyone to have sex with me.'

She raised her arm and hit him hard across the face.

He blinked and said quietly, 'Ouch. You certainly know how to say goodbye.'

Alberta retreated to the hall and slammed the door behind her. She knew she had behaved appallingly and it didn't worry her at all. She would have very much liked to scream and if it weren't for the fact that she might alarm Evie and Lionel next door, she almost certainly would have done.

Tony rang again on Wednesday evening.

'Hi, Ber—'

'Tony, do you know who came to offer his condolences today?'

'I have no idea. Should I have any idea? Wait a minute I did speak to Daniel this morning.'

'Did you really? What did you speak *about*?'

'The new Dogs of Hell single. He's almost finished it. He's done a brilliant job. He's going to work with the Growlers in Reading in a few weeks.'

'I don't give a damn about the Growlers, did you talk to Daniel about *me*?'

'He asked how you were and I told him. He said he'd try to make time to visit you.'

'Well, guess what? He *did* make time. In fact, he went out of his way to be offensive and gross and I want you to know that if you plan to invite him round any time soon, you'd better let me know first so I can vacate the premises.'

'You won't have to do that; he's leaving Bath in a few days' time. What on earth did he say?'

'Well, let's see. First, he told me there was nothing wrong in sleeping with prostitutes so I shouldn't worry about *that* and then he told me I shouldn't worry about the scandal either because – guess what? – his family had an even bigger and better scandal than my one and then he told me what I am almost certain is a made-up story about his grandparents dying in a car and—'

'That *is* true. My friend, Marty, is a great buddy of Daniel and he told me the story ages ago. Daniel's grandparents were driving somewhere and the grandfather was drunk and drove into a tanker – at least, I think it was a tanker – and the car went up in flames. It was all very nasty. Marty said the car had been a custom-made Jaguar.'

'You're as bad as Daniel! What does it matter what sort of car it was?'

'It's interesting, that's all. It *was* custom-made.'

'What *does* matter is Daniel's attitude. He was entirely flippant about the whole thing. That's one reason why I couldn't believe it was true. And then he was rude and insensitive and making fun of me and I'm afraid I couldn't take any more and so I slapped him.'

'You slapped Daniel Driver?'

'Yes, I did.'

'You *slapped* him?'

'Stop saying that! I don't care. He was completely out of order. He was quite brazenly rubbing my nose in the whole beastly business. He said he had never slept with prostitutes because *he* had women positively begging to sleep with him.'

'That doesn't sound like Daniel.'

'Excuse me, it sounds exactly like Daniel. I knew him at nursery school, remember? He thinks he's so all-round Mr Wonderful . . .'

'Why would he tell you he'd never slept with prostitutes? Why would he think you'd think he *would* sleep with prostitutes?'

'Probably because I *had* – under considerable provocation – suggested he *had* slept with prostitutes.'

'I see. Did *he* slap you when you said that?'

'Look, Tony, you weren't there, you have no idea what he was like. He was *trying* to upset me! I don't want to even talk about him any more. I'm very glad to hear he's leaving Bath. Can we change the subject now?'

'All right. Did you watch a film today?'

'No, I did not watch a film. I was far too angry to watch a film. I rang Diana and told her I'd come back to work and of course she immediately gave me a thousand things to do so I was busy all afternoon and now I'm going round to have a drink with your parents so I have to go.'

'All right,' Tony said. 'I still can't believe you hit Daniel.'

Really, Alberta thought, it would be much better if Tony didn't ring her at all.

# CHAPTER TEN

## *A Distant Trumpet*

There were times when Alberta thought Tony was right about Diana. When Alberta rang her to say she was ready to start work again, she did not expect Diana to immediately offload a sweet pepper and salami salad for thirty on to her. And half an hour after Tony's phone call in the evening, Diana rang again. It was clear she had let all the TCC regulars know that the catering side of the operation was back in business. Consequently, Alberta was asked to spend the next day making two apple pies, one lasagne, one gingerbread birthday cake and twenty-five fairy cakes with pink icing.

In actual fact, though it pained her to admit it, Tony had been right to suggest she should get straight back to work. She had spent a frantic afternoon careering round the supermarket, making the stupid salad and then delivering it to the stupid client; the reward had been the best night's sleep for over a week.

The next morning, she made her shopping list over breakfast and went out to the car, trying to quell the nagging feeling of guilt that had been growing in her mind ever since her conversation with Tony. As she drove off towards the supermarket for the second time in two days, she turned on the radio and concentrated on the *Today* programme. The two presenters were sharing a jocular little comment about reality television, but it was clear that neither of them knew what they were talking about since they referred to *Big Brother* in the same way they'd mention some obscure medical condition. Then one of them started to interview the Education Secretary about the surprising results of a new poll that had shown that large numbers of parents were dissatisfied with their children's education.

There was no doubt about it: Tony's phone call had riled her. She could swear he had been rather amused by the account of Daniel's visit, and if she was right, then that was irritating enough. But she also had the distinct impression that not only had he been shocked by her use of physical violence, he had also felt it was unwarranted.

*Had* it been unwarranted? No, it had not. The man had more or less thrown in her face the fact that Pa had used prostitutes. Alberta stopped at the traffic lights and gnawed her bottom lip. It was true she had suggested that *Daniel* used prostitutes, and that was a pretty wild accusation, but it was also true that Daniel had made it pretty obvious that he thought buying the services of prostitutes was no worse than buying eggs that weren't free-range. Although, actually, Alberta felt very strongly that it was quite wrong to buy eggs that weren't free-range. She jumped as the car behind her hooted and she realized the lights had changed.

She drove on quickly, cursing under her breath. She was furious with Daniel for making her feel like this. She wasn't the sort of person to behave badly and she hated being put in a position where she was worried that she *had* behaved badly. Until she'd spoken to Tony, she'd been fuelled by a self-righteous fury: she had hit out in defence of Pa. In hitting Daniel she had hit out at all those smug people who dared to condemn him.

The trouble was that Daniel hadn't condemned him. Daniel had said the whole scandal was no big deal. But he had also said that *he* had never been to a prostitute. There was, of course, the unlikely possibility that he had been offended by her supposition that he *had* used them. This was ridiculous. She wasn't going to see the man again so none of this mattered.

She raised the volume on the radio and discovered that the debate on education had somehow changed into Gary What's-his-name talking about football. She turned into the supermarket car park and vowed not to think about Daniel ever again. She hoped and trusted that in the present sad circumstances, Tony would have the sensitivity to refrain from making any further comments about him.

It transpired that Tony possessed no sensitivity at all. When she picked him up from the station that evening, he gave her a lopsided grin as he got into the car. 'Have you hit anyone else today?'

'Very funny.' Alberta started up the car and drove out of the station. For fully five seconds she maintained a dignified silence and then, hating herself, asked, 'Have you talked to Daniel today?'

'Yes, I rang him this morning.' He sighed. 'Don't look like that, I didn't ring about *you*. I wanted to talk to him about the Reading job.'

'Did he say anything about me?'

'He said he went to visit you to try to cheer you up.'

'Well?' Alberta glanced at him impatiently. 'What did you say?'

'I think I said, "Did you?"'

'Oh very good, Tony, great response. What did he say?'

'He said he thought he'd made a very strong impression. He said you'd made a strong impression on him.' Tony chuckled. 'I bet you did. I bet the poor man could hardly move his face afterwards.'

'Are you *trying* to make me feel worse? Then what did you say?'

'I started talking about the Reading job. Believe it or not, we didn't talk about you after that.'

Alberta retreated into another dignified silence which she hoped and expected would provoke Tony into a contrite apology. It didn't. Tony yawned and stretched his legs out in front of him. Goaded, Alberta said, 'I know you think I'm being incredibly self-absorbed at the moment . . .'

'Well, of course you are,' Tony said. 'I wouldn't expect you to be anything else. I know how much you adored your father.'

'You never liked him,' Alberta said.

'It's difficult to like someone who makes it clear that my predecessor was the most perfect son-in-law in the world. But it doesn't actually matter what I thought of him. I know how much he meant to *you*. It's not surprising that you want to lash out now and again.'

Alberta turned into Cleveland Walk. 'Are you saying I lashed out at Daniel?'

'Why don't we stop talking about Daniel?' Tony suggested, which was possibly the most irritating comment he could make *ever*, since he was the one who'd started talking about him in the first place.

She parked the car and watched silently as he reached for his bag in the back seat, got out of the car and walked into the house. She turned off the ignition and glanced resentfully in Tony's direction. She supposed she should be grateful that he had at least left the front door open for her. So he thought she was being self-absorbed. Fine. She would be careful not to talk about Pa or her feelings or Daniel or anything else that was worrying her. It was apparent that Diana was not the only one who thought that one fortnight was quite enough time to spend mourning the loss of one's father in scandalous circumstances.

She presumed Tony had gone straight upstairs to change. She went through to the kitchen where Jacob was raiding the cheese box. 'Jacob!' Alberta protested. 'I told you we'd be eating as soon as I collected Tony. I only have to mash the potatoes and cook the beans.'

'Sorry,' Jacob said. 'Revision makes me *so* hungry.' He looked enquiringly at her. 'There's a bottle of wine in the fridge. Shall I open it? You look tired.'

'That's a good idea,' said Alberta, instantly mollified. 'Get yourself a glass too.' She took her apron from the back of the kitchen door. 'You don't have any exams tomorrow, do you?'

'No, my last one is on Monday.' Jacob rummaged around in the kitchen drawer and pulled out the bottle opener. 'It's just as well. I am finding it extremely difficult to maintain the necessary level of interest in these exams.' He took out three glasses from the cupboard, opened the bottle and filled two of the glasses. 'Cheers, Mum.' He raised his glass. 'Here's to you!'

Alberta, about to plunge the masher into the potatoes, paused. 'Thank you, Jacob. What have I done to deserve that?'

'I think you're very impressive. Grandfather dies, which is terrible, and on top of that you have to put up with all the horrible press stuff. A lot of people would have hysterics or have a breakdown. You just watch a few Westerns, think about things a bit and get on quietly and calmly with your life.'

'Well,' said Alberta a little uncomfortably, 'I don't know about that.'

'It's true.' Jacob raised his glass again as his father came into the kitchen. 'Dad, I'm drinking to Mum!'

'I'll drink to Bertie,' Tony said. 'I'll drink to anyone.' He had swapped his blue shirt for one of his oldest T-shirts. 'Pour me a glass, Jacob. Why on this particular occasion are we toasting your mother? What is it you want this time?'

'Dad,' Jacob said, 'you are such a cynic. Can you not accept that there are times when I simply want to say something nice?'

'You and simplicity do not go together. Simplicity is to you what krypton is to Superman.'

'That is such a bad analogy. Krypton had the capacity to destroy Superman. Simplicity can't destroy me, it simply bores me.'

'Well, there you are, my son. You have just admitted that you find simplicity boring. Ergo, you do not practise it yourself.'

Alberta, checking the chicken pie, felt the invisible ropes around her heart begin to slacken. This was the first proper family meal they had enjoyed since Pa's death. She had missed the amiable sparring that was as much a characteristic of Tony's relationship with his son as it was of his relationship with his father. Chucking the beans into boiling water, she cast a quick glance at Jacob. He was so different from Tony; looking at them both, one would never believe they were related. Jacob looked like one of those flowers that grow too quickly. His body was long and thin and never seemed to fit his clothes. Today, he wore his threadbare maroon jersey with his black cotton trousers. As always, his hair looked like it needed a good haircut and his spectacles kept slipping down his nose. Beside him, his father was effortlessly good-looking in his trainers, his denim trousers and his T-shirt proclaiming the 1989 tour of some now extinct pop group. Hannah's university friends had thought Tony was incredibly cool with his soft-spoken, laconic way of speaking and his slim, slight build. Alberta watched him laugh at something Jacob said and realized she hadn't seen Tony look so relaxed in weeks.

Taking the pie out of the oven, she announced that supper was ready and that the table needed to be laid. As her menfolk moved to the dining room, armed with wine and cutlery, she drained the beans. Pa was dead. Pa was dead and she would carry on without him. Pa was dead and she would be quiet and calm.

She joined Tony and Jacob in the dining room. Father and son were having a typically spirited argument about Maud's fifteen-year-old brother. Carton had for the last three months been carrying out a kindness campaign, inspired by a talk given by the Archbishop of Canterbury. Carton, much to the consternation of his parents, had found God. Tony was expressing some doubt about Carton's new campaign on the grounds that Carton was irritating enough *before* he decided he wanted to spread a little love throughout the world.

'I think you're very unfair,' Jacob said. 'He's simply following Plato. Do you know what Plato said?'

'You know very well,' said Tony, 'that I know as much about Plato as you do about the music industry.'

'Well, Plato said the purpose of life was love and that's what Carton believes. Have you heard of the Kindness Crew?'

Tony grimaced. 'I'm glad to say I haven't.'

'They're four Americans who set up this group in 2001 in response to 9/11. They've carried out over fifty-six thousand acts of random kindness since then. Carton says he wants to beat their record.'

Tony shook his head. 'Only in America,' he said, 'could you have people doggedly noting down every time they do something nice. Can you imagine it? Every time Carton smiles at someone or picks up a piece of litter or helps someone across the road, he has to whip out his exercise book and record what he's done. It must be so tempting to bump up the numbers by smiling at one person after another and noting it each time he does so . . .'

'That would destroy the whole point of the exercise,' Jacob said. 'Maud's been doing it as well. He'll miss her when she goes.'

'Where is Maud going?'

'She's going to France.' Jacob smiled at both his parents. 'I am too.'

Alberta, who had been quietly eating her chicken pie and wondering if she had put in enough mushrooms, looked up in astonishment. 'How long for?'

'We'll be back for Christmas.'

There was a stunned silence broken finally by Tony who put down his glass and said without expression, 'It's nice of you to keep us up to date with your plans.'

Alberta, mindful that her son had only recently praised her for her calmness, struggled to keep her voice level. 'So when are you leaving?'

Jacob pushed his spectacles up his nose. 'We're going on Wednesday.'

'Right,' said Tony. 'So let me get this straight. In a few days' time, you are going away for six months. Did you plan all of this a long time ago?'

'Maud's aunt has a hotel in Avignon. She rang about a month ago and asked if we'd like to work there during the summer season. I was going to tell you before but then Grandfather died. We're going to work there till October and then travel round Europe for a bit. I'll try to email you when I can.'

'Thank you,' said Tony. 'That's most kind.'

'But what about school?' Alberta asked. 'Don't you have to be there for the end of term?'

'No. I finish my exams on Monday. There's no reason to go back. Can we have Lionel and Evie over on Saturday evening and have a proper going-away supper?' He smiled at his mother. 'Don't look so worried, Mum. This is a new era! You and Dad can have lots of romantic evenings together.'

'There you are, Bertie,' Tony said, at his most bland. 'Aren't we lucky?'

On Friday mornings, Alberta always rose early to make carrot cakes for local delicatessens which she then delivered in readiness for the lunch-time trade. St James's Square, her last port of call, was a part of Bath that Alberta was particularly fond of. The leafy square itself was quietly elegant and it had a cluster of interesting little shops nearby. Today, with the trees in blossom and a gentle breeze in the air, it looked even more enticing than usual.

Alberta parked the car and took out her last remaining carrot cake. As she crossed the road, she was aware that she was being watched. Standing in front of the delicatessen, with what she couldn't help thinking was a somewhat exaggeratedly wary expression on his face, was Daniel Driver.

Alberta felt the blood rush to her head. She gripped her cake tightly and made herself walk over to him. 'Daniel,' she said. 'I'm very glad to see you.'

'Are you sure about that?' he asked. 'You don't want to hit me again, do you?'

'No, of course not.' She pushed back her shoulders and looked up into his face. 'I want to apologize to you . . .'

'In that case,' Daniel said, 'you'd better come and have a coffee with me.'

He walked into the deli without waiting for her response, leaving her to follow along behind. It was, she felt, absolutely typical that he should just assume she *would* go with him. The trouble was that since she had hailed him in order to say sorry, she couldn't very well be so ungracious as to refuse his suggestion but it also meant that what she had hoped would be a quick, brief moment of embarrassment would now be anything but.

She delivered her cake to Annie behind the counter. Annie turned out to know Daniel since he was staying with his friends up the road and had become a regular customer. Annie's eyes sparkled with interest as Daniel asked for two coffees for himself and Alberta. Alberta gave what she hoped was an unconcerned smile and went over to a table by the window. She sat down and tried to compose herself, first crossing her legs one way and then the other, folding her arms and wondering if that looked too confrontational. She quickly unfolded them and placed them on her lap instead. She could see Daniel chatting easily to Annie. Annie was laughing and telling him he was a smooth-talking bastard. Daniel looked completely at ease. Alberta crossed her legs again.

He brought the coffee over, sat down and looked expectantly at her. 'So,' he said, 'you want to apologize.'

This had been a terrible idea. She took a sip of coffee to give herself time to think and to look as if she was quite calm and unperturbed. That was an even worse idea. The coffee was boiling hot and scalded her tongue, bringing tears to her eyes and making her move her mug too quickly, thus spilling some of the liquid onto the table. So much for looking calm and unperturbed.

Daniel asked her if she was all right and produced a tissue. Alberta muttered her thanks through gritted teeth while mopping up the mess she had made and wishing she was anywhere else in the world. Finally she looked at Daniel and saw that he was still waiting for her to say sorry. Her tongue was hurting and it was his fault because he had bought her the stupid coffee and he was expecting her to say sorry and she wished she had never met him.

'I want to apologize,' she said carefully, 'for being so . . . so . . .'

'Violent?' Daniel suggested.

Alberta stared at him with dislike. 'Well, I wouldn't say "violent" exactly. I was certainly far too . . . unrestrained in my behaviour and I assure you that such behaviour is quite uncharacteristic.'

'Really? Have you never slapped anyone before me?'

'No, of course I haven't,' Alberta snapped and then, remembering that she was supposed to be contrite, said quickly, 'I have never slapped anyone. I don't slap people. I feel very bad that I did slap you.'

'It really hurt,' said Daniel sadly.

Alberta squirmed in her seat. 'I'm sure it did. As I said, I am sorry.' It was very hot in here. She took off her jacket and put it on the chair next to her.

Daniel sighed. 'My face *had* stopped hurting by last night. More or less.'

Alberta's eyes narrowed. He was enjoying this. She straightened her back and looked directly at him. 'I have to say,' she said coldly, 'that you were being very annoying.'

'In that case,' Daniel smiled, 'I shall be very careful to never say anything to you in the future that you might regard as even slightly annoying.'

'I don't think you'll have to worry about that,' Alberta said. 'Tony tells me you're going back to London soon so you won't have to put up with my appalling temper any more.'

'I'm going back today,' Daniel said, 'and I'm glad to see

you before I go. It gives *me* an opportunity to apologize to you. I don't know why I find myself behaving so badly when I'm with you but I do. I was tactless and unpleasant last time we met and I can quite understand why you felt the need to hit me. May I say that I am very sorry about your father?'

'Thank you.' She was unprepared for his sympathy and took another sip of her coffee to prevent herself from crying. It was definitely time to change the subject. 'So you're going back to London today?'

'Yes. And then I'm off to Iceland next week.'

'Really? Is that business or pleasure?'

'Both. I always jump at the chance of producing stuff out there. Iceland is probably the most wonderful country in the world.'

'I don't know anything about it,' Alberta confessed. 'Why is it so wonderful?'

Daniel laughed. 'I could give you so many reasons. It has only three hundred thousand people and yet it has the most exciting music industry in Europe. It's the only member nation of Europe not to have any armed forces. It hasn't had any since the fourteenth century. It's also one of the safest places you can visit. Do you know what its annual murder rate is? Guess.'

'I have no idea. A thousand? Five thousand?'

'Five! Just five! And the entire prison population is about one hundred. What else can I tell you? It has a superb health service: it's so good that chemist shops are virtually unknown. And the capital – Reykjavik – is amazing. The restaurants are great. You haven't lived if you haven't tasted reindeer carpaccio. And at this time of year, you can have a meal and walk out onto the pavement at midnight and the sun is still in the sky.' He stopped to have a sip of his coffee. 'Am I boring you?'

'Not at all. I didn't know any of this.'

'Not many people do. And yet it is unbelievably beautiful: mountains, glaciers, green hills, you name it, Iceland has got it.'

'You make me rather envious,' Alberta said. She laughed. 'I wish I could go with you!'

'I wish you could too.' For a moment, Daniel's eyes held hers and then she looked away.

She hoped she hadn't blushed but her face was burning. It was possible he was flirting with her but, more likely, he was just being polite in which case it was all the more excruciating that she was so obviously thrown by his comment. She gave a slightly forced laugh. 'Well, unfortunately I can't as I have quiches to make and my house to clean.' She made a point of glancing at her watch. 'I must get on, I had no idea it was so late.' She stood up and said quickly, 'Please don't get up. Thank you for the coffee.'

He stood up anyway. 'It's my pleasure. I've enjoyed meeting my old nursery school companion . . . after all these years.'

'That would be more impressive,' she said lightly, 'if it weren't for the fact that you have no recollection of me at all! Whereas I remember Disgusting Daniel only too well!'

He gave a slight nod of his head. 'I shan't forget you this time.'

'I'm sure you won't! Once again, I apologize for my bad behaviour.' She picked up her bag and her jacket. 'Goodbye, Daniel.'

She walked out of the deli and couldn't resist glancing back. Embarrassed to see that he was still looking at her, she gave a quick wave and walked away.

Her car was in Northumberland Avenue and as she unlocked it and got in, she realized she was happy. She was glad she'd apologized to Daniel and she was pleased that their brief acquaintance had ended on a harmonious note. His enthusiastic description of Iceland had acted like a distant trumpet call amid the gloom, reminding her that there was more to life than death and depression and horrible press cuttings. And there was also the fact that, while it probably meant nothing, he had looked at her in a way that made her feel special and interesting instead of hysterical and crazy. She put on a Roxy Music tape and sang along to 'Let's Get Together' all the way down Lansdown Hill.

# CHAPTER ELEVEN

## *Goin' South*

On Saturday evening, Lionel and Evie came bearing gifts for the intrepid traveller. Evie gave Jacob a moleskin-covered notebook, a jar of Marmite and a wallet containing one hundred euros. Lionel brought a bag containing compass, peppermint lozenges and a book of Maupassant's short stories. 'Keep it with you at all times,' he said. 'It has all you need if you get lost in a French forest.'

'I don't think there are any French forests in Avignon,' Tony said.

'Nonsense,' Lionel retorted, 'of course there are French forests in France. You don't get French forests anywhere else.'

'Sometimes,' Tony told his father, 'your logic is very exhausting.'

'That's because I'm a philosopher,' Lionel said. 'Which reminds me, I'm giving my talk on Hume's principle of causality in two weeks. We will miss you there, Jacob.'

Lionel was an enthusiastic member of Bath's philosophy society. It held open meetings every month and encouraged members to take their turn in producing papers for discussion. Twice a year, Lionel would spend weeks preparing a speech comprising thousands of words that would then be ruthlessly culled by Evie. The whole family attended these occasions. Jacob would invariably delight his grandfather by asking a follow-up question that to Alberta was just as impenetrable as the lecture that preceded it.

Over dinner, Jacob, inspired perhaps by the hundred euros, was unusually expansive, regaling his family with information about Maud's aunt. She was evidently a woman of strong character. Her French husband had recently confessed to a long-dead affair and its living consequence: a twenty-year-old daughter called Marianne. Maud's aunt had not only forgiven her husband but had invited the girl to work in their hotel, an act of great generosity that had led Gaston to fall at his wife's feet and cover them with kisses. What Gaston didn't know, Jacob said, was that Maud's aunt had once had an affair with his brother and was only too happy to find that her husband had revealed a frailty to match her own.

'Did she tell her husband she had had an affair?' Alberta asked.

'What would be the point?' Jacob said. 'Her husband thinks she is wonderful and he continues to be very fond of his brother. Why would she want to spoil all that?'

Tony raised an eyebrow. 'Is *she* still fond of her husband's brother?'

'Dad!' Jacob grimaced. 'She's really old now. She's got to be fifty at least.'

'Right,' said Tony. 'No one has affairs over fifty.'

'I do think these hidden histories are fascinating,' Evie

said. 'I've just finished reading a book about Stalinist Russia. It's quite heartbreaking. It details the appalling purges Stalin carried out against the kulaks.'

'Who were the kulaks?' Tony asked.

'I suppose one could best describe them as a rural middle class. They were wealthy peasant farmers and Stalin set out to destroy them. Thousands were killed. There's a girl in the book called Antonina Golovina. Her father was branded a kulak in the 1930s and at eighteen she forged new papers and went to medical school. She told no one the truth, not even the man she married. And then, many years after Stalin's death, when *glasnost* came and people started talking about the past, she discovered that for more than two decades she'd been married to a man who, like her, had spent his youth in labour camps in Siberia. Like her, he'd never dared mention his past. Isn't it extraordinary that a couple could live together for so long and know so little about each other? Can you imagine finding out after more than twenty years that you and your partner had such similar experiences?'

'I can't imagine that at all,' Lionel said. 'I would find it impossible to keep secrets. One of the many joys of having a family was to be able to come home from work and discuss everything that was on my mind.'

'I know,' Tony said. 'I am scarred for life by your zeal for telling your family everything on your mind. I remember bringing my first girlfriend back after school and you walked in and said you'd been worrying all day about the fact you'd never talked to me about sexual diseases. She couldn't leave the house fast enough.'

'I remember that girl,' Lionel said. 'She wasn't right for

you. Her eyes were too close together and she had a silly name.'

'Dad, she was called *Fiona*.'

'Exactly. Never trust anyone called Fiona.'

'I'm not sure you're right there,' Evie mused. 'A very interesting study was presented to the Royal College of Psychiatrists in 2000. Apparently, the name Fiona had the most positive associations for psychiatrists. They were far less likely to consider a patient to be a malingerer or a drug addict if she was called Fiona.'

'I used to have a friend called Fiona,' Alberta said. 'I was very fond of her. She became an estate agent.'

'There you are,' Lionel said, 'I rest my case.'

It was a good evening and made Alberta all the more aware of the childless state in which they would soon be living. As she finished cleaning her face that night, she glanced wistfully at Tony. 'It's going to be so odd without Jacob. I still can't believe he's going on Wednesday. Why don't you come home on Thursday evening? We could cheer ourselves up by going out. We could try the new fish restaurant.'

'That's a nice idea,' Tony said slowly. He got into bed and rubbed his neck. 'But I can't come back till Friday.'

Alberta climbed in beside him and reached for her book. 'We could go out on Friday.'

Tony took off his watch and studied it carefully before putting it next to his radio alarm clock. 'I might be a little late for that. I'm going to Lydia's wedding in the afternoon.'

'Lydia's wedding?' Alberta repeated sharply. 'I didn't even realize a date had been set. Have I not been invited?'

'Yes, of course you were. The thing is I had no intention of going but Lydia's worried about Dylan. She's asked me to keep an eye on him. You know he gets a bit overexcited at times.'

This was true. Dylan's voice after a couple of drinks accelerated rapidly in both volubility and volume. The memory of the speech he had made at his twenty-first birthday party still had the power to make Alberta cringe. It had been very long and very frank and he had finished by thanking everyone for his presents but confessing that better than any of them would be the forthcoming birthday shag from his girlfriend. He had then raised his glass and voiced the hope that all present would soon be having as good a time in the sack as he would be. Alberta's eyes had shied away from the appalled expressions of sundry elderly relations and settled on the white-faced girlfriend, who looked almost catatonic and certainly didn't look like a girl who was looking forward to a good shag.

'As a matter of interest,' Alberta said, 'when exactly did you get the invitation to the wedding?'

'I can't remember.' Tony's voice was suspiciously offhand. 'At the time, it didn't seem important since I didn't think I'd be going. I can't say I'm looking forward to it.'

'Were you ever going to tell me about it?'

'Yes.' Tony glanced at her and repeated defensively, 'Yes, of course I was. It just got buried under everything else that's happened in the last few weeks.'

'And I take it – since you kept it quiet – that you'd rather I didn't come with you?'

'I didn't see why we should both have to give up a day's work. I know it's not your sort of thing.'

'I wouldn't mind. I'm sure I could shift engagements if you'd like me to go with you.'

'No, you'd hate it. There'll be loads of Lydia's barrister friends impressing themselves with their brilliant conversation. It will be terrible. At least there's one positive outcome.'

'What's that?'

'Dylan's coming back with me for the weekend. So we won't be on our own after all.'

'Right,' Alberta said, switching off her light and lying down with her back to Tony. 'That *is* good news.'

Driving back from Bristol Airport on Wednesday, Alberta surprised herself by bursting into tears. This might have been understandable if she'd been thinking about the Jacobless house that awaited her. But she did not think she was unduly upset by that prospect. Jacob had spent vast swathes of time at Maud's house in the last two years and it was not as if he was the sort of son who enjoyed a close and touching relationship with his mother. *Neither* of her children enjoyed a close and touching relationship with their mother but now was not the time, Alberta thought fiercely, dashing a hand across her eyes, to try to work out the reasons for that particular state of affairs.

It had been fun driving Jacob and Maud to the airport. Maud, a girl whose demeanour was almost always grave, had laughed three times while Jacob had tried to converse with them in execrable French. When the time came to say goodbye to them, Jacob had actually hugged her. Admittedly, if there had been a record for the quickest hug in the history of the world, Jacob's hug would have topped it, but nevertheless it was a hug. And it had been good to watch them both stride off towards their new adventure with such enthusiasm.

So, no, she didn't cry for Jacob. She cried for her father. One minute she was driving along, past the Chew Magna reservoir, admiring the sun skipping on the water, the next she was crying for her father. She couldn't understand why. She had accepted that the patina of gloom that had settled on her life would be with her for some time to come but she had assumed that at least the initial shattering grief would have been subdued by now. And yet, here she was, three weeks on, crying like a baby.

It didn't help that the press continued to be fascinated by the scandal. In yesterday's paper, for example, there had been an article in the health section about premature ejaculation; the journalist, with a bizarre synaptic leap, had suggested that Lord Trussler's much reported predilection for sado-masochistic sex could possibly be a consequence of this condition. Alberta had had no idea that so many reporters were amateur doctors and psychiatrists. So far, her father's private preferences had been attributed to childhood abuse, parental coldness, hatred of women, hatred of himself, hatred of everyone, a desire to retreat into childhood and a straightforward enjoyment of slapping female bottoms, an enjoyment which the writer of this theory, judging by his lingering description of the beauty of said bottoms, clearly shared.

Alberta had no idea which, if any, of these theories was correct. All she knew was that as day followed day, the father she knew and loved seemed to slip further and further away. In place of the father who was so eloquent, so authoritative, so wise, there was now the man who liked spanking. Or being spanked. Or both. And then in that horrid kiss-and-tell piece that she wished she had never read, there was the suggestion that he liked dressing up in *nappies*! That Lord Trussler should henceforth be associated in the public mind with dodgy women and funny nappies was bad enough. What frightened Alberta was that henceforth her own memories would be similarly tainted.

On Thursday evening, she watched *Rio Bravo* on TCM. She had seen it before, of course, but enjoyed it nonetheless. There was big John Wayne, most rugged of sheriffs, trying to maintain law and order with only the help of funny old Walter Brennan, drunken Dean Martin (whose character was obviously an alcoholic because his hands were too shaky to roll his cigarettes), good-time girl Angie Dickinson and young Ricky Nelson, who had to be using a ton of hairspray to keep his quiff so vertical during even the toughest gunfights. At first, Big John thought he could manage on his own but he found out he needed their help and they needed his and in the end everyone was happy. Funny old Walter Brennan got to kill lots of baddies. Drunken Dean Martin got to beat up the horrid baddy who smirked all the time, and was so pleased he stopped being an alcoholic and was able to roll his own cigarettes again. And best of all, Big John Wayne realized he loved Angie Dickinson, who might be a good-time girl but she had proved she was brave and loyal and true, and one knew they would live happily ever after even if the kisses they exchanged were surprisingly chaste and rudimentary, more like pecks really, which was a bit disappointing given that she was a good-time girl and he was a rugged sheriff.

Perhaps, Alberta thought as she showered the following morning, she should try to be a bit more like Angie Dickinson and show Tony she was brave and loyal and true. On the other hand it was difficult to be brave and loyal and true to a man who was still in love with his ex-wife. He didn't want her to go to Lydia's wedding because he didn't want her to see how much he still cared about Lydia. Did he really think she didn't know how much Lydia meant to him? It was true that for a long time she had assumed he *was* over Lydia but she knew better now. When she thought about it, he had been unlike himself ever since that phone call from Lydia on the night of the Erica fiasco. She felt unutterably depressed and her depression wasn't helped by the fact that she had to cope with Dylan in the evening.

In the event, she was given a temporary reprieve. She had a call from Dylan at seven. His booming greeting suggested that, like Dean Martin, he was in no state to roll any cigarettes. 'Hiya, Bertie! How *are* you?'

'I'm very well. Are you on the train?'

'No, we're outside Dad's flat. Dad asked me to ring and tell you we won't be coming down till tomorrow. We've only just left the wedding party. Dad's paying off the taxi.'

'Have you had a good time?'

'Yeah, there was lots of champagne. There wasn't enough food. Dad and I are going to find somewhere to eat. There were loads of speeches. I wanted to make one but Dad said we had to go. The newly-weds couldn't stop groping each other. It was pretty gross. You'd have liked the wedding cake. It was a great big mountain of profiteroles covered in chocolate sauce. I dropped my plate.'

'Oh dear.'

'No worries, I got another one. Dad drank too much. Hey, Bertie, I'm sorry about your father. I've told all my mates about it. We think it's really cool.'

'You've lost me there,' Alberta said. 'What is it that's cool?'

'Well, having a shag in a brothel must be the very best way to go. I'd like to go like that. I'd like to have a couple of prostitutes, one on—'

'Dylan, is Tony still paying off the taxi driver?'

'No, they're talking about music. It turns out the taxi driver likes one of Dad's bands so now he's his new best friend.'

'That's nice. Well, Dylan—'

'I'd better go or Dad will stay talking to him all night. See you tomorrow. I'm sorry we can't come tonight.'

'That is *quite* all right. Goodbye, Dylan,' Alberta said, pressing the Off button with a flourish. She put the phone down and breathed in deeply and then exhaled slowly. It was easy for Angie Dickinson to be brave and loyal and true to John Wayne. John Wayne didn't have a vulgar, stupid, rude, unpleasant, obnoxious twat of a son. And if Dylan *dared* to mention her father again this weekend she would go down to the end of the garden and scream.

She went to the fridge and took out a bottle of Sauvignon. She opened it and poured herself a large glass of wine. She deserved it. It was Friday night and she had not lost her temper with Dylan. She took a cool, refreshing gulp. At least she hadn't started cooking the vegetables. She took the casserole out of the oven. They could eat it tomorrow. She ought to ring Marma. She hadn't spoken to her for days. But in order to ring Marma, she needed to be in a good mood and at the present moment she wasn't in a good mood at all.

It was the wedding. Perhaps it was silly to be offended by such an unimportant oversight. The truth was, Alberta wasn't sure it *was* unimportant. She didn't care about the fact that Lydia would notice she wasn't at the wedding. Well, all right, she *did* care but she cared far more about the fact that Tony had kept the invitation from her for as long as he had.

Alberta knew she had been difficult and self-absorbed in the last few weeks. But given the circumstances, wasn't she allowed to be a little difficult and self-absorbed? If Tony had told her he had wanted her company at the wedding, she would have been happy to go. He hadn't wanted her company and he hadn't wanted to talk about it.

The phone started ringing again and Alberta glowered at it. It was probably Dylan, ringing to share with her yet another perceptive thought about her father's death. It might, of course, be Tony and she would very much like to share with him her views about his son. She picked up the receiver.

'Hi, Mum.' Hannah sounded tired.

'Darling, how lovely to hear you.' Alberta pulled out a kitchen chair and sat down. 'I've just had a very annoying phone call from Dylan.'

'When is Dylan *not* annoying?'

'He surpassed himself this time. He and Tony have been to Lydia's wedding. Dylan thought I'd like to know that he's told all his chums about Pa's death and they think it's cool and Dylan says he'd like to die in just the same way.'

'He is such a moron.'

'I can't talk about him any more. Just thinking about him makes my blood curdle. Tell me something new. How is Alfie? Has he finished filming the Queen Isabella drama? Is it going to be successful? Has he done the sex scene with his princess yet?'

For a couple of moments there was silence and then, 'He certainly has!' followed by what sounded like a sob.

'Darling?' Alberta gripped the phone and stood up. 'Hannah? Hannah darling? What's happened?'

A full-blown torrent of weeping ensued, while Alberta, horrified, walked round the kitchen and then through to the hall and into the sitting room. 'Hannah, what *is* it?'

Hannah gave a huge sniff. 'He had the sex scene,' she gulped. 'He had the sex scene. He had the sex scene in my bed!'

For a moment, Alberta tried to work out why a film crew would want to film a scene in Hannah's bedroom. 'Do you mean,' she began, 'he has . . . I don't understand.'

'I came back from Grandfather's funeral and I saw him and Princess Blanche on my bed. They were having sex! I saw them having sex! And as soon as they saw me, Alfie tried to pretend they were rehearsing their latest scene.'

'Well, perhaps they were,' Alberta said. 'Perhaps Alfie was doing a bit of method acting . . .'

'Right,' Hannah said, 'in that case it was remarkably thorough method acting. They had no clothes on, she was on her hands and knees and Alfie was attacking her backside like he'd been without sex for a year!'

'Oh, Hannah, how horrible for you!' She was amazed

that Alfie had been able to come up with an explanation so quickly. It was pretty impressive in a really hideous sort of way. 'Oh, darling, I'm so sorry. Why didn't you tell me before?'

'I haven't felt like telling *anyone*. I only told Kitty at first and I only told her because she came back to find that her brother was no longer living with us.'

'It must be so awkward for her.'

'She's furious with Alfie. She's been great, actually.'

'Is she there this evening?'

'No. She's gone out. I'm on my own.'

'Why don't you come down here tomorrow? We've only got . . .' Alberta hesitated. 'We will have Dylan.'

'I'm sorry but Dylan is the second to last person in the world I can take at the moment. Anyway, I've got lots of work to do this weekend. I'll be all right.'

'You don't sound all right.'

'Oh well. It's not very nice to find that someone you really cared about doesn't care about you.'

'I know. It happens to us all and it's always devastating. I still remember that time in Mallorca . . .'

'Please, please, *please* don't tell me about Red-Haired Boy in Spain who chatted you up for twenty minutes and broke your heart by not turning up the next day. If that's the only incident you can dredge up to show that you understand how I feel, then all I can say is you have no idea what I am going through.'

'You're right. I'm sorry,' Alberta said humbly. 'I only brought it up to show how easy it is to get people wrong. It happens to us all at some point and of course it's terribly disappointing.'

'It's always happening to me and disappointing doesn't begin to describe what it's like! It's a little more than disappointing to find that the man I thought I would love for always has turned out to be a complete bastard. It is a very *lonely* consequence.'

'Oh, darling, I know about loneliness—'

'No, Mum, you do not! You haven't lived on your own *ever*! You are a *bouncer*!'

'I'm a what?'

'It's what Kitty and I call women like you. Women like you can't live on their own. Women like you bounce from one man to another. So when Mr Red Head hero fails, you go home and fall in love with Daddy and when Daddy dies you move in with Tony and if Tony died you'd probably move in with someone else. You don't have any idea about loneliness. I don't even know why I'm bothering to talk to you about this!'

'Well, I do—'

'Look, I'm sorry, forget everything I said, I feel so *horrible* at the moment. I have to go, I've work to do. Don't worry about me, I'll be fine. I'll see you soon.'

Which meant that she might come back once before Christmas. Alberta looked at the phone and wondered why it was that she was so useless with her only daughter. Diana's daughter lived in Manchester but still managed to come home once a month. Diana's daughter rang her mother at least three times a week.

Alberta had only herself to blame. She had always been a little overawed by her daughter. Even as a child, Hannah displayed amazing confidence about who she was, where she was going, what she wanted to do. Alberta couldn't remember a time when she hadn't felt that Hannah found her really rather stupid.

She took another gulp of wine and cursed herself for her ineptitude. She should have told Hannah that she had at least discovered in good time that Alfie was not right for her. She should have told Hannah that she was very young and would one day find someone worthy of her. She should have told her that somewhere there was a soulmate for everyone.

Alberta sniffed and tried very hard to erase the thought that burst into her mind like a tidal wave. There was nothing to be gained by dwelling on the fact that her own soul-mate had died twenty years ago.

# CHAPTER TWELVE

## *Rancho Notorious*

Philippa was not enjoying her widowhood as much as she had thought she would. She had always assumed Michael would go first; he was, after all, nine years older than her. She had often imagined life after Michael and although it was some time since she had looked forward to it with a considerable degree of wistful anticipation, it had never occurred to her, even in these later, more congenial years, that she would find it difficult to be without him.

Of course, she could not have foreseen that his demise would leave in its wake a welter of scandal and prurient interest from the press. And even then, she took it for granted that life would soon return to normal. Well, she had been wrong about that as she had been wrong about so many things in her life. Christopher could barely bring himself to mention his father, Alberta continued to sound utterly stricken and most people in the village still failed to make eye contact with her.

Time, as Philippa knew only too well, was a great healer. Her children would eventually recover their equilibrium, in time her friends would stop reacting to her as if she were a bad smell that had hung around for too long, and with any luck some other scandal would soon divert those journalists who continued to pester her with demands to hear her side of the story.

In the meantime, she should shake off this silly depression that had unaccountably taken hold of her and start being positive about her life. It was in pursuit of this sensible objective that she was now sitting in her husband's study with a pad of A4 paper in front of her and a pen in her hand. She picked up the pad and surveyed her handiwork:

WHY I AM LUCKY

I do not have to cook Irish stew or shepherd's pie ever again.
I am able to listen to *The Archers* without being interrupted.
I am able to watch American comedies and repeats of *Inspector Morse* and Agatha Christie dramas.
I have the bed and the pillows to myself and can switch the light out whenever I wish.
I can play any music I want.
I can have sardines on toast for supper.
I do not have to have any supper.
I do not have to make cooked breakfast any more.
I can stay out in the garden as long as I like.
I can have a dog at last.
I can go and see Christopher and Alberta whenever I like.
I do not have to keep the house immaculate any more.

Philippa adjusted her reading glasses and studied her work. She was indeed pleased that she no longer had to eat Irish stew or shepherd's pie. Michael had loved them and insisted on eating them at least once a fortnight. And it was a joy to listen to *The Archers* in the knowledge that no one could come in and say, 'How can you listen to that rubbish? Nothing ever happens.' Philippa had once tried to defend her programme by insisting that actually a great deal happened. Emma slept with her fiancé's brother just before the wedding, resulting in a bitter fight over the paternity of the baby that followed some months later. Ruth got cancer, got better and nearly left David for the cow-man. Brian had an illegitimate son and persuaded his wife to take him in when the mistress got cancer and died. Kathy was raped by the chef at Lower Loxley, Adam fell in love with Ian, the vicar fell in love with Usha, John died under a tractor, Fallon fell in love with Ed . . . She could, she said, go on for ever at which point Michael said he would very much rather she didn't and made a quick retreat to his study.

So now she could listen to *The Archers* without turning down the volume. That was a definite plus.

And as far as TV was concerned, she at last had possession of the remote control. She no longer had to watch *Newsnight* – so depressing to see that politicians in the twenty-first century were every bit as duplicitous, hypocritical, sanctimonious and self-serving as they had been in the twentieth century. (How wise Camus had been when he observed that great men did not concern themselves with politics.) Now she could watch whatever she liked and was at last finding out why *Friends* had been so popular for so long. Another definite plus.

She was sleeping better too. Michael used to get up to go to the loo at least four times a night and he always woke her up every time he did so, yanking the bedclothes over to his side as he returned to bed. Now she had the pillows and the duvet to herself and could make a veritable cocoon out of them. Really her life was so easy. She could eat what she wanted when she wanted, she could garden all day and watch telly all night. She could go off and visit the children, she could buy a dog, she could do all manner of things she had never done before.

It was perverse, therefore, that now that she was able to garden all day, she found that she didn't want to. Now that she could at last get the dog she had always wanted, she found she didn't want one. The idea of being sole owner of a pet and being responsible for its welfare and its training was far too worrying. She was quite sure that any dog trained by her would be the sort of dog that barked all day and bit the postman's trousers. Now that she no longer needed to keep the house as spotless as Michael liked, she realized she had long since stopped being the Bohemian free spirit she had so fondly considered herself to be. She didn't actually like living in a mess. She liked the smell of polish on the dining-room table and the sharp tang of disinfectant on the kitchen floor.

As for visiting the children, she knew there was little chance of her jumping into her car and driving off to London or Bath. Christopher and Helen led such busy lives and would want to look after her and take her out and she would feel dreadfully guilty. And as for Alberta, Philippa was pretty sure Alberta would have no idea what to do with her.

Philippa stretched her arms behind her and stood up. These days, the thought of her daughter seemed to have a Pavlovian effect on her, requiring instant sustenance in the form of sherry or coffee. Regrettably, it was too early for sherry. Alberta had rung yesterday morning, her voice sounding resolutely cheerful and upbeat. Everyone was well. Jacob had arrived safely in Avignon and was happy despite finding that he was to be a menial cleaner. Alberta said he had apparently assumed he would work behind the bar and, given his tendency to break glasses just by looking at them, it was just as well his assumption was misplaced. Tony sent his love and was in the garden with Lionel trying to light the barbecue. Dylan had come to stay for the weekend and they were all having a very jolly time.

If Philippa had been injected with a truth serum, she would have replied that she might not be brilliant, but even she knew that no one could have a jolly time if Dylan was around. She would have said that she knew Alberta was unhappy and that she knew she missed her father. If the truth serum was really strong, she would probably have added that even *she* was missing Michael and that that was extremely odd since she had never thought she would.

Philippa spooned coffee into a mug and smiled. She could just imagine how Alberta would respond to all of *that*. It was just as well that there had been no truth serum around. When Alberta asked her mother how she was, Philippa said she was very well, she was keeping busy and she was very pleased because Hilda had invited her to go on holiday to Crete with her. At least the last of the three statements had been true.

A truth serum would definitely not be a good idea. If

she took a truth serum, she would be forced to admit to the vicar that when she followed his sermon with such rapt concentration she was in actual fact simply fascinated by the violent movement of his Adam's apple. If she took a truth serum she would have to rush over to Joan Cartwright and tell her she knew the only reason why Joan wouldn't talk to her was because she had fancied and flirted with Michael for years and felt personally betrayed by him. If she took a truth serum she would be forced to tell Maurice Cartwright that he was the one person in her life who had made her feel she was interesting and intelligent and his cruel exit from her life had made her realize once again that she knew nothing about anyone. If she took a truth serum, she would want to jump in the car and drive down to Alberta and that . . . that would make a nonsense of the last twenty years.

Philippa filled her mug with boiling water and took it out into the garden. The roses were looking wonderful this year. She had gone to the Chamberlains' summer party on Saturday and had taken some over. She had only decided at the last moment to go and she was aware of a collective intake of breath when she walked through the door. She had made a point of going up to all those guests who seemed to be most embarrassed by her presence. She chatted fiercely to Angela Mann about greenfly. She exchanged views with Marion Farton about the state of the economy, which had actually been quite fun given that neither she nor Marion knew anything at all about the state of the economy. She had even cornered Jessica Mayhew in the conservatory and when Jessica expressed her surprise that Philippa should want to come partying at 'such a painful time', Philippa said very loudly that Michael had always enjoyed the Chamberlains' summer parties and would have wanted her to be here. When Philippa mentioned Michael, Jessica's face went a most unbecoming puce colour and Philippa felt almost exhilarated. And then the Cartwrights arrived and Philippa caught Maurice's eye and he looked away quickly, and suddenly the party wasn't fun any more. Philippa slipped away and went home and watched a *Midsomer Murders* story on the television. It was rather good and was about a little old lady who set about killing all of her neighbours in turn. Philippa knew just how the little old lady felt.

She had read something rather interesting about crocodiles the other day. Researchers from the University of Queensland had trapped three crocodiles, fitted them with satellite tracking devices and then airlifted them round the coast. Within a few weeks, all three of them had found their way home and one of them had had to make a journey of two hundred and fifty miles in order to do so. It was almost as if they had been programmed. Scientists were baffled as to how they had been able to find their way back.

She knew just how the scientists felt. She found her own feelings at the moment just as baffling. No matter what had happened during her marriage, no matter how unhappy she had been, in the end she couldn't get away from the fact that, for some inexplicable reason, now that Michael was dead she couldn't function properly without him. She would go out into the garden full of plans to weed the front flower bed and somehow find herself standing for ages staring at a worm. She would drive to Marlborough and go into Waitrose and forget what she wanted to buy. She would decide to go for a walk and get halfway down the drive and decide to go back again.

Of course a reasonable person would say that after fifty years of marriage, it would be impossible not to miss her husband. But a reasonable person would not know that Michael had once broken her heart with such efficiency that ever after it had remained a poor limp shadow of its former self, stuck together with fraying bandages. A reasonable person would have no idea that for years she had only stayed with him as an act of penance, of justly deserved self-mortification. She had always assumed that his death would relieve her from this burden of guilt, but it was still there, bumping along behind her.

And in the meantime, somewhere along the line, something very odd had happened. Nothing had been said – it had been years since she and Michael had talked about their feelings for each other – but since his retirement, they had somehow acquired the art of living comfortably together. Who would have thought it? He had once told her he could never forgive her. She had once thought she would rather die than live with him. And yet here she was, standing in their garden, aware that she missed him. Perhaps a scientist could explain it because she couldn't.

# CHAPTER THIRTEEN

## *Un Autre Homme, Une Autre Chance*

Hannah had nearly taken Alfie back. She had finally agreed to meet him for a drink and he almost convinced her that bonking Princess Blanche had been a desperate attempt to overcome a feeling of emasculation, a consequence, he said, of living with a girl who owned her own flat and earned a great deal more money than he did. She had no idea, he added, how difficult it was to find a halfway decent flat to rent in London. Hannah had picked up her bag and told him she'd be sure to send him the names of some good letting agencies.

She was aware she was in danger of losing the plot completely. Only the other evening, unable to cope with the bitterness and rage that had colonized her brain, she had rung her mother of all people and vented all her frustrations on her, which was not only completely unfair but downright selfish and cruel given that Grandfather had died less than a month ago. She had rung again in order to apologize but had continued to berate herself.

Tony, possibly primed by her mother, had rung a few days later when he was in London and suggested lunch.

She intended to tell him how guilty she felt but in the event they barely mentioned her mother or Alfie. Tony talked about his ex-wife's wedding. He said he had found it rather moving since it was clear that Lydia had at last found someone she could wholeheartedly love and apparently the lucky man was all right too, even if he had weird taste in shoes. It was only at the end of the meal that Tony mentioned Alfie.

'I'm sorry to say this about a brother of Kitty but the man's a complete bastard. To paraphrase the immortal words of the Swinging Blue Jeans, he's no good, he's no good . . .' Tony paused for dramatic effect, 'baby, he's no good.'

'I keep telling myself that.' Hannah gave a watery smile. 'But it doesn't seem to help.'

'I know,' Tony said, 'but it will. You keep saying it. You're a star, Hannah Granger, and you deserve only the best.'

Hannah gave him a quick, fierce hug and then left the restaurant before he could see she was crying.

And that was another thing. She *hated* the fact that she was currently crying like she'd been force-fed emotional laxatives. She *never* cried. And she hated the fact that she wasted so much time on being angry and sad and thinking about *him*.

Part of the trouble was that the two people to whom she would normally turn were no longer available. Harrison's behaviour continued to be strange and extremely hurtful. He had sent her a card saying he was sorry he had had to leave her flat so abruptly, but he had given no explanation as to *why* he had left. He had also told her he was sorry to hear about her grandfather, which was kind except that he had added nothing else. She emailed him after the Alfie disaster to tell him they'd split and that she'd love to see him. She got back a few lines telling her he was still doing temporary work but was starting a new position with Environmental Watch in a few weeks and had loads of reading to do. Hannah had immediately picked up her phone before slowly putting it down again. For some reason that she didn't understand, Harrison no longer wanted to see her. To pester him with phone calls was not only humiliating but would probably earn her his contempt. And that was something that Hannah could not bear.

Meanwhile, Kitty's help was equally out of bounds. She was, Hannah could see, in an appallingly difficult position. Kitty had been furious with Alfie and had fully supported Hannah's decision to throw him out of the flat. Ever since it happened, she had been kind and sensitive and assured Hannah she was perfectly happy to discuss her brother's failings any time at all. But, of course, Hannah couldn't and they ended up avoiding a subject that they both knew preoccupied Hannah beyond anything else. And whenever Kitty was out or late back from work, like tonight, Hannah wondered if she was seeing her brother and if he was telling her his side of the story. What *was* his side of the story? She would give a lot to know the honest-to-God, unvarnished Alfie side of the story. Would he say she was spoilt and selfish, only interested in her work and with no sex appeal at all, unlike the fabulous Princess Blanche?

Worst of all was the fact that when she was on her own in the flat, she spent her time doing stupid things like looking Alfie up on Facebook to see what he was doing and who he was doing it with. This was what she found most difficult to accept: that Alfie had transformed her from a tough, independent, ambitious woman into a lachrymose, self-pitying, self-hating female who was actually beginning to wonder if she had *ever* been tough, independent and ambitious.

Tonight, for example, she was sitting at her kitchen table, preparing for her final examination paper in the morning, and was finding it impossible to concentrate.

She heard a key in the door and quickly closed her laptop. She heard Kitty call, 'Hell – oo!' Pre-Alfie drama, Kitty would walk straight in, talking away as if continuing a conversation that had been randomly interrupted. Post-Alfie drama, she would walk in, glance anxiously at Hannah and say, 'Hell – oo!' in a voice that combined both hope and anxiety: hope that Hannah was miraculously restored to her old self, anxiety that she would never return to her old self.

'You're late,' Hannah said brightly. 'Have you been anywhere nice?'

'I have had,' Kitty said, 'the most extraordinary day. Have you eaten?'

'Not yet. I was going to open a tin of tuna. There's some salad in the fridge.'

'Great, I'm starving. I must have a pee and then I must get out of these shoes. You will never guess what happened!'

While Kitty got changed, Hannah put the dinner together and tried very hard to guess what had happened. Had she seen Alfie? Had he told her he'd been offered a starring role in a Hollywood blockbuster and had been promised a fortune and wanted to lay it at Hannah's feet so that she would see he had not simply slept with her in order to get a free flat? Had he said he couldn't go on like this, that he realized Hannah was the core of his existence or something equally superb and soppy?

The trouble with being obsessed with someone was that one assumed that the rest of the world would automatically share that obsession.

Kitty came in and said, 'What do you think happened today?'

'Tell me,' Hannah said, sitting down at the table and trying to look cool and calm.

'You will never guess what happened at work!' Kitty filled her glass with water, took a great gulp and pulled out a chair. 'Melanie stormed up to my desk this afternoon. She tells me the blurb I've written for the new *Colditz* film is way below standard and then she says she's been very patient with me but the fact is I'm not up to the job and she's going to have to let me go, and I sit there and . . . you know how I get when I feel something's completely unfair?'

Hannah did know. Their economics teacher at school had never used sarcasm again after a verbal lambasting from Kitty that had lasted at least twelve minutes according to a grateful Grace Bartlett, who had been the constant target of the aforementioned sarcasm.

Kitty helped herself to a liberal portion of salad. 'I just sat and looked at her and I could feel this fury gathering up inside me and I was just about to let rip when Conrad – *Conrad!* – says very quietly, "If you fire Kitty, then you can fire me too." And I *gape* at him and Melanie gapes at him too and she says, "*What* did you say?" because she can't believe what she heard and I can't believe what I heard either and Conrad is still really quiet and calm and polite but he says again, "If you fire Kitty, then you can fire me too." And then he says – just as if he's having a conversation about the weather – that I'm efficient and I work hard and I produce great stuff and he doesn't want to work in a company that gets rid of good people like me, and Melanie looks as if she's going to explode and then she says she will have to talk to David.'

'Who's David?'

'Hannah, you *know* who David is. He's our managing director – he has a thing about spinach, remember? So then she storms out and I look at Conrad but Conrad's looking at his computer screen as if nothing's happened and I can't say anything because I think I'm going to cry. So I go to the Ladies and I sort myself out and then I come back and Melanie comes in and starts talking about her mother, who's apparently very ill and bad-tempered, and then she looks like she's swallowed a frog and says she thinks she might have been unfair to me and she never actually meant she was getting rid of me and shall we put the past behind us and forget anything ever happened, and she actually tried to smile at me which she can't quite manage but at least she tried and then she goes out and I still can't talk so I write a message to Conrad and he writes back and says yes.'

'What did you write?'

'I asked him if he'd let me buy him a drink after work and he said yes and we went to the Redwood Wine Bar, which is why I'm late and starving.'

Hannah watched as Kitty expertly speared with her fork two lettuce leaves, a tomato and a huge wodge of tuna. 'So why did Conrad ride to the rescue? I thought he hated you?'

'I thought so too. He says he thought I hated *him*.'

'You did.'

'No, I didn't. I only hated him after I thought he hated me.'

'I'm on Conrad's side here. You do have a tendency to scowl at people you don't know.'

'I do *not*. That is so unfair.'

'You do. Half the time you don't even know you do it. You have this scowl you present to the world. I mean, I know you don't mean it but people who don't know you can find you pretty scary.'

'I don't scowl at people. I scowled at Conrad because I thought he was trying to get rid of me. He said he finally spoke up because it was so obvious that Melanie was picking on me. He thinks she's jealous of me but there's no reason why she should be. The good thing is that Conrad and I shook hands and agreed we would be friends from now on and work together. We talked about the Cannes Television Festival in the autumn and he reckons we should both ask to go and oversee the display boards, and for the first time ever I actually think it might be possible to enjoy my job. Isn't it funny how you can discover that people are completely different from the way you thought they were?'

'Yes,' said Hannah soberly, 'I think it's very funny.' Her grandfather had frequented brothels, her boyfriend had turned out to be an adulterous liar and her best friend from Oxford had suddenly stopped liking her. People were very funny. Hannah didn't understand any of them.

It was partly because of Harrison that Hannah decided to

go to Emily Faraday's party two weeks later. Emily had been working in Swindon since leaving Oxford. She had recently moved up to London to take a post on a national paper. Emily was a good friend of Harrison – she had been one of his flatmates in their second year at Oxford – and it was inconceivable that he wouldn't be there.

Hannah was also conscious of the fact that Kitty was anxious about her. It was time to at least give the impression that she had recovered from Alfie's treachery. Besides, Hannah was fond of Emily; it would be good to see her again.

Hannah dressed up for the occasion. She put on her black wrap-around dress and her fake-tiger-skin shoes, sprayed her neck liberally with her best Stella perfume and applied far more eye make-up than usual. She arrived at Emily's house at nine and was happy to see that she knew most of the people there. Someone called her name and she shouted, 'Back in a minute!' because, first, she wanted to find Harrison. She fought her way through the crowded sitting room into the even more crowded kitchen.

Harrison was standing by the sink, opening a bottle of wine. He was dressed in blue jeans and a cream T-shirt with the face of Britney Spears emblazoned in red across his chest. She struggled over to him and said, 'Hello, stranger.'

'Hannah!' He held up the bottle. 'Would you like a drink?'

She looked down at her empty glass. 'Thanks.' She neatly side-stepped someone's elbow and wedged herself between Harrison and the sink. Emily's kitchen was not spacious and there had to be at least fifteen people in here. 'How are you?' she asked.

Harrison filled her glass. 'I can't hear you,' he said. 'What did you say?'

'How are you?' Hannah moved her glass to her left hand and held it away from someone's gesticulating hand. 'Look, let's get out of here,' she suggested and, holding her glass aloft like Florence Nightingale with her lamp, she led the way through to the hall. 'I've missed you,' she said again. 'I haven't seen you since . . .'

'I know. I've been pretty busy. Did I tell you about the new job?'

'Yes. Yes, you did.'

'I was so sorry to hear about your grandfather.'

'Thank you.' It was no use. She had to find out why he'd been behaving so oddly. 'Harrison,' she began earnestly, 'I wanted to say something—'

'Hannah!' Emily burst upon them and hugged each of them in turn. 'Oh it's so lovely to be in London and have my old friends about me! I was so lonely in Swindon! I used to talk to myself as I walked along the pavement, and nobody noticed; and I only realized I was doing it when I saw someone else doing it too. I reckon Swindon is full of lonely people all talking to themselves wherever they go! Harrison, you must go and talk to Sam. He's lost his job and doesn't know what to do. Hannah, I want to borrow you for a bit, you can talk to Harrison later.'

With barely concealed reluctance, Hannah followed Emily into the sitting room and towards a tight little group by the bay window. Emily plucked a man from the group and delivered him to Hannah. 'Hannah, this is Rando. Rando, this is Hannah.'

If Rando were an actor, he would have made a perfect

Doctor Who. Thin and pale-faced, he had protuberant eyes and hair that shot forward from his head in spikes. He looked like a cartoon character come to life.

Emily took Hannah's hand. 'Rando is a friend of mine from work and he's been dumped by his girlfriend and is very sad.' She turned to Rando. 'Hannah is a friend from Oxford and she and *her* boyfriend have just broken up and she is very sad too. I think you'll both get on. Do talk!'

She dropped Hannah's hand and smiled at them both before returning to the group of people by the bay window.

Rando shook his head in admiration. 'What an introduction!' he marvelled. 'Can you beat that? Hey, you two are both losers, come and be lost together! Let me assure you, Hannah, I am still a functioning human being and you do not have to spend time talking to me if you would rather not.'

'I'm glad to hear it,' Hannah said gravely. 'Perhaps we should talk to each other for a few minutes since Emily has made such an effort.'

'I'm not sure we should encourage her. I don't think I want her to go on bringing pretty girls over, only to tell them I've been dumped. It's not terribly good for the ego.'

Hannah smiled. 'I know what you mean.' She had been planning to get straight back to Harrison but there was, after all, no hurry.

Rando glowered in Emily's direction. 'I suspect she's been planning this for some time. I'm sure it was you she was talking about the other day. Are you the granddaughter of Lord Trussler?'

Hannah stiffened. 'Yes.'

Rando gave a satisfied nod. 'He's one of my heroes. At the risk of confirming what you probably think of me, I'm one of those sad geeks who used to watch *Question Time* while all my friends were getting laid. I'm not a Conservative like your grandfather but I do believe passionately in Europe.'

'How refreshing. Most people seem to think we're in dire danger of surrendering all our powers to Brussels.'

'Of course we're not. We still have control over justice and home affairs, social security, tax, foreign policy and defence. The European Union is a modern miracle; it enables some twenty-seven countries to live and work together in a more or less peaceful manner. And if you look at the problems we face today – terrorism, the environment, globalization – you'll see there is no way we can tackle them on our own. It beggars belief that—'

Rando's words had tumbled over themselves with such speed and energy that his abrupt silence was all the more surprising. He smiled an apology and said, 'I'm sorry, I'm sorry, I must stop doing this! I must be boring you rigid. My girlfriend – my *ex*-girlfriend – always said I should carry a soapbox with me. I know I shouldn't lecture people about Europe but I find it so difficult. It's just something that seems terribly important to me.'

'Don't apologize,' Hannah assured him. 'I always feel guilty for not caring enough about things like that. As it happens, I agree with you.'

'Thank you. I say –' Rando grinned and Hannah instantly saw what he must have looked like as a little boy – 'Emily is looking at us.' He gave Emily a smile and waved at her.

'I thought you said we shouldn't encourage her? Emily has an addiction to matchmaking lonely hearts. She was always doing it at university.'

'Do you have a lonely heart?'

'I think I'd describe it as battered rather than lonely. What about you?'

Rando shrugged. 'It's difficult. My girlfriend – my ex-girlfriend – is now seeing the man who lives in the flat below me. So I still bump into her on a fairly regular basis. I've perfected this cool way of greeting her: I say, "Hiya, Grace!" and smile like this –' Rando paused to bare his teeth – 'just to show her I'm not bothered. What do you think?'

'Well,' Hannah said, 'I think I'd cut the smile and the "Hiya". Otherwise, it's fine.'

'I see. That gives me great confidence.'

Hannah smiled. 'You could always move. Why are you called Rando? Is it a foreign name?'

'My parents called me Randolph. I think they thought it would give me instant gravitas. Instead, of course, everyone called me Randy Randolph at school. When I went to university, I decided to call myself Rando, which is better except that some people *will* call me Rambo. You don't know how lucky you are to have a nice, normal name. Do you have a nice, normal job as well?'

'I'm not sure. I work for Associated Metals.'

'That sounds very serious and extremely grown-up. What's it like to be a fully-paid-up member of the corporate world?'

'I don't know. I don't feel like I *am* a member most of the time. I still feel very much the new girl.'

'I bet you're brilliant.' Rando held up his empty glass.

'I need another drink. Can I get you one?'

'I'm fine, but you go ahead. There's someone I have to catch up with. I'll see you later.'

'All right. I promise I'll leave my soapbox behind.'

'I've told you,' Hannah said, 'I like your soapbox.'

Talking to Rando had done her good. By laughing at his own heartache, he had also diminished her own sense of hurt and humiliation. He had obviously liked her as much as she liked him and she thought it was highly likely that she had found a new friend. All in all, she felt far better equipped for her confrontation with Harrison.

She made her way through the sitting room, into the kitchen and then into the hall where she found Emily standing a little unsteadily beside a very tall man in glasses.

'Hannah!' she exclaimed. 'Do you know what Ralph here has just told me? Have you heard of the expression, a white elephant? Apparently, that goes back all the way to a very cunning king of Siam. He used to give white elephants to his enemies because he knew they were very expensive to feed but too rare to be destroyed and so his enemies would go bankrupt trying to feed them! Isn't that a great story? Ralph, I must have a word with Hannah, I'll see you in a bit . . .' As they walked away from him, Emily lowered her voice. 'That man is so boring. I don't know why he is here, I didn't invite him.'

'Emily,' Hannah said, 'I'm trying to find Harrison. Where is he?'

'He left a few minutes ago,' Emily said. 'I think he said he had to meet someone. Oh look, Rando's coming over. Now, tell me quickly! What do you think of him?'

* * *

She had a text from Rando a few days later. It was still making her smile when she went running on Sunday morning. 'Saw ex-girlfriend on stairs and did non-verbal nod. V. successful. Am sure she now thinks I'm cool.'

She was glad they'd exchanged mobile numbers. She was glad he'd been at the party. She had spent the last hour of it in a convoluted discussion with him about the meaning of love but it had made her laugh and had taken her mind off the hurt caused by Harrison's abrupt departure.

The running was part of Hannah's new campaign for getting over Alfie. It certainly beat looking at Facebook. On a sunny day like today, it was even quite enjoyable and it allowed her brain to skim gently over her various preoccupations. So, today, she was able to appreciate the beauty of the two young black men jogging in the opposite direction to her while also trying to accept the sad truth that Harrison no longer wanted to be her friend. Today, she could appreciate the green expanse of Clissold Park while finally working out what had been different about her recent phone calls with her mother. Usually, Hannah was the one to answer questions and terminate the conversation. In the six weeks since Grandfather had died, her mother had definitely become increasingly withdrawn.

Later, as Hannah walked home, she thought about the effect of her grandfather's death on the family. Of course it was upsetting – very upsetting – to see him hauled up as a figure of ridicule: an old-age pensioner who couldn't keep away from dubious females and even more dubious practices. It was upsetting to realize that he had a secret life which bore no relation to the man they all thought they had known. But then, if Hannah had learnt anything in the last few weeks, it was that most people *did* have secret lives and that one shouldn't expect too much of anyone. And if it was difficult for her mother, how much worse was it for Marma? And yet Marma continued to be her sweet, sunny self. Marma was a lesson to them all, Hannah thought, and later she would think how extraordinary it was that she should be thinking of Marma at the very moment her eyes fell on the billboard outside the newsagent's with the words firmly emblazoned LADY TRUSSLER'S LOVER TELLS ALL!

# CHAPTER FOURTEEN

## *Blood Money*

### LADY TRUSSLER'S LOVER TELLS ALL!

*Meg Leakey's exclusive interview with Peter Repton*

The man sitting opposite me celebrated his fifty second birthday last month. His hair is flecked with grey and his forehead is etched with deep lines that suggest he has suffered. When he smiles, his blue eyes light up and dimples appear on either side of his mouth. When he smiles, it is easy to see why Lady Trussler risked her marriage, her position in society and her reputation for him.

Peter Repton lives in a stone cottage in the pretty village of Ardfern, near the seaside town of Oban in the highlands of Scotland. We sit, drinking tea, in the small sitting room that looks out across the lane onto the beautiful loch that sparkles in the summer sun. The setting is calm and tranquil. It is hard to believe this man's life was torn apart by an explosive affair which to this day continues to haunt him. There are those who say his subsequent marriage to Penelope Dangerfield, heiress daughter of the diamond tycoon, Sir James Dangerfield, never stood a chance.

I ask Peter what made him decide to speak now after so many years of silence. He answers hesitantly, softly. At times, I have to lean forward to hear him. From time to time, his fists clench involuntarily, revealing the tremendous strain he is under, belying the gentle, quiet voice.

'Philippa was the love of my life,' he says. 'When I read about the sordid death of Lord Trussler and thought of the pain and humiliation she has suffered and must continue to suffer, I knew I had to— ' He stops, gives a little shake of his head and struggles to retain control of his feelings. 'I felt compelled to speak out. The world should know what sort of a man he really was.'

I notice that he glances frequently at a framed photograph on the small table beside him. He follows my eyes and hands me the picture. 'That's Philippa,' he says. 'I took the photo. I remember it like yesterday. Isn't she beautiful?'

The face of a mature woman looks back at me. She is indeed beautiful with her blonde hair falling about her shoulders, a smile hovering around her generous mouth, her eyes radiant with love. It is a photograph of a woman gazing at her lover, a woman who is confident of her own sexuality. I find it almost unbearably moving.

I ask, 'How did you meet her?'

'I was a friend of her son-in-law, Ed Granger. Ed and I had a lot in common. We were both chief aides to Ministers, we were young and ambitious and looking for parliamentary seats. Ed was selected for one in the Midlands. It helped that he was married to Michael

Trussler's daughter but everyone knew he was brilliant. Trussler threw a party for him and I was invited. I remember seeing Philippa across the room. She wore a pink dress and I thought her husband was a very lucky man. And then she came over and she asked me who I was and our eyes met and all I could do was tell her that she was the most beautiful woman I'd ever met.'

I look at the middle-aged man opposite me and I hesitate to speak for I can see he is lost in the past. I remark tentatively that he had been a young man without wealth or position while she was the middle-aged wife of one of the most powerful politicians in his party.

He gives a small, sad smile. 'I know. It was insane. Our eyes met and we were lost. We both knew it was crazy but we were powerless. We became lovers within the week. Nothing else seemed to matter. We took ridiculous risks. I'd go to their house in Surrey and we'd make love for hours on end. Sometimes we'd hear the doorbell ring and we'd hide under the bedclothes and giggle like children.'

'You were sleeping with the wife of Michael Trussler. Did you never think you were putting in jeopardy any chance of getting into Parliament?'

'I didn't care.'

'Did you feel no guilt?'

He sits forward and pounds his knee with one hand. 'Their marriage was a sham! There are things I could tell you . . .' His voice trails away and the anger gives him strength. 'All I will say is that he tried to persuade her . . . tried to subject her to unimaginable perversions . . .' He stops again and then sighs. 'I'm sorry. I don't want to speak ill of the dead. But no, I did not feel guilty. Philippa was twenty years older than me but it was I who taught her the joys of sexual love. The first time we made love, she cried and told me she had no idea it could be so beautiful. And then she laughed and asked if we could do it again. She was like a child and yet . . . I'm sorry . . . I can't go on.'

I suggest a break and I go for a short walk along the shore. An old man is rowing across the water in a small, weather-beaten boat. In the sky, I can spot a buzzard, its huge wings gliding elegantly in the gentle breeze. It all seems a million miles away from the miserable intimacies of the Trussler marriage.

When I return, Peter is making another pot of tea. He offers me shortbread and I decline. I have to watch my weight, I tell him. He studies me and tells me I have a perfect figure. From most men, that would be a polite, insubstantial compliment. When Peter says it, he speaks as if he means it. He is a man who likes women, I think.

We return to the sitting room and I ask him to tell me about the end of the affair. 'I had a visit from Ed Granger,' he says. 'I couldn't believe it. He was so cold and brutal. I should have known that in a contest between friendship and ambition, he'd always put ambition first. He told me if I tried to contact Philippa again, my political career would be over before it began. I told him I didn't care. It was pretty unpleasant. Of course I wasn't deterred. But something he said really got to me. He told me if Philippa left her husband for me, her friends and family would never speak to her again. I felt I couldn't let that happen. So I rang Philippa and told her we had to stop seeing each other.'

I prompt him gently, 'And then what happened?'

'I regretted it almost immediately. I knew I couldn't give her up. I wrote and then I rang. I kept ringing her but she wouldn't answer my calls. I was prepared to give up everything for her. I was young and idealistic, I believed love could conquer all. I should have known that Philippa wouldn't have the strength to stand up to her husband. Perhaps if I'd been older or if I'd had a degree of financial security, she might have followed her heart. I wrote to her again and begged her to see me. I told her I would come to their London flat and wait all day if necessary. When I arrived, Ed was there. He told me there wasn't a constituency in England that would take me, he told me Philippa had gone to visit her son in Canada and wanted me to leave her alone. He told me if I made any attempt to pursue her, my life could become very unpleasant. I told him he sounded like a second-rate gangster. I told him a few other things too, none of them complimentary. Then I walked away and spent the day thinking about Philippa. I think I went a little mad. I wanted to tell the world how I felt.'

Almost timidly, I ask him why he didn't.

'Something completely unexpected happened. Ed was killed in a car accident. Trussler had adored him and his daughter was left widowed with a small daughter. I couldn't add to their suffering. So I kept quiet. I had lost the love of my life and I had to let her go.'

'And yet,' I remind him gently, 'a few months later, you married Penelope Dangerfield.'

He shrugs. 'I was determined to put Philippa behind me. I had to, for the sake of my sanity. I convinced myself I was in love with Penelope and from the moment our marriage began, I was determined to make it work.' He shrugs again. 'In the end, though, the past has a way of catching up with you.'

'You've paid a heavy price,' I muse. 'You never became a Member of Parliament and your marriage is in ruins. Do you regret what happened all those years ago?'

He looks at me proudly and says, 'Not for a moment.'

'And finally,' I say, 'Lady Trussler is still alive. What would you say to her if she were here now?'

'I would tell her I loved her. I would thank her for what she gave me. I would tell her I bear her no ill-will. I would tell her I have never known happiness since she left me.'

As I take the Oban train back to London, I gaze at the majestic Scottish landscape and muse on the conundrum that is Peter Repton. Many people would say he is a lucky man. He married one of the richest women in the country and has two teenage daughters. He lives in a comfortable cottage in one of the most beautiful places in the world. And yet, I come away with a great feeling of sadness. He is a courteous, still handsome man but there is an emptiness and a loneliness about him. He is, I feel, a man who, twenty years on, still mourns the loss of his one true love.

'Yuck!' Tony said, glancing up at Alberta who was standing at the sink, watching him anxiously. 'Pass the sick-bag!'

Alberta nodded. 'I know,' she said. 'It's vile.'

Tony stared at the paper with disgust. 'It's far worse than that. It's the rank hypocrisy that makes me want to vomit. It's all so obvious. Lover-boy has been dumped by his rich wife and now your father's safely dead, he sees a way of making a quick buck. The journalist obviously fancies the pants off him. I bet she *did* get the pants off him too. And did you notice how she couldn't resist telling us he thought she had a perfect figure?' He flicked back a page. 'You must have been at that party Repton talks about. Do you remember meeting him?'

'No. There were loads of people there. I don't remember Ed ever talking about him so he can't have been that great a friend.'

'And Ed never hinted anything to you about Marma's private life?'

'No, he never said a word. I can't believe he never told me.'

Tony nodded. '*I* can't believe he never told you.'

Alberta shot a fierce look at him. 'Don't say that.'

'I was simply agreeing with *you*.'

'*You* mean there's something sinister about Ed not telling me. *I* mean I can't believe that Ed was able to keep such a huge problem secret from me. In fact, I know why Ed didn't tell me. Ed was trying to protect me. Ed always had a very protective attitude towards me.'

'I see,' Tony said.

The studious neutrality of his response was infuriating. And why was he going on about Ed anyway? Ed wasn't the one who'd had an affair.

'Thank God your mother's in Crete at the moment,' Tony said. 'I can't get over the man's sheer effrontery: all that stuff about Marma being the love of his life while gleefully ensuring that thousands of people will be slavering over the details of her sexual awakening. He's hanging her out to dry, he's deliberately setting out to make a laughing stock of an elderly lady. It's beyond contempt.'

'I agree. But then Marma's behaviour was pretty appalling too.'

Tony glanced up sharply. 'I don't understand you.'

'I mean that Marma had an affair with a man who was young enough to be her son. She took him to the family home, she made love with him in the marital bed and she told him all about her husband's most intimate personal details. Oh my God!' Alberta put her hands to her face.

'What is it?' Tony asked.

'I understand it now! After Ed died, Pa sold our home. It was the most beautiful place and he wouldn't tell me why he did it. He obviously couldn't bear to go there once he knew what she'd been doing. I'm amazed he was able to forgive her.'

Tony sat back in his chair and put his hands behind his head. 'Since when have you become so sanctimonious? What that interview does show – if you can believe anything that man says, which I doubt – is that your mother must have been terribly unhappy. Why else would she fall for such a corny chat-up line? She was married to someone who was obviously pretty screwed up about women and—'

'Do you mind if we don't discuss my father's sex life?'

'But that's the whole point,' Tony said. 'If you want to discuss the reasons for Marma's infatuation with Peter Repton, then you can't ignore your father's sex life. And there's something else. For God knows how long, you've resented the fact that Marma didn't rush back from Canada when your husband died—'

'Even a phone call would have been nice! I didn't even get a phone call!'

'I know. She let you down badly and—'

'She didn't *ring* me when Ed died, she didn't even write to me when Ed died. I got nothing! She stayed with Christopher and Helen *for a year* and I heard nothing! I know Helen was ill after Richard was born and I'm sure Marma was busy looking after them both, but nothing excuses the fact that she never once got in touch with me! She just didn't care.'

'You see, I don't think that's true. The first thing she did when she got back to England was come over to see you. I can remember opening the door to her and she had tears in her eyes. I'd never met her before and she said, "I'm Alberta's mother and I don't know what to do."'

'Of course she didn't. She *never* knew what to do. Because of her, Pa sold our home and I had nowhere to go after Ed died. Because of her, I had to live with Ed's parents. I bet she never even realized that.'

'You didn't *have* to move in with his parents.'

'Oh really? I suppose Hannah and I should have stayed on in the rented flat in Peterborough where we didn't know anyone? Pa was spending huge amounts of time in Brussels that year and couldn't really help. Ed's parents were mad with grief and virtually demanding that Hannah and I go and live with them. It seemed to be the only answer at the time.'

'Bertie, this all happened twenty years ago.'

'And it still hurts! And this stupid—' Alberta stopped, grabbed hold of the paper, tried without much success to screw it into a ball and hurled it onto the floor. 'This piece of *shit* doesn't help!'

'Well, perhaps it could.' Tony left his chair to pick up the paper and fold it neatly before returning to the table. 'It puts your mother's absence in a rather different light. You thought she went to Canada for the sole purpose of helping Christopher and Helen. I never did understand why she didn't fly straight back to you as soon as she heard about Ed's death. This interview provides an explanation. Marma left England immediately after the end of a very passionate affair. It seems more than likely that she got out to Canada and had a sort of nervous breakdown. She must have been unhappy and confused. Perhaps she couldn't cope, perhaps she didn't call you because she wasn't mentally strong enough to do so.'

'That would be a great theory if you hadn't forgotten something. Why didn't Christopher tell me if that's what happened? When he and Helen moved back to London, he said they couldn't have managed without Marma. He said she used to take Richard for walks and rock him to sleep and make delicious puréed meals for him. Now I may well be wrong but I wouldn't have thought that someone suffering from a nervous breakdown would be able to do all that.'

'How do you know what someone in that situation might do? And anyway, this is crazy. We are talking about something that happened some *twenty* years ago. Can't you let it go?'

'That's very easy for you to say. You're not the one reading an article that tries to justify your mother's immorality by deliberating vilifying your father. My father was a proud man. It must have been hell for him to find out that his wife had betrayed him with some juvenile political wannabe. I tell you something. I am actually sorry Marma's in Crete. She ought to read this. Someone should show it to her.'

Tony looked at her curiously. 'You really think that, don't you?' He pushed his chair back and stood up. 'What has your mother done to deserve a daughter like you?' he asked.

She was too upset to say anything. Tony had jumped to her mother's defence without even considering what *she* must be going through. It was clear he had never tried to understand the full horror of her life after Ed's death. Her mother had abandoned her and yet, somehow, *she* was the one at fault. It wasn't fair, it wasn't fair at all. She couldn't even look at Tony and it was only after he left the room without saying anything more that she looked up and started to cry.

Jacob had been pretty wide of the mark when he'd suggested his parents would soon be enjoying romantic evenings together. Barely bothering to offer an excuse, Tony returned to London on Sunday evening rather than the following morning and he didn't ring till Wednesday and then it was only to say curtly that he wouldn't be home till Friday.

Alberta didn't want to see him anyway. She was having a rotten week and was in no state of mind to try to improve relations with him. Just a few weeks ago her beloved father had died in scandalous circumstances. Now, her less beloved mother was the focus of yet another scandal and, while she was enjoying the sun in Crete, her daughter was answering phone calls from reporters who wanted to know how she felt about having a sex pervert for a father and a randy adulteress for a mother. The one person in whom she might understandably look for support was instead wilfully refusing to see that she had any reason to be even slightly upset by the turn of events. And she hated the way he'd so obviously wanted to believe the worst of Ed.

'Ed was trying to protect me,' she'd said and Tony had said, 'I see,' and looked at her as if he were about to say something but had then thought better of it. She hated people who looked as if they were about to say something and then thought better of it. People who did that usually had a smug expression at the back of their eyes which could be loosely translated as: I could say something very wise right now but I won't because you are too emotionally fragile/needy/pathetic to take it.

She *knew* what Tony had meant when he had not said anything. Tony meant to say that her relationship with Ed was not the beautiful relationship she had always thought it to be. Tony meant to say that Ed had kept secrets from her and that therefore her relationship was somehow flawed or inadequate.

Tony thought that, because Tony hadn't known Ed and Tony didn't have a protective bone in his body. His idea of relationships had been forged during his apprenticeship with Lydia and Lydia was as tough as old boots. Tony thought men who wanted to protect their women were dysfunctional and controlling which was why Tony had never liked Westerns. Tony thought John Wayne, Spencer Tracy, Randolph Scott, James Stewart, Gary Cooper and Clint Eastwood were emotionally frozen dinosaurs and he thought Alberta was a dinosaur for liking them.

Alberta had a busy day on Friday and didn't get back till after five. She could hear the Dogs of Hell singing their hearts out in the kitchen so Tony was home. He was not only home, he was repairing the stair carpet, which meant he felt bad about last weekend since she had been nagging him to repair it for months. When he told her Kenny had rung to suggest they all meet for a curry that evening, she looked again at the stair carpet and resisted the temptation to say she was not feeling sociable.

Tony had obviously warned Kenny and Jane about the minefield that was her mother. No one mentioned the latest press revelations. Instead, subjects covered included children, alcohol intake – Jane had been reducing her consumption for three weeks now but had decided she felt far healthier when she drank more – and the failings of Diana as a business partner.

This last proved a popular topic since, as Jane pointed out, it was always enjoyable to slag off people who were too terrifying to be slagged off directly. In the past Alberta had always defended Diana against Tony's criticisms. Tonight, she was less inclined to do so. Diana had returned from her holiday with a detailed new agenda for the business. She wanted to expand the catering side – a bit rich, Tony said, since she did so little catering herself – and she wanted to make her friend, Pam, a partner as soon as possible. On the one hand this made sense since Pam was doing quite a lot of cooking for them these days and had gone to the trouble to refurbish her kitchen and get it cleared by Health and Safety. On the other hand, Pam was a woman whose slavish devotion to Diana made her a deeply depressing prospect as a business partner to Alberta. Ken and Jane and Tony were all sympathetic and although their suggestions – explain her fears to Diana, kick ass with Diana, walk out on Diana – were all out of the question, she was grateful for their interest. Later, as she and Tony went up to bed, she was sufficiently mollified to compliment him on his stair-repair work and he was sufficiently pleased to suggest he might even put up the new curtain rail in Jacob's bedroom at last.

Consequently, Alberta was completely unprepared for the storm that broke the following day. She came back from the farmers' market in high good humour and was putting away her purchases when she noticed Tony sitting on the garden bench outside. Later, she realized she should have concluded that something was wrong since he was not reading the paper or on the phone. He was just sitting.

She put away the last of the vegetables and went out to join him. 'Do you want some coffee?' she asked. 'It's a bit cold to be sitting out here, isn't it? You'd never think it was the middle of summer.'

He didn't smile or say hello or ask her what she had bought. He said, 'Your mother rang.'

'Of course, she came home last night, didn't she? Has she had a good holiday?'

'I didn't ask her. She was anxious to know how *you* were. She told me she's been going through her post. Someone sent her – anonymously – a copy of that paper with the interview in it. She wanted to know if you'd seen it.'

Alberta could feel her face roasting under the glare of

Tony's disdain. She stammered, 'I-I didn't send it,' and even as she said it she knew he didn't believe her.

'It's funny,' he said, 'I've always respected your mother. At that charade of a funeral where most of her so-called friends failed to turn up, she was the perfect hostess, seeing to people's drinks, making sure they had food to eat. I've never known her say an unkind word to anyone. I always thought you were like her. But you're not. Admittedly, you don't go on for hours about the European Union and as far as I know you don't get your kicks from being spanked by prostitutes but in other ways you are very like your father.'

Alberta stared at him in disbelief. 'I don't mind you insulting me,' she said at last, 'but I do mind you insulting Pa.'

'I'm sorry,' Tony said. 'I don't feel I know you any more. I would never have thought you could be so vindictive or so cruel to an elderly woman who is living on her own.'

'I see.' Alberta folded her arms. 'Is that all you want to say?'

Tony stood up and put his hands in his pockets. 'Since you ask,' he said, 'I think you have a father-fixation that at your age is pretty weird.'

'I'd love to hear more,' Alberta said, 'but I have your lunch to prepare.'

'Don't worry about it on my account. For some reason, I think any food at the moment would stick in my throat.' He walked towards the kitchen door. 'I'm going out. You might think about ringing your mother.'

Alberta took Tony's place on the bench and kept her face firmly fixed towards the pond. A couple of minutes later, she heard the sound of a car driving away. She shivered and pulled her sleeves down over her hands. It was only when a great grey cloud inched its way towards the sun and finally covered it, that she returned to the house.

She opened the fridge door, stared without enthusiasm at the hummus and the cheeses she had bought and instead took out the bottle of wine and poured herself a glass. She took it through to the dining room and sat at the table, with her fingers plaited together in front of her. She sat there for a long time, letting her thoughts chase around her brain like rabbits in a field. When they at last settled into a final damning conclusion, she felt a little sick.

She went through to the study and switched on the computer. She was aware that her hands were trembling. An hour or so later, she picked up the phone and rang first Christopher and then Diana. She went back to the kitchen and opened the fridge door again but she still had no appetite. She went back to the computer, looked at her watch and wondered when Tony would come home.

# CHAPTER FIFTEEN

## *The Misfits*

Rando had rung Hannah a week after Emily's party to suggest meeting up for a drink. Hannah agreed but had to cancel it at the last moment due to a meeting at work that had gone on for two hours longer than it should have done. A few days later, Rando rang again and they agreed another date.

Had it not been for the fact that she had already let him down once, Hannah would have cancelled this evening's engagement. It wasn't that she didn't like Rando. She liked him very much. And if it hadn't been for her mother's phone call a few nights earlier, she would be walking to the pub with great enthusiasm. Instead, she entered the noisy bar with a determination to leave it as soon as possible.

Rando was already buying drinks and looked so pleased to see her that she felt ashamed of her reluctance to see him and wished she were in a better mood. 'See if you can find a place outside,' he called. 'White wine all right?'

She nodded and went through to the small garden at the back. It was a warm and pleasant evening, unusually so given that the last couple of weeks hadn't felt like summer at all. Around her, people had taken off their jackets and were enjoying the heat of the evening sun. A couple stood up to leave and Hannah quickly grabbed their table. She sat down, took off her own jacket and put it on the ground along with her bag. In normal circumstances, she would be enjoying the good weather and the prospect of a pleasant drink with a charming companion. She sat back in her chair, folded her arms and tried yet again to make sense of what her mother had told her.

She looked up when she saw Rando come out with the drinks. His dark suit and tie made an odd contrast to his spiky hair; he looked like a boy who had dressed up in his father's clothes. He passed her a glass of white wine and a packet of crisps. She murmured her thanks and tried to smile.

Rando sat down opposite her and sipped his beer. 'Either you've had a rotten day at work,' he said, 'or you really don't want to be here.'

'I'm sorry,' Hannah said, 'I didn't know it was so obvious. It's not you. I had some bad news the other day. I'm afraid I'm not very good company at the moment.'

Rando had a swig of his beer. 'Do you want to talk about it?'

'I don't think I do, really. My mother rang me a few days ago. She and my father are splitting up. I haven't really taken it in yet.'

Rando loosened his tie. 'I know what *that's* like,' he said.

Hannah looked at him sharply. 'Did it happen to you?'

Rando pulled again at his tie before taking it off. 'I remember it like yesterday. I finished my last A level in the afternoon and went home to get ready to celebrate at the pub. My parents were both there. They'd waited until my exams were over to tell me. My father had been seeing another woman for over a year. He left that night. He's married to her now. She's a dog trainer and she looks like a dog too. I still can't work out what Dad sees in her. A few months after he left, my mother met a widower and sold the house to move in with him and his three daughters. When I go there I sleep on the sofa. I see my father once a year. His wife doesn't like me and I don't like her.'

'That's so sad.'

'It is very sad. I still don't feel I have a home any more. Do you know the weirdest thing of all? I had no idea my parents were even a little unhappy.' He gave an apologetic smile. 'I'm sorry, I'm not being very helpful, am I? Let's change the subject.'

'No.' Hannah shook her head fiercely. 'It's good to talk to someone who knows what it's like. And what you said just now – about not knowing – I was like you. I had no idea anything was wrong. I thought it had to be me being thick. I do get things wrong with people sometimes. I know Mum's been very depressed since Grandfather died. It only happened two months ago. But she and Tony have always been fine.'

'Tony's your father?'

'He's my stepfather but he's always been like a father. My real father died when I was three. Tony's great. He and Mum never argue. They've always laughed a lot. None of it makes any sense. I asked her if there was someone else. She says there isn't. She says it's complicated. She says that now that my brother and I have left home, they can see they have little in common. It's so stupid. Jacob only went away a few weeks ago. She sounded so odd on the phone. She's got this catering business in Bath, she runs it with a friend. She's spent years building it up. Now she says her friend's agreed to buy her out. She's got interviews for jobs in London and she's going to live with my uncle and his wife until she finds a flat. She's leaving Bath in a few weeks' time. She *loves* Bath. It's like she's tearing everything up for nothing. And I can't help thinking it's all about my grandfather . . . You probably read about him in the papers.' She stopped and took a gulp of her wine.

'That must have been difficult for her,' Rando said gently.

'It was for all of us, especially for Marma, my grandmother. People are such hypocrites! Marma lives in this pretty little village in Hampshire, she's known everyone there for years and now no one will speak to her. And Mum hasn't helped. It's almost as if she blames Marma for . . . for Grandfather doing the prostitute thing. I think she's gone a bit mad.'

'Have you talked to your father – your stepfather yet? What does he say?'

'I rang him last night. I told him how *I* felt. Tony's never been someone who likes to talk about how *he* feels about things. He just said it was very sad but they both think it's right for them to live apart. Actually, he couldn't wait to get off the phone. I told him they'd always seemed so happy and all he could say was, "Things change." What sort of answer is that? I feel as if my family is falling apart and there's nothing I can do about it.' Hannah took another sip of her wine and then sighed. 'I'm sorry. I told you I'd be bad company tonight.'

Rando smiled. 'You couldn't be bad company if you tried.'

'Rando,' Hannah said, 'that's the nicest thing anyone has ever said to me.'

'It happens to be true.' Rando picked up his bottle and finished his beer. 'Do you want to go home now or can you stay for another drink?'

'I think,' Hannah said, picking up her bag, 'you've had quite enough of my problems for one evening. I'd better go.'

'I like hearing about your problems. I haven't fitted in with my family for years. I know what you're going through. Let me get you another glass of wine and I'll tell you more about my dog-faced stepmother.'

Hannah hesitated. 'I do have work to do.' She laughed and put her bag back on the ground. 'But I *would* like to hear about your dog-faced stepmother.'

# CHAPTER SIXTEEN

## *Ride Lonesome*

Evie had invited Alberta round for a sherry. In normal circumstances, Alberta would be looking forward to this but these were not normal circumstances and she was dismayed to see that Lionel was coming out of the house as she was coming in.

'Lionel,' she said, reaching up to kiss his cheek, 'aren't you staying for the sherry?'

Lionel gave a sad smile. 'Alas, dear one, I have been dispatched. I have been instructed to post these letters and furthermore I have been told to ignore the first two post boxes. Evie wants to have A Talk with you.'

'Oh dear,' Alberta murmured.

'Courage, my love! Evie is very wise. Be guided by her. As Theodore Roosevelt once said, "Nine-tenths of wisdom is being wise in time."'

'I promise you,' Alberta said, 'I am trying very hard to be wise.'

'Good girl, good girl! I am sure you are!'

Alberta sighed and waved as Lionel raised his walking stick in a farewell salute. She knocked on the door and tried to work out what she was going to say to Tony's mother.

Evie was dressed in black linen trousers and a knee-length green kaftan. Her hair was pinned precariously in a loose bun at the nape of her neck and she wore the silver chain Alberta and Tony had given her last Christmas. Alberta wondered if it was supposed to imply an unspoken rebuke. 'Alberta!' she said. 'How lovely to see you!'

Evie's sitting room was small and comfortable. Every inch of wall was covered with framed photos, at least half of which featured Tony, Alberta, Hannah, Jacob and Dylan. Evie could not have chosen better surroundings in which to pitch her case. She presented Alberta with a very large glass of sherry and motioned her to sit down on the strawberry-coloured sofa.

'Right,' she said briskly, 'I'll get straight to the point.'

Alberta took a sip. The only time she drank sherry was when she came round here. The amber liquid warmed her throat and made her feel a little less nervous.

Evie joined Alberta on the sofa. 'I want to say right away that I am not going to talk to you in a professional capacity. I can't be professional where you two are concerned. And I should tell you that right now I am seriously beginning to doubt my professional credentials since I would never have guessed in a million years that you and Tony would ever even contemplate splitting up. I have always felt,' she said, 'that you and Tony are very good *friends*.'

'We always have been,' Alberta agreed. 'We always have been until recently.'

'You've been under stress,' Evie said. 'When one is under stress, one tends to take one's anxiety out on one's partner.

It's a sad fact but it is the way people are.'

'I'm sure you're right. I know you're right. And as a result of that, we haven't been getting on very well. And because we haven't been getting on very well, it's made us see that apart from our friendship, we haven't really got anything else.'

Evie adjusted the cushion behind her back. 'I think I can say with complete confidence that there are a great many couples who have been together as long as you and Tony have, who would love to be able to say they are friends with each other. I don't think either of you appreciates what a huge achievement it is to live with someone else for as long as you have done and be *able* to say you are truly friends.'

'I know and we've been very lucky.'

'You have been lucky. Over the years I have had to help many patients through troubling times. I remember one man I saw shortly after I'd qualified. He and his wife had been together for twenty-three years. He told me that for the last four years he had loathed his wife. He had only stayed with her because she made a rice pudding for him every Wednesday. He said it was the best rice pudding in the world. One Wednesday, she said she was fed up with rice pudding. Instead, she produced a lemon meringue pie. He left her the next day.'

'That's pretty harsh.'

'I had another client, a woman. She and her husband had been married for twenty-eight years. He bored her. She said they had run out of things to say to each other years before.'

'Did she leave him?'

'She contemplated leaving him. She said that somewhere along the way she had become boring too and that since she had nothing of interest to say to anyone else, she might as well stay with him.'

'That's so sad.'

'And I had another client – a very sweet man, I grew extremely fond of him – who told me he hated his wife. But when she died, he came to me for help. He'd discovered that it was his hatred that had made him feel alive and without it he felt he was nothing.'

'Evie,' Alberta said, 'you're not exactly selling long-term relationships to me.'

'I am trying,' Evie said patiently, 'to show you that many, many marriages are unhappy. I am trying to indicate that what you and Tony have is very special. One reason why Lionel and I love coming round to you both, is because there is an atmosphere of laughter and of comfort that cannot be simulated. Everyone loves to come to your house.'

'Hannah doesn't,' Alberta said. 'She hasn't been down here for months.'

'Very healthy,' Evie said without a pause. 'If you bring up your children properly, they will stay away after they leave home, while they build their own lives. We never saw Tony when he left home. But he came back. He came back with you and Hannah and Jacob. And you have delighted us ever since.'

'Oh, Evie!' Alberta took a quick gulp of her sherry. 'I sometimes think that you and Lionel are one of the reasons why Tony and I have lasted so long. I've loved being next door to you both. I've been very happy.'

'And you can be happy again.'

'The thing is,' Alberta said, 'once you work something out, you discover all sorts of things you'd never understood before. I know it looks like this has come out of the blue but I promise it hasn't. We haven't been getting on well for months, for all sorts of reasons. We've both been . . . uncomfortable. And when you feel like that, you start to think. There've been odd times over the years when I wondered if we should stay together. But I've loved living here, I've loved our life here. Tony's been a wonderful father to Jacob *and* to Hannah and any doubts I had seemed ridiculous. But lately, when Tony and I have been so cross with each other, I've felt that it just isn't working any longer. Tony agrees. When I told him I wanted to leave, he *wasn't surprised*. He was *relieved* I said it first. It was almost surreal. He opened a bottle of wine and we sat down together and it was just like it used to be. We sorted everything out. There were no recriminations, no bitter words. He's my best friend, he probably always will be.'

'In which case,' Evie persisted, 'you should both be trying harder to save what has been, as you yourself admit, a very satisfactory life together. Look at the facts. Your father has died in distressing circumstances. Your mother has been the victim of a disgraceful newspaper article. Your son has suddenly left home. Do you really think that *now* is the time to make big decisions about throwing away your job and your home and your partner?'

'Perhaps if none of these things had happened,' Alberta conceded, 'we'd still be together. But these things did happen and they've made us see things differently. You know what I'm like! I'm the most indecisive woman in the world! But

I decided I ought to leave and as soon as I made that decision, I *knew* – I still know – it was right.'

Evie studied her glass and had a sip. 'You're like a daughter to me,' she said. 'I can't pretend to be impartial. Nothing you've said convinces me you're not making a terrible mistake.' She took a tissue from her pocket and blew her nose.

'Evie,' Alberta said, 'I wish—' The lump in her throat was growing bigger by the second. 'I have to go,' she whispered and fled from the house.

'I want you to know,' Jacob said, 'that you have all my sympathy.'

'Thank you.' Alberta pulled her duvet up to her neck with one hand, while cradling the phone in the other. 'That means a lot.'

'I *do* understand what you're going through. I've talked to Hannah.'

Alberta's fingers intensified their grip on the phone. 'Oh, have you? I'm not sure Hannah understands at all.'

'Well, I do. You're going through your second adolescence. I've only recently emerged from a very similar stage. You and I have a lot in common.'

'Jacob, I am not going through a second adolescence.'

'Mum, you are forty-five.'

'Thanks for reminding me,' Alberta said.

'I am merely trying to point out that you are forty-five and therefore almost certainly menopausal.'

'I am *not* menopausal. I should know!'

'Maud says that most women—'

'I do wish,' Alberta said furiously, 'that you and Hannah

would stop consulting all and sundry about intimate family concerns!'

'Maud,' Jacob said a little stiffly, 'is not all and sundry.'

'I know. I'm sorry. It's just a little annoying to find that my children assume I am pursuing a self-indulgent, possibly hormonally driven whim when in fact Tony and I have spent a very long time making a very painful decision.'

'The point is,' Jacob said, 'you haven't.'

'I haven't *what*?'

'You haven't spent a long time. When I left home in June, you and Dad were fine. Now, some six weeks later, you've decided to end a relationship that's nearly twenty years old. I think you should wait till I come home and the three of us can discuss it together.'

Alberta had a brief vision of Jacob sitting between his parents, passing out judgement while they listened gratefully. 'When *are* you coming home?' she asked.

'Well,' said Jacob, 'I'm working at the hotel till October and then Maud and I plan to go and visit Pompeii and possibly Rome if the money lasts. I expect I'll be back at the end of November. What I suggest is that you and Dad sit down together and make a list of all the advantages of staying together and another list of all the disadvantages. You could start the advantage list by noting that you will be sparing Hannah and me a great deal of unhappiness.'

'I know but—'

'And if you want any help, don't hesitate to email me. In fact, when you complete your lists, you can send them to me if you like.'

'Thank you but—'

'And in the meantime, try to get some exercise. It will do you good. At your age that's very important.'

What Alberta did not – could not – say to Evie or Lionel or Hannah or Jacob was that her relationship with Tony had never been designed to last. It was like a temporary classroom, erected for a specific and transient purpose and, as with so many temporary classrooms, it had somehow become permanent.

She and Tony had been drawn together by the need for comfort rather than love. Each had regarded the other as a plaster that would protect the heart during the healing process. When Tony had originally invited her and Hannah to move in with him, it had been on the basis that it was a good interim arrangement while they sorted themselves out. She had known he was still in love with Lydia and *he* had known she was still in love with Ed. Both of them found succour in the fact that the one understood what the other was going through. Tony told her that he never wanted to love anyone as much as he'd loved Lydia and Alberta knew exactly what he meant. As for their own relationship, they took from each other physical and emotional comfort and expected little else.

The arrival of Jacob had, it was true, rather undermined the practical nature of their relationship. But even then, neither of them had fully grasped the fact that a baby might change everything. When Tony had suggested the move to Bath, he was quick to preface the idea with a laughing promise that she could leave whenever she wanted.

In fact, Alberta had loved Bath from the moment she arrived. Hannah had run straight out into the garden and made it quite clear she loved it too. The small primary school was perfect and was just ten minutes' walk away. Alberta was very fond of Evie and Lionel and she relished the fact that the house was minutes away from hills and fields.

For a long time, they *had* been happy. Evie was right about that. Tony made her laugh and she made Tony laugh, even if she wasn't always sure why. Hannah adored Tony and her feelings were fully reciprocated; from the very beginning he had treated her as if she were his daughter. Lionel and Evie were terrific grandparents, available on request but never intrusive. They had all been happy.

What Alberta did not say to Evie or Lionel or Hannah or Jacob was that the end had come about not because she was derailed by family tragedy or mid-life depression or hormonally induced restlessness. Certainly, she and Tony had fallen out over the sordid revelations resulting from Pa's death and it was true that their arguments had taken on a bitterness that had hitherto been absent. But, as she pointed out to Tony when he finally came home after that scene in the garden, he would never have reacted with such anger if something else hadn't happened. Something *had* happened. Lydia had married again and Tony had discovered that the plaster hadn't worked. Lydia had fallen in love and Lydia's happiness had prompted Tony to take a long, painful look at what he didn't have with Alberta.

She had said all this to him and he had not disputed it, for which she was grateful. What he did do was to throw the ball back at her. He had watched her, he said, that evening he brought Daniel Driver round to supper. 'I've never seen you like that before,' he said. 'Your eyes were sparkling, you never stopped talking, you were flirting . . .'

'I was *not* flirting!' Alberta protested. 'I actually thought he was conceited and arrogant!'

'You fancied him like hell,' Tony said and even as she denied it, she remembered the moment she had first seen him at the Bath Spa. She had stared at his long, lean torso and had, if only for a few moments, wondered what it would be like to have that torso pressed against her.

It was, nevertheless, an unfair comment to make. The fact that she had been physically attracted to a thrice-married, probable ex-alcoholic, probable ex-drug addict, was hardly on a par with Tony realizing that he still loved his ex-wife. She had never, as she told Tony with righteous indignation, dreamt of having a relationship with Disgusting Daniel and not just because she knew that Disgusting Daniel would never even consider having an affair with *her*. Men like Daniel flirted automatically with all women but men like Daniel only bedded pert bottoms and flat tummies. The only reason Tony brought up Daniel was because he didn't want to face the fact that it was he, as much as Alberta, who was responsible for the end of their partnership.

The one unexpected advantage of Pa's death was that Pa had made it easy for her to leave. Throughout the long hours in which she had waited for Tony to come home, she had sorted out her future with an efficiency that she had never known she possessed. She had studied job vacancies and letting agency details on the Internet. Christopher had told her how much money she had been left in the will and when she would receive it. She had had an extremely difficult conversation with Diana but they had finally worked out the terms of her departure from the business.

As for the immediate future, she had made a tentative suggestion to Christopher. Her brother, after expressing his shocked dismay at her decision to leave Tony, said he would first need to consult Helen. The consultation had been very short since he had rung back within thirty minutes. Alberta would move into their spare room and in return she would agree to cook for them as often as she could manage. Alberta put down the phone and set about writing a job application.

Consequently, when Tony came back, she was able to tell him *what* she intended to do as well as why. She had expected him to try to talk her out of leaving. Instead, he agreed that things weren't working. He took issue over the reasons for this state of affairs but he accepted Alberta's proposed solution and, in fact, seemed relieved that she had made the decision for him. He opened a bottle of wine and they sat down and talked about finances and the children and he smiled at her just like he used to, just as if nothing had happened. He raised his glass and said he hoped she'd be happy and she raised her glass and said she hoped he would be too. It was all very civilized.

# CHAPTER SEVENTEEN

## *The Lone Granger*

Alberta had decided to move away from Bath for two reasons. The first was in order to be near her children. Jacob had a place waiting for him at University College London and Hannah had no plans to leave the capital. The second was less easy to explain but its origin lay in an accusation levelled at her some weeks ago.

This often happened to Alberta. She supposed it was because her brain took rather a long time to process all the data it received on a daily basis. Often, someone would say something to her and she would hardly notice; the comment would drop like a lead capsule into the murky pond that was her brain. And then, bit by bit, it would release half-formed thoughts and ideas that would be virtually impenetrable at first but would gradually coalesce into a pristine, perfectly formed message.

When she was fourteen she had a boyfriend called Frankie. Over breakfast one day, her mother made a random observation – Marma was prone to random observations. 'Have you noticed,' she said, 'that Frankie always shows his gums when he smiles?' Marma hadn't meant anything derogatory by it, it was simply something that had occurred to her, and Alberta had not even bothered to respond, being far more preoccupied with a magazine questionnaire aimed at helping her discover if she was an introvert or an extrovert. Yet four weeks later she broke up with Frankie and it was mainly because poor Frankie's gums were now seriously irritating her.

It had happened again a year or so later. She overheard Aunt Hilda tell Pa, 'Of course, Christopher has inherited all the brains.' Pa had replied that that might be so but he'd rather live with Alberta than with Christopher and Aunt Hilda had said that was only because Alberta could cook. Pa had laughed but said quite seriously that in his view cooking was a grossly underrated talent and that Philippa's culinary gifts had been a major factor in his decision to marry her. At the time, Alberta had been rather miffed that her intellectual faculties had been so summarily dismissed but it was that snatch of conversation that had led to her deciding to go to domestic science college rather than to university.

And then when she married Ed, her friend, Sally, said to her after the wedding that she had always known Alberta was a one-man woman and that once she had found her man, she would never fall in love with anyone else. When she thought about it now, Alberta felt that it was one of those gushing, sentimental comments that a girl tends to make at a wedding after drinking excessive amounts of champagne. Nevertheless, it remained in a dark corner of Alberta's mind and she was sure it had been a major factor in her later deciding to throw in her lot with Tony.

And now, Alberta was haunted by an angry comment

her daughter had made weeks ago. Hannah had accused her of being unable to cope on her own. Admittedly, she was in a state about Alfie at the time and had apologized later but it continued to hurt.

The reason *why* it hurt was because Alberta wasn't at all sure it wasn't true. She had never, ever lived on her own. She had lived with her parents and then with Ed and then with Ed's parents and then with Tony. It was time to stand on her own two feet and that meant leaving Bath. In moving to a strange new environment, she would prove she was bold and brave and fearless. She even allowed herself to indulge in a pleasant daydream in which Hannah would admit that she had gravely underestimated her all these years.

Before that could happen, Alberta had to make a success of her fearless new life. She did see that it was not particularly fearless to move in with her brother and sister-in-law but it was, after all, temporary and she was anxious to make it clear to all her family that it was only agreed on the basis of a sound business proposition. In this spirit she had asked if she could invite Hannah and Kitty to lunch on Sunday, and in the same spirit she had made it clear that, on her arrival in Brixton, she would be going straight out to buy supplies for both the lunch and the rest of the week.

When her taxi deposited her at Christopher's house, her new landlord and landlady rushed out to greet her and insisted on taking her cases up to her room for her. Christopher announced that he and Helen were taking her out to dinner that evening and that, furthermore, they were happy to go out for lunch the following day as well.

Alberta blinked and said quickly, 'I would love to go out with you both tonight but I *want* to do lunch tomorrow. You have to realize I can only stay here and be *happy* to stay here, if you help me keep to the terms of our arrangement.'

'Of course,' Christopher said, 'but—'

'I think,' Helen said, 'we should leave Alberta to unpack. Alberta, the shower room next door is for your use alone. You can do whatever you like in the kitchen. There is a set of keys for you on the hall table. We are going out at seven. Make yourself at home.' She took Alberta's hands in both of hers, gave her a quick kiss on the cheek and ushered her husband out.

As soon as the door shut behind them, Alberta sat down on the bed and swallowed hard. She and Tony had only stayed here a couple of times and she had forgotten that the bed squeaked at the slightest touch.

The room had a large airy window but otherwise there was little to recommend it. It was dominated by a huge, oppressive wardrobe and an equally ugly chest of drawers. Above the bed was a framed, faded print of a pheasant shoot with two dead pheasants in the foreground. Alberta stood up and went to the wardrobe and opened the door. There was a mirror on the inside of the door. Not only was it cracked but it made her look curiously square-shaped and even shorter than her five feet and one inch.

She shut the door and looked around at the heavy maroon curtains and the threadbare carpet. She tried not to think of the bedroom she had left behind, with its brass bedstead, soft coffee-coloured carpet and cream curtains. She had known what this would be like and, besides, it was only for a few weeks and then she would be moving into a flat of her own.

Don't panic, Alberta told herself and promptly did so. What had she *done*? Had she torn up a perfectly good life in Bath in a moment of *temper*? What was she doing in this depressing and alien house? There was a basin near the window with a blue plastic beaker by the cold tap. She filled it with water and drank it greedily. Then she sat down on the protesting bed and reminded herself of a few facts. She had broken up with Tony because she was no longer content to be with a man who still held a candle for his ex-wife. She had broken up with Tony because he respected her so little that he actually believed her capable of sending an anonymous package to her mother. And when she had told him she thought their relationship had exceeded its sell-by date, she had seen in his eyes that he thought so too.

So. There she was. Or rather, *here* she was and she might as well make the most of it. She took her clothes out of her suitcase, carried the empty trolley bag downstairs, scooped up her keys from the table in the hall and sallied forth towards the shops. She had food to buy!

At first, she felt a little self-conscious, with the tartan pull-along in tow. In fact, within a few minutes of hitting the high street, she realized she had no need to worry about attracting attention since she could never compete with the vast diversity of colour and noise and people around her. In Bath, most of the population were white and were either on their phones or consulting their shopping lists or talking to their companions in discreet murmurs. Here, the air was full of a hundred different languages and in the course of just ten minutes, she passed two full-blown arguments, one joyful reunion and three heated discussions, any of which she would have loved to listen in to. She was given flyers about a gospel church choir, a second-hand boot sale and at least three different art exhibitions. She was offered drugs once and love and redemption through Jesus twice and narrowly missed having her feet flattened by a boy on a purple bike. She returned to the house, exhausted but also rather exhilarated. She had wanted change and she had certainly got it.

There was no sign of either Christopher or Helen and at first she assumed they had gone out. Then she heard a slight cough from an upstairs room and realized they were probably working in their studies. This was a very different household from the one she had left behind. She wondered if they would like a cup of tea and decided not to bother them. She opened the fridge and stared at the contents: two pints of milk, two antique courgettes, a half-empty tin of baked beans, a pack of cheese slices and a carton of Flora.

She closed the fridge door and began to unpack her purchases. Whatever else she did, she would enjoy giving her brother and sister-in-law some proper food for a change. She was touched that they were taking her out to dinner and her appreciation of their kindness only intensified her guilt at approaching the meal with such a lack of enthusiasm.

Christopher was a good man, certainly the most conscientious man Alberta knew. As a teenager, he had been a passionate socialist and had spent most of his weekends volunteering his services at a hostel for refugees where he spent many hours teaching basic English. He was uninterested in pop music and parties and as far as Alberta knew he had only had one serious girlfriend, who had been prone to both acne and depression. Alberta presumed he had liked the fact that the girl had hair like Joan Baez.

Christopher met Helen while he was teaching at the University of Toronto. Helen was a schoolteacher and they met while attending a lecture on the fate of the planet. They married quietly a couple of months later. Christopher sent Alberta a letter – she still had it – in which he wrote that he had been impressed by the happiness she had found with Ed and, until Helen, had never expected to be blessed in the same way. He said Helen was beautiful. He enclosed a photograph which indicated that while love might not be blind, it could certainly be short-sighted.

While Helen was pregnant with Richard, Christopher wrote the book – *Chaucer and the Twentieth Century* – that would make his name. Two years later, he accepted a place at University College and bought the house in Brixton, and had remained in both places ever since. Helen had taken a variety of teaching posts and was now Head of Geography at a comprehensive in Hackney.

Their son, after a difficult adolescence, had developed into a charming and cheerful young adult who loved all things American. He was now at Harvard and had a stunning girlfriend called Macy, who modelled part-time. His stated aim was to live in New York and make as much money as possible. His parents regarded him with a mixture of awe and affection. They could not understand where the confident, good-looking young capitalist came from but they adored him nonetheless.

Alberta loved her brother and was very fond of Helen. She had never been close to either of them since goodness was not a characteristic that encouraged intimacy and Christopher and Helen were full of goodness. They abhorred selfishness, resentment, envy and greed. Naturally, Alberta abhorred them too but it was a sad fact that most personal conversations, unseasoned by such emotions, remained anaemic in character.

There was also the fact that the main link between her and Christopher – their parents – was a subject they had agreed to steer clear of many years ago, when, two months after they had returned to Britain for good, Christopher and Helen had brought their small son down to Bath for the weekend.

Alberta had never asked her mother why she hadn't contacted her during her year in Canada. She had assumed Marma would give her an explanation on her return and when Marma failed to do so, Alberta retreated into injured silence.

At some point on the Saturday evening, Alberta tried to express her bitterness and bewilderment to her visitors. Christopher made some awkward comments about Marma's fragile emotional state at that time and added that Alberta had constantly been in her thoughts. Alberta said that was all very well but any normal mother would have rushed home to comfort a grieving daughter. Christopher blustered again about Marma's health and eventually lost his temper and told his sister she was being completely unfair and uncharitable. Alberta lost her temper too and the evening ended in tears and recriminations. It was the first proper quarrel they had had since the time Christopher had, with complete fairness, accused her of stealing his Pocket Solitaire. The next morning they both apologized and agreed to avoid the subject in future.

Now, of course, Alberta knew that Marma's long exile was a probable consequence of her ill-advised affair with the Repton man. She could remember Christopher telling her that she had no right to judge Marma when she had no idea of the state of her mind at the time. She had responded with what she felt was a reasonable observation that of course she had no idea of Marma's state of mind because Marma had never bothered to tell her what it was.

Most siblings in the current circumstances would probably debate endlessly the latest revelations about their parents. If Christopher was less partisan towards Marma and less high-minded about everything, it might be easier. As it was, Alberta felt that she would only talk about the recent press revelations if Christopher brought up the subject.

So it was with mixed feelings that she walked down the stairs at seven that evening and met her dinner companions in the hall. She could not, however, help smiling when she saw Christopher's face. Christopher had the same small eyes and narrow face of his father but where Pa had always exuded authority, Christopher's features had often reminded Alberta of a sparrow anxiously foraging for food. And Christopher did love his food. Tonight, his eyes were alight with anticipation and he smiled happily at the sight of his sister and said, 'I've been thinking and thinking about what I want to eat. Shall we go?'

On the walk to the restaurant, Christopher was like a small child on a birthday outing. He told Alberta that they had been to this particular place twice before and then proceeded to tell her exactly what he had eaten. On stepping through the sacred portals, they were shown to their table and Alberta watched Christopher and Helen discuss the menu with all the gravity of heads of state at an international summit. Finally, the choice was made and Christopher sighed with pleasure, poured out the wine and sat back in his seat.

'Well,' said Helen, 'isn't this lovely?' She looked rather summery in a green linen dress and a pink cardigan. Helen was one of those women who look better as they grow older. When Alberta had first met her, she had been thin and angular and her limbs had looked as if they had been insecurely fastened to her body. Her teeth had been prominent – Ed had declared she looked just like his aunt's favourite horse – and her hair had been tied back in a limp ponytail. She had clearly been in awe of Alberta, possibly because at the time Alberta exuded the confidence that comes from being loved by a gorgeous husband and a beautiful baby daughter. The next time Alberta saw her was when they returned to England with their small son. Helen was a fearful and nervous mother and told Alberta more than once that she wished she could be more like her.

Now, as Alberta smiled at her sister-in-law, she couldn't help thinking that fate had somehow rewarded Helen for her youthful humility and punished Alberta for her equally youthful assumption that her life would always be perfect. Helen had a son who was frequently in touch with his parents and who confided in them freely. Alberta had two children who told her as little as possible about their personal affairs and who often talked to her in the patient tones that doctors reserve for their most tedious patients. Helen was still happily married to Christopher whereas Alberta had just left a man who, in twenty years, had never stopped loving his ex-wife. Helen's hair was now short, she had put on some much-needed weight and she certainly bore no resemblance to horses. Alberta currently felt as attractive as an old sponge.

'I think we should make a toast to you, Alberta,' Helen said. 'Let us drink to . . . to your new . . .'

Alberta was about to suggest the word *life*, but in Helen's moment of hesitation, she understood that her brother and his wife regarded her separation from Tony as a temporary aberration, perhaps even a whim. Were Alberta to provide the word *life*, she would probably provoke a discussion in which she could properly enlighten them. Of course, in the process, she would be able to hear their own views on the virtues of Tony, the damage to her children as a consequence of the split, the need to think carefully before breaking up the family and the advisability of seeking some sort of therapy.

'Why don't we toast my new job?' Alberta suggested.

They duly did so. Helen congratulated Alberta on finding new employment so quickly and Alberta said she had been very lucky since it was the first job she'd applied for. She had instantly clicked with her new boss at the interview. Francesca Simon was charming and dynamic and just a little scary. The company, the Quality Food Company, was only five years old but had an enviable list of well-heeled and well-connected customers. Christopher and Helen were convinced Alberta would have no trouble settling into her new position there. This would have been more reassuring if it weren't for the fact that they were impressed by *anyone* who could cook a half-decent meal.

After their first course arrived, Alberta asked about her nephew. Richard, unsurprisingly, was doing brilliantly and had sent a hilarious email just that morning. He'd spent a weekend with his girlfriend's parents and had met her grandfather, who kept pushing his head forward in the manner of a tortoise and who loved to hear Richard speak because he adored the English accent.

Helen asked about Jacob and Alberta told them about Jacob's surprisingly good exam results and wished *she* could refer to some hilarious emails too.

It was during the main course that Christopher refilled their glasses and cleared his throat. 'I think I should tell you,' he said, 'that Helen and I have invited Marma to come and live with us.'

Alberta blinked. 'You'd never get Marma to leave her garden. She loves it.'

'I know she *did* love it,' Christopher said. 'I don't think you understand the pressure she is under, living in that small village. We went there last weekend and Marma met us from the train. Two girls walked past us and when they saw Marma, they started sniggering. I wanted to say something but Marma wouldn't let me. She said that since that horrible interview came out, it has happened a lot. She said she didn't mind, she just ignored it, but I could tell she *was* upset. So I talked to Helen on the train home and Helen agreed we should . . . how did you put it, Helen?'

'I said we should offer her sanctuary!'

'Exactly. At the moment, Marma is determined to stick it out. She says people will soon get bored with talking about her but I'm not so sure. I have told her she has only to ring us and we'll organize everything. That man, Repton, has a lot to answer for. I still can't believe he could stoop to such *baseness*! If the libel laws were halfway decent, I'd take him to court for defamation of character!'

'But basically,' Alberta said tentatively, 'isn't what he says true?'

Christopher and Helen exchanged looks and then at exactly the same moment filled their mouths with chicken. Alberta took a sip of her wine and waited.

'Basically,' Christopher said at last, 'very, very basically, it was true. I suspect Repton made up virtually all the details.'

Alberta took a deep breath. 'So did Marma go out to Canada to help you and Helen with the baby or was it to get away from Peter Repton? Was it to get away from *Pa*?'

'Well,' said Christopher uneasily, 'I suppose there was an element of *escape* in her decision to leave England but I think she would have come out to us anyway. Helen was in a terrible state: she had lost a lot of blood during labour. Richard nearly died and so did she. They both needed looking after.'

'I know they did,' Alberta said quickly, 'I wouldn't dispute that for a moment. And I am not – I promise I am not – going to have a go at Marma. I just would like to understand why she didn't get in touch with me after Ed died.'

Helen shifted in her seat. 'She wasn't well,' she murmured and looked at her husband.

'She was in a very bad state,' Christopher said firmly. 'I know you won't accept this, Alberta, but it's true. I'm convinced she was having a breakdown and yes, in the circumstances, you might think it's odd that she was able to look after her grandchild so well but I don't think it's *that* odd. She knew about babies and she felt safe with babies and she didn't have to explain herself to babies. She didn't know what to say to you, so she said nothing. She didn't know what to say to us either for a lot of the time but she always knew what to say to Richard. I know you've always been hurt by Marma's silence and I'm sorry about that but at the time she wasn't capable of helping you, however much she might have wanted to. You may doubt me if you want to, but I am telling you the truth.'

'I believe you,' Alberta said. She could see that Christopher had worked himself into a state and tried to lighten the atmosphere. 'What a rat that man Repton is! Tony reckoned he was out for a quick buck after his wife booted him out.'

'Tony,' Christopher said with great deliberation, 'is very perceptive.'

'He's such a lovely man,' Helen sighed.

'He is,' Alberta said lightly. 'You know he always said Richard should go into politics? Do you think that is likely?' She was back on safe ground. They talked about Richard for the rest of the meal.

It was only later, as Christopher was collecting their coats, that Helen took Alberta's arm. She whispered quickly, 'If you could have seen her! She cried for you so much! She could have flooded Canada with her tears!'

Sunday lunch the next day was surprisingly successful. Alberta had been dreading an inquisition from Hannah about her departure from Bath but Hannah was far too well-mannered to make a scene in the presence of her aunt and uncle. Conversation flowed easily not least because at every available moment, Kitty and Helen and Christopher praised the quality of the beef and the Yorkshire puddings and especially the gravy. By the time Christopher was on his second helping of lemon tart, Hannah had forgotten she was cross with her mother and Alberta was sufficiently relaxed to help herself to a second glass of Christopher's excellent wine.

Kitty was in particularly good spirits. She had learnt on Friday that she was to be part of the team that would be going to the Cannes TV Festival in October.

'I'm so glad you're doing well,' Alberta said. 'I thought you were thinking of looking for somewhere else.'

'Basically,' Kitty said, 'everything's changed since Conrad and I became friends. He supports me and I support him and we're both stronger as a result. I never thought I'd say this but work is actually fun.'

'It's so nice when that happens,' Alberta said. She raised her glass to her lips and sipped her wine thoughtfully. 'I expect Conrad fancies you.'

Hannah rolled her eyes. 'I *knew* you'd say that!'

'He doesn't,' Kitty said. 'And even if he did, it wouldn't change anything. We both agree we're rubbish at relationships and it's much safer to be friends.'

'My mother,' Hannah told Kitty, 'has never understood the concept of platonic relationships between men and women. She's always thought *Harrison* fancied me.'

'I have a theory,' Kitty said, taking off her glasses and rubbing them with her sleeve, 'I think he might be gay.'

'He might just be confused,' Alberta said. 'Or perhaps he bats both ways.'

'Do you think so?' Helen asked. 'How very perceptive of you!'

Alberta tried not to look pleased. She had forgotten there had once been a time when she'd been regarded by Helen as a sophisticated woman about town.

Kitty exchanged glances with Hannah and started giggling. 'I'm sorry,' she said. 'It sounds so funny when you say that.'

'Just because I lived in Cleveland Walk for twenty years,' Alberta said, 'doesn't mean I don't know about things like . . . like that.'

'As a matter of interest,' Hannah said, 'how many people do you know who *do* bat both ways?'

'None,' Alberta conceded. 'At least, none that I *know of*.'

Hannah laughed again but it was a good-humoured laugh and when, a few minutes later, she asked if she could have second helpings, Alberta felt she could at last relax. Hannah might well think her mother had made a mess of things – an opinion with which Alberta was ready to concur – but at least she had stopped looking at her as if she was beyond the pale.

When they finally left, Alberta felt happier than she had done for weeks. Perhaps now she was in London, she would have a chance to get to know her daughter better.

She wondered if Marma ever had similar thoughts about *her*. It occurred to her that she had spent far too much time thinking about her own unhappiness since Pa's death and far too little time thinking about Marma. She must be pretty lonely living in a village which had by all accounts turned its back on her. Then there was the whispered comment made by Helen last night. Alberta wondered why Helen had waited until Christopher was out of earshot before telling her that.

She spent the rest of the afternoon clearing up the lunch, having had to virtually push Helen out of the kitchen. She then set about making a shepherd's pie and a lasagne before returning to her room, picking up her phone and punching in a number. 'Marma?' she said. 'Are you busy tomorrow? I wondered if I could come and stay for a few days.'

# CHAPTER EIGHTEEN

## *Once Upon a Time in Hampshire*

Alberta emerged from the underground onto the busy concourse of the railway station. She was checking the platform she needed when she heard her name being called. She looked round and saw a well-dressed woman, with glossy black hair, waving her right arm energetically. Her left arm was wound round the waist of the tall, equally well-dressed man beside her.

'Berta!' the woman called. 'I knew it was you! I'd recognize that crazy blonde topknot anywhere!'

Alberta put an instinctive hand to her hair and her brain did a quick mental scan as she walked towards the couple: Lizzie Masters PAST – malicious, poisonous, evil, pretty friend from childhood whose parents had been equally unreliable friends of *her* parents; Lizzie Masters PRESENT – still pretty, well-off judging by the shoes and the handbag, new relationship almost certainly, smug, very definitely. Damn!

'Hi, Lizzie,' she said. 'How clever of you to recognize me! How *are* you?'

'I am *so* well! And this is Jeremy! Isn't he gorgeous?'

'Lizzie, you're embarrassing me,' Jeremy murmured. He didn't look embarrassed at all.

'I can't believe it's you!' Lizzie said. 'I was talking about you only last week. The last time I saw you was at your husband's funeral! *Doesn't* time fly? Jeremy, do you remember we talked about Berta's family at Tiffany's dinner party on Saturday?' She dropped her voice by a fraction. 'You must remember, Jeremy. Berta's father was Lord Trussler who died in that brothel and Berta's mother had an affair with a man young enough to be her son.' She turned back to Alberta and smiled sympathetically. 'How *is* poor Lady Trussler? I always thought she was *so* pretty and *so* sweet. I felt *so* sorry for her when I read that piece in the paper about her. She must feel *so* humiliated!'

'I don't see why,' Alberta said lightly. 'It was utter rubbish. I'm not even sure she bothered to read it!'

'She must have done,' Lizzie said. 'Everyone's talking about it. I can't imagine how I'd cope with something like that. I wouldn't be able to leave the house!'

'I'd probably be the same,' Alberta said. 'But then you and I are very different from my mother. I mean, you and I are not particularly attractive and we're not the sort of women people bother to talk about. My mother, on the other hand, is very beautiful and has always been accustomed to being the subject of envious gossip. I must get on or I'll miss my train. I hope you and Johnny are very happy.'

She turned on her heel and walked away, ignoring the shrill response, 'His name's *Jeremy*!'

There was no justice in the world. People like Lizzie should grow into horrible old crones with fat, smelly husbands. Alberta comforted herself with the fact that Jeremy had teeth that were far too white to be natural.

At first, she was too angry to do anything other than look out of the train window and fantasize about bigger and better put-downs she could have said. Finally, she got out her book. She didn't want to think about Lizzie any more.

*Confessions of a Retired Schoolmistress* was turning out to be much better than she had thought it would be. She'd been a little nonplussed when Diana had presented it to her as a farewell gift, expecting it to be a trashy account of barely credible sexual couplings. In fact, thus far at any rate, the salacious episodes were few and far between and were laced with a sharp intelligence and a malicious wit. In her preface, the preposterously named Felicity Fullock – surely a pseudonym – assured her readers that all the names had been changed, which was just as well, Alberta thought, given that the excitable vicar, the gruesome caretaker and the doughnut-loving headmaster had been described with such detached precision.

Alberta settled down to read and became so engrossed that she barely registered the changing landscape. It was only when she was one stop away from her destination that she abruptly looked up and then down again and frowned. She skimmed through the second half of the chapter once more. It wasn't possible. It had to be a coincidence. She went back to the first page of the book and noticed that Ms Fullock had a website. It was probably nothing, nothing at all; nevertheless, Alberta knew she would be sending Ms Fullock an email on her return to London.

* * *

Marma flung open the door and said, 'You should have rung me from the station! I would have collected you!'

'I enjoyed the walk.' Alberta came in and gave her mother a slightly awkward kiss. 'It's lovely to be here.'

'I've put you in your usual room,' Marma said. 'Why don't you take up your bag and make yourself comfortable? We'll have lunch when you come down.'

As usual, Marma had put flowers in the room. Alberta took off her jacket and went over to the window. The garden looked a little shaggy, which was worrying. There were even weeds in the front border.

Alberta inspected her appearance in the mirror and wondered if perhaps it wasn't finally time to get rid of the long, thick hair she kept so precariously knotted above her head. Then she realized she was only thinking this because of the evil Lizzie's comment. She went downstairs.

On the table, Marma had set out a bowl of salade niçoise, a slab of Brie and a newly baked loaf. She had opened a bottle of Sauvignon and was pouring wine into two glasses.

'Marma!' Alberta exclaimed. 'This is a feast!'

'I enjoyed preparing it. Sit down and tuck in. I want to hear all your news. How are you finding London? Of course, you've only been there a couple of days! Is it all a bit strange?'

Alberta sat down and took a sip of her wine. 'I don't know yet. I've hardly had a moment to myself. I went out with Christopher and Helen on Saturday evening and Hannah and Kitty came to lunch yesterday.'

'How *is* Hannah? Do you think she's still missing that very unsatisfactory boyfriend?'

'It's hard to say. You know what Hannah's like. I hope I'll see more of her now.'

'I'm sure you will. And when do you start your new job?'

'I'm going in on Thursday and Friday but it starts properly next week.'

Marma beamed. 'It was clever of you to find a new job so quickly and to find it on the Internet! Do you think Jacob would give me some lessons when he gets back from France? I do feel it's high time I became part of the web thing. I've got a book for beginners but I don't even understand the first sentence . . . Alberta, you have hardly anything on your plate, do take some more.'

'I'm fine, honestly. I'm going to have some of that delicious bread in a moment.' Alberta hesitated. 'I'm sorry I haven't been down for so long. The last few weeks have been crazy.'

'I quite understand,' Marma said briskly. 'I'm just pleased to see you *now*.'

'So,' Alberta said, 'how *are* you?'

'I have a new project! See if you can guess! *Buenas dias! Como estas?*'

'You're learning Spanish?'

'*Excelente! Es muy dificile!* I've bought a dictionary and a book of exercises and a set of CDs. The man who does them has the most marvellous voice and you just know he'd never get cross however many times you muddled your tenses. He has two students, a boy and a girl, and he teaches them phrases and sentences and leaves pauses for me to say them first. The girl is rather good and the poor boy is rather hopeless and I've become very fond of all three of them. I know my numbers up to twenty and I can tell how to turn right, though I always forget how to turn *left. Espero aprender mucho!'*

'I haven't a clue what you said,' Alberta confessed, 'but it sounds good. You should have gone to Madrid rather than Crete.'

'Oh but Crete was lovely! It was *muy guapa*! Hilda and I went to Knossos. It's where Theseus was supposed to fight the Minotaur and it did look just like a place where a minotaur would live, but apparently it never actually existed, which was a little disappointing. We had a wonderful holiday and Hilda was very sweet, although she read this terribly sad book about Charlotte Brontë and she insisted on reading out all the really sad bits – and there are a great *many* sad bits in Charlotte Brontë's life. Her sisters kept dying and her brother died and her father died and the teacher she fell in love with didn't fall in love with her, and then, of course, *she* died as well. Hilda has this theory that now we're so old we ought to prepare ourselves for death by reading about the deaths of other people, but it does seem an awful waste of time to me. I said to Hilda, "You might die in your sleep, Hilda, and how do you prepare for *that*?" But Hilda is convinced she won't. She says it's all a matter of self-discipline.'

'I have to say,' Alberta mused, 'Aunt Hilda would not be my first choice of holiday companion.'

'I did get a bit tired of Charlotte Brontë,' Marma conceded, 'but otherwise we got on very well. And the sea is so wonderful there, so clear and so warm! I didn't want to come home at all.'

'I'm not surprised.' Alberta speared a piece of tuna with

her fork and asked hesitantly, 'How's it been since you got back?'

'Well,' said Marma, 'I've had one *serious* drama. Keith – you remember Keith? He's been helping in the garden for four years now – he's done his back in and won't be able to do anything in the garden for at least six weeks. I'm trying to keep up but it's difficult and—'

'I'll help you,' Alberta said. 'It's a beautiful day. We'll do it together.'

'*Excelente!*' Marma said. '*Muy, muy excelente!*'

Later, Alberta remembered that afternoon as strangely dream-like. They did not bring up Alberta's separation from Tony or Peter Repton's revelations about Marma. Instead, they concentrated on weeding the garden while making random observations about the tame robin hovering nearby, the unknown creatures who were attacking the delphiniums, the particular delight of the climate in September and the possible frustration felt by slow-moving slugs.

At four, they had a break for tea and shortbread and sat on the patio discussing the advantages and disadvantages of bedding plants. Almost, one could imagine that everything was as it had been before Pa died.

Except, of course, this rural idyll was anything but and Alberta had her first indication that evening of just how bad things were. They were drinking coffee and Alberta had almost jokingly brought up the subject of Christopher's suggestion that Marma move in with him and Helen. 'You do realize,' she said, 'that Christopher hopes you'll save him from a lifetime of undercooked meat casseroles and overcooked cabbage?'

'I'd be happy to do so,' Marma said. 'I would only go there if I thought I could be useful.'

Alberta raised a disbelieving eyebrow. 'You're not seriously considering it? You would *hate* to live in London! You adore the countryside. You can identify virtually every bird in the area, you know the names of cowslips and campion and chickweed and a thousand other wild flowers and you love the smells of newly mown lawn and your nicotiana at night. I don't think I've met anyone who loves a garden as much as you do.'

'Yes,' Marma said, 'but things change.' She glanced up at the clock and said, 'There's a documentary on orang-utans starting now. Shall we watch it?'

So they did and by the time it had ended, Alberta felt the time for further probing had gone.

A second indication came the following morning. Marma wanted to make an onion tart for lunch and suggested they drive to Marlborough to buy the onions.

'The weather's far too good to waste time in the car,' Alberta said. 'I think we should carry on with the garden. Why don't we walk to the village and get the onions there?'

'If you get them for me,' Marma said, 'I'll make the pastry and then we can do the garden together when you come back. That would be *muy fantastico.*'

It was only as Alberta walked down the lane with Marma's shopping basket in her hand that it occurred to her that Marma might have wanted to buy onions in Marlborough because she didn't want to buy them in the village. The thought was reinforced by the fact that she was passing the Cartwrights' house at the time and she could have sworn she saw a curtain twitch.

The village shop was excellent. It sold locally grown produce and organic meat from the farm up the road. It sold newspapers and magazines and toiletries and cards and a decent variety of general groceries. It was also at the moment empty of customers. Mrs Webster was behind the counter talking to her daughter and another girl. She stopped talking when Alberta came in and all three of them stared at her.

Alberta smiled at Mrs Webster's daughter. It seemed to be no time at all since Kathryn had developed from being a sweet, chubby-faced baby to a shrill, pig-tailed child to her present incarnation as a plump, spotty teenager with Cleopatra-like black eye-liner and a tiny skirt. 'Hello, Kathryn,' she said. 'No school today?'

'The teachers have an in-training day,' Mrs Webster said. 'I can't think why they don't do it in the holidays.' She smiled at Alberta. 'It's nice to see you. Are you here for a long visit?'

'Only until tomorrow unfortunately. My mother wants some onions but I think I'll have a couple of the raspberry punnets too. They look terrific.'

'They're a lot better than the supermarket ones. Help yourself. We haven't seen Lady Trussler for a long time. I hope she's all right?'

Alberta turned suddenly as she heard a muffled giggle and was in time to see the two girls nudge each other. Mrs Webster must have noticed the smirks as well because she said sharply, 'If you two girls have nothing better to do, you can go and clear up the crates at the back.'

Kathryn rolled her eyes and said, 'We're going for a *walk*! Come on, Tracy.' She flounced out of the shop, her little skirt struggling bravely to conceal her bottom as she did so. Tracy muttered something that might have meant goodbye and followed her friend outside.

Alberta started filling a brown paper bag with onions.

Mrs Webster gave an embarrassed cough. 'I'm sorry about that,' she said. 'People do like to talk and with Lady Trussler, as you know, there's so very much to talk *about*! Kathryn and her friends can't help but pick things up and they seem to have this knack of always being around whenever there's even a hint of gossip.'

Alberta put the bag of onions on the counter and said, 'I'll collect the raspberries on the way out.'

Mrs Webster's face went a dull pink. 'Just because people talk . . . I don't want you to think . . . I've always thought your mother was a very nice lady and I still do, no matter what most people round here might say.'

Mrs Webster might possess the tact of one of the orang-utans in the film last night but she did mean well and although Alberta's eyes glittered at the reference to 'most people', she simply nodded and took her purse from her bag. When she came out of the shop, she could see the two girls sitting on the bench by the village pond. She wondered if they had been the ones who had enraged Christopher at the station.

She walked back up the lane and tried to imagine how her mother must feel. Marma had always been in and out of the shop. Christopher had warned Alberta that the local gossip was becoming unpalatable and Alberta should have realized that Marma would no longer feel easy about shopping in the village. Marma had always possessed an other-worldly quality, an ability to sail through life, unencumbered by other people's perceptions of her. Now, it seemed she was more vulnerable than Alberta had thought.

And what a pitiless community this turned out to be! For all her failings, Marma was a kind and courteous woman who would never dream of judging anyone on the hearsay of others. Perhaps she was right to consider leaving the village. It was perfectly obvious that the village didn't deserve to have her.

Despite having no coherent plan in her head, Alberta stopped outside the Cartwright house and turned into the Cartwright drive. Someone in there had been watching her; the door opened almost as soon as she rang the bell. Maurice smiled and said, 'Hello there!'

Joan stepped out from behind her husband. 'Alberta! How *are* you?'

'I'm very well,' Alberta said. 'I'm staying with Marma and I thought how nice it would be if you could both come and join us for a drink this evening. I'm leaving tomorrow and I'd hate to go without seeing you.'

If Joan was surprised or embarrassed by the invitation, she gave no sign of it. 'That is very nice of you,' she said, 'and you know me too well to expect me to give you some feeble excuse as to why we can't come. If we did come over, it would be an act of complete hypocrisy and whatever else I am, I am not a hypocrite. I feel very sorry for you and I feel very sorry for your children. I have to tell you that your parents have turned out to be very different from the couple we thought were our friends. To be honest,' Joan said with a sigh, folding her arms and adopting a more-in-sorrow-than-in-spite smile, 'had we known what your father was like, we would never have gone near him and now your mother has been shown to have an equally tenuous grasp on what is decent and true. In the circumstances, it would be utterly wrong of us to accept Philippa's hospitality. Perhaps it's unfair but I feel they have both betrayed our trust over the years. I know this must all be deeply unpleasant for you, but I have to tell you what I really think.'

'I assure you,' Alberta said, 'there is no need for you to feel sorry for me and my children. Hannah and Jacob and I are all very proud of Pa and Marma. And if I may follow your example and tell you what I really think . . .'

'Of course you may,' said Joan graciously.

Alberta paused to think of a suitably scathing and superior summation of her thoughts. 'Screw you both,' she said. 'Screw you both with knobs on.'

She had calmed down by the time she reached The Gables. She told Marma she had enjoyed the walk and that Mrs Webster had asked after her. The visit to the Cartwrights had, however, crystallized a feeling that had been growing in her ever since she'd arrived. She was going to have to bring up the Repton interview – preferably over a very large glass of wine.

In her present mood, Alberta decided to forgo the decorous weeding she had planned to do and instead marched over to the back border with the garden fork and spent a couple of satisfying hours digging out the ground elder and imagining the lanky weeds were bits of Joan Cartwright as she flung them into the wheelbarrow.

She was quite surprised when Marma called her in to lunch. It was extraordinary how quickly time passed when one was furious. As she walked back to the house, she wondered if there was a tactful way in which to bring up the subject of her mother's ex-lover.

When she sat down at the table, she realized there *was* no tactful way. 'Marma,' she said, 'I don't want to leave without mentioning that interview with Peter Repton. I just want to tell you that I thought it was outrageous and I didn't believe half of it. I think the man is a total rat. I actually think *you* come out of it rather well.'

Marma set the onion tart on the table and removed her oven gloves from her hands. 'Would you dress the salad, Alberta?' she asked. She cut two slices of the tart and with a palette knife eased one of them onto Alberta's plate and the second onto her own.

Alberta dressed the salad, put some on her plate and handed the bowl to her mother.

'Thank you,' Marma said. She put some salad onto her plate, took a sip of wine and ate a mouthful of the tart. 'What do you think? Is it all right?' she asked.

'It's delicious,' Alberta said.

Marma glanced in the direction of the window. 'Most of what he says is true,' she said. 'I wish it wasn't. I don't particularly like talking about it because it reminds me of a time when I behaved very foolishly and it's a little humiliating to know that all the world, not least my own daughter, knows now how very foolish I was.'

'That is exactly why I brought up the subject,' Alberta said. She paused. She had spent a long time preparing what she wanted to say and she didn't want to get it wrong. 'You were a middle-aged woman who, I presume, was not as happy as you thought you should be. I can understand that.

I feel the same. In my case, I've decided to leave Tony and Bath and change my life and move to London. In your case, you fell in love with a man who turned out to be a total piece of rubbish. That doesn't make you foolish. Most women fall in love with appalling men at some point in their lives. And I bet that most women reading that interview would be appalled that he could be so un-gallant as to bring up your affair in such a public context. I'm sure you had your reasons for being unfaithful to Pa and I don't expect or need you to tell me what they were.' Alberta hesitated in case Marma *did* want to tell her what the reasons were; if she did, Alberta would be more than ready to listen. 'What's important is that you should realize you have nothing to be ashamed of and you shouldn't let that rat of a man stop you from going to the shop or anywhere else. And if you really feel you can't be happy here any longer, then perhaps you *should* move to London and live with Christopher and Helen.'

'May I ask you a question?' Marma said. 'Is that why you and Tony broke up? You felt you were not as happy as you could be?'

Alberta sighed. 'We always knew,' she said, 'that we both got together for comfort rather than love. We were still in love with our former partners. In the circumstances, it's pretty incredible we lasted as long as we did.'

'I don't think that's true,' Marma said. 'I've always liked Tony. He is a good man. Do you know, he has rung me almost every week since your father died?'

'No,' Alberta said. 'I didn't know that.'

'I always thought you complemented each other beautifully. So you came together for reasons of comfort. Is that so terrible? Being comfortable together is an exceedingly underrated state of being.' She paused to take a sip of wine. 'He's going to be on television in a couple of weeks.'

Alberta shot a startled glance at her mother. 'Who? Tony?'

'Peter,' Marma said, 'Peter Repton. He's been asked onto a daytime programme. They want him to talk about his Great Affair.'

'How utterly nauseating! Will you watch it?'

'They asked me to go on it too.'

'They didn't! You wouldn't!'

'Well,' Marma said, 'I confess I was rather tempted. I thought I could put on an old black dress and a blanket round my shoulders and walk in with a stick and put my hair in a bun and I would go up to Peter and say, "Take me, Peter! The love of your life has returned to you!" It would be so exciting to see what he would do. Don't you think it would be marvellous?'

'Marma,' Alberta said earnestly, 'please tell me you won't do that!'

'I did turn them down,' Marma said. 'In the end, I was just too vain to go on television and make myself look like an old crone.'

'Thank heavens for your vanity,' Alberta murmured. 'And besides—' She stopped as her telephone announced its continued existence with its annoying little tune. Alberta leant back and took the mobile from the dresser.

'Alberta?' The voice sounded breathless. 'It's Francesca Simon. I have a tremendous favour to ask of you. I know you're not supposed to start till Thursday and you were going to have a lovely easy day with Tom explaining everything before he left but I have a *disaster*. Tom has a really bad earache and I've had to send him home. I'm going to take his place in the kitchen this afternoon but tomorrow we have to produce fish pies for eighty and a lorry load of soup and I'm supposed to be meeting two new clients and I hate to ask you but could you possibly come in tomorrow and cook like the world's about to end?'

'Of course,' Alberta said. 'I'll see you in the morning.'

'Alberta!' Francesca sighed. 'You are my *saviour*!'

Alberta put down the phone and raised her eyebrows. 'That was my new boss. She wants me to go in tomorrow. I feel quite nervous!'

'You'll be brilliant,' Marma said. She paused. 'It must have been difficult . . . giving up your business in Bath.'

'I shan't miss working with Diana. I *shall* miss some of my elderly clients. I'd grown so fond of them. I know Diana and Pam intend to do only corporate work in the future and I do feel I've let them down. I hated saying goodbye to them . . .' Alberta blinked and smiled a little too brightly. 'However, onwards and upwards! I suppose I'd better go and pack. I'm sorry I have to leave you.'

'So am I,' Marma said, 'so am I.'

A couple of hours later, Alberta sat back in her seat on the train to London and decided that it was perhaps just as well she had had to leave Marma so suddenly. She was pretty sure that Marma had found it as difficult as she had to discuss such intimate subjects as Pa and Tony and the Repton man. Neither of them was used to talking to the other about such things and it was a little like trying to speak a foreign language: strenuous, stressful, with the ever-present danger that the other might misunderstand what one was trying to say.

Still, she had made some interesting discoveries. It was only after she told her mother that she didn't blame her for being unfaithful to Pa that she realized it was true: she *didn't* blame her. What was even stranger was that she had finally forgiven Marma's puzzling silence in the months after Ed's death. Somewhere, somehow, she had lost the great sack of resentment she had been lugging behind her for so many years. Certainly, Helen's whispered revelation the other night had played a part in that. Christopher had told her she should not blame Marma for not coming home when Ed died. Now, at last, she no longer did so. Marma might not be the most perfect mother in the world – she had after all lumbered her daughter with a terrible name – but Alberta had hardly proved to be the most perfect daughter. She had been so wrapped up in her own grief that she had not given a thought to what it must be like for Marma to face the whispered smiles and the disapproving glances.

While they waited for the train, Alberta told Marma that she must remember that anyone who was rude or unpleasant was someone who was not worth bothering about and that applied particularly to Joan and Maurice Cartwright.

'I don't miss Joan,' Marma said. 'I do miss Maurice.'

And it was then that Alberta realized that she would probably never understand her parents' marriage and she would probably never know exactly what happened when Marma went to Canada for a year, but what she did know was that she didn't like her mother being unhappy and that from now on she would try very hard to help her stop being so. As she got into the train, she remembered the parting words of the red-haired English boy in Mallorca long, long ago. She leant out of the window and waved to Marma and called out, '*Te quiero!*'

# CHAPTER NINETEEN

## *The Beautiful Blonde from Bashful*

All in all, Alberta decided, it was a good thing that her first few days in her new job took place in an atmosphere of panic.

At her interview she had discovered her future employer was nine years younger than she was. Francesca had warned her she would sometimes have to work evenings and weekends and that the job would be physically exhausting. Alberta left the interview feeling old and deflated and tired and was surprised to be offered the job two days later. She was conscious that Francesca was perplexed by the fact that someone of her age was happy to take on a position that had such erratic and demanding hours. Alberta told her she was looking for a challenge, which sounded better than saying she wanted a job that would make her too tired to wonder how she'd managed to mess up her life so spectacularly.

Given that in the company of the glamorous Francesca and the gorgeous assistant cook Jo, Alberta felt as ancient as Methuselah, she had been anticipating her first few days there with the deepest gloom. In fact, from the moment she arrived at the premises in the business park in Vauxhall, she had no time to feel anything at all. On Wednesday, she and Jo cooked industrial quantities of soup and fish pie along with enough chocolate roulades for seventy, one hundred mini Peking duck pancakes with dips, one hundred mini toads in the hole and sufficient smoked mackerel pâté to put her off eating smoked mackerel pâté for at least a month. On Thursday, they prepared a dinner for fifty and in the evening went to the event with Francesca and a small army of waitresses, most of whom seemed to be university students or struggling actresses and all of whom seemed to be utterly beautiful. On Friday they made nothing but canapés and on Saturday morning they made all the food for a child's birthday party in the afternoon, an event which, thankfully, Alberta was not required to attend.

When she finally finished work on Saturday, she was pretty sure that Francesca no longer feared she might be too old for the job and she knew that although Jo and she might be separated by twenty years, they worked extremely well together. Better still, she knew that in Francesca she had an employer who was hard-working, straight-talking and a woman whose good opinion she valued. At home that evening, she was too tired to do anything but sit slumped in front of her brother's television. She was grateful that Christopher and Helen had gone to Hampshire for the weekend. She had an omelette for supper, watched a very bad film about a couple who wanted to murder each other and went to bed at ten o'clock.

* * *

She rang Tony two weeks later and he said, 'Bertie!' with great enthusiasm and then stopped as if he wasn't sure how to continue.

'I've been given a day off on Monday,' she said, 'and so . . .'

'How *is* the job? Is it very different from the Bath operation?'

'I have to work a lot harder and I don't deliver apple pies to nice old ladies or starving widowers. It's all posh charity lunches, directors' dining rooms, weddings and parties. Last week I was out three evenings in a row. That's why Francesca is giving me a day off on Monday. I just thought I ought to let you know I'm planning to come to Bath and collect some things. I can't believe I left my coat behind.'

'Bertie,' Tony said, 'it's good to hear you but you really don't have to let me know when you want to come to Bath. You have a key. You come down whenever you like. It's been your home for goodness knows how long.'

'Well,' Alberta said, 'that's rather the point. It isn't my home any more.'

'That's up to you. As far as I'm concerned, you have a key and you can come and go as you like. You don't need my permission.'

'Thank you. By the way, the girl I cook with, Jo, she's a fan of the Seeds of Persephone.'

'Tell her from me she has excellent taste.'

'I will. Goodbye, Tony.'

'See you, Bertie.'

She wondered when she *would* see him again. She wished he hadn't been so considerate. She almost felt angry with him. How was she supposed to stop missing him as long as he behaved with such good will towards her?

She arrived at Bath Spa Station at midday on Monday and walked up to her former home, wheeling her empty suitcase behind her. The sky was congested with thick grey clouds from which a smattering of rain dropped half-heartedly onto the city. Even in these dispiriting conditions, the long Georgian terraces still looked stunning. Her Brixton residence and the business park in Vauxhall seemed almost like some unconvincing backdrop to an even less convincing play in which the weary heroine makes endless mini Yorkshire puddings while trying to convince her audience she is striking out on a bold and fearless new path.

The chrysanthemums by the gate had come out and the front wall was covered in the peacock-blue flowers of the clematis. Alberta glanced at them before taking out her house keys and letting herself into the house.

There were two notes for her on the hall table. One was in Lionel's flowery writing instructing her to come and have lunch with him when she arrived. The other was from Tony and said simply, 'Bertie, your coat is in Waitrose bag in kitchen.' She could see that Tony had been working in the garden. His mud-caked boots were under the table surrounded by enough crumbs of earth to fill a dustpan twice over. She parked her case by the door and walked through to the kitchen. Given the stringent regulations surrounding her profession, Alberta had always kept it spotless. It was not spotless now. The Sunday paper was spread out on the table, next to a packet of cornflakes, a mug half full of very cold black coffee and an almost empty carton of Flora. She returned it to the fridge and stopped to frown at the contents. There *were* no contents apart from a tub of hummus, two tomatoes, a carton of orange juice and a wrinkled carrot. She closed the door of the fridge and her eyes scanned the sink and the draining board, and she knew she could not go round to Lionel without cleaning them.

When she finally knocked on his door, she was greeted with a warm hug. 'My darling girl,' he said, 'this is *such fun*! Evie's at a conference in Bournemouth and sends her love. I have made my spinach soup for you! Come on in!'

Over lunch, Lionel regaled her with the story of his latest victory over his old sparring partner, Arthur Quiggleton, the result, according to Lionel, of an extraordinarily powerful speech he had made that had proved beyond doubt that Jean-Paul Sartre knew as little about philosophy as he did about fidelity. Arthur had been so devastated by the effect of Lionel's arguments that he had slunk from the meeting without a word and when he'd seen Tony in town on Saturday, he'd—

'How *is* Tony?' Alberta asked and then wished she hadn't as Lionel sighed and said, 'He's all *right,* dear girl, but he's lost . . . What's that French thing people lose when they feel unnecessary? He's lost his *joie de vivre*! I wish you'd come home, old girl, we do miss you! We all miss you!'

Alberta toyed with the piece of bread on her plate. 'I miss you too but . . .'

'You see, what I can't understand,' Lionel said, 'is how all this *happened.* I mean, usually it's easy to see the signs: A stops making B laugh so much, B stops bothering to chat to A, A starts looking at other people, so does B and B falls in love with C who has long since stopped talking to D, and wham, bang, before you know it, a marriage is killed.

But you and Tony have always enjoyed each other's company and you split up so suddenly. It doesn't make *sense.*'

'We split up so suddenly,' Alberta said, 'for the simple reason that we didn't want to go through all those stages and end up hating each other. We knew things were beginning to go wrong and we split up before they could get any worse.'

'Yes, but, my darling girl, if I followed that argument to its logical conclusion, I would cover the garden in tarmac as soon as I saw a weed, I would stop going to my painting classes because I know my friend is better than I am and I would give up driving because I reversed into the gate last week. Isn't it worth taking the risk that things might get worse in order to fight one's hardest to make things better?'

'I think,' Alberta said, 'we both felt pretty sure that things weren't *going* to get better.'

'Do you *still* think so?'

'When I'm not sitting talking to you, I do!' Alberta said. She pushed back her chair, stood up and went over to kiss Lionel's cheek. 'I must go. I'm getting the four-fifteen train and I have to sort through some things.'

'Come again soon,' Lionel said, 'and think about what I said!'

'I always think about what you say. Give my love to Evie.' Alberta kissed him again and made a quick exit back to the other side of the house.

She almost felt sorry for poor Arthur Quiggleton. If she'd spent another four minutes with Lionel, she'd be ringing up Tony, begging him to take her back. She closed the door behind her and let her eyes wander round the hall. She had once caught six-year-old Jacob standing on a chair, scrutinizing his reflection in the mirror there. 'What are you doing?' she had asked and he'd turned and said, 'I'm thinking what a funny sort of boy I am.'

She went through to the sitting room and was struck by the familiar objects on the mantelpiece. There was the wonky little pot that ten-year-old Hannah had made in her art class. A little further along was the small oval frame containing a photo of Jacob at the age of three. He was sitting on the beach with his bucket and spade between his legs and he was laughing. That had been the year they'd gone camping in France and Tony had taught Hannah to swim.

The third item was a small silver cup on the mantelpiece. Alberta picked it up and smiled as she read the inscription: ALBERTA GRANGER: TOP MOTHER. Tony had given it to her a week after Hannah had gone up to university. Alberta swallowed hard and rebuked herself. She had not come here to wallow in nostalgia. She must get on.

It was when she was on the train back to London that she noticed there was something else besides her coat in the Waitrose bag. She pulled out a square package on top of which was a pink envelope with her name scrawled across it.

She tore open the envelope and looked at a pretty card with the word SORRY printed in the form of small roses. Inside was a message that she read once and then immediately read again.

*Dear Bertie,*

*I wanted to tell you on the phone but I funked it. I*

*rang Marma the other day and we were chatting about the Cartwights. She told me she'd discovered it was Joan who sent the newspaper interview to her. Apparently, she found their newspaper bill stuck in the paper. I'm sorry I thought you sent it. I'm sorry about everything. I wish things were different. You will come home for Christmas, won't you?*

*Tony*

Alberta stared out of the window and watched the villages of Bathampton and Bathford slide away from her. That note was so typical of Tony. That *question* was so typical of Tony. What the hell did it mean? Did it mean 'You *WILL* come home for Christmas'? Or did it mean 'You will come home for *CHRISTMAS*'? Most likely, Tony wasn't sure. And what did he mean by 'I wish things were different'? Did he mean that he wished they were still together or did he simply mean he wished he hadn't misjudged her?

She never had been sure what Tony meant when he talked about the two of them. She remembered going out for a curry with him, when she lived with Ed's parents. She'd been moaning about her circumstances, telling him she was going to have to move somewhere else. He'd listened and said carelessly, 'Why don't you move in with me? We can pool our broken hearts. I'm bored with cooking for myself.' She'd said, 'Are you serious?' and he'd said, 'Of course.' But even after she and Hannah had moved in, she wasn't sure that he was. The trouble with Tony was that he had a way of sounding as if nothing mattered too much and it seemed almost pedestrian to try to pin him down. She had never known how he felt about her. She still didn't know how he felt about her. You *WILL* come home for Christmas? You will come home for *CHRISTMAS*?

Alberta opened the package and pulled out a DVD: *Un Autre Homme, Une Autre Chance*. There was a note taped to the back of it.

*I thought you'd like to try a French Western for a change.*
*I am very, very, very, very, very sorry.*
*Love,*
*Tony*

She took out her phone and looked at it for a long time before settling on the right choice of words. Then she sent her text: 'Apology and present accepted. Christmas in Bath good. Have taken my silver cup.'

Back at Brixton, she unpacked her booty: the silver cup, her Elizabeth David cookery books, the small marble Buddha given by Marma during her world religion phase, her brown leather boots, a rug for her bed and the silver-framed photo that had lain at the back of her wardrobe in Bath.

The photo had been taken three months before Ed's death. He sat there, laughing at the camera and she and Hannah were laughing too. Alberta had kept it hidden for years in case the blatant happiness and vitality exposed by the lens might reflect adversely on the years following. It was silly really, because Tony wasn't the sort of man to feel jealous or threatened by someone else.

She set the frame on the shelf next to the Buddha and stared at the face of her late husband. Did he know at that time that Marma was involved with his friend? Try as she might to convince herself of his good intentions, she was finding it increasingly unsettling to know he had told her nothing about his involvement in her parents' marital affairs. She was no longer sure she could justify his silence on the grounds that he had wanted to protect her. She couldn't help thinking that if that were true, it was a rather patronizing stance. She looked intently at her husband's face. He certainly didn't look like a man who was hiding a secret from his wife. But there again, he didn't look like a man who might try to bribe his mother-in-law's lover.

She jumped at the sound of her phone and when she heard Marma's voice, said impulsively, 'How funny! I was just thinking about you!'

'Oh dear,' said Marma. 'How very alarming.'

'Not at all. Can I come down this weekend?'

'That would be lovely! In that case . . .' Marma paused. 'Would you like me to record a programme for you? Do you remember I was asked to be on a morning chat show with . . . with Peter Repton? It's going out on ITV tomorrow.'

'Don't bother,' Alberta said. 'I can't wait till the weekend. I'll record it myself and watch it in the evening. Do you promise you won't suddenly turn up there?'

'I can't.' Marma sounded rather wistful. 'The plumber is coming over to look at the washing machine.'

'Thank God for that,' Alberta said. 'I will be able to sleep peacefully tonight.'

Actually, Alberta did not sleep peacefully that night. She slept fitfully, her slumbers punctuated by nightmares of a Christmas in Bath during which Peter Repton, looking very like Clark Gable, jumped out from behind menacing snowmen while Tony threw mince pies at her in the kitchen.

The following evening, she took a glass of red wine and a pizza through to the sitting room. Christopher and Helen were both out at meetings. Christopher had suggested they watch the programme together the following evening but Alberta couldn't wait that long to see it. She pushed in the video and settled down to watch her mother's former lover on television.

His interviewer was a sweet, cuddly woman who could be seen chatting animatedly to her guest as the credits came up. When the music stopped, she turned to the camera and said, 'Good morning! How are you all? I'm Peggy Painter and I have a fabulous collection of guests for you this morning! I'll be talking to one of the sexiest actresses on television today, who tells me she's tired of being a sex symbol and wants to be taken seriously. She has an extremely naughty fitness DVD out this week and promises to give us a demonstration! I'll also be talking to the vicar who left his wife *of* twenty-five years, in order to live with one of his choristers who *is* actually twenty-five – so there's a coincidence! He believes that God approves of his choice and I'm sure you can't wait to find out why! But first . . .' Peggy paused to cross one sturdy leg over the other, 'many of you may remember reading about the shocking death of eighty-two-year-old Lord Trussler, a former Minister for three Conservative Prime Ministers, famous in recent years for his appearances on *Question Time* and *Newsnight*. He died in somewhat embarrassing circumstances while in bed with a prostitute in a house in south London.' She raised her eyebrows. 'I'm sure I wasn't the only person to feel very sorry for his widow. A few weeks ago, we learnt a bit more about the Trussler family when my next guest revealed that he had once been Lady Trussler's lover. He's here to talk to us now and I'd like you to give a big hand for Peter Repton!'

The camera turned to the man on the sofa next to her and he gave a sad, almost weary smile. Alberta stared at him with distaste. She could imagine him practising that smile in the mirror.

'Before we start,' Peggy said, 'I'd like to offer you my commiserations. I understand you have recently separated from your wife, the diamond heiress, Penelope Dangerfield. I'm so sorry.'

'Thank you.' Peter bowed his head slightly.

'But today,' Peggy continued brightly, 'we are more concerned with your recent startling revelation about Lady Trussler. It's a fascinating story, because you were good chums with Lady Trussler's son-in-law, weren't you? That's an odd situation, don't you think?'

'I suppose it was,' Peter mused. 'I never thought of Philippa as Ed's mother-in-law. To me, she was just a woman, beautiful, bashful, blonde and very sad . . .'

'. . . Who was twenty years older than you.'

'I never thought of the age difference. We saw each other at a party and we fell in love. I remember every minute of that evening. I couldn't stop looking at her and when she came over and smiled at me, I knew I was lost.'

Peggy sighed. 'It sounds so romantic!'

'What can I say?' Peter gave a little shrug of his shoulders. 'It *was*.'

'And yet,' Peggy leant forward, 'what fascinates me is that the object of your love was a fifty-three-year-old mother of two and a wife of one of the most powerful men in the Conservative Party, while you were just a young political researcher. Didn't you have any qualms at all?'

'You see, I didn't.' Peter gave an apologetic smile. 'I was a young man in love. When you're young, you're not interested in reason or practicality. When you're young, you can be pretty wild.'

'I'm sure that's true but Lady Trussler was *not* young and yet she was also – according to you – pretty wild.'

Peter nodded and gave a little laugh, as if remembering some distant memory. 'We had some fun.'

Alberta shouted out, '*Fuck* you!' and realized she really did hate the man smirking so smugly in front of her.

'I'm sure you did,' Peggy said. She sounded rather envious. 'Did Lady Trussler talk to you about her marriage?'

'She did,' Peter said, 'she told me things that made my skin crawl . . .' He stopped and sighed heavily. 'I'm sorry. I don't feel comfortable about revealing intimate details told to me in confidence.'

'*Hypocrite!*' Alberta yelled.

Peggy nodded sympathetically. 'I quite understand. Why did you decide to end the relationship?'

'It was the most difficult decision I've ever had to make,' Peter said. 'I felt—'

'I'm sorry,' Peggy threw up a hand, 'I'm a little confused. In a recent interview, you seemed to imply that it was Lady Trussler who finally finished the relationship. Did I misunderstand that? It *was* you who finished it?'

For the first time, Peter looked unsure of himself. 'It all happened so long ago,' he murmured. 'It's difficult to be sure about things.'

'And yet, you said she was the love of your life. You must have some recollection of how it finished.'

'Well,' said Peter, 'of course it all happened so long ago . . . I think what happened was that I initially bowed to outside pressures and told Philippa we had to stop seeing each other and she decided to go to Canada to see her son. I knew almost immediately I had made a mistake and tried to contact her. She wouldn't speak to me. So, I suppose, you could say we both finished it. I didn't know what to do.'

'Did Lord Trussler offer you money to help you decide what to do?'

Peter fingered his tie. 'He may have done,' he said. 'I'm not sure.'

Peggy gave a sympathetic nod, as if she were an agony aunt, trying to help. 'And did you accept the money?'

Peter hesitated. 'I was confused,' he said. 'I was very young. Lord Trussler was a formidable man. I knew that Philippa was the most wonderful woman I had—'

'I'm afraid we've run out of time,' Peggy said, her voice abruptly changing gear. 'We did ask Lady Trussler to come on the programme but she declined. She did say, and I quote: "I find it difficult to understand why Mr Repton wants to add to my unhappiness at this time in my life." I'm sure Lady Trussler will be very happy to know she was the most wonderful woman you have ever had. Thank you for speaking to us so candidly this morning, Peter.'

For a moment the camera caught Peter Repton looking at his hostess with eyes that seemed to suggest he wanted to cut her up in a thousand pieces.

Alberta switched off the television and yelled, '*Yes!*' She put her tray to one side, got up and reached for her phone. As soon as she heard Marma's voice, she said, 'I've seen it! Wasn't she brilliant? Wasn't he creepy? Don't you feel fantastic?'

'No,' said Marma. 'I feel rather foolish. I feel very foolish.'

'*Why?* The Peggy woman was completely on your side. Everyone will be on your side. And actually you come out of it all amazingly well. Peter Repton is a rat but he's a very good-looking rat and he was madly attracted to you even though you were twenty years older than him. I would *love* to be a sex symbol at your age. In fact,' Alberta said thoughtfully, 'I would love to be a sex symbol at any age. You are a senior sex symbol. You are up there with Honor Blackman and Jane Fonda and Joan Collins. You are amazing!'

'Am I?' Marma asked. 'Do you really think so?'

'I do. You should walk into your village shop tomorrow with your head held high. There isn't a woman over forty who wouldn't feel a little bit wistful about your romantic past!'

'Goodness!' said Marma. There was a brief silence and then she said, 'Do you really think I'm like Joan Collins?'

# CHAPTER TWENTY

## *Unforgiven*

Alberta could not describe herself as happy in her new life, but she had never expected to be. For a lot of the time, she was not *unhappy*, for which she was grateful.

The job was tough and stressful and occasionally terrifying, never more so than when, on an engagement in Windsor, she discovered she had left half the canapés behind. The hours were long: usually, she arrived at half past eight and rarely left before six. At least two evenings a week she would be required to work, usually in London but sometimes in one of the surrounding counties.

Most days, she cycled to work. She had bought a second-hand bicycle with a frayed wicker basket and this, along with the black helmet she acquired at the same time, was the subject of much amusement among her colleagues, who dubbed it the Granny Bike. Alberta did indeed feel like a granny as she wobbled precariously along Great Elm Road. Often, she felt as if she'd jumped a decade or two. The girls at work – and Alberta thought of them all as girls, even Francesca – told Alberta about their boyfriends and their would-be boyfriends and their sex lives. (They were getting either too much sex or not enough sex. No one seemed to be having just the right amount.) They never asked Alberta about her own sex life. They all quite correctly assumed she didn't have one.

In Bath, Diana had treated her as if she were a much younger and rather wayward little sister who needed to be told what to do. Now, for the first time in her life, Alberta was surrounded by colleagues who sought her advice and treated her like the mature woman she ought to be, and Alberta rather enjoyed the experience.

When she thought about Diana, she couldn't blame her for her patronizing attitude. Alberta could see that she had almost encouraged Diana's assertiveness by her own indecisiveness and willingness to be led.

Perhaps she was also to blame for the fact that Ed had not told her anything about her parents' turbulent private life. She had always enjoyed being her father's little girl and it had seemed natural for her to let her husband take charge. It had actually never occurred to her that he *shouldn't* take all the major decisions in their lives. He was older than her, he was in her eyes far wiser and cleverer than her and it was just so very easy to assume he always knew best. It was pretty pathetic but at last, and certainly not before time, she felt she was beginning to grow up.

This cautiously optimistic attitude was enhanced by the fact that in mid-October she moved into a flat of her own. It was a second-floor apartment in a big old house in Effra Road, just half a mile away from Christopher and Helen. She was more than ready to leave her brother's house. It was difficult enough holding down a full-time job, let alone making time to cook quality meals for him and Helen. On top of this, their party and the two dinner parties she'd prepared for them in the last two weeks of September had left her exhausted. There was also the fact that however kind they were, she would always be a guest in their house. The new place might not be to her taste but it was – for the next six months at least – *her* place and no one else's.

Her new sitting room was dominated by two big, black leather sofas and a huge bay window that looked down onto the road and provided generous amounts of sunlight. On either side of the window were shelf-lined walls that would look great if only Alberta had anything to put on them. The bathroom was small, with twin circular basins, chocolate-brown walls and amber tiles. The bedroom was dominated by a kingsize bed and this, together with the black walls and red curtains and carpet, gave it the appearance of a French bordello, or at least what Alberta imagined a French bordello might look like. The galley kitchen had a very good oven, a hob and a stainless steel sink on one side and an enormous gilt-framed mirror on the other. Alberta deduced that her landlord was a sex-obsessed bachelor who enjoyed looking at himself while he cooked. She had never had the least desire to have a black leather sofa and nor had she ever wished to sleep in a French bordello but as soon as she had seen the flat she had known it was right.

Increasingly, Alberta felt she was beginning to get her life in order. She was seeing more of her daughter and was less worried about her mother. Marma had stopped talking about moving and had joined a reading group in the neighbouring village of Little Crackton. So far, she had read Bob

Dylan's *Chronicles* and had even written him a letter which he had hitherto failed to answer.

Alberta knew she was lucky. She had a good employer in Francesca and an interesting job. She might be exhausted a lot of the time but she was never bored. For the most part, she was content. Really, her new life in London was pretty satisfactory.

And then the Ringwood party happened and her new London life slithered to the ground like melted chocolate from a saucepan.

It began with such promise. As the occupants of the Quality Food Company van made their way to Mr Ringwood's penthouse flat, there was a general mood of high spirits. It was half past five on a Friday afternoon, the last job of the week and ahead of them all stretched a work-free weekend, pristine and promising. Both Jo and Francesca were expecting great things from the weekend. Jo had been conducting a delicate dance of flirtation by text for over a fortnight. It had started with a casual message of bland banality from a man she had met at the pub. She had spent days trying to analyse and deconstruct and reconstruct it, before sending off a reply that was carefully purged of anything that might suggest interest or attraction. Now, a dozen texts later, they had agreed to meet for a drink on Saturday.

Francesca was also going out and was almost as excited as Jo since she was meeting a man she hadn't seen for fifteen years. 'He got my number from a friend,' Francesca said. 'He just rang me out of the blue. He lives in Suffolk and he's in London for the weekend. He's staying at Blake's, so he has to be pretty rich. I can't *wait* to see what he's like . . . There was always something between us and when he rang me, it was weird: it was still there, that *buzz*!' She laughed and turned down a side street. 'What about you, Alberta? Are you doing anything nice tomorrow?'

'Very nice,' Alberta said. 'I'm going down to Hampshire. My mother and I are going to rake all the leaves and build bonfires.' She was aware that yet again she had failed to impress her colleagues and said a shade defensively, 'I *like* building bonfires.'

'Right,' said Francesca, turning into a small car park, 'we're here. Now, remember, folks: this is a nice, new client, who happens to own one of the biggest record companies in the business, so let's show him what we can do.'

Alberta felt her heart lurch. 'Francesca,' she said carelessly, 'what did you say the client's name was?'

'Ringwood,' Francesca said.

'What's his full name?'

'He's called Jason Q. Ringwood,' Francesca said. 'I don't know what the Q stands for but I do know he's very rich!'

Alberta had never met Jason Q. Ringwood but she knew all about him. Jason Q. Ringwood was a friend of Tony and a fan of the Hartfelt Records label. Six years ago, Tony had nearly sold it to him. It was more than likely that Tony would be here this evening.

Mr Ringwood was quite clearly very, very rich. The door to his apartment was opened by his personal assistant and Alberta had time only to notice stunning views over the Thames, wide oak floorboards and a carefully lit pre-Raphaelite painting – 'It's genuine,' hissed Francesca – before being hurried into the enormous kitchen that gleamed with immaculate black granite.

By the time the first guests arrived, the granite could hardly be seen since every available surface was covered with an array of dishes: miniature cottage pies, baby beef burgers filled with ketchup and melting cheese, tray after tray of sun-dried-tomato filo tartlets and tiny bacon quiches. The client appeared, resplendent in a silver waistcoat that strained to cover his generous girth. He smoothed back his suspiciously black hair and beamed at the team. 'I just want you to know I have my best buddy coming here tonight and I promised him a good spread! It looks like I don't have to worry! Bachelors like myself,' he added, his eyes resting on Alberta, 'are totally dependent on talented women like you. And it's just a bonus –' his eyes now falling on to Jo – 'to have such pretty ones in my kitchen.' He went to the door and turned. 'I have a very good feeling about this party!'

'What a lovely man,' Jo said. She looked at Alberta who rolled her eyes. 'He *was* a lovely man,' Jo protested. 'He said you were talented.'

Within an hour, the noise from the vast living room was as great as a tidal wave, and every time the door was opened it felt as though it might flood through the kitchen. Francesca and her team of waitresses were in and out the whole time, departing with full platters and returning within minutes with empty ones. As the laughter from the party increased, so the crates of empty champagne bottles grew.

It was another hour before Alberta felt she could take time out to pour herself a drink and it was while she was filling a glass with water that she heard a voice say, 'Bertie?'

She spun round and nearly dropped her water. 'Tony!'

she said and managed a shaky laugh. 'You made me jump. I wondered if you'd be here.'

Jo was checking out Tony with the appraising glance of a woman who's forgotten she has a hot date the next evening. Alberta could see why. Tony was wearing his grey suit, which might be old but was beautifully cut, and which, together with his light grey shirt, was undeniably stylish.

'Jo,' Alberta said, 'would you check the cheese tarts? I'm sure they're ready to come out of the oven.' She walked over to Tony and said, 'It's good to see you.'

'I saw the food van outside when I arrived,' he said. 'It's taken me all this time to work out why I'd heard of the Quality Food Company.'

'Are you enjoying the party?'

'I am. I'm sorry I have to leave it. I'm meeting Dylan and I'm already late but I couldn't go without saying hello to you. How are you? You look tired.'

'I'm fine. It's a bit frenetic here at the moment.' She was aware of Jo studiously – *very* studiously – checking the cheese tarts.

'I'll let you get on. You should come down to Bath soon. Everyone misses you.'

'I'd like to,' Alberta murmured. 'I was going to tell you that I need to come down one Saturday and collect more stuff.'

'Bertie,' Tony said urgently, 'I've told you before. You don't have to say anything. It's your home. Come down whenever you like. I shall be very upset if you feel you have to ask me.' His eyes searched her face and then he leant forward and kissed her cheek. 'Look after yourself,' he said. 'I'll see you soon.'

Alberta watched the door close behind him and felt a strong desire to cry. She swallowed, turned her back on Jo and drank her glass of water.

Francesca came in with a stack of empty plates and cast a practised eye over the cheese tarts. 'Well done, girls,' she said, 'we're getting lots of compliments. I'll take these out and then we can give them the sweet stuff. Are you all right, Alberta? You look a bit hot.'

'I'm fine,' Alberta said. 'I'm glad it's all going well. I'll put the pavlovas together.'

She looked hot. She looked tired. She looked talented. She was beginning to feel like Cinderella without a fairy godmother. It was, of course, absurd to be upset that she was talented rather than pretty and it was even more absurd to mind that the first time she should see Tony since their separation was when she looked hot and tired and talented. It was absurd to be thinking about any of these things in the middle of a job.

The door continued to open and shut as waitresses began to take out the brownies and the treacle tarts and Alberta had no idea what made her lift her head when it opened yet again just as she had finished squirting cream onto the meringue nests.

It was Daniel Driver.

Worse, it was Daniel Driver looking magnificent in a charcoal jacket, white shirt and thin grey tie. The fact that he was here looking like *this* when she was looking like *that* only intensified her quite irrational rage at his presence. She watched him nod at Jo before walking over to her. With his heavy-lidded eyes, his wild thatch of hair and his five o'clock shadow, he looked like he'd just got out of bed.

For a brief moment, she found herself wondering what it would be like to be with him in his bed and felt her face flushing yet again.

Daniel put down his glass of champagne and looked at the pavlovas. 'They look good,' he said. 'Tony was going out as I was coming in. He told me you were here.'

'Really?' Alberta raised her eyebrows. 'How thoughtful of him.'

'It's good to see you. Should I say sorry about you two, by the way?'

Alberta said lightly, 'I don't think you need to say anything at all.'

The door opened again and a blonde young beauty in a tight red dress that left nothing to the imagination stared irritably at Daniel. 'What are you doing in *here*, Danny? I need you to rescue me from that pervy friend of Jason.'

'I won't be long,' Daniel said. 'I'm just saying hello to an old friend. We were at nursery school together.'

The woman rested her eyes fleetingly on Alberta and raised her eyebrows. 'Well, do *hurry*. I'll get some more champagne.'

Daniel waited until she had gone and then turned back to Alberta. 'You look exhausted,' he said. 'Is it hard starting again in a new place and a new job? Do you find it odd being single again?You should let me take you out to dinner.'

Alberta laughed. 'I might be single,' she said, 'but I'm not desperate.' She regretted the comment as soon as she had uttered it. It was not at all funny, it was actually appallingly rude and it had seemingly come from nowhere. Perhaps she was flustered and tired or perhaps she was cross because both Tony *and* Daniel thought she looked tired, which meant they thought she looked awful. Perhaps it was because the blonde in the red dress had looked at her with such contempt. Perhaps it was because she hated the fact that he was looking so desirable when she knew she was looking so gross. 'I'm sorry,' she said, 'that was a terrible thing to say.'

Daniel regarded her without any noticeable change of expression. 'I think,' he said softly, 'there is a misunderstanding here. I wasn't suggesting anything *other* than dinner. I'm not desperate either. Goodbye now.'

Her face felt as if it was on fire. She watched him walk out of the kitchen and then she picked up his glass of champagne and drained it in its entirety.

Jo was looking at her as if she'd turned into a vampire.

'Is there anything wrong?' Alberta snapped.

'N-no,' Jo stammered. 'I just thought you'd like to know . . .'

Alberta squared her shoulders. 'You just thought I'd like to know what?'

'It's only . . .' Jo said, 'it's only that you look a little . . . flustered.'

'Thank you for that piece of information,' Alberta said. 'I think I knew that already.'

'No, I mean you look ill. And Alberta . . .'

'*What?*'

'It's only . . . I thought you'd like to know. You have a bit of cream on your face, under your left eye.'

'*What? Fuck!* Why didn't you tell me before? I mean, for God's sake . . .' Alberta reached for a piece of kitchen paper.

The door opened again and Molly, one of the waitresses, said, 'Francesca says we need to bring the rest of the puddings out, so make sure they're ready.' She looked helpfully at Alberta. 'You have cream on your face,' she said and walked out before Alberta could throw something at her.

Jo had taken the mixed berry sauce out of the fridge and was drizzling it over the pavlovas. Alberta rubbed her face with the kitchen paper and went over to shut the door. She could see Daniel talking to some man and narrowed her eyes. She put her hand on the door handle and then stopped as her heart began to pound furiously.

She left the door open and walked back towards the pavlovas. 'I'll be back in a moment,' she said and picked up the plate before Jo could add any more sauce.

She walked out into the party. She was Gary Cooper in *High Noon*, she was Alan Ladd in *Shane*, she was Clint Eastwood in *The Good, the Bad and the Ugly.* She stepped up to Daniel and his companion and waited for them to notice her.

'Excuse me,' she said, ignoring Daniel, 'is your name Peter Repton?'

The man nodded. 'It is. Have I met you before?'

'I'm not sure that you have,' Alberta said, 'but I'm the daughter of Philippa Trussler and this is for my mother.' She gripped the dish of pavlovas and with all the strength at her command hurled it against Peter Repton's chest.

# CHAPTER TWENTY-ONE

## *Alberta and the Stranger*

Alberta had a pleasant weekend with Marma. They built an impressive bonfire and lit it on Saturday afternoon; the resulting smells of smoky leaves and roasting twigs transported Alberta back to happier times when the children were small and she had never heard of a man called Peter Repton.

She said nothing to Marma about the circumstances in which she had lost her job. She mentioned casually over dinner that she had decided to move on and try something a little less demanding. Marma had responded with a wise nod of her head and a 'Very sensible, darling,' followed by a 'Have you been in touch with Tony lately?'

It was predictable that Marma, a big fan of Tony, would assume that the answer to her daughter's possible employment problems lay with a reconciliation and return to Bath. It was far less understandable that Alberta should have the same thought. She did at least have enough self-respect not to even think of contacting Tony while she was unemployed. *If* – and it was a big if – she was ever to go back to him, it must not be because all other options had closed down.

As for Friday night, the entire experience had been a nightmare, but she would never regret what she had done. As she sat on the train back to London on Sunday afternoon, she kept replaying the pavlova incident. She would never forget either the smug manner in which Repton had said, 'Have I met you before?' or the look of outraged horror as the pavlovas splatted his suit. Those memories would always outweigh the subsequent horror and humiliation: her speedy ejection by Francesca from the apartment along with the fierce command to wait outside; the eventual embarrassed arrival of Jo who handed over her coat and bag and said, 'I'm really sorry but Francesca told me to tell you . . . she's fired you and you're to come in at quarter to eight on Monday morning to sort everything out.'

It was only on Sunday evening when she sat at the small bar in her kitchen, cradling a mug of tomato soup, that the full gravity of her situation struck her with as much force as the blade of a guillotine. She had been fired from her job. She would receive no references. In any subsequent interviews she would have to lie, or at the very least be creative with the truth. And even if she overcame that hurdle, the chance of finding a position with such proximity to her flat was unlikely. It had, she realized now, been unbelievably stupid to fritter away so much money on renting such an expensive place. She had been stupid and arrogant to assume she'd have no problems at work. She might not be at fault for failing to envisage the unendurable sighting of Repton, but she should at least have spent a few months in her job before moving to a flat of her own.

And then there was Hannah, Hannah who had at last

begun to believe that her mother could run her life without the support of a man. Now that Alberta was in danger of losing it, she knew just how much Hannah's respect meant to her. How was she going to tell Hannah she had been fired?

And what was really, really sad and pathetic and stupid, she thought as she lay in bed on Sunday night, unable to sleep, was that what depressed her more than the financial worries, the problem of finding a new job, even Hannah's reaction, was the fact that she had been so gratuitously unpleasant to Daniel Driver and he had responded by telling her he would have to be desperate to sleep with her.

The last time she had felt like this was when, at eight years old, she had waited outside the headmistress's office after inadvertently breaking a classroom window while playing her first – and last – game of football with the boys.

Alberta tried to remind herself she was now a sensible, middle-aged mother of two; she was much older than Francesca and had no reason to feel like throwing up in the litter bin. The indisputable fact was that on Friday night she had not behaved like a sensible, middle-aged mother of two who was much older than her employer.

She was at least dressed appropriately in funereal black trousers and shirt. She took a deep breath and knocked on Francesca's door. She heard a crisp, business-like 'Come in, Alberta,' and felt a crazy urge to turn and run.

Francesca was sitting at her desk, looking at her computer screen and said, 'Please sit down.' Then she pushed back her chair and folded her arms. 'As a result of your actions, I had an extremely uncomfortable conversation with Mr

Ringwood on Friday evening,' she said. 'He told me that the man you attacked . . .' she let the verb hang in the air, 'a man called Peter Repton, was his best friend.'

Alberta gulped. 'Oh,' she said.

'I assured him we would, of course, reimburse Mr Repton for any cleaning costs and that I would substantially reduce our bill. I also told him I had fired you. I have *never* –' she fixed Alberta with steely eyes – 'never *ever* had to grovel to a client like that before.'

'I'm sorry,' Alberta whispered, 'I am so sorry.'

'Mr Ringwood,' Francesca said, 'is a very unusual man. He sent me an email yesterday. He said . . .' Francesca paused to move her chair forward so she could look at the computer screen again, '"I have to admit the party was a little flat and your cook's behaviour, while thoroughly reprehensible, certainly got the party going." He also said that while Mr Repton had been extremely shocked and upset, he had no wish to press charges against you.'

'Oh,' said Alberta.

'None of this means I can condone what you did. Most clients would have taken us to the cleaners along with Mr Repton's suit.'

'I know,' Alberta said miserably. 'I quite understand.'

'However,' Francesca said, 'I had another phone call yesterday from a man called Daniel Driver. He told me he was with Mr Repton when you attacked him. He also told me about your parents and in particular about your mother's former relationship with Mr Repton. He said he was quite convinced you meant no harm when you approached him and Mr Repton with the pavlovas. He told me that when you approached them, Mr Repton was describing in very unpleasant terms his . . . his bedtime activities with your mother. He said it was quite obvious that you couldn't help yourself in the circumstances.'

'But . . .' Alberta hesitated and glanced down at her shoes.

'He asked me not to say anything to Mr Ringwood since Mr Ringwood was a good friend of Mr Repton and Mr Repton would probably deny he had said any such thing.'

'I'm sure,' Alberta said slowly, 'that that is exactly what Mr Repton would say.'

'In similar circumstances,' Francesca said, 'I'd probably have done the same as you. Perhaps I'd have pushed the puddings into his face rather than his suit.'

'You would?' Alberta gasped.

'That does not mean I endorse what you did. Next time you feel like throwing food at a guest, come and see me first.'

'Next time?' Alberta asked. 'You mean I'm not fired?'

'You're a very good cook,' Francesca said, 'and I presume this won't happen again. Just keep to your kitchen in future. I don't know why you were handing round pavlovas anyway. Why do you think I hire waitresses?'

'Right,' Alberta said, 'I'm sorry. I wasn't thinking. Thank you, Francesca, thank you so much.'

'To be perfectly honest,' Francesca said, pushing back her chair and then stretching her arms towards the ceiling, 'after the Saturday evening I had, the last thing I wanted to do was start looking for a new cook.'

'Did you have a bad time? How was the old school friend?'

'He turned out to be married. He only wanted a bit of slap and tickle. I gave him a slap and withheld the tickle.'

She glanced at her computer screen. 'So, shall we discuss today's assignments?'

When Alberta went down to the kitchen unit, Jo was already there and taking off her coat. 'Oh, Alberta! I thought . . .'

'You thought you'd be cooking with Francesca today,' Alberta said. 'I thought you would be too. I've been given a reprieve along with a list of everything we have to do this week. Shall we get on?'

Within half an hour she realized her desire to avoid bringing up Friday was unfeasible. Within an hour she saw it was also insulting to Jo. It was optimistic to assume that their easy rapport could simply continue without an explanation. Jo almost jumped every time Alberta tried to talk to her. Eventually, Alberta said, 'I'd like to talk to you about Friday.'

'Really,' Jo said, 'it's none of my business.'

'I think it is,' Alberta said. 'You are a colleague and you've become a friend and I *want* to tell you. Sit down for a moment. You've worked like a dervish this morning.' She waited until Jo had settled herself on one of the stools and then leant against the cooker and folded her arms. 'You remember the two men who came into the kitchen at the party?'

'The good-looking man with the light-coloured hair and the good-looking man with the big, dark hair?'

'Yes. Well. Well, the first man was my ex-partner. We split up a few months ago.'

Jo hesitated. 'He seemed very fond of you.'

'I'm fond of him too. It's all very amicable. We simply decided we didn't want to live together any more. He's a friend of the other man, the one with dark hair.'

'He seemed fond of you too.'

'He isn't. He does like Tony, though, and I think he just called in on me to say hello. Anyway, the third man . . .'

'The one who got the pavlovas? Is he a friend of your ex-partner too?'

'No,' Alberta said firmly, 'he is nothing to do with my ex-partner. He was a friend of my mother a long time ago. He behaved very badly. When I saw him at the party, I felt rather upset and so I . . . well, what happened was . . .' Alberta stopped and reached for Daniel's lie with all the enthusiasm of a desert-parched teetotaller reaching for a whisky. 'I heard him tell Daniel intimate details of his relationship with my mother and so I—'

'You clocked him with the puddings!' Jo crowed. 'Well done! What a bastard! Why on earth did Daniel let him speak like that?'

'I can't imagine,' Alberta said with genuine fervour, forgetting for a moment that Daniel had done no such thing. 'Anyway, the point is, I behaved appallingly. As Francesca said to me this morning, it could have had serious repercussions for the Quality Food Company. Luckily, Mr Ringwood has been quite magnanimous and Francesca has been very understanding and has let me keep my job. I'm telling you all this because I didn't want you to think I had some sort of exotic secret life which involved hurling puddings at men on a regular basis.'

For the first time that morning, Jo gave her throaty laugh. 'I did wonder,' she said, 'with all those gorgeous men queuing up to speak to you. I had no idea your life was so exciting.'

'It isn't,' Alberta said reassuringly, 'it's incredibly dull, which suits me just fine. By the way, how did your hot date go on Saturday?'

'A mixture of hot and cold,' Jo said. 'We did lots of flirting which was nice and then after about an hour he said he had to meet some friends and would I like to come along. I said I had to go anyway because I was meeting friends too.'

'*Were* you meeting friends?'

'No, of course not, but I didn't want him to think I kept the whole evening free when he obviously hadn't. I wish I didn't find men so difficult to understand.'

'So do I,' Alberta said, 'so do I.'

Alberta stopped off at the supermarket on the way home and bought some groceries, including a bottle of wine. She let herself into her flat and felt a warm glow of relief at the realization that she would be able to go on living there without fear of debt. Then she remembered who was responsible for her salvation. She put the wine in the fridge. She had a disagreeable task to perform and she would need the wine to help her through it.

She took off her jacket, spent a few minutes trying to remember where she had put her writing pad and then, having found it, sat down and frowned. She studied the blank paper carefully and sighed. She looked out of the window and sighed again. Perhaps, while she was waiting for the wine to chill, she should ring Marma and tell her the good news about her job.

She was a little vague about the reasons for her change of plan. She mentioned misunderstandings and clearing the air and patching up differences. Fortunately, Marma seemed uninterested in the details and was simply pleased Alberta's future was once again set out in a straightforward manner.

'I think we should celebrate,' Marma said. 'Why don't you come down again at the weekend? Hilda will be here and she'd love to see you.'

Alberta glanced at her copy of *Confessions of a Retired Schoolmistress.* In all the excitement of the Repton business she had forgotten about the recent email she had had from Felicity Fullock. 'I can't,' she said, 'I'm visiting a friend of Ed on Saturday.'

'Right,' Marma said. She paused and then said again, 'Right.'

This always happened. Alberta had forgotten that this always happened. For a moment, she was tempted to say something, to drag this entire murky area into the light and in so doing rob it of its power. Now that she was seeing so much of Marma, the idea of remaining silent about that year when Ed died struck her as absurd. It was wrong that Marma should continue to feel so constrained every time her late son-in-law was mentioned.

But now, on the telephone, was not the time. Some future evening, when she and Marma were sitting together with a couple of drinks inside them, she would bring up the subject and say it was all in the past. She would tell her mother she quite understood, even though she didn't, and she would take her hand and tell her she loved her. But not now, not over the phone.

So instead she said, as if she had noticed nothing, 'Marma, what are you doing at Christmas?'

'Oh Christmas!' Marma said, sounding instantly happier.

'I meant to talk to you about Christmas. Christopher and his family are coming to stay and possibly Hilda. Will you come too?'

'Not this time. Tony suggested I go to Bath. Jacob will be home and he'll want to see both of us.'

'Of course he will,' said Marma warmly. 'I must say you and Tony are a very civilized ex-couple. But then, I have always thought Tony was a very civilized man.'

'I agree,' said Alberta. This was another subject she didn't feel like discussing at the moment. 'I'd better go,' she said, 'I'm cooking my supper.' Really, she was getting very good at telling lies.

After she'd rung off, she went to the fridge, opened her wine and poured a large glass.

Fifteen minutes later, she was sitting at the table with her writing paper in front of her. Forty minutes and seven drafts later, she read what she had written.

*Dear Daniel,*

*I would like to apologize for my ungracious response to your kind invitation to dinner the other evening. I was rather busy at the time and expressed myself badly. When I said I was not desperate, I meant that I was not desperate to have social engagements of any sort. If I had had more time I would have been able to explain that my working hours are long and strenuous and that I have therefore too little time to pursue a social life. If you interpreted my words differently, I can only say I regret them. I would also like to thank you for taking the trouble to ring up my employer and justify my actions regarding Peter Repton, although since you saw fit to reveal Repton's relationship*

*with my mother to my employer, I don't know why you felt it was necessary to concoct a made-up story, which was smutty, actually, and I was quite justified in bashing Repton anyway, but I suppose you meant well.*
*Yours sincerely,*
*Alberta*

Alberta, now on her third glass, reread the letter and wondered if the last sentence was a little too long. She read the letter again and immediately tore it up. She didn't actually see why she should be so grateful. She had not *asked* Daniel to rescue her and even if she *had* been rude to him, he had been even ruder to her. She could just imagine him smirking smugly as he read her faltering attempts to explain herself.

One mushroom omelette, two more glasses of wine and three crumpled attempts later, she finally felt satisfied.

*Dear Daniel,*
*I understand that you rang my employer and spoke on my behalf after my intemperate action on Friday evening. I would like to express my appreciation for your help even though I didn't ask for it.*
*Yours sincerely,*
*Alberta Granger*

By this time it was quarter past eleven. Alberta quickly folded the letter and put it in an envelope. She reached for her phone and sent a text to Tony, asking him for Daniel's address. In the morning she would post the letter and put Daniel Driver out of her mind.

When she came back from work on Friday, she found a letter waiting for her.

*Dear Ms Granger,*
*Mr Driver has asked me to thank you for your letter and to assure you he was happy to be of service.*
*Yours sincerely,*
*Merrily S. Trumpet*

Alberta let out a growl and tore the letter into a mass of little pieces.

On Saturday morning, at ten past ten, Alberta stepped off the train and looked about her. She had had no idea stations like this still existed. Manningtree had only two platforms and was surrounded by fields. She could easily imagine E. Nesbit's railway children here.

Alberta had spent the entire train journey rehearsing what she was going to say and how she was going to say it. Now, with fifty minutes still to spare, she spotted a public footpath sign and decided a quick walk would clarify her thoughts.

The conditions were perfect for this: a blue sky with the odd cotton-wool cloud and a light breeze. At first, the path ran along below the station but once she had walked through the old brick tunnel, she emerged beside wide fields with only the sound of birdsong to distract her.

She hesitated when she came to a signpost. It pointed in one direction to Flatford and in the other, back to Manningtree. She had heard of Flatford. Constable had done his famous painting of the hayrick there and it was supposed to be charming and unspoilt. It occurred to her that she had a choice. She could just walk on and take a look at Flatford and ring Miss Fullock and make her excuses. Miss Fullock, after all, could have nothing but pain and aggravation to offer.

Except, of course, that wasn't quite true. Miss Fullock could also provide some answers. Alberta took one last look at the leafy path ahead and then turned and went back the way she had come.

She found the pink terraced cottage without difficulty. Miss Fullock's directions had been admirably clear. Alberta opened the little gate and walked up the path. She had no clear expectations of the woman she had come to meet. Her imagination had veered between a little old lady with a roguish twinkle, a jolly Miss Marple sort of figure, and an elderly siren with a voice like Lauren Bacall.

The woman who opened the door bore no resemblance to either of these fantasies. She was broad of beam with a big bosom and short grey hair and was dressed in sensible shoes, blue slacks and an Arran sweater.

'Miss Fullock?' Alberta queried. 'I'm Alberta Granger. It's very kind of you to meet me.'

The woman smiled. 'When I received your first email, I was intrigued . . . and a little apprehensive as well. But I see we will like each other! Do come in and I'll make us some tea. Hogarth, get down at once!'

Hogarth, an enthusiastic terrier with an obvious fascination for Alberta's long, grey cardigan, gave a protesting bark before following his mistress through to a small ochre-coloured kitchen with a door that opened out into a small cottage garden.

Alberta gazed out at the glowing red acer, the Michaelmas daisies and soft white hydrangeas and said impulsively, 'Oh it's lovely! How clever you are!'

'I'm a novice really,' Miss Fullock said. 'I only took up gardening when I retired and now it is my passion, along with Hogarth, of course. I think it's warm enough to sit outside. I love these autumn days, don't you? If you take the tray there – that's the one – I'll bring the tea out in a minute.'

Miss Fullock had gone to some trouble. The tray had pretty porcelain cups and saucers and matching milk jug and a plate of ginger biscuits that had to be home-made. Alberta took it outside and set it on the white-painted garden table. Hogarth followed her out and made a spirited attempt to reach for Alberta's cardigan but she was too quick for him and hastily gathered it up around her waist. 'Down, Hogarth,' she said. 'Good boy!' She thought of the questions she had planned to ask. In this setting, they seemed presumptuous, vulgar, impossible.

Miss Fullock came out with an old-fashioned floral teapot and sat down at the table. 'I hope you don't mind, it's Earl Grey. Do you take sugar?'

'No, thank you,' Alberta said. She sat down at the other side of the table and, aware of Hogarth's interest, folded the ends of her cardigan on her lap.

Miss Fullock gave Alberta her cup and saucer and poured out tea. 'Now tell me a little about yourself. Do you work? What do you do? Where do you live?'

Alberta didn't want to talk about herself but innate good manners made her respond as briefly as she could. 'I work for a catering company in London. Until recently, I lived in Bath.'

Miss Fullock was either unaware of or unruffled by Alberta's coldness. She said she had only visited Bath once but had found it quite fascinating. 'Why did you move away?' she asked. 'Don't you find London rather loud and noisy?'

Alberta put down her cup. 'I find it fascinating,' she said, 'as I did your book. I would very much like to talk to you about your book.'

'*Confessions of a Retired Schoolmistress*! Isn't it a good title? My editor thought of it, I'm afraid I can't take any of the credit. I have to say, I was surprised by your email. I've heard from so many people in the last few months. At least a dozen were from readers who thought, like you did, that they knew one of the people I wrote about. The reason why I found you particularly interesting was that, so far, you are the only one to offer a correct identification.' She looked approvingly at Alberta. 'That was very clever of you. I took great trouble over my pseudonyms.'

'At first I wasn't sure,' Alberta admitted, 'and then when I reread the relevant chapter, it was obvious: Oxford, politics, premature death and then there was . . .' Alberta blushed and took a sip of her tea.

'The foot fetish!' Miss Fullock said triumphantly. 'You recognized the foot fetish! It's what I particularly remember about Ed Granger! He loved to lick my feet.' She sighed. 'Who needs vibrators when one has memories like that?'

'Right,' said Alberta faintly.

'I never expected the book to do so well. It's sold over eighty thousand copies! Eighty thousand! Of course the cover helps. It's very *racy*, don't you think?'

'I think the whole book is rather racy and very . . . unusual. What made you decide to write it?'

Miss Fullock beamed. 'Malice,' she said.

'Malice?'

'I'm afraid so. I feel no resentment towards the men in the book. I don't even feel anger about your late husband and he treated me particularly badly. I wrote the book to spite my family.' She stopped and nodded at the biscuits. 'I insist you try my biscuits. Everyone loves my biscuits.' She nodded approvingly as Alberta reached for the plate. 'Now, where was I? Ah yes, my family. My parents were horrible people. I see now they were horrible because they were unhappy but the fact remains they made their children unhappy too. How they ever conceived three children I cannot imagine. Having grown up with parents who hated each other, I vowed I would never marry. I have never regretted my decision. I am sure I am happier living with Hogarth than are any of my married friends living with their husbands. My sisters *did* marry and somehow believe their status gives them permission to treat me with extreme condescension. They assume I must envy them their unattractive spouses and their hideous offspring.' Miss Fullock gave a wicked smile. 'You might have noticed that I dedicated my book to Margaret and Virginia in the hope that they would receive as much pleasure in reading it as I did in researching it. In fact, I confess that I dedicated it to them in the earnest expectation that they would be absolutely appalled.' She clapped her hands together. 'And they are!' She cast a shrewd glance at Alberta. 'But of course you want to know about your husband.'

Alberta nodded. 'The episode at school – it seems so . . . so unlike him.'

'It was a long time ago,' Miss Fullock said. 'Ed was very young. People often do things when they are young that they would never dream of doing when they are older.'

Alberta picked up the ends of her cardigan and started plaiting them together. 'Miss Fullock,' she said, 'you say in your book you taught him English at school. You say you began an affair with him after he went into the Sixth Form. You say he used the affair to blackmail you into helping him produce an essay that won him a prestigious national writing competition, a prize that he knew would help him to get into Oxford. You say he gave you a box of chocolates when he won his place there and I have to say that that is the only action of his you describe that I find remotely credible.'

'I remember that. He gave me a box of Milk Tray which made me so cross because I knew I'd told him more than once that I only liked *plain* chocolates.'

'It doesn't really matter about the chocolates—'

'I *did* mind about the chocolates!'

'Yes, I'm sure you did but what is really bad is . . . is the fact that you say he blackmailed you. I've been thinking a lot about this and are you sure you didn't misunderstand him? I mean, was it possible that, actually, Ed simply wanted your help and perhaps just jokingly threatened you?'

'Mrs Granger—'

'Alberta. Please call me Alberta.'

'He showed me a letter he had written, Alberta. In the letter, he supplied dates, locations and detailed accounts of our meetings. There was no misunderstanding. Unless I helped him, he said he would show the letter to the headmaster.'

'It seems so unlike him. He never mentioned any of this to me.'

'As far as I can remember, your husband was extremely adept at forgetting anything he didn't wish to remember. He was also one of the most ambitious students I have ever met. As I said in my book, I am quite convinced that were it not for his untimely death, he would now be one of our most celebrated political leaders.'

'But if it is true – if he did that – then it's *terrible.*'

'I was very upset at the time. But then it was stupid of me to put myself in such a position in the first place. He was seventeen. He only behaved badly because I gave him the wherewithal to behave badly.'

'That's no excuse.'

'No, but it's an explanation.'

'It doesn't help to explain Ed to *me*. I'm beginning to feel I didn't know him at all.'

'Did he make you happy?'

'Very.'

'Then that's what counts. He made you happy. He was good to *you*. How well does anyone know anyone else? We are all a bundle of contradictions. People are fascinating just because they are impossible to understand. I'm sure that one reason for the success of my book is that people can't believe that an unmarried English teacher can have a strong interest in sex. I'm writing another book, you know.'

'Really? What are you going to call it?'

'I have always had a liking for alliteration. I suppose it's to do with having a name like Felicity Fullock. At the moment I'm toying with the idea of Fullock on Fellatio but my publishers think that might be a little too *strong*, if you know what I mean.'

'I do. If I can go back to the blackmailing incident . . . I have tried to imagine Ed doing this – and of course I didn't know Ed at that time – but I cannot imagine him threatening you like that. He was always so polite to people.'

'My dear, he was charming! Even when he blackmailed me, he was charming! He assured me he hated to be so unpleasant, and once I agreed to go over his essay he took me to bed and—'

'You went to bed with him after he blackmailed you?'

'I can see I have shocked you. He was an accomplished lover even at seventeen. And I have a very strong sex drive. Happily, it has abated a little in the last few years, though I do have a very pleasant arrangement with a gentleman down the road.'

'I'm glad to hear it.' Alberta smiled. She had expected to loathe Miss Fullock but it was impossible to loathe someone who was so full of good humour and so disarmingly honest. She glanced at her watch. 'I must go. I have a train to catch.' She picked up her bag and stood up. 'Your biscuits are delicious.'

'You only ate one,' Miss Fullock said reprovingly. 'Come along, Hogarth, let's show our visitor out.' She pushed back her chair and waited for Alberta to go into the house before walking along behind her.

Alberta tried and failed to think of something to say and it was only when she stepped out onto the path that she said hurriedly, 'I am so sorry about . . . about the past.'

'Oh goodness, it's not your fault. And anyway,' Miss Fullock smiled broadly, 'it gave me something to write about.' She took Alberta's hand and shook it warmly.

Alberta walked back to the station in a pensive mood. It was all very well for Miss Fullock to say that Ed had been very young when he had resorted to blackmail, but most people, whether young or not, did not do such things. If Ed was ambitious enough to use blackmail, then he was ambitious enough to do all sorts of things. Would he, for instance, have been so attracted to her if she had not been the daughter of Michael Trussler? Would he have been attracted to her at all?

Sex with Ed had been fantastic. He couldn't have faked that. And yet, and yet . . . There was the foot business. For years now, she had assumed she had amazing feet, despite the fact that their charms had mysteriously failed to grab Tony. There were two possibilities: one was that Miss Fullock and she had both had equally charismatic feet, the second was that Miss Fullock was correct in saying that Ed had a thing about feet, presumably *any* feet.

Alberta stood on the platform and waited gloomily for the train. She had a father who apparently liked kinky sex and a dead husband who had had a foot fetish. No wonder the two men had got on so well.

## CHAPTER TWENTY-TWO

### *The Command*

It had been a horrible day. Amid a sea of horrible days, this had been a classic. Up until a few months ago, Hannah's world had seemed so certain and so satisfactory. The more she thought about her life until a few months ago, the more she wondered why she hadn't been jumping for joy every morning. *Then*, she had been in charge of her life, she had been confident, she had been certain of her job and her boyfriend and her family. *Now*, she knew that nothing was as it seemed and everything was different.

The name of her illustrious grandfather had become a byword for sexual deviancy and the butt of numerous and invariably unfunny jokes. Her beloved friend Harrison had chosen to cut off all relations with her. Alfie, her true love and soulmate, had turned out to be neither her soulmate nor true. Her mother, for no good reason, had decided to break up the family home and set up house on her own. Kitty, a chronic failure with men who was always available for an instant review of the night's television, was now wildly and happily in love with a man who had until recently been the scourge of her working life. And most tragic of all for Hannah was the fact that Hannah was equally fraudulent. She had thought she was sensible, successful, confident and mature. In fact she had turned out to be anything but.

She was not only immature, she was downright nasty. All those months she had been with Alfie, she had never once thought that it might be difficult for Kitty to share a flat with the two of them. It had never occurred to Hannah to set aside time just for Kitty. And Kitty had never complained. Yet now that Kitty was at last enjoying a relationship with a man, Hannah's whole being was curdled with jealousy and self-pity and resentment at Kitty's quite understandable preoccupation. When Kitty stayed with Conrad, Hannah felt lonely and abandoned. When Kitty brought Conrad home, Hannah felt her home was being taken over by an outsider. So far she had resisted the temptation to articulate her poisonous thoughts but she knew she was bad-tempered and sulky and hateful. It was no wonder that Kitty spent increasing amounts of time with Conrad in his flat.

And then there was work. Having passed her exams, she had assumed she would begin to relax a little. She was wrong. All the insecurities engendered by the catastrophes in her private life were leaking into her professional life. She was sure that her colleagues didn't like her. And today – while it was possible she was succumbing to some form of paranoia – she could swear that people were laughing about her behind her back.

The truth was that everything seemed to be falling apart. Here she was, walking home on a Friday evening, in the knowledge that the only highlight of the next two days was

Sunday lunch with her mother. How had her life become so sad?

She knew the answer to that one. When Harrison was in Vietnam, she had missed him and longed for his return. Somehow, between Harrison going abroad and Harrison coming home, there had been a dramatic change in her friend. She had given up trying to contact him now because his evasive answers and feeble prevarications were just too painful to receive. He didn't want to see her and that was that. With Harrison's support, she could have coped reasonably well with the fact that she was the granddaughter of a national joke and the ex-girlfriend of a real rising star. Alfie had recently appeared in the pages of both *Heat* magazine and *Grazia* due to his new relationship with the Princess Blanche actress, who was apparently a soap-opera star and therefore a genuine celebrity. Without Harrison's support, she was all too aware that she understood the world about her as little as the world understood her. The one small light in the darkness was her new friendship with Rando. It helped to alleviate the huge hurt caused by Harrison's defection.

Hannah spotted the supermarket ahead of her and made a decision. At least if she was going to spend yet another evening feeling sorry for herself, she would do it with a few creature comforts. She turned into the shop, picked up a basket and chose a bottle of wine, a bar of milk chocolate and a four-cheeses pizza.

It was when she was standing in the queue, her eyes listlessly wandering over the journals and magazines, that she saw it. There, on the top right-hand corner of one of the papers, was the headline emblazoned in red capitals: THE

TRUSSLER SCANDAL REVISITED. SEE PAGE 10. Hannah reached for the paper and quickly turned to page ten. She stared in horror at the words above the picture of her grandfather: THE TRUSSLER SCANDAL REVISITED BY RANDO CHEATHAM.

As soon as she paid her bill, she shot out of the shop and marched at a panic-fuelled pace along the pavement, trying to conquer the nauseous fear she felt. She tried desperately to remember the conversations she had had with Rando. What had she *said* to him? The more she tried to remember, the blanker her mind became.

She arrived home at last. She threw off her jacket and put her groceries on the table. Never had her flat felt so empty. She opened the wine and poured herself a large glass. Then she sat down with the newspaper, turned to page ten and began to read.

It was terrible. She couldn't believe Rando could be such a devious, treacherous snake. She couldn't believe she'd been such an idiot. The man was a journalist and she was the granddaughter of Lord Trussed-Up Trussler. Of course Rando would find her interesting. Of course he would encourage her to discuss her family. How could she be so naive? With every line that she read, she could feel the waves of panic rising, threatening to engulf her. What had she *done*? What could she *do*? She stood up and walked round and round her flat, alternately biting her nails and gulping her wine. She wished Kitty was here, she wished Harrison was still her friend, she wished she had someone in whom she could confide.

She poured herself another glass and made herself read the article again.

Years ago, I read about the Irish leader Charles Stewart Parnell and was fascinated by the tragedy of the man: the fact that his glittering career was ruined in 1890 by revelations about his affair with a married woman. The papers had a field day. He died of a heart attack two years after the scandal broke, in the arms of the woman he loved. I remember I felt sorry for him.

I love gossip as much as anyone. Don't we all love reading about the scandals of the great and the good? Don't we swallow every salacious detail? Don't we laugh at every humiliating revelation? If a man aspires to be a public figure, doesn't he forfeit a right to our sympathy if he's found with his metaphorical, and more often than not actual, pants down?

As a connoisseur of political gossip, I have to say that the Trussler affair was hard to beat. We had Lord Trussler, charismatic Tory grandee, acknowledged authority on all matters European, TV and newspaper pundit. He died in a sordid brothel in Streatham, a long-term devotee of the sort of sado-masochistic practices one would see in a bad porn movie. You couldn't make it up! How we laughed!

And then I met his granddaughter. We became friends and now the story doesn't seem so funny after all. Hannah is a thoughtful, serious-minded . . .

Oh it was too bad! She couldn't bear to read what he said about her, it made her want to puke. She skimmed over the next couple of paragraphs and then swallowed hard.

> For the public, it's an excuse to laugh at people we envy. We read the story, we chat about it, we forget about it. Lord Trussler's daughter couldn't do that. Her father was her hero and when he fell off his pedestal, she fell into pieces too. Estranged from her mother and separated from her long-term partner, she lives alone, unable to . . .

Hannah let out a long, low moan. Why the hell had Emily introduced Rando to her? Did she not know that the man was an amoral, opportunistic, unpleasant little jerk? Was it possible Emily had even been in collusion with him? Hannah, in a fire of self-righteous fury and stomach-churning despair, strode into the sitting room, reached for her bag, pulled out her phone and scrolled down for Emily's number.

She waited with increasing rage for Emily to pick up. She presumed she was in a bar somewhere and certainly, when Emily at last answered the phone, there were other voices in the background.

'Hi, Hannah,' Emily said. 'How are you?'

Hannah took a deep breath. 'I'm not very happy, Emily, and I am going to tell you why. I had an odd day today: I kept thinking people at work were talking about me. And when I was coming home this evening, I decided I'd been imagining it, and then do you know what I saw, Emily? Would you like to have a guess?'

'Hannah, listen to me, I know what you're trying to—'

'I bought a paper on the way home. I bought it because on the front page there was a reference to an article on my family on page ten. So I bought it and now I have read the article on page ten. Do you know who wrote it, Emily? Your friend, Rando, wrote it. He talks about his good friend

Hannah Granger and he describes in great detail just how the scandal of Lord Trussler's death has affected the Trussler family . . . according to Hannah.'

'Oh, Hannah, I saw the paper this morning. I'm so sorry. I swear I knew nothing about it.'

'He's very frank and open, Emily, he confides in his readers all sorts of details about me and my mother and grandmother and he concludes with a pious little homily about the pernicious effects of press intrusion. It actually makes me want to vomit, Emily, and I probably will do just that when I put the phone down.'

'Hannah, I promise you, I had no idea he wanted to write about you or your family and I certainly haven't talked to him about your grandfather. Where did he get all his stuff from?'

Hannah swallowed hard. 'I presume it was from me. I laboured under the delusion that since he was *your* friend, he must therefore be a trustworthy sort of person. We had the odd drink together and he's taken things I've said and twisted them and made them sound terrible. My family will be appalled and hurt and desperately upset and I can't believe your friend could do this to me. I can't believe you had no idea—'

'Hannah, I know you're upset but I resent your implication that I am somehow involved in all this. I haven't even seen Rando since my party. I'm just as appalled as you are but it's no good blaming me just because you decided to shoot your mouth off to him. The man is a journalist, your family is newsworthy.'

'I thought I could trust him! He was your friend and then I thought he was my friend too.' She tried to stifle an angry sob. 'I can't trust anyone, after all. Everything's gone wrong and I don't understand people. Rando turns out to be a creep, Alfie turns out to be a rat and Harrison won't talk to me any more.' She sniffed furiously. 'I'd better go. If you see Rando, tell him I hate him, will you?'

Hannah put her phone on the table and covered her face with her hands. Oh God, she thought, oh God. She could imagine what Emily must be thinking. Poor Hannah, poor hysterical Hannah had finally lost the plot.

She bit her lip. Now was not the time to get hysterical. She must ring her mother first; then after she had rung her mother she would get extremely hysterical and very drunk.

Alberta answered the phone immediately. 'Hello, darling!' She sounded cheerful so she obviously hadn't seen the offending paper. 'How lovely to speak to you. I've only just got in from work so you've timed it beautifully.'

'Mum,' Hannah said, 'I have something to tell you.'

'Oh dear,' Alberta said. 'That sounds serious. Is anything wrong?'

'Yes, something is terribly wrong. Do you remember me telling you about a friend called Rando?'

'Of course I do. He's quite a new friend, isn't he? Has something happened to him?'

'He's a journalist,' Hannah said. 'I've been out for a few drinks with him from time to time. We swapped stories about our families. I didn't think anything of it. The thing is—'

'When you say you swapped stories,' Alberta's voice had developed a precision Hannah had rarely heard before, 'what exactly do you mean?'

'Well,' Hannah gulped, 'you know what it's like when

you're getting to know someone, they ask you questions and you . . . you answer them?'

There was a silence at the other end of the line during which Hannah could almost hear her mother's brain whirring and then Alberta spoke slowly and deliberately. 'A few months ago, your grandfather's name was splashed all over the press. You meet a journalist, he takes you out for a drink, he asks you questions about your family and *you answer them*?'

'I know it sounds terrible but it wasn't like that. I'd met him at Emily's house. He's a friend of Emily. We got talking at the party and I thought he just liked me. The next time I saw him, I hardly remembered he *was* a journalist. I was upset because you'd told me you were leaving Tony. He was sympathetic, he told me about *his* family. His parents were divorced and he . . . he was kind. And then this evening, I was coming home from work and I saw a headline in the *Daily Telegraph*—'

'That's Marma's paper! *What did he say*?'

'The headline said, "The Trussler Scandal Revisited. See Page 10." So I bought the paper and I turned to page ten and there was a big article by him. At first, it's not too bad. He mentions the . . . the pernicious effects of scandal on the people involved. He talks about Charles Stewart Parnell. Parnell was a—'

'I know who Parnell was.'

'Well, he talks about Parnell and then he gets on to our family. He says he interviewed me – but he *didn't* interview me, I'd never have agreed to an interview, we just talked. You *know* I would never have talked to the press if I'd known! You know I wouldn't do that!'

'What did you say to him, Hannah?'

'I can't remember exactly. I know I didn't say what he said I said, at least I didn't say it in the way he said I did. He twisted everything!'

'Since you say you can't remember what you said, how do you know he twisted it? What does he say you said?'

'Well, he goes on about Grandfather's death and the publicity and the way it's changed us. He concentrates on you and Marma. He says Marma's become a nervous recluse, living in a village which refuses to have anything to do with her. He says a lot about you as well. Mum? Are you still there?'

'What does he say you said about me?'

'I didn't say those things, I'm sure I didn't. I think he probably *inferred* . . . he must have made various assumptions and has made them sound like I said them. He says you found the press interest particularly difficult to handle and you blamed Marma for speaking to journalists. He says you felt it was Marma's fault that Grandfather visited prostitutes. He says you had a breakdown and that's why you left Tony to go and live on your own. I never said that! I promise I didn't say any of that! Mum? I am so sorry!'

There was a deafening silence at the other end of the phone.

'Mum?' Hannah prompted.

'I'm here. I'm trying to think. Marma will have read this. You must ring her right away and tell her he made most of it up. I'll ring her myself in a little while.'

'All right. I'll see you on Sunday.'

There was a brief pause. 'Do you mind if I cancel Sunday? I need time to think about all of this.'

The phone went dead. Hannah couldn't believe her mother had hung up on her. She put the phone down, stared at it for a few moments and then burst into tears.

Alberta couldn't remember the last time she had felt so consumed with rage. She stood in front of the bay window with cheeks aflame and heart pounding. She couldn't believe that her daughter, her own daughter, had stoked up the embers of the whole ghastly scandal. And how could Hannah, clever, sensible Hannah say such terrible things to a reporter? She must have had some inkling, some slight suspicion that he would use what she said. And Marma would have sat down this morning with her muesli and her coffee and she would have reached for her paper and the first words she would have seen would be *The Trussler Scandal Revisited*. And she would have read the article and read those terrible things that Hannah said she had not said . . . Oh it was unforgivable!

Alberta glanced at her watch. She would wait half an hour and then she would ring Marma and offer to go down first thing in the morning . . . No, she couldn't do that, she was doing a lunch in Epping. She would ring Marma and suggest taking her out to lunch on Sunday and she would tell her – she would tell her what?

The sound of the phone made her jump and she returned to the sofa, took a deep breath and picked it up.

'Alberta?' The voice sounded as shocked as she felt. 'Have you seen the *Telegraph*?'

'Oh, Christopher, I'm glad it's you. I haven't seen it but I've just had Hannah on the phone.' Alberta threw off her shoes and tucked her legs beneath her. 'She told me about it. She only met the man who wrote it a little while ago. She knew he was a journalist but she didn't wonder why he proceeded to ask her so many questions about her family. I feel so cross with her, I can't think—'

'Alberta,' Christopher said, 'please be quiet.'

'What did you say?'

'I asked you to be quiet. I think you are being extremely hard on Hannah.'

Alberta put her feet down on the floor and sat up straight. 'I don't understand. Are you trying to say none of this is Hannah's fault?'

'Of course I'm not. But you know as well as I do that Hannah doesn't tell lies. If she said half the things she's reported as saying, then it's because she believes them to be true. And if she thinks you didn't give a thought to Marma's grief when Pa died and if she thinks you blamed Marma for Pa's visits to prostitutes, then she's based those views on things you've said to her.'

'Now, listen—' Alberta was too agitated to remain seated. She stood up and began to pace the room, walking back and forth like a lion in a cage.

'Please let me finish, Alberta. I need to say this while I'm angry. I am about to break a promise I have kept for twenty years. I cannot endure the fact that you continue to think of Pa as some saintly figure while persisting in believing that Marma is a thoroughly unsatisfactory mother—'

'I've never said that!'

'You've come pretty close to it. You've never forgiven her for not coming home when Ed died.'

'Well, I'm sorry but—'

'If you want to know what really happened in the year that Ed died, I advise you to keep very quiet and stop interrupting me because this is the only time I am mad enough to tell you! Do you understand?'

Alberta came to a sudden stop by the window and took a deep breath. 'Yes.'

'These are the facts. Marma fell in love with Peter Repton, which is not surprising given that she had been unhappy for years. They were going to run off together. Your late husband discovered this and for some reason known only to himself, felt it necessary to tell Pa. The two of them decided to bribe Repton to break off the affair. Repton accepted the money and made some noble renunciation speech to Marma. After a few weeks, he thought better of it and tried to get her back. So Ed went round to Marma and told her a few home truths about her great love. He suggested she visit me and Helen in Toronto for a few weeks. He'd even bought her ticket. Marma told me later she was in such a state she'd have agreed to go to Siberia if he'd told her to. So Marma goes off to Toronto and Ed goes off to see Repton. On his way over, he has a collision with another vehicle and dies. Now this is where you have to listen very carefully. Pa rings Marma. He's in a terrible rage. He tells her she is responsible for Ed's death—'

'But that's ridiculous!'

'I know it's ridiculous. I told her day after day and week after week how ridiculous it was. But Marma believed it and she has gone on believing it. Pa tells her to stay in Canada until he feels ready to have her back. He tells her if she tries to contact you in any form he will instantly tell you why *she* is to blame for your husband's death. Pa was always very persuasive. Marma has always known that next to Ed, Pa was the most important person in your life. She decides that her penance is to go back to Pa, to be a good wife and to never let you know the true reason for her year-long exile. So while she is in Toronto, she does not write to you and she does not ring you. She also makes me promise I will never tell you any of this since her penance would become instantly worthless.'

'But,' Alberta shook her head, 'this is crazy!'

'I know it's crazy but it's very important to Marma. The only way she can reconcile what she thinks she did to your husband is to go on enacting this cover-up. So she has spent years knowing that you think she let you down in your darkest hours. In fact, it might please you to know that when she was in Toronto, she cried every day for you and I suspect she cried every night too. So now you have to start a penance of your own. You have to live with the fact that for twenty years you have misjudged her, and you have to live with the fact that you can't ask her forgiveness because you are not supposed to know.'

Alberta gave a long, shuddering sigh. 'Christopher,' she said, 'I don't care if you believe me or not – well, actually, I do care – but ever since I came to London I have tried to make things right between Marma and me. I *did* resent Marma and it probably was pathetic, but I don't any more and I haven't done for some time. It . . . it just *went*.' She pulled a tissue from her sleeve and blew her nose fiercely. 'When Hannah told me what that article said I thought, I felt *sick* and I suppose I felt sick because I knew that's what I did think and I don't think it *now* and I can't bear that Marma thinks I *do* think that. I really can't bear that.'

'Alberta,' Christopher said, 'I wish you wouldn't cry.'

Alberta sniffed. 'I'm sorry.'

'I'm sorry too. I was unfair. I lost my temper. I don't often do that.'

'I know,' Alberta said. 'Neither do I.'

'Oh dear,' Christopher said, 'we're not very good at this sort of thing, are we? Helen always tells me I'm too buttoned-up for words but on the rare occasions I undo the buttons, I find it frighteningly difficult to do them up again. Why don't you come round to dinner? Helen can cook us a meal.'

Alberta managed the ghost of a smile. 'I don't mean to be rude about Helen's culinary abilities, but I think I'd prefer it if you both came to supper with me.'

'To be honest,' Christopher said, 'so would I.'

'Come over next Friday. I'm pretty sure that's free. Talk to Helen. And Christopher . . .'

'Yes?'

'When Ed fixed up the Canada trip for Marma, did he ring you first?'

There was a pause, followed by a cautious, 'Yes.'

'Did he talk to you? What was he like?'

'He was very business-like and to the point. He told me he and Pa wanted you to be kept out of it all. He said it would only upset you. I remember being rather annoyed that Pa didn't say all this to me himself.'

'I see. Thanks, Christopher. I'm going now.'

'Right. I'll get back to you about next Friday.'

Alberta put the phone on the sofa and wiped her eyes with her hands. She heard the phone ring again and felt overcome with exhaustion. She was tempted to just let it ring and then she was glad she didn't.

'Alberta,' Marma said, 'I've just had Hannah on the phone.'

Alberta threw herself down on the sofa. 'Oh, Marma, I'm so *sorry*. That horrible article . . .'

'Forget about the article. I hate so-called intelligent pieces about gossip. They're every bit as prurient as articles in the gutter press but they're dressed up with historical references to make the reader think they're full of great truths. I can't be bothered with them. The point is your daughter is distraught.'

'I know she is and—'

'She was crying down the phone! I haven't heard Hannah cry since she was a small child! She has made a mistake. So have I. So have we all. I've invited her to lunch with me on Sunday and I hope you'll come too. And do ring her, Alberta, she's very unhappy.'

'I will. I was going to anyway. And Marma?'

'What is it, darling?'

'Have I told you I love you?'

'Not lately, dear.' Marma cleared her throat. 'I love you too.'

'I know,' Alberta said. 'I know you do.'

# CHAPTER TWENTY-THREE

## *When the Legends Die*

The *Telegraph* article had unexpectedly beneficial consequences. Since everyone in Marma's village took the *Telegraph*, everyone in Marma's village read that the serene Lady Trussler was now a neurotic wreck. Marma's village felt a collective guilt and, in the next few days, Marma's phone began to ring more often, invitations were issued, visits were made. Marma, who was not one to bear a grudge, received all overtures with grace and tried not to mind that the Cartwrights remained stubbornly silent.

For Alberta, the repercussions of Rando's article were far less gratifying. All her doubts, all her tentative attempts at reassessing the past had now coalesced into one final, damning verdict. Her ignorance of her husband's true character was matched only by her blindness towards her father's flaws.

Pa had been vindictive and cruel. He had instigated Marma's year-long exile in Canada. Worse, after Ed's death, he had ensured she remained incommunicado. He had sold the family home, possibly because Marma had taken Peter Repton there, more probably because he knew it was a house she loved. Alberta did not doubt that her father had loved her but his desire to punish his wife was clearly more powerful than his wish to help his daughter.

She could remember Pa talking to her about Marma's abrupt departure for Canada. He had been careful not to directly criticize her but she could see now that he had painted a devastating picture of a self-absorbed, restless woman searching for self-fulfilment. She always threw herself wholeheartedly into her projects, he said; it was no surprise that she was behaving like this. Her desire to cut herself off from her family in England was all part and parcel of it. 'Never mind,' he had told Alberta, before flying off to Brussels for a fortnight, 'you have me to look after you.'

She could understand Pa feeling angry, vengeful even, over Marma's infidelity. Even so, his response seemed hugely disproportionate to the offence. The only possible explanation, if not justification, was that he genuinely believed Marma was responsible for Ed's death.

But how could any sane man hold Marma responsible for what was just, after all, a tragic accident? At night, Alberta lay in bed and tried to think back to the terrible period after Ed's death. Certainly, Pa had been as stricken as she had been. She could remember an evening when he took her out to dinner at some place near her in-laws' house. They did nothing but talk about Ed and after he had called for the bill, he had given a bleak smile and confessed that for him the fun had now gone out of politics. There was no doubt about it. He had loved Ed like a son. In fact, he had loved Ed more than he had ever loved Christopher.

And then there was Ed. What was she to make of Ed? With every new revelation he became more of an enigma.

She had thought they were as close as two people could be. Yet he had been able to come home after a day spent bullying her mother and bribing her mother's lover and be the loving husband and the gentle father. She could think of nothing in the weeks before his death that betrayed anything untoward. True, he spent more time in London and he said little about what he was doing. But that was not unusual. Ed had always said that when he came home he liked to switch off and forget about work. And yet that *wasn't* true. Most weekends, Pa would ring Ed about some problem and she would watch him spring into action, listening eagerly and talking with fluency and enthusiasm. He loved all the intrigues and the deals and the manoeuvrings as much as Pa did.

She had known Ed for nearly five years and apart from the red-haired boy in Mallorca – she obviously had a tendency towards hero-worship – she had never been so sure of her feelings before or since. Throughout their brief married life she had believed wholeheartedly in his honour and his decency and his brilliance. Only now, two decades later, was she beginning to realize that the love of her life was as much of a myth as any of her Western heroes.

Had Ed loved her? Was it possible to love her when he excluded her from so much of his life? She had spent all those years with Tony in the belief that what they had was a poor second to what she had had with Ed. In those circumstances it was miraculous that she and Tony had lasted as long as they had. Her entire life with Tony had been based on the assumption that she had had the perfect, once-in-a-lifetime sort of perfect relationship with Ed. It was too easy to think she'd been absurdly naive. She knew, of course, that she *had* been absurdly naive – no man could be that perfect, no relationship could be that easy – but how could she have known that Ed was quite so unlike the principled man she had thought he was? Why *hadn't* he told her about Marma? Was it really because he wanted to protect her or was it because he knew that if she *did* know the truth she'd be appalled at his own very active part in her mother's humiliation and retribution?

She wished she had her shoe box with her. She knew exactly where it was. It was under the high chair in the back of the attic in the house in Bath. The shoe box contained all the cards, notes and letters she had had from him. If she read them again in the light of what she knew now, perhaps she would be able to find out if her perfect relationship had been based on nothing but the fact that she was the daughter of Michael Trussler.

It was a good idea to go to Bath. Apart from anything else, it was high time to bid a proper farewell to the house in Cleveland Walk. She had embarked on her brave new life, she realized now, in the comforting belief that if things went wrong, she could always return to her old one. It was time to fold up that particular safety net. She owed Tony that much at least. He had been an unwitting casualty of the whole sordid drama. Was it surprising that she had been unable to make him happy when she had continued to hero-worship a man who never actually existed?

She had an unexpected free day coming up after a client cancelled a birthday party. On Monday, Alberta rang Evie and asked if she could go round for lunch on Thursday; she was coming down to collect a few final things, she said. She didn't mention the shoe box.

*　　*　　*

Hannah had been exhilarated by Harrison's email. She had read it repeatedly, which, given its brevity – 'Fancy a drink, Wednesday, 6.15?' – did not take long to do. On Wednesday morning, she washed her hair with extra vigour and before she left work that evening, she spent at least twenty minutes in the Ladies, fixing her make-up.

She arrived at the Copper Arm promptly at quarter past six and looked round impatiently. He was there at the table by the window. He was sitting, hunched over his mobile, wearing a vivid green jersey and a thin grey scarf. She could see he had bought her a drink, which was courteous and thoughtful and somehow rather ominous. When he saw her, he stood up and smiled and Hannah's heart froze. She had seen that smile two or three times before, but it had never been directed at *her* until now. It was the smile of a man trying to extricate himself from the clutches of a woman.

In all her life, Hannah could never remember feeling as scared as she did at this moment. She had read once that Mary, Queen of Scots, had insisted on dressing up in a beautiful gown before going to her execution. And now here was Hannah in her best pink silk shirt and most flattering grey trousers, on her way to be told she was going to be cut out of Harrison's life for now and forever.

She went over to him and said lightly, 'Thank you for buying my wine.'

'It's nice to see you,' Harrison said.

She watched him turn off his mobile and slip it in his jacket pocket. He didn't *look* as if it was nice to see her. 'You're looking well,' she said.

'So are you. You look great.' He glanced down at his

drink and then out towards the bar and then finally, awkwardly, at her. 'I'm afraid I can't stay long, I have loads of paperwork to do . . .'

'That's fine,' Hannah said miserably, 'I've got work to do too.'

'So,' Harrison took a sip of his wine. 'How's the job going?'

'It's better than it was,' Hannah said. It was no use. She had never been any good at polite conversation. If she was going to meet her doom, she might as well go down fighting. She took a gulp of her wine and fixed him with a sudden, challenging stare. 'Someone caught me crying in the Ladies the other day and now people seem to be a bit nicer to me.'

'Why were you crying? Was it to do with the *Telegraph* article?'

'Did you read it?'

'Yes,' Harrison said. 'Emily showed it to me.'

'I expect she told you about my phone call to her.' She saw his eyes flicker away from her and swallowed hard. 'You were round there that night, weren't you? You were there when I rang her and went off into that hysterical rant. What did everyone say? Did you agree that poor old Hannah had finally lost it?'

'No, we didn't. Emily rang her journalist friend and told him she never wanted to see him again and we then spent a rather good hour or so tearing his character to pieces.'

'Oh,' Hannah said. 'I must give Emily a ring. I seem to remember I was rather horrid to her.' She clasped her hands tightly in front of her. 'I seem to remember I mentioned you in that phone call.'

'Yes,' Harrison said. 'That's actually why I wanted to see you.'

'Harrison,' Hannah said urgently, 'if you are meeting me out of *pity*, then I would really rather you left now.'

Harrison shifted uncomfortably in his seat. 'It's not pity . . .'

'Then what is it?' Hannah demanded. 'I don't know what I've done wrong! Why can't we be friends any more? What's gone wrong?'

'It's difficult,' Harrison said.

'It's only difficult because you *make* it difficult.' Hannah put her elbows on the table and leant forward. 'I've been trying and trying to work out why you don't like me any more and nothing makes sense. I mean, I can't believe it's that you're gay and if—'

'You think I'm gay?' Harrison appeared to be genuinely puzzled. 'Why do you think I'm gay?'

'Well, I don't really,' Hannah said a little uncertainly, 'but you told Kitty there was something you'd never told me and I couldn't think what else it could be.'

'Hannah,' Harrison said, 'for an intelligent person, you are remarkably obtuse.'

'I know I am,' Hannah said humbly. 'I've never been very good at understanding people. But I really *hate* not understanding you.'

'There isn't a lot to understand,' Harrison said. 'In fact, it's really very simple. I haven't stopped being your friend because I don't like you any more. I have to stop being your friend because I like you too much.'

Hannah put a hand to her forehead and stared intensely at Harrison before shaking her head in frustration. 'I don't understand,' she said.

'The first time I met you,' Harrison said, 'I fell in love with you.'

'But . . .' Hannah stopped and then realized she had no idea what to say.

'More to the point,' Harrison said, 'I'm still in love with you.'

'But . . .' Hannah repeated and tried to clear her throat.

A quiver of amusement brushed across his face. 'Do you want me to get you some water?'

'No, I'm just . . . It's just . . . Harrison,' she whispered, 'why didn't you *tell* me?'

'I never got a chance,' he said. 'The second time I saw you, you came bounding into my room to tell me about the god that was Russell and as soon as you stopped going out with him, you fell for lanky Ludovic. One reason I decided to go abroad for a few months after university was to try to get over you. When that didn't work, I decided I had to stop seeing you. I'm sorry I ran out on you after your supper. I lost it for a while.'

'I never knew,' Hannah said.

'That is perfectly evident.'

Hannah sat up straight. 'Listen,' she said, 'I have something to tell you. I may be stupid but I do know that there's something very odd about the fact that losing you has made me a hundred times more miserable than losing Alfie. I hated the fact that you didn't like me any more. I couldn't bear the idea that you wouldn't see me. The point is, Harrison . . .' She looked expectantly at him and then smiled. 'Now who's being obtuse?' She reached forward to take his face in her hands and kissed him hard on the mouth.

She was still kissing him when an unpleasantly familiar

voice said, 'Now this I cannot believe. Is Hannah Granger kissing a man?'

Hannah broke away and looked up. 'Hi, Dylan,' she said.

Dylan laughed. 'I hope I'm not interrupting you.'

'Well, actually,' Hannah said, 'Harrison and I thought we'd go home and indulge in some serious sex. Do you want to come along?'

Dylan blinked, apparently trying to compute this new piece of information. 'Either you're trying to be funny,' he said, 'or you are seriously weird. Since I know what a great sense of humour you don't have, I assume you are trying to be funny.' He was clearly rather pleased with his quick-witted response because he gave them a smug smile before he left the pub.

'Yuck!' Hannah said. 'I can't believe someone as nice as Tony can have a son as hideous as Dylan.'

'Perhaps he's nice when you get to know him,' Harrison said charitably.

'I *do* know him,' Hannah retorted and then wondered if perhaps she didn't really.

'Tell me,' Harrison asked politely, 'are we really going to go home and have some serious sex?'

Hannah blushed. 'I thought you had to get back and do some work.'

'I thought *you* had to get back and do some work.'

'If you want to know the truth,' Hannah said, 'I don't give a damn about my work.'

Harrison put a hand to her forehead. 'Hannah,' he said with exaggerated concern, 'are you sure you are well?'

'I am now. Do you know something? My mother always said you fancied me.'

'Your mother,' Harrison said, 'is a very perceptive woman.'

Hannah nodded seriously. 'She is,' she said, leaning forward to kiss him again. 'She really, really is.'

At nine o'clock on Thursday morning, Alberta was about to board the train at Paddington when she heard a voice behind her call, 'Ed! I'm here!'

Alberta glanced to her right and felt a shudder of recognition. A tall, dark-haired young man in a familiar tartan scarf waved his arm and ran towards her. As the man passed her, Alberta exhaled. He looked nothing like Ed after all, and the colours of his scarf were different from the one Ed had always worn.

Alberta boarded the train and found her seat and, as it eased out of the station, she turned her head towards the window.

What was it about memory? Why were some things so easy to remember and others so easy to forget? That first time she had met Ed was as clear as yesterday, which was all the more extraordinary given her two-decade-long attempt to block out all thoughts of him.

Ed had been one of the first guests to arrive at her parents' drinks party. Pa introduced them but almost immediately a big fat MP with a ridiculous moustache had interrupted them with 'Can I have a quick word?' and she watched, dismayed, as Ed was borne away for what must have been ten thousand words. As the room filled up, Alberta had inane conversation after inane conversation. She talked to a courteous young man who was polite to the daughter in the hope the father would notice; she talked to elder statesmen who flirted benignly and a couple of well-known lechers whose attentions were not benign at all. And every time she looked around for Ed, she caught him looking at her.

At last, when people began to leave, she noticed with despair that he had his scarf on and she responded dully to the well-upholstered baroness who seemed to be going on and *on* about the necessity for ambition in twentieth-century women. And then, quite suddenly, he was there, apologizing to the baroness for running off with her companion and bemoaning the fact that they had another engagement.

'But I don't,' Alberta whispered as he led her away. 'I'm not going anywhere.'

'But you are,' Ed insisted. 'I've told your mother. I'm taking you out to dinner. Unless,' he paused to look down at her, 'you'd rather stay here and continue your conversation with the baroness. She has some impressive statistics about the proportion of women to men in Parliament.'

'I'll get my coat,' Alberta said.

At dinner, he made her laugh with scurrilous stories of the great and the possibly not so good. He plied her with questions. Did she like working in a restaurant? Why had she wanted to be a cook? Did she enjoy eating food as much as she enjoyed cooking it? Did she have a boyfriend? Why not? Who had been her last boyfriend? Why had they broken up? When she tried to draw him on the subject of his own romantic past, he said, 'None of that matters any more,' and he looked at her in a way that made the blood course through her body like an unblocked dam. But he didn't touch her, even when he took her home and she deliberately took her time in finding her keys. She mentioned in a careless way that couldn't have deceived him that her parents were going away for the weekend. Would he like to sample her culinary skills on Saturday evening? She couldn't believe she was being so forward but he didn't seem surprised. He said he'd come over at eight and he left her with a smile that kept her awake for hours.

The next evening he rang to say he'd forgotten he had a dinner engagement. He said he was sorry. He said he had enjoyed the previous evening. He did not say he would see her again. Alberta knew she could be gullible and gauche but she was not so stupid she couldn't see when a man was trying to get out of an unwanted date.

On Friday evening she got back from work and poured a third of her mother's bath oil into her bath. She lowered herself into the water and vowed she would refuse to attend any more of her parents' drinks parties. When she emerged from the bath, she wrapped her towel round her and studied her reflection in the mirror. She wished she had straight hair, longer legs and anything else that might have attracted Ed.

She went to her bedroom and put on pyjama bottoms and an old T-shirt and then she heard the doorbell.

It was Ed. He wore a suit and tie and had obviously come straight from work. He was holding a bottle and held it out. 'Do you have time for a drink?' he asked.

She was tempted to say she was getting ready to go out but she was terrified that if she sent him away he would never come back. She compromised by giving him what she hoped was an indifferent shrug.

They sat with their glasses, at either end of the sofa.

'Alberta,' Ed said, 'I told you I had a previous engagement tomorrow. That was a lie.'

'Oh,' said Alberta, tossing her hair back, 'I know *that*.'

'I got cold feet,' he said.

She took a sip of the wine and put her glass down on the little table to her left. 'I see,' she said.

'No, you don't.' He mirrored her gesture, taking a sip of wine and putting the glass down. 'I've just started working for your father. I like him very much. I think he likes me. I can't afford to go out with his daughter and then screw things up. And I do have a tendency to screw things up.'

She pulled her legs up onto the sofa and rested her face on her knees. 'I wouldn't mind,' she said.

'Yes, you would. What I came here to say was that if . . . if you hadn't been the daughter of your father, I would have asked you to come back with me on Wednesday night.'

Alberta looked up at him. 'I would have said yes.'

He stared at her. 'You're wearing nothing under that T-shirt.'

'And I'm wearing nothing under my pyjama bottoms.'

'Really?' He raised his eyebrows. 'I wish you hadn't told me that.' He glanced down and frowned at her feet. 'Your toe is bleeding,' he said. 'What happened?'

'It's nothing. I caught it against the tap.'

He sat up and took her right foot in his hands, as if he were a scientist inspecting some precious specimen. Then slowly, very slowly, he lowered his head and licked the wounded toe. With each gentle flick of his tongue, she felt an answering lash of red-hot lust. At last, he put down her foot and stood up. He stared at the door for what seemed forever. Then he took off his jacket and loosened his tie. 'Oh hell,' he said, reaching for her hands and pulling her up against him, 'let's take a gamble, shall we?'

They married six months later. A year after that, Hannah was born. When Ed was selected for a constituency in the Midlands, they rented a small flat above a hardware stall in Peterborough. When Ed wasn't working in London, he was visiting local hospitals, spearheading a campaign for school playing fields and grabbing every opportunity to arrange photo-shoots for the local paper. And then he died.

Alberta looked out at the passing landscape. The streets and office blocks and housing estates were giving way to fields and small hamlets and sheep. She rested her head against the back of her seat. The truth was, she thought, that as each year had followed another, the relationship with Ed had been mummified by a thick patina of romantic nostalgia. She wasn't sure it was possible to break through that and disinter the true reality of it. Perhaps the shoe box would help.

She decided she needed a coffee. She hoisted her bag onto her shoulder and made her way through the carriages to the buffet car. It was just after she took her place in the queue that she glanced through the glass door and saw Daniel Driver walking along the aisle. There was nowhere to hide. Alberta remembered what she'd said to him the last time she'd seen him. She remembered what he'd said to her. She pulled her book from her bag, opened it and desperately pretended to read.

She could *hear* Daniel come and stand behind her. She could *feel* him looking at her.

'Alberta?' His voice sounded almost apologetic. 'Did you know that you are reading your book upside down?'

She blushed furiously and snapped her book shut. There was no point in dissimulation or prevarication. She squared her shoulders and turned to face him. 'I panicked,' she confessed. 'I saw you through the door and I panicked. But actually, I'm glad you are here. I want to apologize for being so rude at that party. I was hot and bothered and I took it out on you. There is no excuse. And to make it worse, you went out of your way afterwards to stop me from getting the sack. I feel very ashamed.'

'Wow,' Daniel said. 'I don't know what to say. I'm not used to you being so *nice*!'

Alberta gave a reluctant smile. 'I have behaved badly, haven't I? You must let me buy you coffee. Would you like black or white? Or perhaps you'd rather have tea?'

'A black coffee would be fine. Thank you. I'll wait by the window.'

Alberta turned back to face the queue and discovered there were only two people left in front of her. She took out her wallet and waited her turn, keeping her eyes fixed resolutely in front of her.

When she joined Daniel, she found him standing by the window with a smile on his lips.

'What's so funny?' she asked, handing him his coffee.

'When I saw you just now, you reminded me of something I haven't thought of for years,' Daniel said. 'A long time ago, I was on holiday and I was sitting in a bar and I spotted this stunning brunette. She picked up her book – it was *War and Peace*, which rather impressed me – then I noticed she was reading it upside down. So I went over and asked her why and she said she did it to exercise her brain. I'd forgotten all about her until I saw you doing the same thing.' He stopped and stared at her. 'Do you *know* you are looking at me as if you've seen a ghost?'

'I-I'm sorry,' Alberta stammered, 'but I think I might have done. This is really rather odd. A long time ago, I was also on holiday, in a bar. I could see a red-haired boy looking at me and I was so embarrassed, I picked up my book without realizing it was upside down and then he came over and— But this is impossible. It couldn't be you. He had red hair.'

Daniel looked at her for a few moments and then gave an incredulous laugh. 'The first time I saw you,' he said, 'in that open-air pool, I *knew* you looked familiar and I couldn't think why. But your hair is blonde.'

'I had dyed it brown,' Alberta said. 'I was going through a phase of wanting to be taken seriously. That's why I was reading *War and Peace*. I never did manage to finish it. What about your red hair?'

'I had to dye it red after a particularly vicious game of forfeits. It's all coming back to me now. I really liked you. I meant to meet up with you the next evening and then the next day we visited some friends on the other side of the island and I got wasted and we ended up staying there a couple of nights.'

'I waited for you the next evening. I was very upset when you didn't show up.' Alberta studied Daniel's face carefully. 'I'm just trying to remember what you looked like. This whole business is so peculiar. First of all, you turn out to be Disgusting Daniel, and then you turn out to be the Man I Fell in Love With on Holiday.'

'Did you really fall in love with me?' Daniel asked. 'I wish I'd known.'

'I've thought about you so often.' Alberta felt quite light-headed. 'And all the time, you never had red hair at all.'

Daniel gave a half-smile. 'You know, if I believed in this sort of thing, I'd say that fate was trying to tell us something.'

'Don't you believe in fate?' Alberta asked.

'I'm beginning to think perhaps I do,' Daniel said. 'Don't you think this is all rather extraordinary? We met when we were children. We met again in Spain years later. And now we've met again. It sort of makes you wonder, don't you think?'

'Yes,' Alberta agreed. 'It sort of does.'

'Do you remember me telling you about Iceland?' he asked. 'Do you remember you said you'd love to see it?'

'Yes,' Alberta said. 'You made it sound so beautiful.'

'Well,' Daniel began and then clasped both his hands round his polystyrene mug as the train lurched to a stop. 'We're at Reading,' he said. 'This is where I get out. Alberta, at the risk of getting slapped or insulted again, I am going to be brave. I am going back there for a few days, just before Christmas. At this time of year it has a magic all of its own. Why don't you come with me?'

# CHAPTER TWENTY-FOUR

## *The Good, The Bad and The Devious*

As Alberta walked along Cleveland Walk, she glanced at her watch. Evie had suggested that she come over at one. She had a good hour and a half until then.

She let herself into the house and picked up the mail that was scattered over the carpet. She sifted through the letters: an animal charity envelope stuffed with greetings cards of black-eyed seal pups, a couple of bills, a wine merchant catalogue and a postcard addressed to the two of them from a one-time neighbour who'd moved to Australia – 'Hi, you two, How are you? When are you coming to see us? How is Hannah? How is Jacob? GET IN TOUCH!'

Alberta put all the correspondence on the hall table and glanced at the coat stand just in case Tony's green jacket was there. Of course he would still be in London. She wondered how often he *did* come home these days.

She had come here to get her shoe box. She put her bag under the table and went upstairs.

Some time – not now, but some time – she and Tony must clear out the attic. It was a tip. The old high chair was in the corner, there were boxes of toys, a broken railway set, a stringless guitar, a bag stuffed with Hannah's glowing school reports and another with most of Jacob's less glowing ones. There was Lionel's school trunk containing a variety of fancy-dress clothes, a science set that Jacob had loved for all of two weeks and a huge stack of long-playing records. Alberta went across to the high chair and knelt down to pick up the shoe box. She picked it up, blew the dust off it and opened the lid. Inside, there were a few yellowing notes, a couple of Valentine cards, confetti-crisp newspaper cuttings, a thin volume of selected poems by T.S. Eliot. She opened the book. On the frontispiece, Ed had written, 'My darling Alberta, if one is to give and to take, then to you I give what I can give and from you take only in honesty and happiness, Ed.'

Alberta sighed and put the book back in the box. Ed had given her happiness at least and she was no longer sure she'd have kept even that if he hadn't died. She was not going to learn anything new here. She already knew more than enough. What she must not do was spend the next twenty years wondering if he had really loved her. Felicity Fullock had asked her if Ed had made her happy. He *had* made her happy. A long time ago, he had made her happy. It was time now to leave him and her love for him in the past where they belonged. She replaced the lid and put the box back where she had found it.

She went downstairs and wandered into the kitchen. The answerphone was flashing and without thinking she went over and pressed the Play button.

'Hi, Tony, it was nice having you to dinner last week. I hope you're well. I was only ringing because I've been given tickets to the theatre for next Saturday. It's a Tennessee

Williams play. I wondered if you'd like to come with me? Give me a ring and I'll speak to you soon.'

She knew that voice, although she'd never heard it sound so tentative and so gentle before. Tony was seeing Erica Wright. Erica Wright! What on earth could Tony see in the terrifying Ms Wright? And immediately, Alberta knew exactly what Tony saw in her. Erica was tall and clever and elegant with auburn hair just as Lydia was tall and clever and elegant with auburn hair. At Christmas, she would probably find Erica ensconced in what had been *her* kitchen and *her* bedroom. She would have to ask Erica if she wanted help in the kitchen and Erica would say no thank you and they would all have to eat Erica's horrible turkey.

She pressed the Play button and listened again. Oh, Erica, she thought, you are smitten, you are definitely smitten.

Something made her turn round. Tony was standing in the doorway. He was holding a couple of Waitrose bags and she watched him put them on the table. She blushed and turned off the machine. 'I-I'm sorry,' she stammered. 'I wasn't prying. I put it on without thinking.'

Tony took off his jacket and put it over a chair. 'You don't have to apologize. It's nice to see you. Are you down here for long?'

'I've arranged to have lunch with Evie. I'll go back this afternoon. I was given a day off and thought it would be good to see her and Lionel. What about you? You're not usually here on Thursdays.'

Tony gave a short laugh. 'I've had rather a difficult few days. I thought I'd come down and work from home for a bit. Do you remember the Growlers?'

'Aren't they the band that always sings about death?'

Tony nodded. 'They gave an interview a few months ago in which the lead vocalist, a very profound thinker, declared that Death was the new Life.'

'What does *that* mean?'

'I have no idea. I suspect it doesn't mean anything at all. They brought out a record in March . . .'

'I remember you playing it. It was all about suicide.'

'That's the one. Great sound and appalling lyrics. There were these lines:

'"*Cover your head with a bag,*
*And then you will feel it sag.*
*Have your Crunchy Nut Cornflakes first,*
*And then you will feel a burst,*
*Of mind-emptying death.*"'

'Don't tell me,' Alberta said. 'Some fan has decided to do a Growler-type suicide.'

'You've got it,' Tony said. 'The boy was found in his room, which was covered in Growler posters. His mother decided to sue us. You wouldn't believe the conversations I've had with the lawyers. They think we'll be all right since he was eating Coco Pops not Crunchy Nut Cornflakes before he killed himself. It's all been pretty unpleasant.' He walked over to the kettle. 'Do you want some coffee?'

'That would be nice.' She sat down at the table and it was only then she noticed the postcard. 'I see you've got one from Pompeii too. "Maud and I loved all the petrified corpses, especially the dog with his legs in the air."' She smiled. 'Those two are so well-suited!'

'Did you notice his PS? He'll definitely be home in time for Christmas.'

'Good,' Alberta said. She didn't want to think about Christmas. 'Everything's looking very tidy. I'm impressed.'

Tony took out the cafetiere and gave a little bow. 'Thank you. I know it's not up to your exceptionally high standards.'

'It looks fine.' Alberta watched Tony putting mugs on the table and taking milk from the supermarket bag. It was odd that it felt so natural and at the same time so unnatural to be sitting here with him in the kitchen. She said, 'I haven't seen you since the Ringwood party.'

Tony filled the kettle with water and switched it on. 'I heard about the meringue incident. I wish I'd seen it. Did you tell Marma what you did?'

'No, of course not. I nearly lost my job over it.'

'I think it was brilliant. I take it you have an understanding boss.'

'She wasn't *that* understanding. She was going to sack me, but Daniel Driver –' Alberta was aware that she blushed as she mentioned his name – 'Daniel got in touch with her and persuaded her to keep me on. That's why I asked you for his address. I wanted to thank him.'

'He's a good man,' Tony said. 'Have you seen him since?'

'Funnily enough,' Alberta said, 'we met on the train today. He got off at Reading.'

Tony nodded. 'He's doing some work with the Seeds of Persephone there. Did he say it was going well?'

'We didn't talk about that. Actually, we made a rather extraordinary discovery. Do you remember me telling you about the red-haired boy I once met in Mallorca?'

'I think,' Tony said gravely, 'you might have mentioned him once or twice over the years.'

'Well,' Alberta said, 'it turns out he was Daniel!'

'Daniel hasn't got red hair.'

'Apparently, he had to dye it after a game of forfeits. Isn't that weird?'

'It certainly is.' He gave a half-smile. 'It's almost like some supernatural force is bent on getting the two of you together.'

'That's what Daniel said.'

'I bet he did. So when are you going to see him again?'

Alberta laughed. 'How do you know that I *am*?'

'I know Daniel.'

'He *did* invite me to go to Iceland with him.'

'Are you going?'

She wished he would stop spooning coffee into the cafetiere. She wished he would turn round and face her. 'In the last few months,' she told his back, 'I've discovered some pretty nasty facts about my husband and my father. As a result, I'm pretty wary about any idea of resurrecting the red-haired romance of my youth.'

'He's a nice man.'

'I know he's a nice man. He's also incapable of looking at a woman without flirting with her and, actually, there is something a little *sleazy* about him.'

*That* made him turn round. 'Sleazy?'

'He is definitely a little bit sleazy.'

He grinned and poured boiling water into the cafetiere. 'Poor Daniel. I'm beginning to feel almost sorry for him.'

'Poor Daniel, my foot!'

'You know that message you heard from Erica,' Tony

said carelessly. 'I bumped into her in town a few weeks ago. She invited me over to dinner . . .'

'You don't need to tell me anything about this,' Alberta said quickly. 'It's none of my business.'

'It sort of feels,' Tony said slowly, 'as if it *is* your business. We had dinner and nothing happened. We just had dinner.' He pressed the plunger down until it hit the coffee.

'Oh,' Alberta said. She watched him bring the coffee over to the table and felt suddenly self-conscious. 'I mustn't be too long,' she said. 'Evie's expecting me.'

'Actually,' Tony said, 'she's not.'

'What?' Alberta threw him an anxious glance. 'Why not?'

'I have a confession to make. Do you want milk?'

'What? No, I don't want any milk.'

Tony sat down opposite her and put his hands together on the table. 'Evie rang me on Tuesday. She told me you were coming down to have lunch with her. I asked if she'd mind if I hijacked you. Then I made some calls and rearranged a few meetings. I caught the early train this morning. I did some shopping and then dropped in on the parents. I was over with them when you arrived.'

'But . . .'

'The advantage of having a mother like mine is that she gives me free advice whenever I want it. The disadvantage of having a mother like mine is that she gives me free advice whenever I don't want it. She keeps telling me I'm hopeless at expressing my feelings. I *am* hopeless at expressing my feelings.' He gave a short laugh. 'Of course it's always been easy for Mum to express her feelings because she's always had a clear idea of what her feelings *are*.' He poured out the coffee and passed her a mug. 'Do you remember the evening I first met your father? You'd told him we were planning to move in together and he invited us out to dinner. Halfway through the meal, you realized you'd forgotten to tell your mother-in-law where you'd put Hannah's cough medicine if she woke up. You went to make a call and your father took the chance to put me right about a few things.'

'What did he say?'

'He thought I should know that Ed was the most brilliant young man he'd ever met. He wanted me to know I could never match up to him and that you knew that too.'

Alberta stared at him in dismay. 'How could he do that?' She shook her head slowly. 'I always knew Pa loved Ed. I think his death seriously unhinged him. Oh Lord, it's no wonder you didn't like him!'

There was a ghost of a twinkle in Tony's eyes. 'It certainly made it difficult to relax with him.'

'Oh, Tony, I'm sorry!'

Tony shrugged. 'It's not your fault. And, anyway, I knew you loved Ed. I told myself it didn't matter. After all, I still loved Lydia, didn't I? As long as I told myself that, it didn't seem to matter too much. It only started to matter when Lydia decided to remarry. I *thought* I was very upset. I didn't even know why at first. And then it dawned on me: I was jealous of her. She was so happy and certain and I . . . I wasn't certain of anything. I could see you were fascinated by Daniel Driver . . .'

'Tony, that is so unfair!' Alberta said furiously. 'I was cross with you because *you* hadn't bothered to tell me Lydia was getting married again even though it was obvious that it was *painfully* on your mind. And as for being fascinated by Daniel Driver, if I did find him fascinating it was only because I'd forgotten what it was like to be in the company of someone who *did* find me attractive! And then you didn't even *tell* me about Lydia's wedding date. How do you think *that* made me feel?'

Tony gave a twisted smile. 'Bertie, I'm not trying to blame you for my pathetic neuroses. Lydia's announcement threw me into a thoroughly self-indulgent depression and your father's death didn't make things any easier. I was bad-tempered and angry and I didn't really understand why I *was* bad-tempered but I somehow felt it had to be your fault and then you said you wanted to leave . . .'

'I said I wanted to leave after you accused me of sending my own mother an anonymous letter.'

'I know.' Tony looked straight at her. 'I pretty much fucked up, didn't I?'

'I think we both did.'

'The funny thing was,' Tony mused, 'when Marma told me it was Joan Cartwright who'd sent that article, everything became clear . . . sort of.'

'What does *that* mean?'

'I mean, I wasn't sure how I'd got myself into this mess but at least I knew it *was* a mess and I didn't like it. I couldn't believe I accused you of doing something so terrible. I couldn't believe I'd messed up so spectacularly. And that's when I asked you to come back to me.'

'Excuse me!' Alberta sat bolt upright. 'You did NOT ask me to come back to you! You sent me a DVD – which was very nice of you although I haven't seen it yet as I don't have a DVD player – and you asked me if I was coming to stay at Christmas.'

'I asked you if you'd come home for Christmas.'

'You see,' Alberta cried, 'that is *so* like you! Won't you come home for Christmas, you said. What does that mean?'

'That I'm rubbish at saying what I want?' Tony suggested.

'You can say that again. I've been listening carefully to everything you've said and I'm sorry my father said those stupid things to you but the fact remains that if Lydia was to suddenly ring you up and tell you she loved you—'

'I don't care a jot about Lydia. I don't think I've cared about her for years. What I do know is that for two people who were supposedly in love with two other people, you and I still managed to make each other pretty happy for a very long time.'

Alberta looked away. 'I *did* think we were happy,' she said slowly. 'And then these last few months I wondered if I'd imagined it all.'

'I miss you,' Tony said. 'I miss you all the time. Even when I went to dinner with Erica, especially when I went out to dinner with Erica, I was missing you.'

'I can't think why,' Alberta said stiffly. 'Erica is just your type.'

'No, she's not. My type turns out to be a blonde-haired midget with a topknot on her head.'

Alberta's eyes welled up with tears. 'Actually,' she said, 'I'm thinking of getting my topknot cut off.'

'Don't!' Tony said unequivocally. 'I love your topknot.'

'You love my topknot.' Alberta sniffed, fished in her pocket for a tissue and blew her nose.

There was a long silence. Tony raised his hands and then let them fall. 'Bertie,' he said, 'you know what I'm trying to tell you.'

'That's the trouble, I never know what you're trying to tell me. *What* are you trying to tell me?'

Tony shifted in his seat. 'That I do,' he said.

'You do what?'

Tony pushed his chair back and stood up. Then he bent down, took Alberta's face in his hands and kissed her. 'I love you,' he said. 'I love you really badly.'

Alberta stared up at him and tried to say something sensible. She really wanted to say something sensible – like, do you really not fancy Erica or do you really not love Lydia any more – but instead she could feel the tears running down her cheeks and it was quite impossible to say anything at all.

Tony sat down and drew her face to his and he kissed her again. And when he had finished kissing her, he looked at her and said, 'You are so beautiful.'

'Tony,' she said, 'I can't remember the last time you kissed me like that.'

'Bertie,' Tony murmured, 'in the immortal words of Bachman-Turner-Overdrive: you ain't seen nothing yet.'

Philippa sat by the fire, sipping her sherry, checking her Countdown to Christmas List and feeling more or less at peace with the world. She had had a lovely phone call from darling Hannah who sounded very happy, which probably had a lot to do with the nice new boyfriend she had, one with a funny name; she had listened to *The Archers* and all she had left to do this evening was to make an omelette at some point. The Christmas tree twinkled in the corner of the sitting room, her presents were wrapped and spread under the tree, the beds were already made up for the arrival of Hilda and Christopher and Helen in a few days' time.

Philippa sat back in her armchair and contemplated her good fortune. She did this quite often, particularly during those times when she felt a little tired of her own company. She was, after all, so lucky to have this house and she was even luckier to have her family.

Philippa felt particularly blessed about Alberta. She had always assumed their relationship would never recover from that terrible year after Ed's death. She had accepted this with the dismal recognition that it was part of the price she must pay. And yet, miracle of miracles, the joy of the last few months had been the gradual flowering of a warmth between them and a concurrent dissipation of tension. She had no idea why or how this had happened and she knew she didn't deserve it, but she welcomed it with open arms. Alberta rang most evenings now, though not tonight. Tonight, Alberta was working till nine at some do in Kensington. It was wonderful to think that she was going to go back to Tony. It had been terrible to be at home and to feel so helpless in the last few months. The most difficult thing she had ever done was to keep silent when Alberta had told her she was leaving Tony, because she had *known* that he was so absolutely right for her and she had known Alberta would have to work that out for herself. And now they were going to be married! When Alberta told her the news, she had felt like cheering. She had been so thrilled! She had said, 'You are going to be Alberta Hart!' and had had to stop herself from saying, 'You are no longer going to be Alberta Granger!'

She had always known that Ed was trouble. She had

known from the beginning that her husband was in love with him and there had somehow been a ghastly inevitability about the fact that Alberta had fallen in love with him too. Philippa had thought that Ed's baleful influence would haunt her all her life. Well, it hadn't. She and Michael had made their peace. And now at last Alberta was free of him too. She had a new confidence about her that was marvellous to behold, she had handed in her notice to her London employer and had plans to set up a new business of her own in Bath. Apparently, it would be aimed at people called Time Consuming Clients, which sounded very odd but she was sure Alberta knew what she was doing. And, meanwhile, darling Tony would be her son-in-law at last. Really, Philippa thought, I'm a very lucky woman.

Her thoughts were interrupted by the sound of footsteps on the gravel outside. For a moment, she thought it must be the motley band of tone-deaf carol singers that had called on her a few nights ago. She had given them ten pounds and thanked them for their singing, so it would serve her right if they came back for more.

When she opened the door, her initial feeling of relief at the sight of the non-carol singing man in the grey coat, tartan scarf and trilby hat was overtaken by the shock of realizing it was none other than Maurice Cartwright.

He took off his hat and said, 'Philippa, I've come to say goodbye.'

It was only then that she noticed he was carrying a suitcase. 'Would you like to come in?' she asked.

Maurice followed her into the hall and put his suitcase down. 'I can't stay long,' he said, 'I have a train to catch.'

'Well, come into the sitting room for a bit,' Philippa said.

'You can warm yourself by the fire.'

He hesitated and then put his hat on his suitcase. 'Thank you,' he said. 'It's very kind of you to be so . . . hospitable.'

In the sitting room, he watched her sit down in her armchair and then he perched on the edge of the sofa. 'I wanted to see you before I left,' he said quickly. 'I didn't want to go without saying goodbye. I wanted to apologize to you. I have not been a good friend to you. In fact, I have been a very bad man.'

'Well, I must say I agree,' said Philippa candidly. 'I always thought you and I were particular friends and it's been disappointing to see I was wrong.'

'I know,' Maurice said, 'and if it's any consolation, I've wanted to come here every day since Michael's death.'

'That isn't *any* consolation at all,' Philippa said. 'Are you sure you can't have a small sherry?'

Maurice glanced at his watch. 'Perhaps a small one would be a good idea.'

Alberta went to the drinks cabinet and poured him a glass. Maurice rather surprised her by drinking it all in one go.

He stood up and put his hands behind his back as if he were about to make a speech. 'This is all very difficult for me. Would you mind not interrupting me until I finish?'

'I don't mind at all,' Philippa said. She returned to her armchair. 'Would you like to begin now?'

'Thank you,' Maurice said. He cleared his throat. 'When we heard about Michael, Joan was extremely upset. It was almost as if she took the circumstances of his death as a personal affront. She became quite irrational and insisted we break off all contact with you. I pointed out to her that such behaviour would be as unfair as it was cruel but she remained adamant that she wanted nothing more to do with you. I realized then that I hadn't actually liked her for a very long time. I suppose that until that moment my feelings for her had been obscured by the guilt I felt.'

'I'm so sorry,' Philippa said, 'but why should you feel guilty?'

Maurice looked at her and frowned. 'Surely you must know that I've been in love with you for years?'

'I certainly did not!' Philippa exclaimed.

'Well, don't worry about it,' Maurice said equably, 'I'm quite used to it now. Anyway, I didn't want to hurt Joan and I certainly didn't want to leave her all on her own. But I knew that her sister was coming to live with us as soon as she had sold her house, and the second piece of good fortune was that Joan told me she would throw me out if I ever tried to see you. All I had to do was agree to have nothing to do with you until her sister arrived. I had no idea how difficult that would be. I can't tell you how many times I nearly came round to see you. But I held firm. Sheila arrived last night. This morning I told Joan I wanted to invite you round for a Christmas drink. Joan said I could not. I said I would. We had a very satisfactory argument which ended with Joan telling me she never wanted to see me again. I packed my case and now here I am. I had no idea I could be so devious.'

'But where are you going now?'

'My nephew and his family are putting me up for Christmas and then I thought I might go and stay with an old pal in Scotland for a bit, while I decide what to do.' Maurice glanced at his watch again. 'I must go,' he said.

'I've left the car for Joan, so I'm walking to the station.' He stepped up to her and squeezed her hand briefly. 'You have been the light of my life for a very long time. I will never forget you. Please don't come to the door. It's far too cold.'

He left the room quickly and she heard the front door shut behind him. She stood up and listened to the sound of his footsteps on the drive until she couldn't hear anything other than the crackling of the fire.

She could imagine him, hugging his coat to him in the wind, walking briskly down the lane towards the railway station, not looking back. And meanwhile she would have the comfort of knowing why she hadn't seen him for so long. But of course she would never ever see him again.

With a speed she hadn't known she possessed, she ran out of the room into the hall. She flung open the door and stepped out onto the drive, her eyes searching and then finding the figure near the gate. 'MAURICE CARTWIGHT!' she shouted.

The figure stopped and turned.

Philippa ran forward a few steps and shouted again, 'MAURICE CARTWRIGHT! HOW DARE YOU SAY THOSE THINGS AND THEN LEAVE ME ON MY OWN! COME BACK HERE THIS MINUTE!'

## Debby Holt

# Love Affairs for Grown-Ups

*'It's always risky starting relationships at our age . . .'*

Dragooned into driving the female friend of a colleague's wife through France, Cornelius Hedge is not at all happy. How on earth is he expected to make small talk from Boulogne to Montelimar? First impressions are not auspicious: the moment he introduces himself, the woman inexplicably bursts into tears.

But by the time they've reached their destination, Cornelius has grown increasingly fond of the unassuming Katrina. She is interesting, entertaining, amusing; he'd actually like to see more of her.

At their age however, the past has a habit of intruding on the present. Ex-husbands, ex-wives, selfish sisters and sulky teenagers all seem to conspire to thwart the budding romance. What's worse, both Katrina and Cornelius are hiding secrets from their past. Secrets that burst into the open – with rather surprising results.

**ISBN: 978-1-41652-677-3**

**PRICE £6.99**

Debby Holt

# The Trouble with Marriage

*Nobody ever tells you how difficult it is to make a marriage work.'*

When Robin asked Tilly to marry him, it was the happiest moment of her life. Ten years on, the sparkle has faded – household bills, household chores, two small children and a boisterous dog have seen to that – but Tilly is convinced their love can survive even the attentions of interfering in-laws and a glamorous ex-girlfriend.

When dramatic news ignites the simmering undercurrents into a full-blown crisis, Tilly is forced to face the fact that her marriage is under threat. Can she and Robin find a way to recapture the love, lust and sense of fun that filled their early years together? Can Tilly find the strength to overcome the obstacles in the path of true happiness? And when temptation arises in an unexpected form – can she, should she – find the will to resist . . .?

Hilarious and heartbreaking in turn, Debby Holt's delicious new novel explores with coruscating honesty what happens after the 'happy ever after'.

**ISBN: 978-1-41652-676-6**

**PRICE £6.99**

## Debby Holt

# Annie May's Black Book

Entries from Annie May's Black Book:

October 15th, 1974: Miss Baker for telling me how to blow my nose and not believing when I still couldn't do it.

April 12th, 1987: Peter Elton for 'borrowing' my cigarettes and never buying any of his own.

February 9th, 1988: BEN SEYMOUR FOR EVERYTHING FOR EVER!

In her Black Book, Annie May has recorded the name and offence of everyone who has ever done her wrong. The greatest transgressor of them all was Ben Seymour – the man who jilted her at the altar seventeen years before.

Now he's moving into a house round the corner . . .

The bestselling author of *The Ex-Wife's Survival Guide* returns with this warm, witty and bitter-sweet tale of two stubborn people who have a chance to put things right.

**ISBN: 978-1-41650-245-6**

**PRICE £6.99**

POCKET
BOOKS